The Warmth
of Our
Closest Star

A Novel
Chase Connor

Book Cover Designed by: Allen T. St. Clair, ©2022 Chase Connor & The Lion Fish Press

CHASE CONNOR BOOKS are published by

The Lion Fish Press
539 W. Commerce St #227
Dallas, TX 75208

www.chaseconnor.com
www.thelionfishpress.com

eBook 978-1-951860-33-2
Paperback 978-1-951860-34-9
Hardback 978-1-951860-35-6

To "Peter"—everything.

Also by Chase Connor

LGBTQ+ YA Books

Just a Dumb Surfer Dude: A Gay Coming-of-Age Tale
Just a Dumb Surfer Dude 2: For the Love of Logan
Just a Dumb Surfer Dude 3: Summer Hearts
A Surplus of Light
GINJUH
When Words Grow Fangs
Sending Love Letters to Animals and Other Totally Normal Human Behaviors

LGBTQ+ New Adult/Lit Fic/MM Romance

A Tremendous Amount of Normal
The Gravity of Nothing
Between Enzo & the Universe
The Warmth of Our Closest Star
A Straight Line (w/ co-author J.D. Wade)

LGBTQ+ Magical Realism

Possibly Texas

A Point Worth LGBTQ Paranormal Romances

Jacob Michaels Is Tired (Book 1)
Jacob Michaels Is Not Crazy (Book 2)
Jacob Michaels Is Not Jacob Michaels (Book 3)
Jacob Michaels Is Not Here (Book 4)
Jacob Michaels Is Trouble (Book 5)
CARNAVAL (A Point Worth LGBTQ Paranormal Romance Story)
Jacob Michaels Is Dead (Book 6)
Jacob Michaels Is... The Omnibus Edition (all 6 JMI books and CARNAVAL)
Murder at the Red Rooster Tavern (Book 7)

Erotica

Bully
Briefly Buddies
Jake (A Novella from Tricked: The Men of Briefly Buddies)

Kindle Vella

Tricked: The Men of Briefly Buddies (serialized/episodic continuation of *Briefly Buddies*)

Audiobooks

A Surplus of Light: A Gay Coming-of-Age Tale (narrated by Brian Lore Evans)
Between Enzo & the Universe (narrated by Brian Lore Evans; Tantor Media)

Translated

Between Enzo & the Universe – **Spanish**
A Surplus of Light – **Spanish**

Anthologies Contribution

Magis and Maniacs: And Other Christmas Stories (*Frank*, *A Christmas in Pajamas*, *A Surfer's Christmas*, and *The IT Guy*)

Contents

Part Three

Life Goes On

Part Four
Here You Come Again

About the Author

A Coffee Shop
Present Day

If you love the smell of warm sugar, a coffee shop is not a bad place in which to find yourself. With nothing more pressing to do in a day, one of my favorite activities is taking a morning run—or even a brisk walk—and stopping by my favorite coffee shop as a reward for the physical exertion. The coffee shop I love above all others is actually inside my favorite bakery, so technically, it's a bakery. The bakery sells decadent American and French treats that both excite and sadden me. Obviously, the excitement is from knowing that I will feel the grainy sweetness of sugared dough sliding past my lips. The sadness is the result of the bittersweet nostalgia the baked goods produce. Chocolate croissants—as Americans love to call them—éclairs, donuts, cookies of all varieties, Madeleines, palmiers, mille-feuille, and every color and flavor of macaron on display behind a tunnel of glass, seemingly for my eyes only. It never matters how many other customers are waiting in line, I know that the ladies who work behind the counter are waiting for me to approach. They enjoy making me repeat my order so that they can giggle at my accent and use any manner of term of endearment on me.

The first time it happened, the giggling and the request to repeat myself, I was concerned that the ladies' amusement was at my expense. Surely, these women were going to have a laugh at my strange accent and then tell me to *go back to where you came from right now!* That's not the story I have to tell, though. The first time I had walked up to the counter at La Croûte, I felt so alone, though I wasn't. Even though I had assistance available if I should need it, I hadn't found my autonomy in America, and I desperately needed to achieve that goal. So, I had stepped up to the counter, feigning confidence, ready to inform the matronly woman behind the counter that I wanted macarons and croissants. And two black coffees. Coffee is always good.

"Oh, my goodness. Can you say that again?" she had gasped. *"You must be French!"*

Any confidence I had managed to fake quickly abandoned me, creating a treacherous pool at my feet waiting to help my frequent clumsiness make me look even more foolish. However, I had forced myself to repeat my order to the woman with the surprised expression.

"I could listen to you say that all day." She clapped her hands in surprise. *"Lena! Come here. You have got to hear this!"*

So, Lena came from the back of the shop so she could hear me repeat my order. Soon, the space behind the counter was lined with the employees of the shop, listening to me speak, asking me questions, and reveling in my accent. *Are you visiting here, hon? You've moved here? Oh, that's so exciting! We hope to see you here often! Isn't he so precious?* I felt vulnerable and nervous—and somehow, important. Which, of course, made me feel ashamed. Though, I suppose, not in an awful way, since it didn't make me act out of character. The ladies who worked in the shop filled my order and sold me the selected items at a discount, welcoming me to my new home in the process. As I was stepping away, a box with two to-go cups atop it, the lady behind the counter—whose name, I learned, was Nancy—told me: *"If you ever need anything, you let me know, hun!"*

La Croûte became the second place in America that felt like home—a safe space where I could go whenever I felt out of place. Which was why the ladies in the shop got their wish and saw me multiple times a week. As my confidence in speaking with Americans grew, and I came to truly believe these women were as friendly as they seemed, I realized that La Croûte was a magnificent place to practice my American English. I could sit in a booth near the window and watch the city go by as the women of the shop worked and talked to each other, giving me insight into the figures of speech common in my new homeland. Most of the idioms and other expressions they used seemed absolutely ridiculous to me, and my God, how I adored them.

People came and went through the front door of the shop. Some even stopped to enjoy their coffee at one of the café tables, leisurely sipping their coffee and eating their treats, either alone, in pairs, in groups, or while working on a laptop or reading a book. Most of the patrons of the shop took their orders and left, tipping their coffees back frantically as they rushed off to their next destination—which is a very American thing to do. Sometimes people would sit on the bench outside, regardless of the weather, and watch the world pass as they enjoyed their purchases. I was free to watch all of these transactions, actions, and decisions—these choices that were at all times flippant yet deeply personal. I could listen to conversations, pretending I was a man deep in thought as I looked out of the window. Americans are loud, so I did not have to try too hard to listen, though I do not mean this in a scolding way. Americans speak at a volume to be heard. Sometimes they speak in hushed tones if they are trying to have a private conversation, which forces me to concentrate to hear what they are saying as I pretend to look out the window.

To be an American, I quickly realized, you must be unabashedly yourself. You must be self-possessed, though I mean this in neither a good nor a bad way. It is simply one of the characteristics of America and its people. People in the United States carry on their lives in an individualistic way. They don't do it to bother others nor do they let others bother them. People are loud. People are quiet. People are polite. People are rude. Some people drink their coffee at a leisurely pace at a table while others hurry down the street, chugging it as though it is nectar. Americans do not ask permission. They ask forgiveness. But it is an understood agreement—*I'll forgive you if you forgive me.* Then no one has to actually utter the words.

For better or for worse, it is the one thing I have noticed everywhere I have traveled in America. Americans cherish their individuality. No matter which church or government building you step inside, the highest honor goes to the self. Of course, some Americans do not think that others should be themselves—racism, homophobia, misogyny, and other prejudices abound, as in any other country. But those are the people who did not learn quickly—as I did—what it means to be authentically American.

America is not a theme park, as I had often thought, growing up and seeing it through the filter of a film played in the cinema. It is not the interpretation given by many directors and other filmmakers. Though it is loud and bright, vulgar and rude, and often overwhelming, it is a land where freedom is valued above all other things. *Individualism.* Whether you are a person who appreciates this concept or not, it is an idea that deserves respect. The case for whether or not such a system can sustain itself for any length of time is debatable, but what intelligently curious person wouldn't want to find out?

Whenever I spend time outside of my home, among the American masses, I wonder if my family would have loved the country as much as I do. I would have loved to have taken Maman and Mamie to the *Mall of America* and seen their eyes light up at so many shops in one place. To see them wandering around, their eyes bulging as they considered the possibilities. Ila would have adored the year-round Christmas shops where beautiful shiny glass ornaments and sparkling lights hung from the ceiling. I would have loved to have seen my father's expression at the natural beauty of the Midwestern states of America. To see him on a boat on one of the Great Lakes with a fishing pole in his hands. I would have given anything to walk along the peaceful shores with Noe on a calm and quiet spring day, even if we would have had to rest often. Even sitting there, with the chilly water lapping at our toes, would have been heavenly. Then I remember that I never would have been to America if my family was still with me, so I quickly force myself to stop thinking such things.

Labeling oneself by nationality is an odd concept to me, having had to change that label frequently in my short lifetime. *French. French-Canadian. Canadian. American.* They are all labels that have been applied to me and my status. I had been told once that I was a "citizen of the world," so one place was as good as any other, but I'm not so sure that is true. I think human beings—the ones who find a way to live life to its fullest—become part of the place in which they live. We come to adopt and adapt to most of the culture of where we live and let it mold us into the person we are to become. I had always felt mostly French when I was in France. I had never felt Canadian or even *French-Canadian*. I've never felt more uniquely myself than I do in the United States.

Individualism.

Since my final arrival to the United States from Canada, the one that would be my official homecoming, I have thought of myself as American with a French flair. Beyond that, I am Enzo. Both are labels that can be given to an individual. A place and a name. I've never felt more like Enzo than when I am in America. It is where Enzo placed his feet on solid ground, found out who he was, and embraced his individualism. I was no longer the oldest child in a family. I was no longer a brother. A son. A grandson. I became other things when I arrived in America, but becoming Enzo was my first great accomplishment as a new American. It is the land of dreams—and I hadn't known that learning about Enzo was one of my greatest dreams.

In America, I have touched my feet to its dirt, swam in its waters, walked through its forests, climbed on its mountains and hills, ran along its sidewalks and roads, shopped in its stores, slept in many of its beds, met many of its people, spoken its unofficial language with glee, and contributed to its economic power. I have strolled along city sidewalks when I had only the moon to keep me company. I've met people belonging to more ethnic and racial backgrounds than one would expect, and tried all of the foods available. I have discovered secrets my body held and solved one of its major problems. I have even become a son and a brother again, though I have learned that it does not have to infringe upon my individuality. I have endured heartache and joy, pain and pleasure, love and hate. But all of it lends experience to my human experience. It makes Enzo who he is today.

As I walked into La Croûte, my arms full and my raincoat pulled over my head to protect myself and my bundle, I was greeted by a group proclamation of *"ENZO!"* from the staff. Nancy, my favorite of all of the employees, the one who first said she loved my accent during my first visit, indicated that I should sit down and she would come to take my order. The bakery was empty of customers and it was obvious that the heat had not been turned on for this one cold, rainy day in early spring. Of course, with all of the ovens on, and all of the physical labor the employees endured, they would never notice the chill in the air as someone who had come in out of the rain would. There was no reason to complain. Once I had a hot coffee and a warm, sugary treat, all would be well. The chill would not bother me either.

My raincoat got carefully removed and hung on one of the hooks by the door before I made my way to my favorite booth by the front window. Gently, I slid into the cushioned seat laying my bundle carefully on the seat beside me. Nancy walked over and we exchanged a few words quietly before I gave her my order. A large black coffee and an almond croissant. She disappeared to retrieve my drink and treat. Outside, the rain was still coming down in spatters, heavier than a mist but not quite a rain. Everything was gray; heavy clouds hung in the sky and people raced down the sidewalk, trying to avoid getting sprayed by cars driving too close to the gutters. The smile I had been sporting all morning refused to leave my face, even as I shivered and pulled my cardigan more tightly around myself. Minneapolis wasn't always dreary, though, for some reason I've never been able to explain, that was my favorite Minneapolis weather.

Summer in Minneapolis was my first experience with what would come to be my new homeland, so it might seem odd that I wouldn't enjoy sunny, warm weather more. Especially after what seemed an eternity in Montreal. Dreary, rainy days connect me to my past. Even when I've not a care in the world, the gray rain clouds tether me to that which would otherwise be forgotten when it's summertime and the sun is shining its warm rays on my back. A back that would most likely be unburdened by a shirt as I ran through the concrete and steel streets of the city that replaced Montreal as my home. Or maybe dashing through the water to leap headfirst into one of the Great Lakes, only to discover that the water would never be sufficiently warmed by the summer sun. My feet would push me up, to crest the water's surface, an exhilarated shout escaping my throat. I suppose it is unnecessary to say that I enjoy my new home in all of its seasons—when the sun is shining, when it's not. But I do not want to forget my past.

As Minneapolis ties me to who I am today, dreary, cold, rainy days remind me of ties to my past. Both of these things, the juxtaposition of the two, keep me centered in who I am. For better or worse, I find that besides being American, I am also the drops of water that fall from the clouds, and the rays that beam down from our closest star. It's odd how two contrasting elements can both help to define a person. I've found, over the course of my life, that I am a man comprised of many elements—and not just those taught to us in biology or other science classes. I'm not only carbon and hydrogen and oxygen. None of us are, really, because we are all comprised of those things. We are actually all of our memories. Those we have, those we are making, and those we've not even begun to create. The same can be said for our experiences. We are not either our bodies or minds, but what those two parts contain. What it means to be American is all of these things...*and individualism.*

I am Enzo. I am my mother and father. My brother and sister. My grandmother. I am white. I am Cambodian. I am French, Canadian, French-Canadian, and American. I am the doctor's hands I fell into at my birth. I am the grass in the parks I played in as my grandmother followed along, holding my hand. I am the kneelers that dug into my shins in countless churches and the pressure of my hands together as I asked my questions of the universe. I am the running I do to forget myself, even though I know I will always return to me. I am my hopes and dreams. I am my sins and my good deeds. I am unburdened. I carry the weight of the world on my shoulders. I am the love my friends give me and I am the hate I foolishly give to my enemies. I am all of these things. I am everything. We all are. But, somehow, we are all still uniquely individual.

It's a paradox.

Thinking about it too much makes my head throb, though not nearly as bad as it would have years ago. So, I do my best to accept myself and my circumstances as they are in the moment. When life is good, it's only a disservice to self to behave otherwise. Though, it does amaze me how quickly such infinite thoughts can traverse the channels of my brain in what amounts to mere moments. How lost I can get in what is quite literally a thought that lasts five seconds. One moment I'm staring out of the window of a coffee shop as I sit in a booth, staring at people passing with their raincoats and umbrellas, and the next I am turning to greet a waitress as she places a pastry and coffee in front of me.

Nancy set my coffee and almond croissant down on the table gently and we exchanged a few whispered greetings and updated each other on our lives quietly. She was expecting her third grandchild, which warmed me nearly as much as the first sip of my coffee did. Hopefully, she explained, she would be able to take enough time away from La Croûte to enjoy becoming a grandmother for a third time.

When she stepped away from my booth, Nancy laid a light-as-a-bird's-wing hand on my shoulder, glanced down at the booth, then smiled at me. I smiled back and she spun to return to her work behind the counter.

Often, I've wondered what it's like to work in a coffee shop that sells baked goods. How wonderful it must be to constantly smell warm sugar and ground coffee all day long. To have it permeate every fiber of your clothes. Unlike working in a factory assembling products or pushing a mop to clean up other people's messes in bathrooms, or selling clothing in a large department store, the smell of a bakery is a pleasant one to carry home with you. At the end of the day, one doesn't wash away a bakery in the same manner that one would wash away custodial work. You may love to feel the smell of cleaning products and grime sliding away from your flesh, but the smell of sugar leaving your skin is almost like saying a wistful "goodbye."

Maybe because, while people appreciate having their toilets clean when they return to work the next day, there's nothing like the joy you can create when you hand someone a pastry. A person's eyes do not light up at a clean toilet like they do at a croissant or éclair. Certainly, no one moans with satisfaction when they bite into a toilet. I hope.

Not to say that bakers and baristas are more important than those who produce or sell goods, or those who keep our workplaces and homes sanitary, but a baker's work is appreciated in a way that no other work is. The people who work in factories and in shops produce tangible goods, sure. But was it made or sold with love in a way that an éclair from a bakery was?

To create an éclair, a baker must painstakingly make a dough that's just right. Just so. Then it must rest and be chilled. Then it is piped meticulously onto a baking sheet. After this process, which takes hours, a baker places it in the oven at *precisely the right temperature*. If things go wrong during this process—resulting in an éclair that is too soft or too firm—the whole process must be redone. If it works out perfectly, a baker lets the now baked éclairs sit until they are room temperature. Then they are returned to the oven to dry out. Once again, they must be cooled. Then the baker must prepare the custard, poke holes in the delicate baked éclairs, then pipe the custard into the éclairs with an expert touch. Then a ganache is made and the éclairs are ever so gently dipped in the chocolate glaze. Then it's back into the fridge for a while to be sure the chocolate and custard set.

Once all of these steps are complete, the éclairs are ready to consume and/or sell. There are not many jobs that require as much dedication and care. Most people, when they bite into an éclair, don't know any of this. They simply taste the chocolate, custard, and sugar. The smell of sugar on a baker's skin at the end of the day reminds them that, even if the person who bought the éclairs never knows it, they sent them away with love.

Warm sugar is love. I've always known that.

Part One

What It Means to Be an American

A New Favorite Mammal

"Was this your first flight?"

The lady sitting next to me on the airplane had been watching me closely out of the corner of her eye for almost three hours. Upon embarking on the plane and finding out we were seatmates simply by luck of the draw—first-row economy class—the woman had watched me. At first, she only seemed curious, as though trying to decide whether or not I was someone who liked to make small talk with strangers. Of course, she had uttered the obligatory "hello" and "good morning," which I had returned in kind, but she had said nothing further. A few times it looked as though she might try to strike up a conversation—once before the flight safety announcement, once when the drink and snack cart came along, and then again when her e-reader had run out of battery and she was left with nothing else to do. However, each time she seemed about to open her mouth to start a conversation she changed her mind and found something else on which to devote her attention.

Even after the plane had landed—and some odd people decided to clap for, I suppose, the pilot not sending us crashing to the Earth in a fiery ball of death—she remained silent. Her eyes continued to dart over to me as we waited to taxi up to the gate bridge. I sat patiently in my seat, my belt still fastened around my waist like a good, rule-abiding passenger, my hands clasped in my lap. The woman snuck glances at me. Other passengers made noises about wanting to hurry and get off the plane, though the flight had not been that long. The woman snuck glances at me. Finally, when the plane's engine thrust gently to push us towards the gate bridge, her head slowly turned to me. As though she may never have another chance to say something to me, and had been dying to, her mouth uttered those five words.

Was this your first flight?

"No." I turned my head to smile at her. "I have not flown much, but this was not my first flight ever."

"Oh!" She gasped, delighted. "I should have talked to you sooner! I was wondering about your accent. Coming from French Canada and everything."

Gauging her accent, which I assumed was a fairly standard American one, I couldn't help but be amused.

"Well, my accent is because I am French," I said. "I live in Québec now. Montreal is my home."

"Doesn't everyone there have an accent?" she asked as she reached for her purse.

This was an odd question as we had both boarded the plane at the Montréal-Pierre Elliot Trudeau International Airport. Surely, I was not the first French-Canadian she had spoken to in her travels?

"I suppose some have an accent like mine." I relented. "Some do not."

She thought about this. "You know, it just dawned on me that you're right. Anyone who spoke English there didn't have too much of an accent at all."

I heaved my shoulders upward with a goofy smile.

"You don't have to be nice." She chuckled. "That was stupid of me."

"No." I shook my head. "Stupid people do not ask questions."

She threw her head back with a laugh as she unzipped her purse.

"You're right again!" She cackled. It was loud. She was boisterous and making a scene. I liked her immediately. "Are you coming to America for vacation?"

That question made me pause, as though I had no clue as to why I was traveling to the United States of America. Of course, I knew why I was traveling, but I didn't know if "vacation" was the correct word for my reason to travel.

"I suppose," I said, finally. "Yes."

The woman eyed me suspiciously, which was fair. My response had been odd.

"Well," she said slowly, "are you going to do anything special while you're here? How long are you here?"

"Two weeks," I said. "I'm here to see a friend. Yes. A friend."

Once again, I had been unable to help myself. I'd made things even more awkward. As though I couldn't keep from making myself sound like an international spy, slipping into America undetected through Canada, I simply couldn't explain myself well. How does one explain that they are traveling to a different country to see a possible romantic interest they haven't seen in two years and have only talked to via text, letters, and the occasional phone call? Was the woman homophobic?

"That sounds very nice," she said simply, her mouth set in a tight smile.

She said no more and asked no more questions. Obviously, my social ineptitude had helped her make a decision she'd had trouble making during our flight. I hadn't been worth speaking with—I was obviously insane—and she had been right in not speaking with me for the entirety of our flight. As the plane came to a stop at the gate bridge and people began standing, the woman seemed more than eager to unfasten her seatbelt and busy herself with retrieving her carry-on from the overhead compartment. Unfastening my seatbelt as well, I waited patiently for her to retrieve her bag, give me a nervous smile and wave, then join the line of passengers waiting to exit the plane before I stood.

My first social interaction in America resulted in a stranger thinking I was a freak. Great.

Waiting so that I was nearly at the end of the line of passengers disembarking the plane was torturous. Eager to set foot on American soil, I desperately wanted off of the plane. It had always been—for my brief twenty-two years— a lifetime dream to visit America. Of course, saying I dreamed of visiting America was confusing to anyone not from the U.S. To most of the world, "America" could mean North or South America or any of their territories. "America" is not only the United States. However, more than my desire to find out if all I'd learned about the country I referred to as "America" from going to the cinema was true, there was one greater reason that I wanted off of the plane. It had absolutely nothing to do with a new country to visit and foods to try and sights to see.

Peter.

During the flight, I'd done my best not to think of him excessively. It would have made the flight seem like an eternity. Somehow, I had convinced myself that I was merely on my first trip to America and that my excitement was for finally fulfilling a lifelong dream of visiting a country I had dreamed of for so long. It had enabled me to not bounce in my seat, shift uncomfortably, or get bored.

I was on my way to America.

On a plane

Using a ticket that I purchased with my own money.

Nervously, I reached for my carry-on bag—a sad overnight bag I had purchased secondhand at a thrift shop days before my trip—and frantically unzipped the side pocket.

My passport. It was still there. Next to my medication.

I chuckled nervously to myself as I moved the passport from the bag's compartment to my right hip pocket. One last glance reassured me that I had not forgotten my medication. Zipping the bag closed once more, I dragged it from the compartment and slung it over my shoulder. Briefly, I considered whether my carry-on and suitcase—that I'd retrieve at the luggage claim after disembarking—would seem meager to Peter. Would it embarrass me? Would it embarrass him?

For almost exactly two years, I'd been working for a large multi-national corporation that specialized in interpretation and translation services. The job for which Peter had recommended me. I was low on the rungs and was not much more than a glorified office assistant, but I'd managed to catch up on my rent. Though it was secondhand and I'd had to spend an entire afternoon cleaning it well, I had a sofa in my living room. I'd purchased a small television—which sat on a secondhand table—that I could only watch free OTA channels and secondhand DVDs on since premium television services seemed an extravagance. I'd purchased new sheets for my bed. I had three pairs of new shoes. My kitchen was never food bare, though the specter of my impoverished past often demanded that I eat simple pasta dinners so that I did not feel I had overspent. I never made myself eat less than I wanted, however.

An elaborate homecooked meal with a nicer cut of meat or an exotic ingredient once a week was no longer out of the question, however. I had a warm comforter for my bed and a new phone—though nothing fancy—with a charger whose cord was not frayed. There was a large rug in my living room that I'd found at an estate sale for what amounted to twenty dollars, so my feet were never cold on the floorboards in the mornings. It had needed a good cleaning as well and was a bit threadbare at the corners, but I owned a rug.

Somehow, I'd managed to save money to update my passport, buy a plane ticket, and purchase a few new outfits for my trip to America. Luggage that was new and fancy had been out of the question. Thrift store finds were what I ended up with in the end. But they were clean, sturdy, and served their purpose. And they belonged to me.

I found that I was proud of my overnight bag that was slung over my shoulder. Peter would think nothing of the way it looked. I hoped.

Had I achieved enough in two years so that I would not seem the street rat he had met in Montreal two years prior? Still skinny, though I'd managed to gain fifteen pounds since I'd last seen him, I wondered if seeing me would be pleasing to him. Would I look less like the gangly, awkward young man who walked the city streets as long as he could each day to avoid going home to a hollow apartment filled with intangible, yet painful memories?

Would he like to know that sitting on my sofa at home, eating dinner, and watching television didn't feel as lonely as it once would have? In the two years since we'd first and last seen each other, did he wonder how many nights I shivered in bed, praying for the next paycheck when I could maybe, finally afford better bedding? Would he be curious to know that the first pair of shoes I bought were so warm that I actually cried because my toes were not freezing when I got home from the store? Did he want to know that I had a bus pass and didn't have to walk anywhere unless I wanted to get exercise?

Did he want to know that every night, when I lay in bed, and my hand crept under the covers, he was my only thought? That when explosions went off throughout my body and stars danced in my eyes, his face was burned in the sky of my imagination? He was the constellation my ecstasy brought into creation each night—a collection of resplendent stars, and I reveled in their warmth.

Butterflies invaded my belly. Though I'd managed to keep myself from thinking about the real purpose of my first visit to America for two years, and during the short flight, reality had presented itself suddenly. Exiting the plane, and then after having my passport and luggage possibly checked, a face I hadn't seen in two years would be before me. What would come then?

There was nothing to do but force my mind back into a mode of denial. America. That was my goal. Visiting America. Peter had yet to see me and it could very well turn out that the memory of me had not burned as brightly for him. Maybe I was not his constellation any longer. Not even a single star. Perhaps a flame that burned dimly in the recesses of his brain, but more appealing as a concept than a reality. My first trip to America could merely be my first trip to America. Nothing more.

At the front of the line of people disembarking the plane for the bridge gate, I was surprised, though I shouldn't have been, when the flight attendants welcomed me to the U.S. Embarking in Canada, I had been greeted in French and English. Now it was only English. Reality sunk deeper into my mind as it became clear that I was a stranger in a strange land. Never had I visited a foreign country on my own.

If I couldn't think of the English word for something, who could help me?

My English was fine. I could easily hold a conversation with someone who only knew English. But there were still words that might prove troublesome. Eight years in Canada had not exactly perfected my English. *Particularly.* I had to avoid using *particularly.* I always got tongue-tied with that word. If I could avoid certain words, I would be fine. My heart raced, though not for entirely unpleasant reasons. Monsieur Paquette, whose ESL classes I still attended in the classroom over the Chinese restaurant—and still paid for with housekeeping duties—thought my English constantly needed improving. However, the pride in his silent grin when I told him I was to visit America alone was obvious. He'd offered me the use of his personal luggage for the trip, but I was determined to procure my own, even if it was secondhand.

In the months leading up to my trip, I'd studied American currency and Imperial measurements and weights. I'd taught myself the difference between Celsius and Fahrenheit. I was amused to find that Canada and the United

States were not greatly different compared to France and the United States. I'd studied maps of Minneapolis and looked up locations of interest in the city. I tried to learn as much as I could about customs that were unique to America. *People in America love smiles and warmth and small talk and appreciative, uproarious laughter. Do not discuss politics or how things are "weird" in America. Do not insult the culture, even if there seems to be none.* I would be fine. Even if Peter did not greet me as warmly as I wished, I could do well in America for the two weeks of my trip.

"Enjoy your stay in the U.S.!" The flight attendant exclaimed brightly as I stepped off of the plane and onto the gate bridge. "Thank you for flying with us!"

"Thank you," I said with a smile.

A warm "thank you" goes a long way when one isn't sure what else to say. For mere moments I was lost in thought about the exchange before I realized I was on a gate bridge leading from a plane into an American airport. It took all I had to keep from running excitedly along the pathway into the airport so that I would officially be in America. When I remembered that Customs was the last stop before I was legally and officially in America, I was able to calm myself. There were more steps to complete before my feet touched down in a new country.

Stepping off of the gate bridge into the bustling airport was enthralling. Even though removed from the bustle of passengers and visitors seeing off or picking up travelers, it was overwhelming. Not necessarily in a bad way, but my senses were overloaded by the sights and sounds as my eyes danced from one person to the next. American airports—from what I could tell—were no different than many others throughout the developed world. People rushed here and there, people spoke loudly, and airline employees worked to provide tickets, check luggage, and help passengers with issues. But this was America. It was special for that reason alone.

The process to get through the line at Customs was neither as stringent nor as nerve-wracking as the picture my mind had conjured. Though it seemed a whirlwind and I could barely process what was transpiring at the rate it was happening. Most people were waved through after their passport was merely given a glance. At my turn with the agent, he simply gave my passport a glance.

"You don't look very Canadian," he said.

"How does one look Canadian?" I asked, confused.

Was I supposed to be wearing a toque even in summer?

He, along with his coworker, laughed, and I was waved through.

And I was in America. Again, my eyes danced around the scene before me. People rushed here and there—many in much more comfortable clothing than I had chosen for my flight. Compared to Americans, my dark slacks and long-sleeve button-down, collared shirt seemed incredibly glamorous. Sweatpants, jeans, t-shirts, and sneakers seemed customary in American airports.

People walked by, shooting casual smiles at me as they held giant coffees and soft pretzels as big as their heads. Suitcases in every color of the rainbow wheeled past, missing my toes by centimeters. Fellow travelers said "hello" and asked "how're you" and wished me a good trip but rarely waited for any kind of response. A smile and a nod became my standard greeting as I stood there, taking in everything around me.

It was everything I had imagined America to be. Without the fireworks and mascots. Though I imagined if I stood there and waited long enough, I would see them.

However, it wasn't fireworks that eventually grabbed my attention. The red that caught my eye was not sparks or flames or a thunderous burst in the sky. It was a stylishly cut mop of hair in the crowd that drew my gaze.

When I imagined reuniting with Peter for the first time since our one perfect night in Montreal, it hadn't involved time stopping. So, I was surprised that everyone around me seemed to freeze as Peter's head turned in slow motion. Then our eyes locked across the distance between us and my feet began to move of their own accord. As though moving underwater, I approached Peter, my overnight bag over my shoulder and my suitcase whirring behind me on its wheels. Peter's eyes stayed on mine as a tentative smile came to his face.

Coming to stand before him, leaving enough room so as to not seem too forward, I let my suitcase come to a stop and gently lowered my overnight bag to rest atop it. I stared into Peter's eyes, unsure of what to say or do next. Two years of our lives had culminated in this moment. Everything around us was a petrified silence as we looked at each other, nervous smiles on our faces. Finally, after what seemed an eternity, Peter brought his hand up from his side.

"I wanted your first American souvenir to be from me," he said, holding out his hand. "I couldn't find a plane. Maybe they were sold out? But this has wings."

Effort was made to pry my eyes from Peter's, but finally, they landed on the object in his hand. A small black plastic bat with an attached keychain lay in his palm. On its belly was "USA" in red, white, and blue. What an odd thing. Resolutely, I decided that bats were one of my favorite animals, though I had never thought much about them until that moment.

It was a perfect first souvenir.

"Thank you," I replied automatically as I gingerly took it from him.

For a few moments, I examined the gift, wondering how it could be more perfect. Then, realizing we were standing in silence, I slipped the gift into my pocket and let my eyes wander back up to Peter's.

"It is perfect," I said.

Peter smiled. Again, we stared.

"Hi," he said.

"Hello."

More silence. The world around us was still frozen and the silence was so thick I could have sworn I could hear my own heart thundering in my chest.

"I don't know what to say," Peter said. "I didn't think I would be nervous to see you again. But here you are. *Finally.* And I'm nervous. I've been thinking about this day—*every day*—for two years, and—"

What came over me I still don't understand to this day. I stepped forward, my hands found Peter's face, and I leaned down to cover his mouth with mine. Peter jerked in shock, and for a moment I was concerned I had misunderstood the intention of our visit. When his arms wrapped around me and his body melted into mine, I leaned into the kiss desperately, feeding at his mouth. Peter's hands clutched at my back as he returned my kiss as passionately. Only the second kiss I'd ever had—and the first I'd ever given.

I finally saw my American fireworks.

Everything around us came back to life and the sounds of the airport rushed to my ears as I slowly, yet reluctantly, pulled back from our kiss. Peter's eyes opened incrementally as my hands slid from his face and I smiled at him. Peter gave a shuddering exhale as a wide grin overtook his face.

A dreamy sigh escaped his lips.

"Welcome to America, Enzo."

It's Not a House, It's a Home

Peter's car was a hurdle I had not expected to have to overcome so early in my visit to America. As we had exited the airport Peter insisted on pulling my suitcase while I carried my overnight bag so that we each had a free hand. Because he immediately laced his fingers through mine as he led me out of the airport to the parking lot. The ease with which we held hands and conversed effortlessly on our way to his car both delighted and unnerved me.

For two years, Peter and I had exchanged texts, emails, the occasional phone call, and even actual physical letters. Having kept in touch almost daily, it should not have surprised me that conversation came easily. However, conversing via the written word makes one feel less self-conscious than having to look someone in the eyes and speak one's mind. I found that, with Peter, as it had been in Montreal on our one perfect night together, everything was easy. I did not feel self-conscious at all. Until he opened the passenger door of his car for me with a flourish and smile.

The gesture, opening the car door grandly for me, was an attempt at chivalry on his part, not an obnoxious display to illustrate his wealth. Regardless, his car was the nicest car I'd ever been invited to ride in that I could remember. Leather seats that were deep, wide, and luxuriously comfortable, proved that "bigger is better" in America. The lights and knobs and buttons on the consoles and doors and dashboard dismayed me.

Don't touch anything, Enzo.

While Peter busied himself stowing my luggage in the hatchback of the vehicle, I fastened my seatbelt and took a deep breath. Peter knew that I was not of extraordinary means. He didn't expect such things from me, so it was not required of me to be familiar with all of the knobs and buttons in his car. Asking questions if I didn't know what something was would not elicit derision from him. Peter would never made me feel lesser than due to our contrasting socioeconomic statuses.

At that moment, I made a promise to myself that I would not spend two weeks—or any time after two weeks—worrying about what Peter thought of my socioeconomic status. Peter had invited me to America to visit him for that time period. All of me. As I was. Worrying about something so arbitrary was a waste of time and energy. Instead, I decided that focusing on the adventure of going to America was the road I'd travel.

The hatchback closed as Peter's phone rang—a simple ringtone fitting a grown man. Not a pop song or a funny little noise or something that would wake the dead within ten kilometers of the car. A typical ringtone. Glancing over my shoulder, I saw the hatchback click shut and Peter bring his phone to his ear through the back window. He stood there, smiling and greeting the caller, so I turned my face back to the windshield to avoid being nosy.

The concrete parking garage was dank and dark, even for a bright and cheerful summer day. So deeply swallowed up within its industrial belly, the sunlight didn't reach our parking spot. I wasn't sure if it felt womb-like or claustrophobic. However, I knew that I didn't want my first thoughts of America to be the airport hustle and bustle and the industrial dark gray concrete walls and sickly blue lights of the parking garage. Mentally, I tried to block out the sights of the parking structure as well as the hollow mechanical noises of cars coming and going. The sounds of airplanes going off somehow managed to reverberate through the car.

I was hungry and thirsty. On the airplane, I'd only been offered small snacks and water or soda to drink. Of course, I'd indulged in a soda since it was an item I often felt was too extravagant to have regularly. Nerves had played subtly in the lowest places in my body, so I hadn't been able to snack on the plane. Though I'd had breakfast in the inky black hours of early morning before catching my flight—a simple breakfast of buttered toast and poached eggs—it hadn't stayed with me. I needed food. I thought to open the compartments of Peter's car and search to see if he had anything available, but I felt it wasn't my place to snoop. My angry belly would have to get over itself.

Peter's door opening scared my thoughts of food away.

"Sorry," Peter chirped as he slid into the driver's seat. "That was just work."

"Is everything okay?"

He waved me off as he closed his door. "Of course. They were just confirming some details of an account that—"

Peter's head turned and our eyes met.

"What?" I asked.

"Nothing." He shook his head with a laugh. "Boring stuff. This is my first vacation in a long time. Let's focus on us."

"Okay."

"What do you want to do first?" Peter reached out to grab the hand I had resting on the console between us, thought better of it, and retracted his hand.

My cheeks felt warm. "If it's not too much to ask…"

Peter searched my eyes.

"I would like for you to do what you were just about to do."

Smiling broadly, Peter didn't hesitate to lace his fingers through mine.

"Better?"

"Better," I said.

"Now what?" He grinned wickedly.

My cheeks grew warmer.

"You're adorable," he said.

"You have gotten more handsome."

"Liar. You have as well. You've gained some weight."

"Is…is that okay?"

"You're perfect. Then and now."

Though this did nothing for the warmth in my cheeks, I couldn't help but grin.

"I'm so glad you're here, Enzo." He sighed.

"I'm glad as well."

The world could have passed us by, the entire two weeks of my vacation, but with Peter's hand in mine, I wouldn't have felt it was wasted. Sitting inside of the car in the giant parking structure, listening to other people's travels echo in my ears was fine. Peter's hand was in mine. Again. Finally.

"What should we do first?" Peter asked.

Husky and ragged, his voice seemed stuck in his throat as his eyes gazed into mine. I desperately wanted to mention anything other than my hunger, but my stomach made a decision for me. Rumbling from my gut broke my staring contest with Peter. He glanced down at my stomach and an amused smile came to his lips.

"I'm a little hungry," I said.

"I see—hear that," he said. "What would my prince from The Great White North wish to eat?"

My brow furrowed with amusement.

"My immigrant from L'Hexagone??" He shrugged.

I laughed and said, "Have you been learning these things for this very day?"

"I already knew the Canadian one," he said as his finger trailed along my knuckles. "I did, in fact, look up the France one."

"Your pronunciation was not bad."

He bowed his head slightly.

"Something...*very American*...would be nice to eat," I said. "If that is not offensive?"

Peter chuckled. "It's not offensive at all. If I remember correctly, you will eat almost anything, right?"

My blush, which I thought had dissipated, warmed my cheeks further.

"I am not...particular."

"Your pronunciation wasn't bad," Peter teased.

"I struggle with that word."

"It's beautiful coming from your lips," Peter lifted my hand and kissed the back of it.

Then his eyes were back on mine.

"This may sound odd, Enzo," he said, "but I missed you. A lot."

Again, warmth flowed over me, but it wasn't only in my cheeks.

"I missed you, too," I replied. "And we're both odd, I suppose."

Peter laughed and a specter of regret flashed across his face as he was forced to release my hand so that he could fasten his seatbelt and drive. I secured my seatbelt as the push of a button started Peter's car. Somehow, I managed to not show my shock at such a fancy feature, but I was impressed nonetheless. The compulsion to start pushing buttons, simply to see what they did, was nearly irresistible. I managed to suppress that urge as well.

Expertly—at least to me—Peter drove us out of the parking lot and away from the airport, zipping in and out of traffic effortlessly, putting distance between us and one of the busiest parts of the city. Once traffic became lighter, the further we got from the airport, Peter asked if I wanted to turn on the radio. Music, though one of my greatest loves, was not what I wanted to hear. I wanted to hear more of Peter's voice, to have him tell me about the city he called home, and I wanted to stare unabashedly like a tourist at the things we passed by in his car.

I declined the offer of the radio and asked Peter to explain where he was taking me. I presented the request in a teasing way, suggesting that I was at his mercy and wanted to be certain of my safety. Which made him laugh. I'd forgotten how Peter's laugh affected me. To miss something that had become a specter of a memory over two years, and not know it until you are presented with it once again, does things to a person. In my case, I found that I wanted to kiss Peter again. More. For how long, I wasn't certain, but kissing Peter was all I could think about for several moments.

Finally, as he began to tell me where we were going, I reluctantly shook those thoughts away so that he would have my attention.

"There's a really nice restaurant," he began, "that serves delicious burgers, fries, barbecue—those kinds of things—that I think you'll love."

"Oh?"

"Huge portions," Peter grinned wickedly as he stared out at traffic, "and nothing there is going to be good for your diet. It's very American."

I chuckled. It was exactly what I had wanted—except for one thing.

"Really nice restaurant?" I asked.

Peter glanced at me before his eyes returned to the road. We sat in silence for a moment as Peter negotiated the highway traffic, but finally, he explained himself.

"I was planning to treat you to lunch and dinner today," he said.

"Peter—"

"I want you to go to two of my favorite restaurants," he ignored me. "And, yes. They are a little expensive."

"I cannot afford *expensive*," I said as Peter took what was apparently our exit.

Peter focused on the road as he smoothly exited the highway onto a city street, guided us through lunchtime traffic, and slowly eased into a parking spot along the curb of a busy street. Looking around, I could see that he had delivered us to a popular and busy section of the city, overrun with what looked like harried business people and fashionable young people. The passing faces on the sidewalk outside of the car were of different hues and ages, which made me smile. I found myself staring out at the deluge of Americans on the sidewalk, though I knew it would have been considered rude if anyone had noticed. Fortunately, people were too busy on their way to wherever one goes in the middle of a Monday to notice.

My eyes were drawn from the people to a sign high on the brick wall of the building we were parked alongside. *Chop House 42.* Was this the restaurant he had wanted me to try? As people passed, and I could glance between their bodies, the large windows that lined the front of the building answered my question. People inside were seated at tables with white tablecloths, eating, talking, and laughing— probably in the loud American way that was as charming as it was startling.

"Enzo." Peter tore my attention from the building.

I turned to look at him.

"I know you can't afford much," he said.

I didn't respond for fear that I would blush and stammer.

"You probably budgeted your vacation down to the last penny," he said.

"I—"

"I want to say," he ignored me again, "that I want you to have the best vacation of your life. I don't want you to worry about if you'll have enough money for something as important as food. And in the U.S., you have to try everything. Because there's so much of it. So, if you don't mind, please let me worry about making sure you're fed while you're here, okay?"

"Peter—"

"It would make me happy," he said, reaching to the console to thread his fingers through mine once again. "I'm a Midwesterner at heart. Hospitality is important to me in general, but it's paramount when it's you."

I looked down at my lap, allowing myself a small smile.

"Also, I know how much this hurts your pride and you don't want to feel that you owe me anything," Peter said softly. "I just want to make sure you eat well. That's all."

"Okay," I said, knowing there was not much else I could do.

Peter was right. I had budgeted for my trip to the last penny that I could afford to spend. A nice meal in a restaurant was beyond my means. It was ridiculous to argue with Peter about my ability to pay for anything beyond fast food. Furthermore, it would have hurt to put my pride above Peter's happiness. So, agreeing was all I could do.

"However," Peter said, "I do have a solution to make you feel less guilty. So you feel that you aren't taking advantage of me."

My curiosity piqued, I looked up at Peter. What would he suggest? Not that there would be anything I would deny him.

"Since I'm taking you to lunch and dinner today," he explained, "let's go to a big American grocery store tomorrow, and you can pick out all of the delicious things you love to make. And you can cook meals for us. My kitchen needs to be used and I'm not a *great* cook."

Grinning, I nodded slowly.

"I would love that," I said. "To cook for you."

"See?" Peter grinned as he unfastened his seatbelt. "If you would just trust me, things work out so well."

I unfastened my seatbelt as I rolled my eyes playfully.

"I will need more proof before I become an ardent believer," I quipped.

Peter laughed and slipped out of the car, racing around to my door to grab the handle and hold it open for me as I slid from my seat. My cheeks warmed at his romantic display, though I did not mind it at all. Though Montreal's population was greater than that of Minneapolis, I found myself anxious in the swarm of people passing by on the sidewalk.

Americans. I found myself thinking. *They do not like foreigners.*

When Peter laced an arm around my waist and guided me from the car, using his fob to lock it behind us, my tension eased marginally. Having him guide me through the intense, though friendly, faces of the people on the sidewalk, I wasn't as anxious.

"They have a hamburger here," Peter began as we made our way to the two glass and wooden doors with brass accents at the front of the restaurant, "that has sauteed mushrooms, caramelized onions *and* crispy shallots, Swiss cheese—it's just so *fucking* good you will want to have sex with it."

I gave a startled laugh at Peter's profane description.

"And the fries and onion rings are delicious," he laughed with me as we approached the door and he slid his arm from around me to open it.

"Well," I said before stepping through the door, "if I don't feel like having sex with something before this is over, I will be very upset."

Realizing what I said, heat raced up my neck and I dashed through the door that Peter was still holding open for me. Unfazed, he laughed and ducked in behind me.

Holding doors was one of the ways in which Peter showed care. After lunch, he took us on a leisurely drive around the city, pointing out places of interest to me—which I stared at with awe as though I had never visited Earth before—before taking us to his house. The place I would be staying at for the length of my two-week visit. Peter parked his luxurious car in his equally impressive garage, grabbed my bags from the hatchback of his car, and led me to the backdoor of his home. Up a few steps, he held the door for me once again.

Though I was fully capable of doing such things for myself and prided myself on my independence and ability to take care of myself, Peter doing such things for me affected me in ways I had no words to explain. Never in my life had I wished for another man to behave as though I was incapable of something as simple as opening a door. However, when Peter did it, his charm easily conveyed that he was expressing his affection, not passing judgment on one's ability. So, I felt I would never tire of his affections.

The backdoor of his home, a gorgeously renovated two-story American Craftsman, led into the kitchen. Taking in the sight of Peter's kitchen made my eyes grow wide. I did my best to quickly correct myself as I took in the size of the room, its décor, and the appliances. Peter's kitchen rivaled my entire apartment, and it was decidedly more luxurious. However, it occurred to me that Peter's kitchen was probably not all that impressive for an American home in an upper-middle-class neighborhood.

As my eyes landed on the stove, I smiled. Eight gas burners—sparkling clean and obviously untouched for a while—greeted my eyes. If we went and purchased groceries the next day as Peter suggested, I would be able to cook delicious meals easily for him. The refrigerator dominated the corner of the room, but I did my best not to stare at its size.

Coffee maker. Toaster. Blender. Stand mixer. Microwave. Large center island on which to prepare ingredients for meals, make pasta or bread dough. A magnetic bar on the wall over the counter by the sink held a selection of knives. A variety of cooking instruments stood tall in a canister by the stove. A small table with four chairs. The multitude of cabinets surely held pots, pans, plates, cups, silverware—everything one would need for a meal.

Peter had everything a home chef would need.

"Your kitchen is nice," I said over my shoulder as Peter stepped inside with my bags and shut the door gently behind him.

"Thanks," he said. "I don't use it much, but—"

"I can tell," I teased.

"—but," Peter nudged me playfully, "it should have anything you need while you're here."

"I am certain I will somehow manage, even if this is subpar at best," I chuckled, my eyes still scanning the room.

Peter laughed appreciatively at my joke as he rolled my suitcase through the kitchen. I found myself unable to move from the backdoor, as though afraid I would stumble and break something. Or trip and scuff his beautiful wooden floor. When Peter reached the door that led out of the kitchen, he turned with a smile, which disappeared when he realized I wasn't following him.

"Is everything okay?" he asked. "Enzo?"

"Your home is very nice," I said, unsure of how else to explain myself.

Peter stared for a moment, then his expression softened.

"Please act like you're in your own house," Peter said. "This is your home for the next two weeks. You can use anything while you're here. Eat anything. Drink anything. Enjoy yourself. Please. For me."

Drawing in a deep breath, which I slowly let out, I managed a smile.

"I will do my best," I said. "But if I break something—"

"It'll be okay," Peter said. "I promise."

"Okay."

He said: "I need to make a quick phone call to the office. Why don't you show yourself around? Open doors. Inspect the place. Make sure I'm not a serial killer and hiding dead bodies or something?"

I laughed.

"Seriously, though," he said. "Looking around while I'm not watching might make you feel more at home?"

"Maybe."

He jabbed a thumb over his shoulder in the direction he had been going.

"Dining room, living room, den, downstairs half-bathroom," he said, before pointing behind me, "basement door—laundry's down there. Pantry. My little office space. If you want to see the bedrooms and bathrooms upstairs, the stairs are off the living room in the entryway. Or you can take the ones behind you."

My head jerked to look over my shoulder, then back at Peter.

"Two staircases?" I asked. "So fancy you are."

He blushed. "It's...the way the house was built when I bought it. It was a *real* shitbox before I renovated it."

I chuckled warmly. "Shitbox?"

He shrugged. "I tried to make sure it kept its original charm, but, you know, updated it for modern living. I think it hadn't been updated in the hundred years since it was built. Until I came along."

I looked around. "It's very charming. You did a wonderful job. At least in the kitchen."

"You'll give me a decision about the rest of the house after my phone call?"

I nodded. "Yes."

Peter meant that he fully expected me to show myself around as he had requested and to not be shy about it while he made his phone call. If that's what Peter wanted, I would somehow force myself to tour his house and be as nosy as possible. Within reason.

"Then I'll leave you to it," Peter said. "Don't forget to put that in the fridge."

Peter's statement reminded me that I was holding a to-go box that contained two enormous slices of cheesecake from Chop House 42. The crowded, boisterous atmosphere of the steakhouse, frequented by both chic young people and proper business types, was in direct contrast to the exquisite food it had to offer. Though a "burger joint," as Peter explained when we were seated at our table, which was covered in a pristine white tablecloth, the food was delicious and refined.

Doing my best to ignore the prices on the menu, I took Peter's suggestion and ordered the burger he had told me about on the sidewalk outside of the restaurant. Peter ordered the same. Since we both waffled over fries or onion rings, we ordered a plate of each to share. Over a dark beer for Peter and a glass of water for myself, Peter explained that I was going to be shocked by the quality of the food. Of course, I didn't believe him, but I nodded along, simply happy knowing that I would soon be fed after my journey.

Peter turned out to be underselling the restaurant. Burgers that covered half of the plates and teetered precariously in height were brought to our table. The fries and onion rings were mountains upon the trays they were presented on. The quantity of food made me certain that it would be no better than anything one could order at a fast-food restaurant.

Upon my first bite of the burger, Peter once again was proved truthful. Buttery, delicate brioche enticed my tongue as tender, succulent ground meat, grilled to medium perfection, melted in my mouth as its juices threatened to escape and drizzle down my chin. Mushrooms that were sauteed until dark brown seduced my tongue with their earthy, savory, umami meatiness. Caramelized onions, sugary sweet, buttery, and creamy slid over my tongue as the crispy fried shallots snapped and crunched between my teeth—a perfect contrast to everything else. The gooey Swiss cheese melted on the burger and the *real* garlic aioli—both pungent and decadent—were a creamy compliment.

It was the perfect burger.

The fries were crispy and salty when bitten into, but fluffy and delicate inside. The onion rings delivered the aromatic, savory onion flavor contained within the crispy coating; a touch of sweetness following behind. It was all too much and not enough. Everything was so delicious that I wanted to eat until I burst. Dessert had been impossible, even though we had managed to eat all of our burgers, fries, and onion rings. So, Peter insisted that we get dessert to go. I found it impossible to argue with his suggestion. I let Peter decide for us, and slices of cheesecake were his decision.

"I forgot that—" I looked up.

Peter was gone with my suitcase and bag. Knowing that Peter would be upset with me if I didn't tour his home and make myself comfortable, I forced my feet into motion and crossed the kitchen to the refrigerator. Inside the door on the right, I found it well stocked. Milk, eggs, a few juices, real butter, condiments, vegetables, beers, a few sodas, and various containers holding leftovers. I slid the to-go box holding our dessert into an empty space.

Since I was curious, and Peter had insisted I sate that curiosity, I opened the left side of the refrigerator and found frozen foods. A tray full of ice from an automatic ice maker, a tub of ice cream, two frozen pizzas, some frozen vegetables, several steaks, and a variety of meats.

Glass beer mugs, frosty and ready to be utilized, lined the shelf on the door. I shut the doors and turned to examine the kitchen. I had no real interest in finding out what brand of pots and pans Peter had in his kitchen, though I did feel that knowing what his dinner plates looked like would be interesting. Since I knew that I would find that out organically, I decided against opening cabinets.

I ventured into the small office Peter kept off of the kitchen. Utilitarian and obviously designed with a focus on function over style, I stepped back out into the kitchen. Behind a door next to Peter's home office, I found a pantry as big as my bathroom in my apartment, well-stocked with dry and canned goods. My mind could not comprehend that room so quickly after everything else I'd experienced in the day, so I closed the door and opened the door next to it.

A dark stairwell led down into the basement. I assumed the best—that Peter was not hiding bodies—and shut the door. My eyes landed on the stairs that led upstairs from the kitchen, but then I realized I hadn't seen the rest of the downstairs.

Stepping into the hallway that led from the kitchen to the dining room, I found a few chic picture frames on the wall at eye-level above the dark wainscoting leading up from the dark cherry floorboards. The pictures within held what I assumed were family photos. I wasn't quite ready to examine Peter's life outside of his connection to mine, so I ventured further down the hall.

The dining room had the same dark wooden wainscoting as the short hallway, but the large windows that lined the wall to my left made it feel more cheerful. A nice, but understated wooden dining table and chairs enough for ten were the focus of the room, naturally. The room was rather plain; décor had not been wasted on it.

So, I moved from the dining room into the living room. Peter was perched on the edge of the couch, talking on his cell phone. My suitcase was standing before him with my other bag nestled atop it. He continued his conversation but smiled up at me as I entered the living room. When I saw that he was still on the phone, I moved to leave, but Peter indicated that I was welcome to keep looking around. So, I did.

I walked around the living room, looking out the numerous windows at the front yard and neighbors' houses, and eyed the furniture discreetly as Peter spoke into his phone. I did my best to ignore what he was actually saying to whoever from his work was on the other end. Like the dining room, the living room felt a bit sparse. Barren. As though Peter hadn't spilled over into the room. It was functional and clean but had none of Peter's personality.

I gestured to Peter, indicating that I was going to tour more of his house, and he gave me another wave and a smile. Another small hallway off of the other side of the living room, like the one between the dining room and kitchen, greeted me. Halfway down the hallway, I found the half bathroom that Peter had mentioned. Toilet, pedestal sink, small medicine cabinet with a mirror. Functional, clean. I had yet to find anything wrong with Peter's house—nothing that concerned me—but I had yet to find *Peter* in his house.

When I stepped out of the bathroom and traveled to the end of the hall, I finally found Peter.

The den.

It was obviously his favorite room. A large sofa big enough to be a bed for two, an easy chair, gorgeous in the obviousness that it had been used lovingly for years, three bookshelves that reached to the ceiling which were full of books, and an obscenely large television greeted me. A cozy, quilted blanket had been draped haphazardly across the back of the sofa—obviously after having been used for a nap. The ottoman in front of the easy chair was askew just so. Three books were stacked on the end table between the chair and sofa, along with a half-full glass of water. Various remote controls and gadgets were strewn haphazardly on the table.

This was Peter.

A smile came to my face as I took in the room. I imagined that Peter spent hours of his free time in his den watching movies, reading books, and taking naps on his sofa. He maybe even ate his meals from his easy chair. When I turned, I noticed the fireplace tucked into the corner behind me. Taken care of and clean, it still showed signs of frequent use. The hearth was large enough for a person to sit upon it comfortably in front of the fire to warm themselves, even with the bin of logs and the tools on either side of the fireplace.

"*Enzo?*" I started at the sound of Peter's voice coming from the living room. "*I'm going to take your bags upstairs if that's okay?*"

I swallowed and responded in kind.

"That is okay!"

Peter didn't respond but I could hear him carrying my things up the stairs. When I turned back to the fireplace, I felt a tear in the corner of my eye. It had been a long time since I had been in a home and screamed a response to a question. Years had gone by since I had been in a home with proof of life I hadn't created myself. I shook my head, refusing to entertain those thoughts, and walked across the room to look out at the backyard from one of the windows that were on either side of the enormous television.

Minnesota was temperate in mid-summer. Though warm, it was pleasant, so it was no wonder that I found the backyard lush and mostly green. The memory of my one perfect night with Peter in Montreal flashed through my mind as I spotted the patio, pergola, and grill that he had described to me then. I wondered if Peter would grill hamburgers and hot dogs or even steaks for us during my visit. Would we sit under the pergola in the evening hours under the stars, eating our dinner and discussing...*everything*?

I found that I was already imagining what life with Peter as a partner would be like, so I chased those thoughts away, too. Vegetation towards the back of the property caught my eye and I gasped with delight. I turned around, as though expecting Peter to be right there so I could tell him what I had spotted. Laughing to myself, I jogged from the den down the hallway and through the living room to the entryway.

Up the stairs, I found a door to my immediate left. A guestroom? A bit further down the hall, I found a large bathroom for guests, then another bedroom after that. When I made my way to the end of the hall, where the stairs down to the kitchen began, I found a door to my right. Light streamed out into the hallway from the large windows in the massive room. Peter was standing at the end of the bed, and my eyes lit up.

"Peter," I said excitedly as I stepped into the room.

He turned to look at me and a grin bloomed on his face. "Yeah?"

"You have sorrel growing in your backyard," I said. "At the edge of the yard."

"Do I?" he asked. "Oh. Yeah. In spring wild garlic grows out there, too. I usually let the lawn guys harvest it for themselves, but I take some to use from time to time."

I grinned. "I bet it is delicious."

"It is," he said. "Is...do you eat sorrel?"

"You can," I said with a shrug. "Some people like it. Some don't. I like it. Maman would make it into a soup, and—"

I trailed off, my eyes lowering. Silence filled Peter's bedroom.

"You like everything even remotely edible," he said, teasing me to lighten the mood, but he wasn't wrong. "It's one of the things that makes you so wonderful."

My cheeks felt red, so I turned to look at his bedroom. After my tour downstairs, I didn't feel as self-conscious snooping around Peter's bedroom, even with him watching. The cavernous room held a bed so large that surely four men could sleep in it. That thought made my cheeks redder, so I pushed it away. Two dark wood tables with drawers sat on either side of the bed, and both had lamps on top of them. A large dresser of the same wood lined the wall next to the door and probably contained more clothes than I had ever owned in my life.

A bay of windows with dark wood plantation shutters was across the room from the bed. Two armchairs sat before the windows, facing the bed. A small round table positioned between the chairs completed the sitting area. A large door on the wall opposite the entrance led into a bathroom, but the angle was such that I couldn't see inside.

Where Peter was standing at the end of his bed was a small knee-high bench, upon which he had set my suitcase and bag. When I saw my bags on the bench, inside his bedroom, something in my stomach fluttered. I felt faint for a moment. Peter noticed my gaze and winced.

"It was probably presumptuous of me," he said slowly. "You don't have to sleep in here with me. You probably saw the other rooms, so—"

"No," I stopped him, taking in and releasing a soothing breath. "No. I suppose I just—"

"Enzo, you don't—"

"I never thought that I would actually be able to visit you in America," I said. "I *wanted* to. Desperately. But I never believed it. I…I have struggled to believe anything for a while. But…now I'm here. It is real."

I knew I wasn't explaining myself well at all.

Peter was nodding along slowly.

"I guess I assumed we could share my bed," he said, his voice measured. "On Sunday, we can have breakfast over there."

He flicked his head at the two chairs and the small table by the windows.

"Have a *perfect Sunday*," he said.

My stomach fluttered again. *He remembered.*

Finally, he cocked his head towards the bed.

"Huge bed," he said. "It's easy to make sure you have plenty of your own space."

I chuckled nervously.

"It looks comfortable," I said.

"Crawl up on there," Peter said jovially. "Test it out."

I cocked my head to the side and grinned at him.

"Really," he said. "Kick your shoes off and get comfortable."

With a shrug, and knowing that it would do no harm, I put the toe of my left shoe against my right heel and extracted my foot from my shoe. Then I repeated the motion for my other shoe. Gently, I crawled onto Peter's bed and rolled over onto my back to stare up at the ceiling. I wished that I could have taken my outside clothes off, so as to ensure Peter's bedding stayed clean, but also for comfort. However, lying in front of Peter in my underwear in broad daylight would have finished me off. My anxiety would have made my head explode.

Peter was right. Again. The pillow cradled my head and the bed felt like a cloud. I could have easily stretched out my arms and legs and not touched both sides of the massive bed. Though it still made my stomach flutter, thinking of sharing a bed with Peter, experiencing the actual size of the bed eased my nerves. If I had difficulty sharing such an intimate space, it would be easy to put distance between us.

"How do you get out of bed each day?" I asked. "This is heavenly."

"Someone's gotta go to work and pay the bills," he said. "And no one else around here pulls their weight."

I laughed and Peter joined me. After a few moments, our laughter died off, and a comfortable silence filled the room as I lay on the bed and stared at the ceiling.

"What is it like?" I asked.

"I'm sorry?"

"Living in this giant home all by yourself," I explained.

The question was rude. If I'd asked it of anyone else. Peter was different. I knew he'd understand and not be offended.

"Lonely," he said. "Often lonely. Hollow. I swear that every noise is an echo some days. In fact, I think the echo sometimes whispers '*lonely*' at me."

I nodded along slowly. When I didn't respond, though I had deeply connected with Peter's explanation, he spoke again.

"Do you want to take a nap?" Peter asked. "I know you've had a long day already."

Somehow, I managed to shrug, though my eyes were indeed heavy. Between the anxiety I'd had to fight during my journey to the U.S., the heavy, though delicious, food from lunch, and the luxury of Peter's bed, sleep sounded wonderful.

Peter chuckled. "Take a nap. You need to be rested for dinner."

An appreciative moan emanated from my throat.

"Dinner," I mumbled as my eyes began to droop.

"I'll be downstairs if you wake up," Peter said softly and began to tiptoe across the room.

"Peter?" I stopped him, lifting my head.

"Yeah?" He turned to me with a soft smile at the door.

Chewing at my lip, I wasn't completely certain my thoughts would be welcome, but I was certain I wanted to share them.

"I love your house," I said. "The den is my favorite room."

Peter's smile grew.

"It's very nice," I said.

"Thank you."

"Also," I said, "do you want…will you nap with me?" I was overcome with the need to make Peter not feel lonely in his home. If only for a short while.

His smile somehow got wider. "You sure? I was going to use the den sofa."

That made me happy, knowing I was right about Peter's favorite napping spot.

"Please," I said. "If you want?"

Peter didn't say anything, but he mimicked my actions, kicking off his shoes. I moved over on the bed, giving Peter room to climb onto the bed from the side closest to the door. Once he was on the bed with me, we didn't speak to each other, but somehow communicated that our nap would not include being uncomfortable with proximity. Peter gently snuggled up to my side and laid his head on my shoulder, draping an arm over my chest. I lifted my head to look at him and he turned his face up to look into my eyes. Without words, we kissed. Then again. Several small, delicate kisses eased us into sleep. I'd never slept with someone snuggling up to me, using my chest as a pillow before.

I found that I never wanted to sleep any other way again.

But that was probably because the someone snuggling me was Peter.

Fancy restaurants always intimidate me. Prohibitive costs are not the only issue, though that is a piece of it. Generally speaking, my experience with fancy restaurants has always involved the waitstaff looking at me as though I don't belong in their place of business. Probably because I don't; of which I'm aware. Being reminded of that fact is humiliating, however.

Butcher's Prime was a steakhouse, and like Chop House 42, it aligned itself with a diverse clientele while still managing elegance and refinement. A few tables were occupied by people with bright hair colors, piercings, and exciting and unique fashion choices. Other tables were full of men in suits and women in elegant evening dresses. People of all races, ages, and sizes surrounded us in the dining room.

I loved the crowd. It made me feel less like I didn't belong. I was appalled at the menu.

"They are charging forty dollars for…chicken breast." I lowered my menu to lean across the table and whisper to Peter.

He looked up from his menu.

"And sauces and sides are an additional cost, Peter," I said.

Peter grinned.

"It's really good chicken," he whispered back dramatically.

Rolling my eyes, I glanced at my menu again before responding.

"I cannot do this," I said as I closed my menu and laid it on the table. "This is obscene."

My statement was meant to be humorous, but I was actually appalled at the prices.

"I'll order for you." Peter reached across the table to take my menu away from me. "Then you don't have to think about it."

"Having you order for me does not change the prices." I pointed at my menu as it lay on the table in front of him.

Peter laughed and continued perusing his menu.

"It's excellent food," he said. "You'll forget all about that when you take your first bite. If you thought lunch was excellent, you are going to have your mind blown here."

"I will choose to trust you."

Though I felt like a child, when our waiter arrived at our table to take our drink orders, and Peter ordered wine, I ordered a soda. Peter smiled at my choice, but said nothing, nor did the waiter. I'd been told by Peter that he wanted me to have the best vacation ever, so I ordered the drink that would make me the happiest. Peter went back to the menu when the waiter left to get our drinks, and I was left to surreptitiously examine the other patrons of the steakhouse.

I wondered if my long-sleeve button-down shirt, slacks, and borrowed tie from Peter made me fit in or made me look as though I was playing a role. When Peter had informed me that we were going to have dinner at a "nice steakhouse" after we rose from our nap, I had spent an inordinate amount of time in his bathroom getting ready. It wasn't only that his shower had a bench, multiple showerheads, and was big enough for ten grown men to use. I wanted to look nice for our…*date*.

Date. That was how I was labeling our dinner. Though, I wasn't going to ask Peter if he felt the same for fear that he might not.

Every inch of my body had been scrubbed to squeaky cleanliness. My hair was styled perfectly, and I had checked myself out in the mirrors in the bathroom from every angle once I was dressed. When I had joined Peter downstairs, his smile upon catching sight of me was all I needed. Of course, Peter was dressed similarly, though, in my opinion, he looked better.

"Have you gentlemen decided what you would like?" the waiter asked as he set our drinks before us on the table.

He turned to me first for some reason, but Peter cleared his throat to get his attention.

"I'm going to have the prime rib with béarnaise sauce and the scalloped potatoes," Peter said, causing my mouth to water. Then he looked over at me. "I think...for Enzo...we'll do the twelve-ounce filet mignon au poivre with cognac cream...medium-rare...blue cheese potatoes, and...grilled broccolini."

My stomach groaned with pleasure.

"Excellent choices," the waiter said, collecting the menus from Peter. "I'll get your order put in right away."

Peter gave him a smile and a nod, then turned his head back to me once he was gone.

"Did I order the right thing?" he asked.

I nodded. "I can't wait for my food now."

"How was my '*au poivre*'?"

"Excellent," I said.

"Good," Peter said, leaning in. "Was this a good choice for our first date?"

My words caught in my throat, so I had to ease myself into taking a deep breath before I responded to him.

"Perfect," I said. "It is perfect."

"I know that Montreal was our *official* first date," Peter said, "but this is the first one we got to actually plan, so it's still a first date."

"I feel that I'm okay with that."

"So," Peter gestured at my glass, "soda?"

I shrugged as my cheeks warmed. "I don't drink."

"Did you remember to pack your medication?" Peter asked nonchalantly as he brought his wine glass to his lips.

Though I hadn't mentioned my need for medication since our one perfect night in Montreal, Peter had remembered. The fluttering in my stomach returned.

"Yes."

"Good," Peter said. "The desserts here are insanely good. They have a crème brûlée that's served in a tart style crust, which sounds weird, but it's ridiculously delicious, and——"

"We still have cheesecake in your refrigerator." I laughed at Peter's dessert suggestion.

He shrugged. "It'll still be there. It would be delicious for breakfast."

Though instinct told me that I should chastise Peter for his suggestion—*cheesecake for breakfast?*—I didn't want to do that. Instead, I leaned in, mirroring his position, and smiled at him.

"I like you, Peter," I said.

"I like you, too, Enzo," he replied. "A lot."

Torpid and bloated, though ebullient, after dinner, Peter and I decided to walk around the neighborhood in which *Butcher's Prime* was located. Even on a Monday, late in the evening, the neighborhood showed no signs of slowing down. People scurried into and from bars and restaurants, sat at outdoor cafes, drank beers and spirits, had late-night meals, and mingled on the street. Peter must have sensed my anxiety, because his hand found mine, and his fingers tangled with my fingers, and he didn't let go as we walked along.

Holding hands with Peter—another man—fed my anxiety momentarily. Queerness, displayed openly, anywhere in the world is a risk. Sometimes it is calculated, based on what one knows about a neighborhood, city, or country. But it is still a risk. In the U.S., I'd been led to believe that unless one was in New York City or Los Angeles, it was best to not display affection openly if you are queer.

However, I found that Peter and I were not the only two men, or two women, or only queer couple, holding hands on the street. I'd whispered a question to Peter, wondering if we were in a "gay neighborhood," but he had responded that Minneapolis was simply a "queer-friendly" city. Though he was forced to admit that some areas were not as friendly—but he wouldn't take me to those areas. I thanked him for that.

The people we passed on the street were cheerful and friendly and loud, greeting us with "hellos" and "how are you's." Peter whispered to me to simply respond with *"Hello!"* and *"Great! How are you?"* and to keep walking.

"Not to sound jaded, but it's just a formality," Peter had explained. *"No one wants to stop for an actual conversation. And they don't want to know if your day sucked. Save that for friends."*

Americans. I had thought. French by birth, I was not predisposed to cheerful, positive displays if that was not how I felt—and sometimes even if it *was* how I felt. *We're all trudging through life to an inevitable death, collecting misery along the way,* my French innermost self whispered. However, I appreciated the efficiency of the American way of greeting people on the street, even if it was disingenuous.

Greet person so they know you have noticed them and are a polite person.

Receive response that does not invite further conversation so you know that you were noticed and they are a polite person.

Go about your day.

Feigned politeness was not necessarily the best way to connect with other human beings, but it was an efficient way to get through a day.

My greatest fear—that someone would hear my accent and comment derisively—was laid to rest quickly. Most of the people we spoke to briefly in greeting either did not care about my accent or responded with delighted comments. No one screamed at me for being a foreigner.

Though I had lived in two different countries and had learned for myself that one never truly knows the culture and mood of a place unless one has spent time there, I was still shocked by my first day in the U.S. I hadn't once been treated poorly or spoken to rudely. Not once had I seen someone with a gun strapped to their waist. I was so amazed by this, that I had to share my thoughts with Peter.

He had chuckled and said: "*Oh, it'll happen. There are some real assholes here—like anywhere else. It's just not as common as people will lead you to believe. Of course, it's probably more common than I've said.*"

That sounded more like the truth than anything else I'd been led to believe.

Stereotypes about countries are neither true nor untrue. Because stereotypes are generally passed along from one ill-informed person to the blissfully ignorant. Stereotypes have no life unless it is breathed into them by those they are used to poorly describe.

I found that I wasn't certain that anything I knew about the world was true—since truth is found in experience. And experience varies based on various factors.

But I knew for certain that any experience was better if I was holding Peter's hand.

"I've never done this before," Peter gave me a conspiratorial grin.

"Really?" I asked. "I am shocked."

He leaned into the table and chuckled.

"I'm full of surprises."

"I am certain that is true," I said.

At the kitchen table in Peter's house, we sat, sipping coffee, two empty plates between us containing the crumbs and smeared remains of our slices of cheesecake we had been saving. Since we had walked so much, we both felt we deserved a treat when we got back to Peter's house. When I had suggested that I make coffee to accompany our cheesecake, Peter had been aghast.

"Caffeine at this hour?" he had asked.

With a laugh, I had ignored him and used his French press to make enough coffee for a small cup apiece.

"Dinner was delicious," I said after taking the last sip of my coffee. "Thank you again."

"You don't have to keep thanking me," he said. "You've thanked me seventeen times tonight."

"I will say it an eighteenth time if I want."

"Ooooh, feisty." Peter chuckled.

He licked his finger and dragged it through the crumbs on his plate, then licked his finger clean. I smiled at his hedonistic display.

"How was your first day in the U.S.?" he asked. "Is your vacation starting off well?"

I sighed happily and sat back in my chair. "It was a perfect day."

Peter seemed pleased with my response.

"Besides tonight—obviously," Peter asked suddenly, "what was the best meal you've ever had?"

I began to speak, but he stopped me.

"And don't mention The Lazy Duck," he warned me, referencing the meal we'd had together in Montreal, "because that's pandering."

"I wasn't even going to say that." I turned my nose up comically. "You are full of yourself. I barely remember anything of that night."

Peter laughed.

"That beet salad at The Lazy Duck was delicious, though." He smacked his lips.

Frowning, I said, "It was a warm salad with lentils and—"

Peter's grin grew and his eyes seemed to twinkle. I smacked myself in the forehead gently.

"You are…you are…"

"An asshole?" He shook his head playfully at me as he leaned into the table.

"No." I smiled and looked down at the table. "You're wonderful. Of course, I remember that night."

Peter smiled warmly.

"But," I said, "if I am supposed to choose some *other* meal, it would be a Christmas dinner with my family. Before…well…*before*."

When I looked up, Peter was smiling sadly and staring into my eyes.

"Do you miss them?" he asked.

My shoulders rose and fell.

"Not as desperately as I once did," I said. "My apartment doesn't feel as lonely and hollow as it did before. But, yes. I think about them every day."

"Are you doing okay in Montreal?" Peter asked. "I worry about you. Probably more than I should. You're a capable, smart…*handsome*…guy. But I find I think about you at least a hundred times a day."

I raised an eyebrow.

"What's he doing? Is he okay? Does he think of me?" Peter laid out his thoughts for me. "You've occupied a lot of my brain for two years, Enzo."

"Have I?"

"You have."

"Are your thoughts always simply about my well-being?" I asked.

Flirtation was my intention, but I had such little experience, I hoped that Peter would pick up on my meaning. When he grinned at me from across the table, I knew he understood.

"Of course not," Peter said. "I've thought a lot of things about you since I last saw you."

I bit at my bottom lip and looked down at the table. Surely, my cheeks were crimson. It wasn't embarrassment at having Peter say such a thing, it was embarrassment at finding that I desperately wanted to know what those thoughts he'd had were, but unsure that I could listen to them without embarrassing myself further.

"Do you want to know what I think about most often?" Peter asked, his voice husky. "I can tell you if you want."

I took a shuddering breath and forced myself to look up at him.

"I feel…I feel that another time would be better," I said. "I don't know if I could hear those things right now."

Peter looked worried for a moment, but when he saw the grin playing along my lips, he smiled.

"Okay."

For what seemed the longest time, we stared at each other across the table. Finally, Peter broke the silence, but his eyes continued to bore into mine.

"Do you want to go upstairs?" he asked. "To bed?"

"Yes," I said. "But I need a moment before we get up."

When I shifted in my seat, Peter chuckled. But it wasn't amusement that rode his tone. It was something deeper, warmer…dangerous. I found that I liked it, but it didn't help my situation.

"Are you sure that you're okay with this?" Peter whispered. "I can sleep in the guest room."

Peter whispering in the dark made it difficult to breathe, though I had been having trouble breathing normally since we had walked upstairs and gotten ready for bed. He was sitting on the left side of the bed, speaking over his shoulder shyly, a shadow in the blue-ish black light that only the deep night provides. I sat on the edge of the right side of the bed, doing all I could to keep my knees from shaking. Though Peter never would have seen it in the dark, surely, he would feel the vibration through the bed, and I'd already made enough of a fool of myself.

In the two years since Peter and I had last seen each other, I'd dreamt of our reunion every second of every day. In my fantasies, events had unfolded much differently. I was sure, though he would have never said, Peter had imagined things going much differently as well. We certainly wouldn't have been in full pajamas, sitting in the dark, the better part of a California king between us.

"I have never been naked in front of another man," I said. "Not—not like *that*."

I felt Peter shift on the bed.

"Enzo," he said, his voice sharper, so I knew he was turned towards me now, "I don't expect anything from you. I'm happy you're here."

"Are you sure?" I asked. "I wanted things to go much differently, Peter. I feel like a horrible guest."

Peter chuckled.

"You're not my guest," he said. "You're so much more."

Though I felt anxious, I smiled.

"I'm scared."

I prayed that maybe Peter hadn't heard me, yet hoped that he had.

"We don't have to do anything, Enzo," Peter said. "All we have to do is crawl under the covers and sleep. Hold each other, not hold each other, it's all okay. I really am happy you're here. No matter what."

"What if I am not good at sex?" I asked.

Ignoring Peter's kindness was not my intent, but I felt that ignoring my feelings and what I was thinking would build an impenetrable wall between Peter and me. One that I would be too afraid to try and climb once the moon disappeared and the sun peeked over the horizon. At best, it would have to be torn down, brick by brick over time. Who knew if the process would take so long that one, or both of us, would eventually lose interest before it was complete? Waking up and finding out that Peter no longer looked at me the way he had all day would destroy me. I knew Peter was a patient man. He'd waited the better part of two years for my first visit, after all. I wanted desperately to do the thing that was on both mine and Peter's minds. I had no idea how to start.

Peter's breathing was a bit more ragged suddenly, as though he was unsure of what to say in response to my question, yet aroused by it.

"I feel that," I whispered, "maybe I will be very bad at it and you will be sorry that I came to visit you."

"I would never be sorry you came to visit me, Enzo," Peter stated firmly. "Ever. Do you hear me?"

I nodded, as though this was an appropriate response in the dark.

"What if I—what if it is over really quickly?" I asked one of the biggest questions I had; the most embarrassing.

"It usually is the first time." Peter chuckled.

"But, for someone like you," I turned my head to speak over my shoulder, "that will be disappointing."

"Someone like me?" He sounded amused. "I do believe you insulted my virtue."

A nervous giggle—*a giggle, for God's sake*—escaped my throat.

"I mean—"

"I know what you mean, Enzo." Peter stopped me. "I'm just teasing you. I've had sex before. You haven't. I'm older. You're young. I get it."

"Okay." I turned my head to look towards the windows again, though all I could see through the slats of the shutters was the blue light of the moon.

The bed shifted and I heard Peter's feet against the floorboards—those gorgeous dark cherry slats that spoke with every tenth or so footstep. Sporadic words and whispers from a house returning the love it had so obviously been given. Peter didn't merely live in this house—the essence of him did, too. Every nook and cranny, each floorboard, every warm accent to this home felt like Peter's arms being wrapped around me. It was a castle, though its grandeur wasn't its size or adornments, but the care he'd shown in restoring it. Peter hadn't made a house. This was a home. Even his bed felt like patience and kindness. I knew that once I was wrapped up in the blankets, I would feel at home. I folded my arms in my lap to hide my obvious excitement since my sweatpants were not capable of such a job.

Peter rounded the bed, a silhouette within the blue light of the moon.

"Do you want to hear about the first time I had sex?"

"I don't know if that will make things better or worse." I was giggling again.

The darkness did my warm cheeks a favor. Peter's eyes, their sclera startlingly white in the dark, were on my lap. He shifted from one foot to the other.

"The first time I had sex," Peter said, "I didn't have sex."

"What?"

"Well," Peter moved towards the bed like a rusty robot and jerkily sat down next to me, "we got into it, kissing and letting our hands do a little above the waist stuff."

"Okay."

The side of Peter's leg was touching mine as I did my best to keep my eyes on his in the near-darkness. It suddenly occurred to me that erections could actually ache.

"But as soon as his hands went below my waist, it was over." Peter chuckled. "His hands weren't even inside my pants. That—that's how my first attempt at sex went. I thought I'd die of embarrassment. I kind of wanted to puke, to be honest. What fifteen-year-old is ready to deal with *that*, ya' know?"

"Fifteen?" I teased. "What a whore you were."

Peter bumped his shoulder against mine gently.

"Wannabe whore," he clarified. "I wouldn't be an official whore for another three years."

"Because of the embarrassment?"

"A little bit, yeah. But I also began to realize that I wanted to make my *official* official first time something special. With someone special."

"Oh."

"If you don't think that I'm that person for you, Enzo," Peter said, "don't force yourself to do anything because you feel you have to—or because you feel you're on some timetable to lose your virginity. I would never feel good about myself again if you had sex with me out of some perceived obligation. My heart would never come back from that."

"Your heart?"

"That's where I hold you," Peter said, his hand reaching for mine. His fingers laced around my wrist, pulled my hand up, and with his fingers, opened my nervous fist to lay my hand flat against his chest. "To know I had any part in making you do something you truly didn't want to do would be something I couldn't recover from."

This was doing nothing to relieve the ache in my groin.

"I'm very skinny."

"I have a bit of a belly now," Peter said. "I've missed the gym for a few months due to work and I've enjoyed too many beers."

"Your clothes must hide it."

"It's there."

"I don't have much hair."

"What does that mean?" He did his best not to laugh.

"My body is not—it's not very...*manly?*"

"Trust me." Peter's hand rubbed against mine and his eyes were on my lap again. I moved my other arm so that it wasn't blocking his view, emboldened in the moment. "It is."

"Okay."

"Do you want to talk about the things you want to do? Or try?" Peter asked. "We can talk about what's okay, not okay, what *might* be okay."

My heart was thundering in my chest and another lower part was throbbing. I had to concentrate so that my hand didn't shake nervously against Peter's chest. Of course, he knew how nervous I was—I hadn't been shy in making that clear—but I didn't want him to know that I was so nervous it was affecting me physically. I didn't want him to know that I wasn't in control of my own body. Peter wanting to make me comfortable made me want to make this moment— and those that followed—as comfortable for him as possible as well.

"Will you take off your shirt?" I whispered my question. "Is—is that okay?"

Peter smiled at me, and then his hand was pulling mine up to his mouth. His lips pressed against my knuckles before he let go, relinquishing control of my hand. My arms returned to my lap and I felt my back hunch, as though my body was trying to shield itself from further embarrassment. But my eyes stayed on Peter. I was unable to look anywhere else, no matter how nervous I was about what was likely to come.

His eyes fixed on mine as his hands reached for his shirttail. Slowly, almost painfully for me, he lifted his shirt upward, a sliver of his stomach exposed at first, then more, then his chest, then his shirt was covering his face. Finally, Peter's face came back into view and his shirt was in his hands. Even in the little light that the moon provided, I could tell that Peter's statement about his belly had been inaccurate. Maybe he didn't have washboard abs, but there was nothing of which to be ashamed. It could have been my imagination, but I felt that I no longer knew how to breathe.

"Breathe," Peter suggested though I wasn't sure if he had read my mind or my body language. "It's just a gorgeous body, after all."

I laughed, which forced me to breathe.

"That is not funny," I said, "because it's true."

"Jokes don't have to make sense," he said, "and you laughed anyway."

Neither of us spoke for several moments.

"Have you ever touched another guy?" Peter asked. "In a sexual way?"

"No."

"Do you want to?"

"More than anything. Well, not just any guy. But, yes." The beginning of my answer overlapped the ending of Peter's question, which made him smile. "I'm nervous."

Peter smiled at me a moment longer, then his hand was reaching for mine again. As before, he brought my hand up to his mouth and his lips pressed against my knuckles, his eyes boring into mine. Then he lowered my hand to his chest and laid it against his bare flesh. *Jesus Christ. I was going to explode simply from the anticipation.* Peter's hand slid from mine and he left me to decide what happened next.

"Enzo," Peter said, "I don't mind if you touch me anywhere."

"Okay."

"Not just now," he said. "Whenever we are together, and it's an appropriate time and place, you don't have to ask permission again. Okay?"

"Okay."

"I'll wait for you to give me permission to do the same. Okay?"

"Okay."

"And if one of us does something that the other doesn't want or like," Peter suggested, "we'll tell each other. We'll learn about each other's bodies together. What we like. What we don't like. What we might like. We'll respect each other but we also won't make each other feel weird no matter what. I won't make fun of you no matter what happens—as long as you treat me with respect. Same for you. I'll treat you with respect and you won't make fun of me."

"Okay."

"Say 'okay' again," he teased.

"Sorry." I chuckled. "I think I am going to pass out."

"Seriously?"

"No." I sighed. "I am just—I am overwhelmed."

"In a good way?"

"Yes."

"Oh. Good," Peter replied. "I think."

"You—you can touch me," I said, though I hadn't known I was going to say it until my lips started to move. "You do not have to ask permission again, either. But I need some minutes before…"

Peter glanced at my lap with a smile.

"Got it," he said. "I don't want you to really pass out."

I was suddenly incredibly aware that my hand was still on Peter's chest, my flesh touching his bare flesh and the sparse hairs there. Were they red like the hair on his head? I had not yet seen them with the lights on. For a split second, I almost asked Peter to turn on the bedside lamp, but I didn't want him to see my obvious predicament. That would have to wait until the next time.

Please, God. Please let there be a next time.

Please don't let me be horrible at this.

"You know," Peter said, reaching up to grab my hand, "even if the first time is quick, you're young. We don't have to stop doing things if you come too quickly. There are other things that can be done until you're ready to try again. I recover pretty quickly for a guy my age, ya' know."

This man can read my mind.

Peter slid my hand down until it was against his stomach. I could feel a thin trail of hairs traveling to lower places.

"Is your body hair red, too?" I asked.

Peter laughed, the little bit of belly he had shaking against my hand. That, too, made me harder.

"Yeah," he said. "Everywhere."

"*Everywhere?*"

"Yes. Everywhere."

A lump in my throat joined the one in my pants.

"Do you want to see?"

"Not this time."

"This time?" Peter's voice was thick.

"Yes." I felt my fingers begin to move against his belly, stroking those hairs and the flesh beneath. "Next time…definitely next time."

"I can live with that," he said, a soft moan escaping his lips as I stroked his flesh, "will I get to see you then, too?"

"Yes." I moved my hand so that my fingers played along the waistband of Peter's pajama pants.

"I want to kiss you." Peter exhaled.

"You never have to ask permission for that, either." I somehow managed to answer even though my heart was in my throat.

Peter moved towards me too suddenly, so that when his lips met mine, my hand was pushed into his lap by his stomach, and I was suddenly touching the most intimate part of him. My whole body shuddered and I almost yanked my hand away out of surprise. Somehow, I managed to leave my hand where I had so agonizingly slowly been working towards. Peter gasped against my mouth, but he recovered and kissed me deeply, his hands coming to cup my face.

Touching another man's erection for the first time nearly sent me over the edge. It wasn't only Peter who shuddered as our lips pressed against each other's. When I felt Peter's tongue gently push against my lips, urging them open, which they gladly did, I knew that Peter had been right about first times. Maybe I wouldn't end up coming too early, but I wouldn't last nearly as long as I would like, or long enough to feel proud of myself. Trying not to be embarrassed by the possibility of coming too soon was getting easier the more we kissed and the more my hand laid against him. All I wanted, now that my fear was melting away, was to make Peter realize how I felt about him.

The most surprising thing to me as Peter's tongue tried to memorize my mouth, and I inexpertly tried to do the same to his mouth, was how warm he felt against my hand. I had only ever touched myself in such a way—and I knew that so much blood in one body part created warmth—but it was surprising nonetheless. Peter was breathing heavier the more we kissed, but when my fingers decided on their own to grab him through the material of his pajamas, he gasped.

When I suddenly felt Peter pull his mouth away and his mouth moved down to my neck, kissing, licking, and gently sucking at the taut flesh there, my fingers gripped him more firmly. I held him firmly in my fist, though I didn't do more, as I wanted to prolong this moment for as long as possible. No complaints were uttered from Peter as his mouth continued moving. I'd never had someone kiss me in a romantic way, let alone in such a passionate and hungry manner that wordlessly explained how much they desired me. It was intoxicating. My whole body seemed to be made of jelly as Peter's mouth moved against my flesh. Peter's mouth on my neck only increased the sensations I was already feeling throughout my entire body. Never, in all of my fantasies, had I imagined that being kissed on the neck would make every part of my body respond.

"I'm going to take your shirt off," Peter managed to mumble as his mouth moved against my neck.

"Fais-le," I moaned. "Maintenant."

Peter froze.

"What's wrong?"

"You just said something." Peter pulled back to look into my eyes. "In French."

I laughed. "Sorry. I—I—my brain. Everything is not working at the same speed right now."

Peter smiled, though his breathing was still ragged.

"Were you giving me permission?"

"I told you to 'do it now.' I just meant to say it in English."

Then my mouth was on his, which surprised him, though not in a bad way. I knew this because his hands were grabbing at the hem of my shirt desperately and pulling it upwards. I didn't have the time or desire to worry if I looked too skinny or if I didn't have enough hair on my chest or stomach. When Peter pulled my shirt off over my head, all I could think about was how I didn't want to pull my mouth away from his long enough to allow it. All I wanted was my mouth on his and our hands on each other's bodies. However, once my shirt was removed, Peter placed a hand against my chest—*a glorious feeling, his flesh against mine*—at the base of my throat, and pushed me back ever so gently.

"What?" I gasped, my lips missing his immediately.

Peter didn't answer, but instead, let his eyes travel over my chest, which was bathed in the soft moonlight. In the dark, it was hard to tell if what Peter saw pleased him, or if instead, it made him question his activities with me.

Am I too skinny?

Do I look boyish?

Are my rib bones showing too much?

"You're so fucking gorgeous, Enzo."

"That is a lie," I said. "But I do not mind it."

Peter laughed, his fingers trailing to the side to trace my collar bone, sending shivers up my spine.

"You're gorgeous to me," he said. "Will that work for you?"

"That works for me." I agreed.

Then I remembered where my hand was on his body; my grip loosened.

"Don't." Peter shivered. "This is okay. For me. Is it okay for you?"

"Yes." I nodded anxiously, my fingers wrapping more firmly around him through his pajamas. "Am I doing everything well so far?"

Peter smiled. "I think your hand has the answer, Enzo."

My cheeks felt hot, but I was more pleased than embarrassed.

"Am I—am I a good kisser?"

"The only way I can answer that…I will kiss you until you can't remember how many times you've been kissed," Peter said. "Your lips should never be without mine on them."

Peter lowered his hand, wrapping it around mine. As he stared into my eyes, he began to move my hand, showing me how to stroke him. His eyes stayed on mine as he moaned softly.

"Is this okay?"

I nodded again, unable to form words.

"Do you want to do more?"

I shook my head, though I wasn't saying "no."

"Stop asking permission," I said. "We said that we do not have to ask permission. We will tell each other if something is not okay."

"Then I'm going to do something I will just have to beg forgiveness for later."

And then his hand was on me. Not my face. Not my neck. Not my chest. Or even my stomach. He was gripping me the same way that I was gripping him. He was wise to not move his fingers once I was in his hand; I shivered as a groan burst from my mouth.

Oh. This is what everyone is so crazy about.

The world makes sense now.

"Well," Peter muttered, his voice like honey, "you're doing better than I did my first time."

I tried to laugh but only managed to groan. Hopefully, Peter understood.

"Enzo," he said, "I need you to know something."

"What?" I gasped as his hand began to move slowly along the most intimate part of me. "What is it?"

"I don't care if you don't last long. I just want to do this. If you want to. I just want us to do this together. We have all night to try again and again to get it right. Okay? Are you okay with that?"

"Okay. Yes. Please." I nodded; my hand was holding him firmly as he stroked me.

Before I could even wrap my mind around what was happening, before it could send signals about how excited I should be, Peter was sliding off of the bed to rest on his knees before me. With the practiced movements of someone more experienced than I, Peter had freed me from my pajamas and he was lowering his head to my lap.

Everything on my body—save one part—stopped working correctly. My legs shook, my hands grabbed at the bed, my head flopped around on my neck, and my toes curled. Thundering in my chest, my heart threatened to explode as my lungs decided that breathing was not so important anymore. What was oxygen when I had *this*? Though I had no experience to compare it to, or with, I knew that Peter was doing an excellent job. It wasn't long before I knew there was no turning back from what Peter was trying to make my body do.

Do I tell him to stop?

Do I warn him?

Does he want me to stop him or warn him?

Will he be upset if I do? Or don't?

My mouth uttered some words, though I had no idea which language they were in, and I spilled forth, which only seemed to encourage Peter to increase his efforts. That only intensified the feelings coursing through my body as I stared down at his head and screamed out in what I could only describe as the most exquisite distress I'd ever felt. Peter's hands reached up to my chest, stroking my flesh as he continued his movements. Even as my orgasm subsided, Peter continued to coax me with his lips, as though now soothing instead of stimulating me. My fingers found his hair, tangling in that fiery field of silk, attempting to express my pleasure without sound.

Moments later, when Peter had moved back up to the bed and was letting me taste myself on his lips and tongue, I knew that not much time would pass before I was ready to try those other things to which he had alluded. Having survived such a joyful embarrassment, I was emboldened, and I found myself sinking to the floor before Peter, who was still more than ready for such a thing. *You will help me?* I had whispered, as I knelt before him. He nodded eagerly as his fingers slid through my hair.

Although Peter had to guide me a bit to begin with, I quickly realized that I took to this act as though it were second nature. At least with Peter. I found myself desperate to please him, enthralled with the sounds I could elicit from him with just my lips and tongue. Though I had to put more work into achieving the same goal he had achieved with what seemed a minimal effort, I still achieved it. As he had done with me, I let him taste himself on my lips and tongue.

The night wore on and I was filled with a hunger to know every inch of Peter's body, to learn all of the dances our bodies could do together. I was like a ravenous and parched man, stumbling out of the desert, ready to feast and drink, to sate every appetite. Every lesson Peter taught me— the use of condoms and lube, how to position his legs, his knees bent over my shoulders, my hands on either side of his body as I held myself above him—was an act I knew I would want to perform over and over, again and again.

I found the universe in Peter's eyes as I slowly slid in and out of him, testing how he looked at me while I was being sweet. Then I saw the devilish charm of him when he encouraged me to see how it felt to be not so sweet, thrusting with abandon. When I would stop, afraid that I was hurting him, he only encouraged me—with a slap on my ass, no less—to continue exploring all of the sexual beings contained within me.

A devil and angel in one skinny body, and someone who enjoyed both equally.

At the end of our night of exploring each other's bodies, Peter and I lay in a heap, unsure of where I began and he ended. The fitted sheet had been yanked away from every corner of the mattress, curled up and inching towards us, which made us laugh. No inch of my body had gone unexplored by Peter's hands, and my hands had touched every bit of his flesh. Not once did either of us have to ask forgiveness. As I drifted off to sleep, holding Peter in my arms, his head against my chest, my chin nestled in his hair, I was left with a single thought.

For once, everything is not between the universe and me.

Right now.

At this moment.

It's only Peter and me.

Peter, not the universe, owns this piece of me.

Getting to Know You

Insanity. It was the only explanation for my behavior the following morning. When I woke, late-morning sunlight was streaming through the opened shutters in Peter's bedroom. Wrapped in the comforter, a smile came to my face automatically. Warm and cradled like a baby by Peter's bed, a content sigh escaped my mouth. My intention was to roll over and wrap Peter up in my arms. Pull him into my body. Inhale his scent and kiss him good morning. However, when I rolled over, I found that I was alone in bed.

Peter was gone.

Typically, such a thing would have created at least a mild panic. However, after the evening and night I'd had with Peter, I knew he hadn't abandoned me, but he wasn't in bed. Staying there and waiting for his return wasn't an option, though. Not having him next to me made curling up under the covers unappealing. I rose from bed, and it took some searching, but I found my underwear halfway across the room, in a heap with my sweat pants. I slid my underwear on—the bare minimum to be presentable—and wandered out of Peter's room after a quick trip to the toilet.

The floorboards creaked a "good morning" as I made my way to the back stairs and tiptoed down to the kitchen. I had barely descended halfway down when the smell of coffee tickled my nose. The sound of something sizzling whispered up the stairwell and I hurried the rest of the way down to the kitchen, pleased that my suspicions on where Peter had disappeared to were correct.

Upon entering the kitchen, I found Peter was across the room, standing at the stove, his back to me. At that moment, I discovered there was a second Enzo living inside of my brain. A brave, amorous, wicked Enzo. That Enzo grinned mischievously and tiptoed across the kitchen like a bandit and snuck up behind Peter. When I wrapped my arms around him, he jumped in surprise. When my mouth found his neck, laying a passionate kiss upon it, he laughed warmly.

"Good morning," he said as he turned in my arms, a spatula in his hand.

"Good morning," I replied, sighing happily as I held him.

Peter cocked his head to the side.

"Step back," he said, his brow furrowed.

Frowning with confusion and worry of rejection, I let my arms fall from around him and stepped back. Peter's eyes scanned my body, from the top of my head to my feet. When he looked back up at me, an impish grin was plastered on his face.

"That's a sight I could wake up to every morning," he said.

Instinctively, I wanted to be embarrassed. I'd never so brazenly been so close to nude in front of another person— at least, not in a way that was intended to be seductive. I found that, though my instincts told me one thing, that Other Enzo told those instincts to shut up.

"I will make sure you have this sight every morning I am here, then," I said.

"Don't," Peter said, pointing the spatula at me in playful reproach. "I'm trying to make breakfast for you. I wanted to be sweet and romantic. I can't be distracted."

"I am terribly sorry," I said, though we both knew I didn't mean a word of it.

Peter rolled his eyes and turned back to the stove, poking at whatever was in the pan on the stove with the spatula.

Insanity.

I found that it couldn't be shaken so easily after the night we'd had together.

Stepping up behind Peter, my mouth returned to his neck and I pressed myself into him, my groin grinding into his backside. Despite his best efforts, Peter moaned and tilted his head to give me better access to the flesh at his neck. I kissed and sucked gently at his skin as my arms wrapped around him to travel down his body and find the most sensitive part of him.

"*Enzo,*" he said, trying to sound annoyed at my distracting actions.

"Oui? *Yes*?" I mumbled against his neck.

"Nothing," he groaned. "Fuck it."

Peter spun and his arms wrapped around me. He pressed himself along the length of me as our mouths found each other, feeding hungrily. Somehow, I managed to reach behind Peter, my hand grasping for the handle of the pan, and I pushed it from the burner. Metallic clatter filled the kitchen and we chuckled against each other's mouths. A bit more groping and I found the knob to turn the burner off. Peter's mouth was on my neck and one of his hands had slipped down between us to slide into my underwear.

Groaning animalistically, I fed at his mouth, my hands holding his face as he stroked me.

Who was the person standing in Peter's kitchen, so uninhibitedly letting another person touch the most intimate parts of him?

"Damn you," Peter whispered against my mouth when I moved to kiss him.

"Damn you," I repeated.

"I'll have to start breakfast over." Peter somehow groaned around my tongue as he stroked me desperately.

"Go upstairs with me," I said. "And I will remake the breakfast. Please?"

"Well," Peter pulled back just enough to look me in the eyes, "since you said 'please.'"

"You're a pervert," Peter said. "The things you just did…"

He was straddling my lap as I laid proudly on the bed, far back enough on my thighs that his now flaccid penis laid lazily next to mine. My fingers were trailing along the hairs on his tummy, tickling at the red hairs that the sunlight caught and turned to waves of wildfire upon his flesh.

"Tell me you did not enjoy it." I sighed happily.

"Why lie?"

"I am only a pervert because I have a good teacher."

"You're a good student."

He laid a hand over mine and guided my hand along his stomach, up to his chest, along his side, helping me to explore his body with my fingertips.

I sighed. "Peter?"

"Yes?"

"What do you think?"

"Of what?"

I blushed and Peter had a moment of realization.

"You're even more attractive with the lights on," he said, bringing my hand up to his lips to kiss it. "I'd ask that you don't wear clothes for the rest of your visit, but I want us to leave the house every now and again without getting arrested."

His lips touched the back of my hand. Then he opened my hand with both of his so that he could kiss the palm, the fingertips, then the back of it again. His eyes never left mine.

The late-morning sunlight shone along Peter's milky flesh as he sat atop me and his lips made love to my hand. Laying my other hand upon his thigh, I sighed happily as Peter stared down into my eyes. I'd never felt so many pleasant emotions at one time before. Flooding through me, I felt I'd be overcome with those feelings. I wanted to kiss Peter. I wanted to trail my fingers over his entire body so that my fingertips memorized every inch of him.

I wanted to pull Peter down and hold him; refuse to ever let go. I wanted to push him off of me and onto the bed so that we could have sex again. And again. I wanted to do things that I had fantasized about many times but had never admitted out loud to anyone before. I wanted to tell Peter those things and see the surprise and hungry desire in his eyes. And I wanted to hold him and kiss him tenderly so he knew how I cared for him.

I wanted to thank him profusely. Like an orphan with a bowl empty of gruel.

Thanks for the mind-blowing sex. Please, sir. May I have some more?

I wanted to thank him for almost effortlessly introducing me to this other side of me.

I wanted him to know that it wasn't only his body that I desired.

And I wanted to stare at him so that every inch of his body was burned as an indelible memory in the deepest recesses of my brain. So even when old age came to claim parts of me and tossed them into the void of time, Peter would always be there.

"I could look at you like this forever," I said.

"My knees are eventually going to give out," Peter teased, but he gave no indication he intended to move. "Then I'll be stuck here. And so will you."

"*Oh, no,*" I cooed happily. "That would devastate me. Whatever would I do?"

I moved my hands to his hips and let my fingers dig into his flesh playfully.

"Again," Peter said. "You are a pervert."

"Do you hate it?"

He laughed.

"Definitely not. I could think of worse things than being trapped on top of you forever."

My fingers dug into his flesh a little harder. Peter looked down.

"No," he said, looking down at my groin. "Breakfast first."

I laughed warmly and groaned with frustration. Not at Peter, but with the sudden unleashing of my libido. Of course, I'd always known that it was there, lurking in the darkest recesses of my mind. It had simply been waiting for the right person to be unleashed. Peter had proven to be the perfect candidate. The genie was out of the bottle, and I knew as long as Peter was near, it would refuse to go back inside. Of course, I wanted to argue with Peter that food was not nearly as important as what was slowly trying to rise and push against his groin, but I knew he was right.

"I…can I request a special favor?" I asked.

Peter grinned wickedly. "What is it?"

"Can we shower together?" I asked. "I would…I've always wanted to do that."

"And then you'll make breakfast for me?" Peter brushed a feather-like finger along my flesh from my sternum down to my belly button.

I shivered. "Yes. But if you do things like that, we may never make it back to the kitchen."

Peter chuckled and lifted himself from my thighs. I grunted with displeasure, though I knew we had to get out of bed eventually.

"Then let's get in the shower." He held a hand out to me as he stood at the side of the bed.

"Fine," I said, reaching out to take his hand.

"Don't worry," Peter said as he led me into his bathroom, his hand swatting my ass, "I'm a great back scrubber. You won't be unhappy for long."

"Who taught you to cook?" Peter asked, bringing his fork to his mouth. "This is delicious."

I set my plate on the kitchen table across from him and slid into the chair. Freshly showered, both of us in jeans, t-shirts, and socks, it was nearly lunchtime before we had breakfast. However, we'd rewarmed the coffee and I'd made scrambled eggs on toast. Buttery, creamy, and soft set, seasoned merely with chives and salt and pepper, the eggs were a sunny yellow against the brown, crispy toasted slices of bread. Peter hadn't been able to wait for me to sit before trying a bite.

"My maman," I said. "Well, she taught me to cook many things. But—"

"Your mother?"

"Yes." I nodded and picked up my fork and knife. "My mother taught me how to cook. My grandmother taught me how to cook things my mother knew nothing about."

Peter smiled at me as he chewed.

"They were very different women from different cultures." I shrugged, though I wasn't remembering them with sadness; I was smiling.

"I wish I could have met them," he said.

"I do, too," I said.

After the last twenty-four hours we'd spent together, I realized that there wasn't anything of Peter's life from which I wanted to be shielded.

"Are the people in the pictures in the hallway your family?" I asked, bringing my first bite to my mouth.

"Mm," Peter said, stuffing more of the eggs and toast into his mouth. "Yeah. I can tell you who everyone is after we eat."

"I would like that."

For a few minutes, we ate in silence and sipped our coffees, though it was not awkward, and each time our eyes connected, it was familiarity that passed between us. Peter's home was quiet, only the sounds of our utensils on the plates and our coffee mugs being set on the table after each drink filling the air. Though, I found that the quiet was not the lonely quiet of my apartment. It was peaceful. The ballad of two lovers spending a moment in time together.

It was a song I'd never known I had been missing from the playlist of my life. A song I found I wanted to be played every moment of every day for the rest of my life.

"We've got to go to the grocery store later," Peter groaned appreciatively as he stuffed the last bite from his plate into his mouth. "I was an idiot to take you out to eat when I have my own little chef right here."

I chuckled, my cheeks warming from the compliment.

"Thank you," I said.

"Other than buying groceries—super exciting stuff, obviously—what else would you like to do on your second day in the U.S.?" Peter asked and sat back in his chair as he brought his coffee to his lips.

I thought about that.

"I had so many ideas when I was studying to come to the U.S. for the first time, and—"

"You...*studied*?" Peter asked.

"Yes," I stuck my tongue out at him. "Your money, units of measurement and volume and weight, customs—"

"You are such a nerd."

I blushed, though I knew he was merely teasing.

"I know," I said.

He sighed. "It's so fucking sexy."

My blush deepened, but Other Enzo forced me to stretch under the table with my foot to run it along his calf.

"So?" Peter asked, smiling as my foot trailed along his leg. "What other American things are on the agenda for your second day?"

I shrugged. "I am here for two weeks."

"It's not long enough."

"The grocery stores stay open very late, yes?" I asked.

"Some all night." Peter nodded.

"Then," I set my fork alongside my empty plate, "I know what I want to do."

"Okay," Peter reached down to rub my foot with his hand. "What is it?"

"I want to go back to bed," I said. "I want to study my new favorite subject."

"You horny little—"

"And we can go to the store later?" I asked. "Please?"

"You know," Peter didn't answer my question immediately, which frustrated me in the most wonderful way, but he brought my foot to his lap and massaged it gently as he stared into my eyes, "I thought having a young man in my bed would make me feel old. You don't make me feel old, Enzo."

"You make me feel…many things," I said with a grin. "That feels wonderful."

"We can go back to bed," Peter said. "But I want to sit here for just a little bit longer and just enjoy having you with me. I've waited a long time to sit across this kitchen table from you."

"Oh?"

"Every morning," Peter said, "I'd think about our night in Montreal, and our emails and texts and phone calls and letters. And all I could think as I ate meals right here was how I wished you were sitting across from me."

I had no words to respond to Peter.

"I saved all of your letters," he said, his hands still massaging my foot absentmindedly. "Sometimes I reread all of them."

"I saved your letters, too."

"How often do you reread them?"

"I will not answer that," I said.

Peter laughed. "Understood."

"I often think of the same things," I said. "Sharing a meal with you again. Especially in your kitchen. Or mine."

"And then we go to your bed or mine and you act like a raging pervert?" he asked.

"Again, I feel that you enjoy that." I flexed and kicked at him gently with the foot he was holding.

Peter laughed. "You don't know how much."

Again, we were left in comfortable silence, staring into each other's eyes.

"Last person to the bed has to wash the dishes when we finally get out of the bed?" Peter suggested with a nonchalant shrug.

Laughing and doing everything we could to be the first to his bedroom, Peter and I rushed from the kitchen and ascended the back stairs.

"We should grill steaks one evening," Peter said as he moved up behind me, pressing himself against my back before kissing my neck.

Even though we were standing in the middle of a grocery store, I found that I was unconcerned that anyone might see. Of course, it was nearly ten o'clock at night, and the store was mostly empty. Anyone who is in a grocery store so late in the evening has likely seen worse things than one man kissing another man's neck.

"I will make the dishes to go with the steaks if you grill them," I said, turning my head to kiss Peter.

Electric tingling seemed to have overtaken my body for the day. Every little touch from Peter since breakfast made my body react in ways I'd never experienced before my trip to the U.S. We'd spent the entire afternoon in bed, and even as the sun set outside, we stayed in bed. Hands, tongues, lips…and other parts…explored every inch of our bodies. When we weren't exploring each other's bodies and moaning with desire, we were laughing and holding each other. Staying in Peter's bed with him for the entirety of my trip began to sound wonderful to me, even if it was unrealistic.

Hunger interrupted our enthusiasm for our activities. We'd finally crawled out of bed, showered for the second time together, and put our jeans and t-shirts back on. Seeing Peter clothed, after so many hours of nothing to hide his nakedness from me, seemed odd. But it was necessary.

Do you want me to put the sheets in the washer? I'd asked after we stood by his bed, freshly showered and clothed.

I wouldn't. Peter had replied. *If we wash the sheets every time we have sex, that's all we'll be doing while you're here.*

Promise? I had asked.

Of course, Peter had been serious. Washing the sheets every day would have been a ridiculous idea. Not having sex would have been worse.

Maybe every three days? I had teased him.

Peter had thought about this. *Maybe we need to use one of the guest rooms for all the sex so our sleeping area will stay clean?*

Laughing, we kissed for far too long as we stood beside his bed, and found that the evening had slipped away. Finally, we forced ourselves to leave the house and drive to the grocery store.

"Why are there so many cereals?" I asked, interrupting our kiss by the meat selections. "But the bakery is…not good?"

Peter laughed uproariously.

I winced. "There is sugar in *everything*."

"Do you hate it?" he asked before giving me another quick kiss.

"I love sugar," I said with a shrug. "I am just wondering. I hope that is not rude."

"No," Peter kissed the tip of my nose, then, with obviously great willpower, forced himself to step back. "Most of the prepared foods here are full of salt or sugar. Or chemicals. You have to kind of expect it here if you don't want to be annoyed all the time. Or don't buy prepared foods, I guess."

"Can we buy some of the cereals?" I asked impishly.

"Absolutely," he said. "You've had cereal before, though. Uh, right?"

"Of course," I said, as though this was the most preposterous thing I'd ever heard. "Don't be ridiculous. I've just never had a cereal with ten spoonfuls of sugar in each bowl."

Peter pinched my side playfully and I laughed, slapping his hand away.

"I know Canada has to have sugary cereals," he said. "I've seen them when I've been in grocery stores there. And I know they have them in France in, like, the American section of grocery stores."

"Of course," I said, "but not in such abundance. And I have never bought them, so I have never tried them."

"Okay," he said. "We will introduce you to the U.S. sugar crisis."

"Wonderful," I said and rubbed my belly hungrily.

Peter and I selected steaks and other meats that I thought we might need for the length of my trip. Then produce and canned goods. We did our best in the bakery, though I was not impressed with the selections. Breads and pastries, being two of my favorite things, had made me particular about the products I chose. Fortunately, I found that American grocery stores carried a wide variety of spices and herbs, though not many that were fresh. Peter selected beer and then put a case of sodas into the shopping cart for me, which made me chuckle.

A variety of cereals were selected—all with too much sugar and startingly colorful—and we visited the cheese and dairy section, which also did not impress me. However, when we finally paid for the groceries and were loading them into the back of Peter's car, I felt we had done sufficiently to feed ourselves for the rest of my stay. If Peter and I ran out of food, we would also have gained plenty of weight in the process.

As we drove back to his house, Peter took one hand off the steering wheel, guiding us through ghostly empty streets, and grabbed my hand. He turned his head long enough from the road to smile at me, then he brought my hand to his lips and kissed it gently. When he let go of my hand, his free hand didn't go back to the steering wheel. He laid it upon my left thigh, gently squeezing my flesh here and there, as though laying claim. Or, maybe, protecting a claim he'd already laid and I hadn't realized until that moment.

Oh. I had thought. *There's that song again.*

Peter set the bowls on the table in front of me, then placed the carton of milk next to them. Next, two spoons clattered into the bowls, and Peter slid into the seat across from me at the kitchen table. I had been so engrossed in reading the back of the cereal box that I had barely noticed him. When he cleared his throat and chuckled with amusement, I pried my eyes from the colorful box and its outrageous ingredients list to look at him.

"Two nights in a row where I have sugar before bed," he shook his head reproachfully at me. "You're trying to make sure I gain ten pounds while you're here, aren't you?"

"What is the big deal?" I asked, my hands moving to the top of the box to open it. "When we go upstairs, we will get exercise."

Peter grinned happily at me.

"I guess if I turned you into a pervert, you can turn me into a chubby guy," Peter said.

"You would be just as sexy," I said, dismissing his thought.

Peter continued to beam at me.

"I promise that you will not gain any weight while I am here, though." I winked at him.

Flirting with Peter—though not as salaciously as I wanted—was becoming second nature to me. There had been a time that looking into another guy's eyes—one I found attractive—would render me a stuttering mess, incapable of coherent speech, let alone charm and humor. Peter put me at ease. He made me feel safe. Though I'd often thought it over the previous two years, after two days in Peter's home, I knew there was nothing he couldn't ask of me.

If he had told me to get up on the table and have sex with him right there, I would have done it. Enthusiastically.

"I'll trust that you aren't lying," Peter said. "I'll be incredibly sad if you are."

The cardboard box popped open and my fingers ripped at the plastic bag inside.

"You will be tired of me in two weeks," I said, grinning over the top of the box at him. "You may ask me to leave early."

Peter looked shocked. "Yeah. Not going to happen."

Laughing, mostly to hide how Peter's words affected me deeply, I finally managed to rip open the cereal bag. Peter held the bowls for me as I tipped the box over each, pouring us both a healthy serving of the colorful nuggets. As I was closing the bag and box, Peter poured milk into each bowl, then passed me mine with my spoon sticking out of the sugary heap.

Neither of us spoke as we dug into the cereal and brought heaping spoonfuls to our mouths. Peter groaned appreciatively as he chewed his bite. When the sugary cereal hit my tongue, my mouth filled with saccharine sweetness, and the crunchy bits of cereal jabbed at my tongue and the roof of my mouth, I was shocked. However, I chewed and thought about the textures and flavors...*and sugar*.

"This is disgusting," I said, finally. "I love it."

Peter laughed; his mouth half full of cereal.

"It's truly vile," he agreed before taking another bite. "It was my favorite when I was growing up. Every Saturday, I'd eat a huge bowl of this—usually out of an old Country Crock tub my mom had saved to store leftovers. That's, uh, a butter-like substance they sell in these big tubs with a plastic lid? Anyway, I'd watch cartoons and get high as a kite on sugar. I was obnoxious all morning long."

I grinned over the table at him, a warm feeling settling over me at hearing about Peter's youth.

"I'm surprised you made it to adulthood," I said. "This is so much sugar."

Peter nodded. "You and me both."

A few minutes ticked by as the two of us ate our bowls of cereal, savoring the extravagance. When our bowls were empty, Peter indicated that he was done, and though I wanted to eat more, I knew that I shouldn't. So, the two of us were left at the table, staring at each other, our bellies full and our eyes wild from the sugar.

"How have you been?" Peter asked suddenly, though softly. "Really? We've kept in touch, but we don't really talk about the important stuff."

I shrugged. "We don't."

"So?" he asked again.

"Okay, I suppose," I said. "I have been working a lot since I finished university. Money is good and it keeps me from thinking too much, so I like to work."

Peter nodded along but made no attempt to interrupt.

"I have a couch," I said happily. "I think I told you that?"

He smiled and indicated I had told him that already.

"And a rug," I continued. "A small television. New sheets and a few warm blankets. I have good shoes now. My pantry and fridge are never empty. I have a bus pass. Which is nice?"

"What about friends?" Peter asked. "You said one time you'd made some new friends in your classes, so—"

"I have been working a lot," I said. "I have not seen them much."

"Are you lonely?" he asked.

I shrugged. Peter was asking me about my life because he actually cared to know about my life. He wanted to know everything about me. I didn't want to lie to Peter. So, I realized a shrug and interjections would not do.

"Yes," I said. "I suppose I'm lonely all of the time."

"I am, too," Peter said.

Our eyes met and we both couldn't help but laugh.

"I have a new, good coat of my own," I said through my laughter. "I brought your coat back to you. I took care of it."

Peter shook his head. "I don't want it back. It was a gift."

"Well, it is in my suitcase if you change your mind."

"I won't," he said. "I like that you have it."

"Okay. Um, yes. I guess I'm okay. My job is good. I really love it, even if it is a little boring."

Peter laughed, as though he understood this concept, so I smiled and continued.

"I'm still taking ESL classes with Monsieur Paquette. He has helped me a lot. Not just with my English but with life, I suppose. He's a very kind man. He retired from his primary job recently and we had a party for him. I think he will not teach ESL much longer, but we have coffee together once a week. I suppose he is a friend, too?"

Peter sat back in his chair and smiled, as though settling in happily to listen to anything I had to tell him about my life in Montreal.

"Sometimes I still clean houses for extra money, but I don't have to if I don't want to," I continued. "My salary is enough. Maybe one day I'll have an even better job and…well, I try not to get ahead of myself."

"You will one day."

I nodded. "It's not so difficult to not have my family anymore, I suppose. I only miss Noe and Ila and my parents and grandmother five or six times a day."

Peter smiled warmly at me; his eyes glistening with understanding.

"I do not have time to go to church every day, but I go on Sundays," I said. "Pray for them—to them. I have started going to the basilica? I…I don't like going anywhere but there now."

Another warm smile greeted me from across the table.

"It's my favorite place now. Besides home."

"Do you ever eat at The Lazy Duck?" Peter asked, sitting up to lean into the table excitedly. "Have you recreated our feast?"

I chuckled. "I would love to, but that is outside of my budget."

"Damnit," he said, sitting back once again. "I wanted to hear what the courses were."

"I'm sorry," I said with a laugh.

"Maybe the next time I'm in Montreal, we'll go together," he said.

"Maybe?"

"We might want to try a new restaurant next time."

"Oh," I said. "Good."

"There will be a next time, Enzo," he said, his foot stretching under the table to rub my calf. "And a next time. And a next."

"How have you been?" I asked, mostly to keep myself from becoming overwhelmed with joy.

"Probably the same," he said as he continued to rub my calf with his foot. "Lonely. I work a lot. I've been skipping the gym a bit, so I need to rectify that. Mom and Dad were here two weeks ago to visit. I think I told you?"

I nodded.

"They're doing well," he said. "Dad's loving retirement and Mom's getting used to having him around all the time, but I guess that's forty-five years of marriage, right?"

My eyes grew wide. "Wow."

"Yeah," he said softly. His eyes seemed glazed over "Imagine finding someone you'd want to spend that much of your life with, right?"

"Or...someone you can't wait to spend forty-five years of your life with?"

"Yeah," he said in the same dreamy voice.

Silence pervaded for a few moments, then Peter shook his head clear of thoughts.

"Every time I found a letter from you in the mailbox it made my day," he said. "I can't believe I'm admitting this, but I rush home every day to see if I have a letter from you. The texts and phone calls and emails are great, but holding one of your letters in my hands is like having you with me."

My cheeks felt warm, but I refused to look down or try to hide it from Peter.

"I've probably read every one of them at least fifty times," he said. "Your letters are poetic."

"I get inside my own head," I said as an excuse, "and forget that I am actually writing a letter to another person."

"I love them."

"I love writing them to you."

"They feel like the truth."

I shrugged. "I suppose they are."

We both laughed.

"I mean—"

"I know what you meant," I said.

"Okay."

"Okay," I teased.

Peter sighed and sat back, pulling his foot away from my calf, which I immediately missed.

"It's after midnight," he said. "If we want to be out of bed at a reasonable hour in the morning so we can do something exciting on your third day here, we probably need to sleep soon."

"True," I said. "After we exercise, of course."

Peter grinned evilly.

"I'm going to wash the bowls and put the milk and cereal away," he said. "Go upstairs and wait for me. Be nude when I get there."

I rose from the table and pulled my shirt off over my head, then slipped my pants off as if sliding out of my skin, looking into Peter's eyes as I did so. He swallowed hard and rose from the table.

"Fuck it," he said. "Let me just put the milk up and we'll go upstairs together."

"I was hoping you would say that."

On my third day in the U.S., Peter and I extracted ourselves from bed—after our morning exercise—showered together, dressed, and had breakfast. We agreed that sugary cereal should be a treat, not a meal, so I made a frittata for us instead. Once we had eaten and washed the dishes—including the bowls from the night before—we actually left the house during the daytime hours. Again, I found myself the passenger in Peter's car, his hand squeezing my thigh as he drove us expertly through Minneapolis traffic. I found that I loved having Peter's hand holding my thigh, though I felt compelled to lay my hand on top of his and twine our fingers.

He didn't seem to mind.

Peter took me to the River Walk. It was supposed to be a self-guided audio tour, but even though we paid the requisite fees, we decided to forgo the audio. Instead, we strolled hand in hand, talking about our lives and the things we found along our walk, and greeted other Americans exuberantly, asking how they were doing though we didn't want an answer. Peter seemed to derive great pleasure from watching me say "hello" and "how are you" to everyone who looked friendly.

After our walk—which lasted much longer than it would have had we taken the audio tour—we returned to Peter's house so that I could make lunch. He had promised me that I could cook for him so that he wouldn't spend more money than necessary on food, and he kept his promise on that third day. Fettuccine with a lemon cream sauce and sauteed chicken was our meal, and we ate until the entire pan was empty. We actually ate from the pan. Bringing it directly from the stove to the table, I set it upon a folded dish towel, and Peter and I ate together from the pan as we told stories and laughed.

After lunch, Peter took us to the Sculpture Garden, and like our time at the River Walk, we spent most of our time leisurely strolling hand in hand, talking about our lives instead of paying attention. The thought that began to form in the back of my mind, as we held each other's hands and walked along, was that no one seemed to care. None of the other visitors to the Sculpture Garden looked at our locked hands with disgust. No one turned up their noses. No whispers or hisses greeted our ears.

It was so peaceful that it had escaped my notice for the first half of the day.

When our time at the Sculpture Garden was over, Peter drove us to his office building so that I could see where he worked. We didn't actually go inside so that I could see his office or meet his coworkers, but he wanted me to at least see where he worked each day. It was an impressive building of metal and glass, though somehow it looked sophisticated instead of coldly and impersonally modern. I imagined dark woods and brass and leather chairs inside, though I figured that was probably not typical for a modern company. Everything was probably all straight lines and minimalism with glass and steel—nothing I imagined when I thought of Peter's warmth.

That night, I made an onion tart and roasted vegetables. Peter had indicated that all of the heavy meals were "going to be the death of him," so something lighter was in order. After dinner and the dishes were washed, Peter led me into his den and we laid in his favorite napping spot on his giant sofa and snuggled as a movie neither of us cared about played. Within minutes, Peter's favorite place to nap became one of his favorite places to do other things.

Eventually, we managed to make our way upstairs to his bedroom for the night.

The following three days were essentially the same, though the places we visited in the city changed. In the mornings, we'd have sex, shower, I would make breakfast, and we would eat. Then we would go on an adventure until lunch. We would return to Peter's home so that I could cook for us. After lunch—and possibly more sex—we were off on an afternoon adventure until dinner started to beckon us. The evenings were spent wrapped in each other's arms, talking about our lives, telling funny stories, teasing each other, and more sex. The nights were Peter's head on my chest, my chin tucked into his hair, and our arms around each other as we drifted off to sleep in his giant bed.

Every day was the same song, whose melody never grew bothersome.

Golden sunlight, the kind that only the earliest morning hours can produce—right as the sun peeks over the horizon—was streaming through the open shutters when I awoke on Sunday. I had washed Peter's bedding the night before, and the crisp sheets and fluffy comforter whispered against the flesh of my legs as I stretched and groaned happily. Though a week of my visit had passed, I tried to push that from my mind. Focusing on enjoying my limited time with Peter was all that mattered. Everything else could be dealt with as it came, including my return to Montreal and leaving Peter behind; returning to my lonely life.

Where a man I cared for deeply wasn't perpetually waiting to be dragged off to bed. Or to have breakfast with each morning. Or lunch. Or dinner. Or to snuggle with and watch an innocuous television show or movie. No one to hold hands with as I walked down a busy city street, jubilant and excited simply to be alive.

Peter was down in the kitchen again when I ventured from the bed to search him out. I'd done nothing more than put on my boxer briefs before tiptoeing downstairs. Peter's home was becoming as comfortable to me as my apartment. When he caught sight of me, he gave me an appreciative, leering assessment, hunger in his eyes, before shaking his head clear of thoughts. Playfully, he ordered me back upstairs for a "surprise." Of course, I couldn't deny Peter anything, so I stomped back upstairs, feigning frustration with him, though I knew he saw right through it.

Barely five minutes had passed, and I was lounging on the bed once more, when I heard Peter coming down the upstairs hallway towards his room. When I heard the sound of his footsteps, I sat up expectantly. I didn't want him to see how eager I was to have him back in his bedroom with me, but I found that, with Peter, I didn't care if he thought me overly eager. I'd done nothing in the last week to show him that I could be cool and calm when around him. There was no need to try and start so late into my visit.

"I made breakfast," Peter said, "to have breakfast in bed. Kind of."

I rose to my knees on the bed so I could clearly what lay upon the tray that Peter was carrying into his bedroom. The coffee carafe and two mugs were clearly visible, but the food—the most important part—was not.

"I'm not the greatest cook, as you know," Peter said, making his way to the table by the windows, "but it's all edible. Maybe even tasty."

I chuckled at the sight of the plate of scrambled eggs, the pile of buttered toast, and the plate of sausages. Peter had not made a complicated or refined breakfast, but everything looked delicious. Sliding from my kneeling position on the bed to lay my feet on the floor, Peter smiled nervously over at me. I didn't leave him in suspense for long as I crossed the room to him and wrapped my arms around him, my lips finding his immediately. Peter's hands went to my hips as he leaned into the embrace.

"I wanted to have a Perfect Sunday," Peter whispered against my mouth once our lips parted. "Like we had talked about? At that fountain?"

"Carré Saint-Louis," I said quietly, staring into Peter's eyes. "I remember."

He smiled.

"We will have breakfast, talk about life and politics and everything that matters, and then we'll be *sweet*?" I asked, punctuating each part of my sentence with a quick kiss on his lips.

"You might have to be not so sweet," he whispered back, "if the breakfast sucks."

I laughed. "It looks delicious. It looks perfect."

Peter sighed happily with relief. "Come on. Sit down. Let's test out the table and chairs. I only sat in the chairs when I bought them. Since then, I've been waiting for you to sit in them with me."

There wasn't a response good enough for what Peter had said, so I let him lead me to my chair and I slid into it, inhaling the savory steam still coming from the plates. The eggs were a little overdone for my liking, the sausages maybe a little too brown, and the toast not quite brown enough, but it was the best meal I'd ever seen. Because Peter had prepared it for us to enjoy together. Because it was a Perfect Sunday. Finally.

Peter slid into the seat across from me as I poured coffee into each of our mugs from the carafe. One thing I had learned in a week's time was that Peter did know how to make a perfect pot of coffee. Once our mugs were full, Peter and I each grabbed a fork, sharing the plates, eating from them communally as we sipped our coffee.

A comfortable breakfast commenced, the two of us eating and sipping our coffee, our feet playing with each other's as we exchanged sly grins. Through the window, I could look out onto Peter's front lawn and the street. Early on a Sunday, with the sun barely above the horizon, the neighborhood was golden and warm. The street was empty of cars and foot traffic, and for a moment, I felt like Peter and I were the only two people in the world. Out of the corner of my eye I could see Peter watching me and smiling, sipping his coffee.

Knowing that Peter was happy to sit at the table, on a Perfect Sunday, and watch me with nothing more than a simple breakfast and cup of coffee pleased me. I wanted to turn and look at him, chide him for being so happy with such simple things; tease him for staring at me and smiling like a puppy dog. However, I didn't want to ruin our comfortable silence and peaceful meal. When he began to softly whistle, I couldn't help but smile, though I kept my eyes on the lawn below.

When I recognized the tune, that changed. My head turned to him automatically, as though controlled by a creature living deep within the most important organ in my chest.

Here Comes the Sun.

As our eyes locked, and Peter saw the look of recognition on my face, he stopped whistling and grinned widely at me. For several moments, we simply stared at each other, Peter smiling, me trying to control the fluttering in my chest.

"I bought Abbey Road," I said. "When I finally had enough money. I have listened to it so much I may have to buy a new one soon."

"Yeah?" Peter asked. "Did you like it?"

"That is the best song on the album," I said, then relented. "Okay. The whole album is brilliant, but that's my favorite."

Somehow, his grin grew.

"Enzo," he set his coffee on the table and leaned in, "would you like to see Lake Superior?"

"Yes. Of course."

"I've been wanting to ask you if you'd like to use two of your vacation days to go," he said. "It's a two-and-a-half-hour drive. We could rent a cabin or a hotel room. Spend a day or two checking out the beaches. Eat lots of food. Hold hands and walk along the beaches at sunset like romantic assholes."

I laughed. "I would love that."

The Day We Felt Superior

Leaning out of the car window, reckless and guileless, my eyes were closed tightly against the onslaught of wind that whipped through my hair. Peter was laughing and singing along to the radio as I sucked in great lungfuls of the Northern Minnesota breeze. Somehow still cool and crisp in summer, it stung my cheeks as we drove along the lakeshore highway. With the lake to our right, the breeze seemed speckled with flecks of icy water, the air scented with things woody and earthy. The warmth of the sun fought against the wind and drops of lake water, warming my cheeks as I smiled up, sightless, at the clear blue sky.

Morning had drifted away as we drove north from Minneapolis to Duluth. We had left as the sun was rising, and breakfast was due when we reached the small port city. Eating at a small diner near the lake's shore, we enjoyed hearty breakfasts that settled in our stomachs like stones, but satisfied our cravings for indulgence and carelessness. Biscuits and gravy, bacon, eggs, pancakes—and bowls of fruit so our guilt could be mitigated—we feasted as though it would be our last meal. When breakfast was over and paid for, we waddled from the diner and resumed our trip north.

Apparently, Duluth was not our intended final destination but a stop on our way to where we would be staying for our miniature vacation. Though Peter shared little of the plan he had in mind for our trip, I was unconcerned. I was simply happy to be invited along on the adventure, I left him to make our decisions for us.

It occurred to me—in passing since I was more concerned with enjoying our road trip—that I was uniquely and immediately comfortable in deferring to Peter's judgment. Following someone without question or concern, and relying on their perceived experience, was an unusual decision for me. A decision I made subconsciously. Relinquishing control over any aspect of my life was outside of what I had considered normal for a great period of time.

Though I'd insisted—and won—in giving Peter money for gas, he had chosen the route we would take on our trip. He'd selected the diner for breakfast when we had arrived in Duluth. He had made reservations for our overnight accommodations. He had asked if I had any preferences as he made those decisions, but I had shrugged and indicated that I was okay with whatever he chose. Which was so unlike me.

As my head hung out the window, and my face was assaulted by the crisp breeze, I realized that, with Peter, I had not a single care in the world. Hedonism, or my version of it, was my motto for the short trip. I could simply enjoy myself, pursue pleasure in the moment, and indulge in the sights, sounds, flavors, and smells without concern for whatever the next day would bring. Because, with Peter, I felt that I was part of a team. Where I ended, he began. And vice versa. I didn't feel alone for the first time in a long time.

I felt like I had a partner who had my back.

That realization forced my upper body back into the car and returned my butt to the warm car seat. Though I left my window open to enjoy the breeze, Peter took notice of the change in my demeanor. Reaching over, he laced his fingers through mine and gave my hand a squeeze.

"You okay?" he asked.

I managed a smile and a small nod as I squeezed his hand back.

"I am just excited," I said, raising my voice to be heard over the music and wind. "The lake is beautiful."

Peter grinned.

"It smells like—"

"Cow shit?" Peter quipped. "Fertilizer?"

I laughed, forgetting my sudden concern with what I'd been thinking.

"It smells like nature," I said. "Don't be disrespectful of this beautiful countryside."

"Nature meaning cow shit?" Peter let go of my hand to jab a finger into my side playfully.

I chuckled and swatted at his hand. "No. Stop that. It's beautiful."

Peter jabbed his finger into my ribs a few more times impishly, but his hand finally returned to mine and our fingers twined together once more. He turned his head briefly to gaze into my eyes.

"It is beautiful," he said. "I can't think of a person I'd rather share this with, Enzo."

As he turned his eyes back to the road, he lifted my hand and kissed the back of it passionately before grinning out at the road that raced up to meet the car. Somehow, I managed to speak around the lump that had suddenly formed in my throat.

"I can't either."

"It'll do for one night, right?" Peter asked as we entered the suite. "It's nice enough."

Setting the duffle bag on the floor at the end of the bed, filled with our combined changes of clothes and toiletries, I look around the room. The suite at the lodge where Peter had made reservations wasn't much larger than a standard hotel room. However, the king-size bed looked comfortable, covered in fresh, clean linens. Two comfortable chairs sat in the corner by the glass door that led out onto a balcony. Lake Superior was a mere stone's throw from it. From anywhere in the room, we had views of the lake.

"Somehow I will manage," I stuck my nose in the air.

Peter laughed. "Turd."

I gave him a wink. "It's wonderful, Peter. Amazing view."

He turned to look through the wall of glass on the other side of the room. After our breakfast in Duluth, we drove less than an hour up the highway along the lake to Castle Danger to the lodge we'd be staying at that overlooked Lake Superior. Comprised of timbers and imposing as it sat upon the shore, the lodge proved to be quaint and homey inside. The rooms were warm and somewhat out of date, though I felt that was intended to seem more charming. There were few frills, but the lodge was meant to be a relaxing getaway for people, not thrilling. It was perfect.

"I thought," Peter said as he sauntered across the room to stand by the windows and stare out at the lake, "you would enjoy sleeping in a room like this. Where we could keep the curtains open and see the stars as we drifted off."

Staring at the back of Peter's head, haloed in the brilliant sunlight that poured through the windows and cast metallic ribbons of gold on the lake beyond, the lump in my throat had returned.

"In the morning, we can have breakfast sent up before we leave," Peter said, the corner of his smile visible as he explained himself and stared out at the lake. "We can sit on the balcony with our coffee and watch the sunrise."

He turned to me.

"It seemed like it might be nice," he shrugged. "There's a brewery up the road. I know you don't drink, but I thought we could stop by there tonight for a pre-dinner drink for me. Then we can go to one of the small restaurants and try the local food. After, we can come back here. Be sweet—or not so sweet—somewhere new."

He smiled at me. Though I would have expected wickedness in the curve of his lips, the gesture implied something else. Something longing and warm. Something that I felt in my chest that was reflected on his face. A thing that scared me. An answer to why I didn't mind relinquishing control to Peter.

"That sounds perfect," I managed to say. "I can drive if you have too many drinks."

He laughed. "I'll try to show restraint."

"The room is beautiful," I said. "The view is gorgeous."

Peter turned back to the windows with a smile and gazed out at the lake.

"I wasn't certain," he said, reaching up to scratch his head, "since you can't trust pictures of hotels online, but it did turn out perfect, didn't it?"

"It's exactly what I would have chosen. It could not be better."

Suddenly, he was turning back to me, excited.

"Just wait," he said. "You might not have noticed, but I saw an ice cream stand down by the lake. We'll go get an ice cream cone and walk along the beach and—"

"Ice cream?" I chuckled warmly, the lump in my throat refusing to vacate. "This early?"

"Well," he said, "once it's a respectable time to get ice cream, we'll go get some and have an adventure. See how beautiful the lake really is."

"Ice cream," I said.

"I know my man has a sweet tooth," he said with a silly, uninhibited wiggle of his head.

"Your...*your* man?"

Peter cringed and took a deep breath, as though suddenly realizing his foible. I hadn't seen it as a transgression on his part—being called Peter's "man" bothered me as much as an ant under an elephant's foot. I had simply been confirming what I had heard come from his lips.

"Well, I," he began, reaching up to scratch his head again, which I found endearing, "no. Yeah. My man. That's...that's what I said. And I know you like sweets. I'm not taking it back."

"In case I forget," I said, "I have loved every minute of my vacation. Thank you."

A stream of green milky liquid ran down the cone and over the meaty part of my palm, but I did my best to slurp it up with my tongue before it dripped off, lost to the ground below. Wasting good ice cream was something I could not abide. Peter chuckled as he watched me lick up the stray stream of ice cream from my hand and the cone. It was surprising to me that my ice cream melted so quickly when it was just warm enough to not need a jacket outside. Regardless, my ice cream had to be saved, and I did my best.

The gentle, languid waves of Lake Superior rolled in, one coming in, one coming out, folding and rolling over each other. What breeze we'd had in the early morning hours had tapered off and we were left with a whisper here and there from the cool, late summer weather. Peter and I had changed into swimsuits and t-shirts to get ice cream and walk along the shores of the lake.

More rocks and pebbles than sand, the shore wasn't meant for long strolls as I'd hoped. However, Peter and I managed to enjoy the beach area and our ice cream just the same. Standing there on the shore of Lake Superior, holding hands while our free hands held ice cream cones, couldn't have been more perfect. The weather was a little too cool for ice cream, but then again, was there ever a bad time for ice cream?

"You are an ice cream master," Peter announced.

"No ice cream shall survive in my presence!"

I made my announcement with a triumphant raising of my head from my hand, my lips, and tongue slathered with ice cream. Peter laughed and reached up to wipe my lips with his thumb. When he licked his thumb clean, I was startled at first. Peter had licked food off of his thumb that he had gotten from my lips. Then I remembered everything Peter's lips had done in the week that I'd been visiting him and realized it was not that strange.

"Delicious," he said, somehow making that one word lascivious.

"You'll find that I am pretty delicious in general," I said, surprising even myself.

Peter leaned in with a grin. "I'm well aware."

My cheeks grew warm, but I gave him a quick kiss on the tip of his nose. I only managed to smear more ice cream on his nose. Laughing, I wiped at the streak, clearing it from his face. Peter, laughing at my clumsiness, lowered himself, pulling me down alongside him. Together, we sat on the rough rock-strewn beach and licked and bit at our cones, staring out at the sun shining diamonds on the lake. Every now and then, Peter would lean over and kiss my neck or cheek; whisper something unmentionable in my ear. Or maybe he'd say something sweet. I was appreciative of all of it. I even returned a few of the kisses.

We didn't care if we got ice cream on each other.

Once our cones were eaten and our hands were sticky with melted ice cream—which we tried to lick clean, but failed—we rose and walked to the water, laughing at our predicament. In the chilly water, we washed our hands, only splashing each other a bit. Enough to be playful, but not enough to soak each other. Then we were standing at the shore with the water lapping at our toes as we looked out over the lake, our fingers twined together again.

The golden ribbons cast on the water by the brilliant sun both warmed me and cast me into melancholy. Being at Lake Superior and only staring at the water seemed such a shame.

"Hey, you," Peter whispered. "What's wrong?"

"It's a shame that it's too cold to swim," I said. "We're here and it's too cold."

He chuckled. "It usually is. Minnesota, eh?"

That brought a smile to my face.

"But it's only too cold if you're scared," he said, daring me. "I mean, if you think you won't be able to deal with the cold…"

"Are you getting into the water?" I turned to him, crossing my arms over my chest.

"I'm not stupid," he said, laughing.

Without another thought, I grabbed my shirttail and pulled it up, stripping my shirt off over my head. Peter's eyes bulged as I held it out to him.

"Please?"

"You're not really getting into the water," he said.

"I am."

"Enzo," he said, "I was kidding. You'll freeze yourself to death."

"Then I suppose you will have to warm me up when I am done?" I suggested.

It took a moment, but Peter finally grinned.

"Tell you what," he leaned in, as though there was someone nearby who might overhear, "if you get in the water and you actually submerge yourself. Get *everything* wet—"

Suddenly, he was glancing all around us, confusing me. Then his eyes came back to mine.

"—I'll take you right over there—"

He gestured at a densely wooded area off of the beach several meters away.

"—and warm you up. Right there. Outside. Any way you want."

I shivered. It wasn't the cold water or the breeze. And it wasn't about being cold at all. I felt very warm.

"Any way I want?" I asked.

"Mmhm."

Before Peter could say anything else, my feet had taken on a mind of their own, dashing away from the rocky shore and out into the water. I was knee-deep in the lake before Peter even reacted.

"*Enzo!*" He laugh-screamed out at me. "*You're crazy!*"

"*This is all your fault!*" I screamed over my shoulder at him as I dashed through the water.

Lake Superior rushed up to greet my knees, chilling me to the bones. Then my thighs. My groin. Then the water was above my belly button and I was equally exhilarated by and contrite with my choice to get into the water. Peter's laughter from the shore urged me on, had me determined to complete my mission. I stopped and stood there with the water halfway up my belly as I stared out at the golden water and it froze my lower half as the sun did its best to warm my upper half. I closed my eyes and lifted my face to greet the warmth of the sun, giving thanks for the day that the universe had given me.

The universe.

And Peter.

Then I was plunging into the water, my legs collapsing beneath me so that I could dunk my head under the surface.

There was a moment, when my head first went under the water, and the world was extricated from my senses, that I felt disembodied. I was left with the muffled sounds of

Peter screaming encouragement from the shore and the thrumming of my pulse in my ears. Cradled in an alien environment where only gurgled sound, my pulse, and darkness lived. An icy planet where chaotic bravado won deserving men favors from the person they...*loved.*

That realization planted my feet against the rocks beneath me and pushed me upwards, sending me soaring out of the water like a rocket. I burst through the surface, gasping for air and warmth, laughing at my stupidity. After mere seconds under the water, the sun was searing—and I welcomed it. I gave it a final thanks and turned to race back towards shore. Peter was laughing and shouting at me still, holding my t-shirt in his clenched fist.

As I raced towards the shore, he cheered me on, forcing a grin to my face. When I stepped onto the shore, soaking wet, shivering, and unsure if I was happy with the decision I'd made, he wrapped me up in his arms.

"You'll get wet," I said through chattering teeth. "And cold."

"I don't care," he said into my ear.

"It was so cold," I said stupidly.

"You're freezing. And I don't have a towel. That was so dumb. I loved it."

I shivered and laughed as he held me.

"Let's go up to the room," he suggested, pulling out of the hug to grab my hand. "Get you dried off and warmed up."

Peter tried to pull me from the shore, but I held fast. He turned to look at me, confusion etched on his face. I squeezed his hand and nodded towards the wooded area.

"I think you owe me something first," I said.

Peter shook his head, though he was amused.

"Seriously?" he asked. "You'd rather claim your winnings than get warm?"

"Are you trying to renege on a bet?" I asked, gasping with faux shock.

"You little shit," Peter said, poking at my side with a finger.

Laughing and chasing each other like idiots, Peter and I made our way to the wooded area along the shore of Lake Superior. There, using a birch tree for balance, Peter helped me warm up. As he'd promised. My skin was dry enough after so that I could put my t-shirt back on. So, I did. And Peter and I found a soft area to lay and hold each other as we whispered and chuckled and said things that only lovers say when they are all alone and the world means nothing.

Because the only thing that matters right then is you and your lover.

"I've barely recovered from hypothermia and now you want to eat...*ice*?" I asked.

The brisk late morning had given away to a still and balmy early afternoon. Peter had finished giving our order to the man in the window of the little camper. When he turned to me, his smile stretched from ear to ear, I knew there was no sense in arguing. That smile from Peter could get me to agree to anything.

"Sno-Cones," Peter said. "You can't have summer and not have a Sno-Cone."

"I suppose?"

"Trust me," he said. "Once you have a Tiger's Blood Sno-Cone, you'll realize that every summer before today was a waste of your time. This. *This* is summer."

"I've never had a Sno-Cone," I said with a shrug. "So, I guess I will just trust you."

"You've never had shaved ice or anything?"

"Not that I remember? No."

"Jeez. If I'd known you came from an abusive home—"

I jabbed him in the side, eliciting a laugh.

"Just trust me," he said. "You'll love this."

"What is—"

I was cut off by the vendor drawing Peter's attention. Watching as Peter paid and then accepted the two giant balls of shaved ice in the white paper triangle cups, I was filled with questions. Did people really eat...*ice*? Flavored and colored ice, to be sure, but it was still ice. The vendor, the Sno-Cones, the paper triangle cups, the sugary syrup—it was all very American. I supposed that France and Canada had shaved ice treats, but I'd never encountered them in my twenty-two years of life.

Shaved ice covered in syrup seemed like a summer fair or carnival treat. Or something one would get at an amusement park. Since my family had rarely attended such events or went to such places, my experience with shaved ice was nonexistent. Sno-Cones would be something America introduced me to—like a million other things during my trip.

Peter held one of the cups out to me. A spoon was jammed into the cup alongside the giant ball of red ice.

"Here," he said. "Try it. You'll love it."

I sniffed the ball of ice. Frosty air shot up my nose, tickling along the way, leaving behind familiar scents I couldn't quite place.

"What is Tiger's Blood?"

"Depends on who you ask what it tastes like," Peter said, watching me intently. "But I'm pretty sure it's a mixture of strawberry and coconut."

Deciding that since I liked both strawberries and coconut, Tiger's Blood couldn't be awful, I dug my spoon into the red ball. My first bite was merely a teaspoon's worth of the icy treat since I was unsure if I wanted a mouthful of something named after an animal's bodily fluids. However, when I slid the spoon into my mouth and the flavors raced over my tongue, I realized Peter had been right. Again. Tiger's Blood—and Sno-Cones—were delectable.

They were ridiculous. And I loved them immediately.

"That's really good," I said.

Peter beamed at me as I shoved my spoon back into the red ball of ice as the small bite I had taken melted on my tongue.

"I told you," he said proudly. "You just have to learn to trust me. I'm never wrong."

I laughed at him as he took his spoon in hand. Peter hadn't even scooped up a spoonful of his Sno-Cone when our attentions were drawn to the Sno-Cone camper by the sound of a child's crying. Peter and I stood, my spoon halfway to my mouth, and watched as a child pulled at his mother's hand and cried about some travesty that was probably more of an inconvenience than anything. After a few moments of listening, it became clear that Peter and I had been given the last of the vendor's Tiger's Blood syrup.

And that was precisely the flavor the child had wanted.

My eyes caught Peter's and he gave me a wink. I watched as Peter stepped over to the mother and her child, explaining that the two of us had gotten the last of the Tiger's Blood. After explaining to the mother that he hadn't touched his Sno-Cone, he offered it to them. Gratefully, the mother thanked Peter as the child gleefully took the treat from him. Offering to reimburse Peter, which he declined, the woman continued to praise him as he made his way back to me, waving her off playfully.

I had nothing but a huge smile for Peter when he returned to me. He shrugged and turned to look out at the lake, sighing happily.

"You don't have a Sno-Cone now," I said.

"It's okay," he said. "I've had Tiger's Blood before."

He patted his stomach.

"It wouldn't help this anyway," he added.

"Stop that," I said.

He shrugged again and chuckled.

"You'll be a very good father one day," I said. "That was incredibly sweet. Letting him have your Sno-Cone."

Peter didn't look at me.

"Do you want to have kids one day?" he asked.

Grinning, I dug into my Sno-Cone and stuffed a spoonful of the icy treat into my mouth before responding.

"Of course," I said. "At least one child. Maybe two? I've always wanted to be a father. I suppose that is weird since…since I'm twenty-two…but I would love to have children. I hope I will be a good father."

The corner of Peter's mouth curled up slightly, but he still didn't turn to me.

"I don't want any kids," he said simply.

Halfway to my mouth with another spoonful of red ice, my arm froze. I found myself staring at the side of Peter's face. He continued to stare out at the lake with its rising and falling layers of glistening golden diamonds.

"I'm pretty sure anyway," Peter said. "I'm in my forties now. You know? I think—if I had ever wanted kids—that time is past. I'm accustomed to being unencumbered by things that depend on me to survive."

Peter chuckled bitterly, and somehow, I managed to chuckle softly, too. My stomach was no longer interested in the Sno-Cone. I looked out at the lake and the golden waves. For the first time during my trip to America, I wasn't enjoying myself. I'd made assumptions. And I'd certainly made an ass of myself. However, as quickly as sadness had overtaken me, I managed to push it away. I was on vacation after all. Peter had done so much to make my trip wonderful.

And it was just a vacation. It didn't have to be more.

That realization made my gut ache like a rope had been tied around it and yanked downward.

It was something, though I'd ignored it since my flight had landed in America, that had been in the back of my mind. Coming to America wasn't a guarantee of anything. It was a vacation. A chance to see a country I'd longed to visit for my entire life. A chance to spend time with a wonderful man I missed every day I wasn't near him. But it held no promise other than that. Forced into remembering that caused my stomach to sink.

"Would you like to share?" I asked, holding my Sno-Cone out to him.

Peter turned to assess me cautiously.

"And get your germs from the spoon?" he said finally. "How disgusting."

Leaning in to be discreet, I grinned evilly at him.

"After what you did over there," I nodded towards the beach, "I think the spoon is safe."

Peter couldn't help it. He laughed uproariously before reaching for my spoon.

"Well," he said, "I guess you can't argue with logic."

I held the Sno-Cone for Peter as he dug in with the spoon and took a healthy bite, moaning with appreciation as the ice slid over his tongue. When he dug out another spoonful and held it out to me, I accepted the bite and smiled as the colored ice chilled my lips and tongue. It slid down my throat to my belly, adding to the block of ice resting there.

As Peter had said, the stars were infinite and gorgeous as we lay in bed that night, holding each other under the covers and staring through the wall of glass. My back was against the headboard and Peter was laid against my chest, his arms around my middle. Trailing my fingers through his hair, combing through the field of fiery silk, we were basking in the afterglow.

After our day at the beach, Peter and I had showered and dressed in more appropriate clothes for dinner. We went to the brewery to find a raucous, but friendly, local crowd watching a game on the flatscreen televisions on the walls. Peter had a local beer and I discovered that he could easily get lost in watching and discussing sports as well as anyone else in the bar. Though I had no interest in sports—American or otherwise—it amused me to see Peter's eyes light up as he watched the game and exchanged commentary with other patrons of the brewery.

Though he'd talked to other people at the brewery, he had paid me plenty of attention, and I was unoffended. I had more fun watching him enjoying his beer and the game more than I would have enjoyed talking.

After his beer, Peter somehow pried himself away from the game, actually saying "goodbye" to several of the strangers he had become friendly with during our short time in the brewery. After a short drive—during which Peter tried to explain sports things to me and failed—we arrived at a local restaurant that served local specialties. Specifically, fish was the main offering on the menu. Never one to enjoy fish or seafood much, I ordered a burger and fries, which was always a safe bet when I dined out.

Peter had fish and chips and coleslaw, though I was unsure what species of fish had been battered, fried, and thrown onto a plate with fries. Peter enjoyed it. That was all that mattered. The food was simple, yet delicious. Though it was nothing extraordinary, it was nice to eat at a local restaurant instead of going to a chain owned by a conglomerate.

When dinner was over, Peter drove us to the lake and we sat on the rocky shore again, holding hands, cuddling, and watching the sun give its final "hurrah" for the day. Then we went back to the hotel, and wordlessly, fell into each other's arms. Then the bed. And we did the thing that we had both grown to crave from each other numerous times a day.

Save one thing, it had been a perfect day.

"You're upset," Peter said softly, his lips fluttering against my chest.

"I'm not."

I wasn't sure if I was lying.

Though I was unsure how Peter was aware. I'd done my best to forget our brief discussion over our shared Sno-Cone. I'd been as cheerful as possible all evening. I hadn't mentioned anything about our time at the Sno-Cone stand since it had occurred.

Peter ignored my protest.

"I'm older than you, Enzo," he said. "Maybe I'm settled in my ways? Who knows? I wanted to be honest, though. I hope you're not mad at me."

"I'm definitely not mad," I kissed the top of his head.

"But you're upset."

"Disappointed."

He nodded against my chest.

"Is it that important to you?" he asked, almost whispering the question. "To have a family?"

"It is," I said. "I'm pretty sure."

Again, he nodded.

"Now what?"

"Maybe," I said, "we should simply enjoy the remaining days we have together? We shouldn't think of it. It will ruin the rest of our vacation together."

"Enzo—"

"It's okay," I said. "This has been the best vacation of my life. That's good enough. You know?"

"I understand what you're saying," Peter said. "Yeah."

"Okay."

We were silent for a moment.

"I could change my mind," Peter said. "It's just too early with us that—"

"I wouldn't ask that of anyone," I said. "To give up the freedom that they enjoy so much. But I specifically wouldn't request it of you, Peter. It's okay. I will be okay. I promise."

Peter sighed. "I wouldn't ask you to change what you want either."

I kissed the top of his head.

"Where does that leave us?" He nuzzled my chest with his face.

His arms seemed to tighten around me, as though afraid I was already slipping away.

I supposed that I was.

"We have some days left," I said, kissing the top of his head again. "Let's have more days like this. Food. Talking. Sex. Let's just enjoy each other for the rest of the trip."

He sighed. "Then what?"

"I will go back to Montreal," I said. "That is what was going to happen anyway, yes?"

"I mean—"

"I know what you mean," I said softly. "I feel that we shouldn't make the obvious outcome harder on ourselves by pretending it is not the obvious outcome. Yes?"

"Enzo," he said. "I want you to know that—"

I stopped him, raising his chin so that I could kiss him softly on the lips.

"I've had a wonderful time," I whispered against his lips when we broke the kiss. "And these next days will be wonderful, too."

Peter stared into my eyes for several moments, some internal conflict like electricity in his eyes. However, the power that fueled those jolts died, and Peter sighed.

"I've had a wonderful time, too," he said.

Our arms tightened around each other, and we said nothing more as we drifted off, watching the stars wink down at us. Knowing winks. Remorseful winks.

It was as if the universe itself was surprised by the turn of events.

I'm not certain of many things. However, if you are able to shock the universe, you have done something very wrong. Or very right.

I hoped my decision and what I'd said to Peter was the latter.

Even if it would hurt for a long time.

Who Wants to Play With a Defective Toy?

Pain. Not at first. Never at first. And never during. Pain comes after. When I would come back to myself. It always felt as though someone had wound up a rubber band, stretched it as far as it could go, then let it snap back on itself. The snap resonated through my body. Made me ache in places I didn't have names for or even know existed. Other than the discomfort, the pain is humiliating. The entire process that brings on the pain is humiliating.

Blindness, followed by the blurry vision that brings me back to the world. The slow realization that I've urinated on myself. My aching jaw that I can't seem to unclench for seconds. Minutes? Hours? I'm never sure. Time means nothing and everything. It means nothing because I don't know how much has passed. It means everything because I wonder how much I've lost.

Anger. That follows the pain and humiliation, though none of them fade completely. They simply get pushed to the background as anger rushes to the surface, screaming and red hot. I can't do anything about the anger because I can't do anything. The anger is at myself. Not others. I'm angry because what has happened is my fault. I got careless. Irresponsible. I was flippant.

Finally, there is fear. It might be the worst because fear is a transient emotion that one has absolutely no control over. It is the most irrational. It is the least human—because it comes from nowhere and everywhere. Everything around me strikes fear into me in those moments after a seizure.

Did I jerk and twitch and bash myself against something? Do I have a gash somewhere? Did I hit my head? Did I even fall? Was I standing, sitting, or lying when it started? Where am I? Am I in a safe place? When will I be able to move and check? How long will I be vulnerable? What day is it? Is it day? Do I know my name? Why am I wet?

Oh. Yeah.

My first blurry vision being the red halo of Peter's hair had the fear and humiliation doing a dance in my head. Anger tap-danced around the two.

I'm calling an ambulance.

N—

Non!

NON!

That halo of red froze in place over me, hazy, like looking through gas fumes as the pain slowly faded from my joints.

Ants crawling on my skin. Briefly. But everywhere.

Then nothing.

You had a seizure.

Temps?

Peter stared down at me as my eyes came into focus.

Combien de temps?

Wh-what?

Tuh-time?

Time? What do...how much time?

Yes.

Uh...thirty seconds. At the most? I mean...I think? It wasn't long.

I shuddered, demanding my eyes to not leak.

It felt like forever.

Peter's voice was shaky. Scared.

Over the course of my life, I'd heard that tone, that fear, in the voices of everyone who had ever meant anything to me. I hated hearing Peter's voice sound that way. But even as the regret flooded through me, so did my memory of what had happened. Peter and I had been getting up from the den sofa to head upstairs for bed. As I went to stand, the seizure must have hit. I was on the hard wooden floor, staring up at Peter as he knelt next to my prone body.

I need to call an ambulance.

No. No.

Peter hesitated, his face screwed up with concern and doubt.

Help me sit. Please.

Together, Peter and I got my body working, sitting, reorienting myself with my surroundings. Making sure that I hadn't bashed my arms or legs against anything. Peter explained that I had simply slid to the floor and jerked spasmodically for a few seconds, and then it was over. My arms and legs hadn't flailed violently, nor had I hit my head violently.

It was a mild event.

If such a thing can ever be described in such a way.

I need to shower.

I refused to look down at the front of my pants. Refused to find out how obvious my predicament was to Peter.

I'll help you.

I don't need—

Peter lifted me from the floor, cradling me against his chest. And I knew that he noticed I was wet, though he said nothing. Made no indication that he noticed. He carried me upstairs and into the bathroom, and I was too embarrassed and weak to protest.

Upstairs, in the master bathroom, he undressed me, and himself, and took us into the shower. We sat on the shower bench together as hot water cascaded over us and Peter helped me wash up. I said nothing, and Peter honored my embarrassment by saying nothing as well.

Once we were clean and dry, and Peter had helped me put on fresh underwear for bed, he did the same. Then he led me to bed and laid me down, cradling my head as I sunk into my pillow. Then he covered me with the warm covers, rounded the bed, and crawled in beside me. Pressing his body gently against mine, but as close as he could, he draped an arm over me.

Finally, I looked down at him in the dark with crystals in the corner of my eyes.

I can't imagine a world without you, Enzo.

The crystals dropped like stones.

I don't want to imagine that. I won't.

He covered my face in kisses so soft I might have imagined them.

At some point, we fell asleep. But not before I could wonder who would want a defective toy when there were so many better options.

Warm on Both Sides

Beginnings are happy, endings are sad, and everything between the two points is what comprises the purest memories. Often, we willfully look back through rose-colored glasses to where things began, refusing to admit that when we set out for our destination, it was little more than a small voice inside of us, daring us to dream. We had no agency; we merely answered a compulsion that, if ignored, would destroy us. A sad ending can bring a man to his knees, but it's nothing compared to the memory of refusing that voice beckoning us to set out on the path we've been traveling along since we took our first breath on this earth. That's why beginnings are happy; it's ignorance with no consideration for the possible consequences should we get lost on our journey. It's also why endings are sad. Either we failed to reach our intended destination and must carry the regret, or we succeeded, and it's always too early to want to leave.

Never is this truer than when one's journey is towards love.

The middle part—the journey—is what I wanted to focus on as the minutes ticked by and Peter and I snuggled on his couch on the final night of my visit to America. Two weeks in America had been glorious, especially with Peter by my side. Even with our few missteps—through no fault of our own—it had been the best two weeks of my life. For the last night of my trip, likely the final night we'd ever spend together, I only wanted to focus on the middle parts. The beginning had been happy, to be sure, but my mind had been such a jumble of anxiety that I couldn't trust my recollection of the event. The ending was going to be sad, so I didn't want to focus on that, either. There, on the couch, and everything that led up until we got into his car to go back to the airport the following day was what I chose to focus my energy on.

For our final evening, I had offered to make dinner for the two of us. However, Peter had suggested that we order takeaway—my favorite, Pad Thai—so that we could focus on our time together instead of cooking and then cleaning dishes. Once our food arrived, Peter and I made a picnic of the takeaway boxes on the dining room table. Over noodles—spicy for me, mild for him—we teased and joked and laughed. We shared stolen kisses and bites of each other's food, though other than spice level, it was virtually the same on both sides of the table. As the dinner wore on, our jovial moods incrementally turned somber as the sun sank and darkness loomed through the windows.

Once our meal was done, we worked together in silence, clearing away the empty containers and cleaning off the table. Without discussing it first, as though we had already fallen into a routine, we went to the den and snuggled into the sofa together. Peter turned the television on and rested his head against my chest. I didn't pay attention to which channel he settled on before cuddling up next to me. I was too busy smelling his hair and holding him in my arms so that I might remember his scent and the feel of his body against me forever.

It would be all that I would return to Montreal with the following day. Forgetting it would have been a sin for which I never could have prayed about enough.

The evening crept on as we held each other in silence and the television played lowly before us, though neither of us paid it much mind. When it became apparent that we were both simply delaying the inevitable, I kissed the top of Peter's head, my lips lingering against that field of fiery silk for as long as they could without being awkward. Then I wiggled out of Peter's arms and stood, offering my hand as I gazed down at him, hoping that my eyes did not look as sad as my heart felt. Peter gazed up at me for the longest of moments, his feelings not nearly as guarded as mine, before he sighed and used the remote to switch off the T.V.

For a moment, as he gazed up at me longingly, I was certain he would say something. However, he simply averted his eyes and slid his hand into mine, and I helped him up from the sofa. In silence, hand in hand, we exited the den, made our way through the dining room, into the living room, and approached the stairs. Before I took my first step up, I let go of Peter's hand and turned to him, taking his face in my hands. His eyes closed and his lips pursed as I moved my face to his. Unlike all of our kisses before, this one meant the most.

It was the last kiss that was simply a kiss.

Our last chance to give each other a kiss that wasn't a "hello," a "goodbye," or something carnal. And the two of us took our time with it. When I finally pulled away, though it was against my better judgment, I did my best to smile down at Peter. He leaned up and gave me another quick kiss, which only made my smile spread, though my heart was anything but happy. I ran my thumbs along his cheekbones and gazed into his eyes, wondering at what point in my life I would no longer remember the feel of his skin or the look in his eyes. When would the day come that Peter's memory was no more than a mere shadow and a wistful dream of what could have been? How painful would it all feel until that day arrived and washed away the ache?

"I don't want to think of you not here," Peter said.

I merely smiled at him.

"This house will feel so empty without you, Enzo," he continued. "I'll feel empty without you. I'll feel—"

"We should have sex," I said.

There was no point in playing coy; no time for pretensions. This was our final chance to enjoy each other's bodies and I didn't intend for there to be any misunderstandings.

Peter nodded, so I smiled, took his hand, and turned to lead him up the stairs. My foot had barely touched the first step when Peter's voice stopped me.

"I love you," he said.

When I was a teenager, a mere fourteen years old, and absolutely certain that I was gay, I had to convince myself of two things. One, I had to convince myself that being gay would not destroy my life as I was terrified it would do. Two, I had to be certain that one day, no matter how long it took, another man would tell me he loved me. He would tell me that I was the person who made life complete for him. That I was lovable. That love was a possibility. And I would feel complete. I would feel like I was home. Hearing those words come from Peter's mouth did none of those things. It made me feel sadder.

I turned to Peter. Instead of the smile I should have produced, I simply stared at him, wondering what we were to do with such a thing.

"I don't mean to," Peter said. "I know we weren't supposed to…do that."

My heart felt hollow.

"But there it is," he said. "I love you."

"We can't do that," I finally said. "We both know that…our lives are different. They're in different places. And times. Love just makes this harder."

Peter sighed.

"You know what?" Peter frowned up at me. "Screw you."

I slumped with a sigh.

"I didn't fall in love," he spat. "I was pushed. By what, I have no fucking clue. But it was something bigger than us. So, it's not my fault and it wasn't a choice."

"But—"

"If you want to blame me for spreading my arms and not fearing the crash, welcoming a joyful plunge into uncertainty, then fine," Peter interjected. "You can blame me for that part. I love you."

I stared at him.

"I love you," he said again, though I wasn't sure if he was making sure I heard or trying to convince me. "And there's nothing you—none of your rules—can do about that. I don't give a shit what you think. Not about this. I won't let you leave here without letting you know that I love you."

Gently, I reached down and took Peter's hands in mine. He sighed as I brought them to my lips and kissed the back of each.

"I know," I said.

"What now?" he asked softly.

With a flick of my head, I managed to give him another smile. "Let's go upstairs."

Peter slumped with a sigh but gave me a resigned smile. Together, we ascended the stairs and made our way to his bedroom. We didn't turn on the lights, but instead, opened the shutters and used the moonlight to undress each other. Hands grasped flesh tinted blue by the moon as we took our time saying "goodbye" to each other's bodies. As slowly and deliberately as I could manage, I used my hands, fingers, mouth, and every sense to commit Peter's body to memory, and Peter repeated the ritual on me.

When we were finally naked and exhausted, holding each other as we drifted off to sleep, Peter's head on my chest, his lips fluttered against the skin of my neck.

"I love you, Enzo," he said. "Marry me."

A soft, sad chuckle escaped my lips.

"No," I said.

Seconds later, the two of us had drifted off.

Peter was in the driver's seat of his car sipping his coffee as I sat in the passenger seat, finishing the last few dregs from my to-go cup. The parking garage was relatively empty as the two of us stared out the windshield at nothing, doing our best not to look at each other. I knew that when my eyes met Peter's, it would most likely be the last time we saw each other's eyes. I hadn't been ready for that, and Peter had given no indication that he was prepared for that final look either. So, we drank the coffees we had picked up at the drive-thru on our way to the airport, trying to figure out the best way to say "goodbye" to each other.

Maybe there would be letters and phone calls and texts in the future, but we both knew the truth. Inevitably and incrementally, the time between the letters, calls, and texts would grow, and finally, there would be no more. We would slowly become strangers. Then we would never speak again or read each other's words. Our one perfect night in Montreal and our fairytale two weeks in America together would be a footnote in the history of our lives when they came to an end. Glorious, joyful footnotes, for certain, but nothing more. Hopefully, upon looking back at the specter of our days spent together, we wouldn't feel regret. Only fondness.

"If you forgot anything, I'm sure work will bring me to Montreal again one day," Peter said quietly. "I can always bring it to you."

I smiled ruefully.

"I did not forget anything."

"Okay."

We had an understanding. Even if I had forgotten anything at Peter's house, it was best that it became a part of the history we were leaving each other with when I got on the plane back to Canada.

"I'll miss you," Peter said.

"I'll miss you, too."

"You know," Peter chuckled bitterly, "I could lock you in the car, start the engine, and just drive off. Make you my captive. Never let you leave."

I laughed softly as I stared out at a man struggling to lift his suitcase into the back of his SUV. Why luggage manufacturers had figured out that putting wheels on a suitcase made it easier to handle but had yet to figure out a way to make lifting them into and out of a car easier was beyond me. Once the man finally wiggled his suitcase into the back compartment of his SUV, closed the hatch, and got into the car, I sighed.

"I suppose it is time."

Peter said nothing.

"You don't have to come with me," I said gently. "I can find the gate fine on my own. I will understand if—"

The sound of the car's electric door locks stopped me. Peter turned in his seat to stare at the side of my face. Refusing to meet his eyes, I stared out of the windshield at the black SUV's brake lights as the man pulled out of his spot.

"Are you taking me prisoner?"

"Look at me."

"No," I said. "That will make this more difficult."

"I won't let you out unless you look at me," Peter said, though his words were desperate, not angry.

"I could get out if I wanted to, Peter."

"I know that. You know that."

I nodded. We both knew that Peter wasn't really forcing me into anything. That had to be clear before I acquiesced. Slowly, I turned in my seat, averting my eyes from Peter's until I was turned toward him. Finally, when my eyes met his, I wished I had simply gotten out of the car. The look in Peter's eyes did nothing to unbreak my heart.

"I need to know something before you get out of the car," Peter said. "I don't want bullshit or rules or common sense. I just want truth."

I shrugged. "Sur ce que? What do you want from me, Peter?"

"I want to know if you love me," Peter said.

"Peter—"

"I just want to know if you care about me the way I care about you, Enzo," Peter said. "I want to know that I'm not an old fucking fool who felt like there was something...*here*...when there wasn't. I need to know that...I need to know that you could find it possible to actually love me. The way I love you."

"I—"

"Just shut up and tell me if I'm stupid or not, Enzo," he demanded. "It's not that difficult. Yes, or no? And I'll unlock the doors and watch the greatest thing that ever walked into my life walk back out of it—regardless of your answer. I don't want to hear anything besides 'yes' or 'no' come out of your mouth."

Peter stared deeply into my eyes, his bottom lip quivering as I stared back at him. Instinctively, I knew that telling Peter I didn't love him was the kindest answer. Out of everything I could say, it would leave him devastated, but not nearly as destroyed as telling him I loved him before walking out of his life forever would do to him. Saying "no" also seemed the easiest answer at first, but considering saying such a thing to Peter proved impossible. My lips wouldn't form a two-letter word. Only three letters would do. Eight letters seemed perfect.

"I love you," I said.

Peter exhaled heavily.

"I've loved you for one year, ten months, seventeen days," I glanced at the clock on the dashboard, "ten hours, and seventeen minutes."

Peter's cautiously relieved expression grew into a grin.

"And what?" I asked with an angry chuckle as I pointed toward the airport. "I have a seat waiting for me. I have a life in another country. I love you, Peter. A Canadian citizen who has no legal right to stay in the U.S. indefinitely loves you. What does that do for you?"

"It proves to me that this wasn't pointless," he spat, though he wasn't angry. "It proves to me that what I've also felt for one year, ten months, uh, uh—"

"Seventeen days, ten hours, and…eighteen minutes."

"Yeah," Peter laughed. "It proves that everything I've thought and felt for all of that time wasn't some insane fantasy in my head."

"I'm happy for you," I said. "I'm sad for us."

"Enzo—"

"I have to get on this plane, Peter," I said. "I have a job and an apartment and I'm not allowed to stay here forever anyway. I can't just—"

"Love is taking a chance on yourself, Enzo."

"What?" I faltered.

"People define love in a lot of ways," Peter said, "but what love *really* is? It's taking a chance on yourself."

"I don't—"

"It's throwing caution to the wind," Peter said, reaching out to take my hand. "It's saying, 'O*h, what the hell,*' and doing what you know is right. Even if you don't have a plan. *Especially* if you don't have a plan, because you can't imagine doing anything else. Because doing anything else would destroy you. That's what love is."

"Well, yes, but—"

"Enzo. Can you really imagine getting on that plane right now? Tell me you can picture yourself sitting in your seat right now, leaving the U.S. Does that even feel real right now? Did you really, *really*, think—when you got on the plane to come here—that that's how this was going to play out?"

I searched Peter's eyes as his hand clutched mine.

"Tell me that when you left Montreal that you actually thought you'd be returning unencumbered. Unattached," Peter demanded. "Tell me you really thought you'd leave America without being in love and deciding that we had to be together. I knew that was how this was going to play out, and so did you. Even knowing that maybe we're not on the same page about some things, I still know this is how it's supposed to play out. Tell me I'm wrong."

"You are not wrong." I shrugged. "I have had that fantasy as well, but—"

"Marry me," Peter said, gripping my hand.

"I—"

"Marry me," Peter said.

"Peter." I gave his hand a squeeze. "It's not legal here."

"It's legal in Minnesota."

"If the federal government doesn't recognize it, that doesn't matter since I'm not a U.S. citizen," I said. "So, it's not legal here."

"Yet. It will be."

"Until then?" I asked. "Two men being married means nothing here. And *when* will it be legal? We don't know."

"We'll get married in Canada," Peter suggested excitedly. Desperately. "I'll fly to Montreal as soon as I can. We'll get married there. Where it's legal. Then we'll use that to start the process of getting you into the U.S. on a more permanent basis. Then...maybe it will be legal here then? Who knows? Then we can get married here and get you citizenship. I can move to Canada and become a citizen there if it comes to that. But you're not getting out of this car unless I know that this is just the beginning. I will hold onto you and you *won't* be able to get out."

Though I wanted to be offended at Peter suggesting he could take away my agency, I couldn't be. Instead, I laughed.

"Peter," I said. "This is ridiculous. It is...I don't know what this is. But my plane leaves in two hours. We can't just—"

"All I need is to know that if I fly to Montreal as soon as I can, you will be waiting to marry me," he said. "That's all I need you to do. Right now, Enzo. Before you get on that plane."

Peter's hand was beginning to sweat and I was certain it was from fear that I might reject his idea. As he gripped my hand tightly to the point of near discomfort, and I looked into his eyes, pondering his madness, I realized two things. One, there was nothing I could do to keep myself from being in love with Peter for the rest of my life. And two, when I had said "no" to Peter's proposal the night before, it hadn't been a real "no."

"I have nothing to offer you," I said.

"What?" Peter frowned.

"You have...you have so much in your life, Peter," I said, all of the concerns I'd held trapped in my brain spilling from my lips. Concerns I hadn't even allowed myself to consider since the entire trip had seemed like a daydream. Now, faced with possibility, those concerns poured from my brain like a flood out of my mouth. "I have nothing. I am...I'm a scrawny French guy with weird eyes and no family or money or...I am poor, Peter. I have no career. Nothing to call my own besides the secondhand things in my apartment and the clothes in my suitcase. I have seizures and pee on myself because I became too distracted by life and forgot to take my medication. You don't want kids. Probably. I do. People might be cruel because of our age difference, and—"

Peter's frown deepened. "Let people be cruel."

"We are not equals in any way," I said. "I have nothing to offer you."

"So...you lied when you said you loved me?"

"Of course not!" I gripped his hand tighter. "I do love you, Peter."

"Then why are you saying you have nothing to offer me?"

"Peter."

"Marry me," he repeated firmly. "Tell me that I need to start planning to fly to Montreal to marry you, Enzo. That— and your love—is all I need. We can work everything else out as it comes. Do you need anything more than that from me? My love?"

"Well, no."

"So?"

I shook my head with amused frustration.

"How will this work?" I asked. "I mean...we get married in Canada? You cannot stay there forever, either.

You will have to come back here until we can work things out, and—"

"Are you going to take a chance or what?" Peter teased me. "Are we living or existing here?"

Groaning with frustrated amusement again, I turned my head to stare out of the window at the gray concrete walls, floor, and ceiling of the parking garage. Where the black SUV had pulled out across the way, a mini-van was parking. I watched as the brake lights lit up, then blinked out. A man clambered out of the driver's seat and closed the door. Stretching his arms above his head, he then dashed around to the passenger side and opened the door. A woman—most likely his wife—stepped out and wrapped her arms around him excitedly. The two shared a kiss, then opened the back sliding door of the van so that their children could exit the vehicle.

As I watched them, and Peter's grip on my hand got tighter and more insistent, they opened the hatchback of the van and started to pull out luggage. Their muffled, yet excited, voices echoed through the cavernous concrete structure as they all gathered their luggage. A happy family full of love and possibility. Once the hatchback was closed and they were all excitedly wheeling their suitcases along behind them towards the airport, I realized something. If love was taking a chance on yourself, what was taking a chance besides creating possibility?

What was a life without possibility? Can one live life well without possibility?

"Yes," I said, finally. "I will marry you."

A Street
Present Day

Family, as one can guess if they know anything about me, is a dangerous subject. It's a word and a concept that holds both promise and pain. One that can produce a paroxysm if I'm in a particular mood. In the past, I could be equally sensitive and playful about my family history. When one finds themselves alone in the world, with no blood-family left to call their own, the emotions that go along with it are indescribable as well as nebulous. There never seems to be a way to describe those feelings that do them the justice they deserve, especially since they can evolve by the minute.

Losing one's family so early in life and being left all alone in the world can carve trauma into a person like a canyon. Though the trauma is a violent slash, creating a sudden wound, it grows over time, bit by bit, widened by grief, until it is so vast that it inspires awe. That was my life. At least for a time. Insurmountable, profound grief that carved a crevice inside me so deeply that it became a nearly permanent scar on the landscape of my soul.

Over time, however, I'd come to realize that the concept of family is so rigidly defined when one is young. Especially when one is young and religious. Catholicism taught a young and impressionable version of myself—one so removed from who I am today that I can't even remember him—that one must obey their mother and father. That family is those with whom you share blood. That blood is thicker than water.

The blood of the covenant is thicker than the water of the womb.

That's an older and more accurate representation of the quote.

Though the "blood of the covenant" means blood shed in battle with comrades creates a deeper bond than family. Also meaning, the bonds you create and nurture by choice with people is stronger than the bonds created simply by birth. This makes more sense to me. Through the church's teachings, my brother and sister were not my real siblings. I knew this to be false. Even from a young age when I felt that family was to be held above all other things. Noe was my brother. Ila was my sister. Nothing would make me believe otherwise.

And the family I've made along the way, in my thirty years of life, are as much my family as my parents and grandparents. In fact, maybe, if I dare say, they are more my family. Because they were chosen to be my family. By me.

This doesn't diminish or invalidate the love I had for my parents and grandparents. Nor does it change anything about our bonds. In fact, this discovery deepened that love and those bonds. Because it provided a deeper understanding of the love one can have for, and the bond one can share with, another individual. Keeping the love I had for my family in my heart was a choice.

Choosing to love is powerful.

Loving and continuing to love someone is a choice, but it is also an endeavor so great that, if at the end of life, you still love the people you chose to love, you've completed a Herculean task. Choosing to love someone is easy. Choosing to keep loving someone day after day, year after year, is difficult. Often, even minute to minute is a struggle.

It's not the kinship we feel for someone when we meet them that sustains love. It's the ordinary, mundane events, day after day, that keep that fire burning. Sometimes...the fire goes untended. Whose fault that is depends on the situation.

Regardless, falling is easy, learning to soar is work. Falling in love can happen whether we choose it or not, but what happens after is completely within our control. What we choose is what makes love so special.

This is true for lovers and friends. And found family.

Choosing to continue to love someone is one of the most profound ways that I see God. Well...maybe not God. But the vastness and benevolence of the universe. Chemicals and particles and elements...*and the dust stars are made of*...set into motion billions of years ago, pinging around in the vastness of space, over nearly immeasurable distance, led to the moment a person looks into another person's eyes and thinks:

You're part of my tribe.

What more proof does one need that the universe hopes for the best for us?

I'm never reminded of this more than when I walk along the streets of my new homeland on a dreary day. When the clouds part, if only briefly, and the sun shines down on my face, warming my flesh and turning the rain puddles into pools of golden light, I remember it.

Invariably, a person walking by me will slow, turn their gaze to me, smile, and say:

The whole day might not be a waste.

I'll smile back. We'll nod. Maybe exchange a few pleasantries. Then we'll be on our separate ways, wishing each other well. The light and warmth of the sun traveled across our solar system at the speed of light for eight minutes and twenty seconds to produce that one interaction between strangers. In the grand scheme of things—the universe as a whole—the sun is a speck. But its warmth reminds me that the universe hopes for the best for me.

Walking the streets of Minneapolis, like it had been for me in Montreal, is therapeutic. For opposite reasons, of course. Minneapolis is therapeutic in that it helps me to clear my head and gives me time to think about decisions I need to make, solve problems I've encountered, or simply work off excess caffeine or sugar. Walking in Montreal was to distract me from my loneliness. So, similar, but different.

When I left La Croûte, my belly full of coffee and almond croissants—I'd ended up eating two—I walked aimlessly at first. The bundle in my arms was cradled against my chest as I strolled along the concrete and metal-lined streets of the city. In the late morning, with the sporadic misty rain, the city almost seemed abandoned. Everyone was staying indoors, avoiding the wet and cold of early spring.

I didn't mind. I liked having the city to myself as I made my way along the sidewalks. It made it easier to exchange a few kind words with the few strangers I passed on my way. Without the noise of the usual foot traffic or the honking of horns of cars racing here and there, the city felt almost like a village instead of a sprawling hub of industry.

These special moments, when people abandoned the streets due to the weather, allowed me to reintroduce myself to the city—and country—that had done so much for me.

Though I had plenty of complaints, for no place is perfect, I owed gratitude to Minneapolis and the United States.

Above all of the things for which I had to be grateful was how it had led me to better understand the concept of family.

Part Two

An Unequitable Marriage

Let Me Come Home

"Okay," Peter said, "I know it's not ideal. But we'll figure it out."

With my bottom lip firmly stuck out, I crossed my arms over my chest as I rode in the passenger seat of his car. I didn't want to be difficult or upset on my first official day in my new homeland, but I couldn't pretend I wasn't upset, either.

"This is so annoying," I grumbled.

"It's just two days, and—"

"Two days without any of my own things!"

Peter suppressed a laugh.

"You're very feisty today, Mr. Bradshaw," he teased.

Even though I didn't want to, I couldn't help but smile as I rolled my eyes.

"I don't know what you're talking about Monsieur Barbier," I snipped, though I couldn't put any heat behind my words.

Peter laughed loudly as he applied the brakes, bringing us to a full stop in the congested line of traffic on the freeway. We had barely been moving to begin with, but now we had come to a complete stop in the traffic jam we'd found less than a mile from the airport.

"So," Peter chuckled, "I still haven't convinced you to take my name?"

"Some other time," I waved him off. "Let's focus on important things. Like the fact that I will not have any clean underwear."

"I'm sorry, Enzo," he said.

"I sold or threw away everything, Peter," I said. "Except for my clothes and *that one box*. It can't be lost. Those are the only things I have left."

Peter gave me an empathetic frown and reached over to grab my hand as we sat in the line of traffic, waiting for a chance to creep forward another inch. I stared out at the line of cars spilling out before us, thankful for the heat pouring from the vents. Arriving at the airport in Minneapolis in early autumn reminded me that I was moving to yet another city where the cold would be relentless and brutal nearly year-round.

Two years of waiting for the day to come that I could call America my home had almost made me forget that fact. As I sat in Peter's car, staring out at the cold, dreary day before us and the string of cars spewing white wisps from their tailpipes, I was quickly reminded. Minneapolis was a city that rarely experienced weather that could be considered hot. Even in the height of summer, it could get warm, but rarely hot. However, I would never again be sleeping alone under all of the blankets I owned in order to stay warm. I would have Peter for that. So, Minneapolis would never seem as cold as Montreal.

Everything would be okay.

"I'm sorry," I said, turning my head to stare out the passenger window. "I can buy new clothes if necessary. I don't have much money, but I will have a job eventually. I cannot replace that box, Peter."

He brought my hand to his mouth and kissed the back of it passionately.

"We'll have that box in two days. Just like the airline said," Peter stated. "If we don't, I will tear this city apart for you finding it. I promise. However, you do have your own things and your own money. *Our* things and *our* money. It's not your things or my things or your money or my money, it's our things and money. I've been telling you this for two years. Remember? We can go buy a few essentials tonight so that you won't feel like you have nothing. We'll solve this problem together."

I smiled. We'd been married for almost two years—one ceremony in Montreal, and then another in Minneapolis— but I still struggled with combining our lives. Especially money. Having almost nothing to my name, it felt unfair to expect Peter to share everything he had with me. Hopping from one socioeconomic class to one much higher seemed unfair since I hadn't earned it. Marriage should not be the determining factor for a person's financial security, no matter their circumstances or biology.

"Okay."

There was no other way to respond. Peter was right. Even if I didn't love it. However, I loved that Peter considered us a team.

"So, cheer up," Peter demanded playfully. "You're finally home, babe!"

Babe. Peter's little term of endearment that had, at first, felt juvenile, made me smile. First uttering it as we walked out of the Palais de Justice in Montreal as legal husbands— at least in Canada—I'd cringed when Peter had used the term of endearment. It felt infantilizing. Over nearly two years of hearing him use it on our many visits to each other, conversations on the phone, in our text messages and emails, and after our second and final marriage at the courthouse in Minneapolis, it had grown on me.

It wasn't that I learned to love the term or that it felt less juvenile as time wore on. I'd simply begun to pay attention to Peter when he used the term for me. The way his eyes lit up. How he couldn't keep a smile from forming on his face when he said it. The sheer joy at uttering the term—as if he was staking claim to me—warmed me to it. Peter had shown his ability to feel joy many times before, but I'd never seen him as joyous as when he called me "babe." I couldn't really hate the term when I realized that.

Our first civil marriage—at the Palais de Justice in Montreal was as romantic as such things can be. Paperwork, birth certificates, signing of forms, meeting with officials, and then standing before one to be married as Monsieur Paquette, my ESL teacher, played witness. Afterward, Monsieur Paquette insisted on taking us out to a nice dinner at Le Canard Parasseux, since it held special significance in our "love story." Newly widowed, Monsieur Paquette was glad to have company for dinner after such an event.

Over another incredible meal, Peter and I regaled our witness with stories of our meeting, our one perfect night together, and everything that had led to Peter's proposal. Our witness informed us he was set to embark on a months-long trip across Europe. A gift to himself to celebrate his retirement. Monsieur Paquette and Peter shared many glasses of wine and I ate jubilantly, even as my belly flipped and flopped with the knowledge that I, Enzo Barbier, was a *husband*. I had my own family. When the three of us left *The Lazy Duck*, my new husband and my ESL teacher raucous and laughing from all of the wine, Peter accompanied me to my apartment. A marriage must be consummated, after all.

Peter had only been able to fly to Montreal for a few days during the week in order for us to get officially married in Canada. We made the most we could of those few days, but Peter eventually returned to the U.S. Again, I was alone in Canada, and he was alone in the U.S.

The following month, I flew to Minneapolis for a few days so that we could begin to establish citizenship for me through our marriage in Canada and to get married at the Minneapolis courthouse. Our marriage in Montreal was legal in Canada. Our marriage in Minneapolis gave us some rights in Minnesota. However, since Peter and I were interested in securing United States citizenship for me, things became more difficult. Marriage equality had not been passed on a federal level yet. The state of Minnesota might not have balked at my moving to the U.S. to be with my husband, but this offered me no protections from the United States government if they wished to deport me back to Canada.

Our immigration lawyer, whom Peter had hired for more money than is seemly, had insisted that we establish residence in the U.S. for me as soon as we could after we were married. None of us were sure if marriage equality would ever pass in the U.S., or if it didn't, if the U.S. courts would uphold our Canadian marriage and allow us to live together as husbands in the U.S. once we completed all of the necessary steps. Even upon its passing, marriage equality didn't ensure my citizenship. However, our lawyer knew that beginning the steps immediately would keep things from being delayed—and would make citizenship more likely— if and when the time came that marriage equality passed.

Not that it is uncommon knowledge, but the immigration process in the United States is rigorous, biased, discriminatory, and unfair. It is also costly. These things are sometimes mutually exclusive. If you have money, it can cancel out all of the other impediments. With our high-powered, costly lawyer, we were assured that securing my citizenship would only be a "matter of time."

Our lawyer was right. As soon as Peter and I were married in Canada, I flew to the U.S., claimed residence at his home with a ridiculous amount of paperwork our lawyer provided, and claimed that I would be living in Canada for periods of time due to my work. And we got married at the courthouse in Minneapolis. Our lawyer made it clear that I would need to travel back to the U.S. and stay at least one week every six months, never letting more than five months and twenty days pass between visits. Otherwise, we would have to start all over.

So, that is what we did.

One would think that getting to see each other more, what with all of our visits back and forth between our two countries, Peter and I would have been happy. However, knowing we were husbands, and having our time together cruelly parceled out by arbitrary laws and regulations, each time we had to leave each other was torture. Every time that one of us had to board a plane, we struggled to let go of each other. To not cry and upset each other. Our first two years of marriage were filled with sorrow and longing.

And far too much phone sex. Though, is there ever too much?

Governments do not care that their rules separate people who love each other. They do not care about the emotional trauma they inflict on those who are bonded by love or blood. They love their rules. That is what they are beholden to; not the people whom they are meant to serve and nurture.

Then marriage equality was passed in the United States. Our American marriage was not valid. And then it was. In an instant.

And I got the call.

As with most major events in my life, food plays a central role. It was a Friday night after a long week at work where I had raced along the halls of the office building where I worked all day long, delivering messages and packages and fetching and getting for people with much higher salaries than mine. To make up for a difficult week, I had roasted chicken and made a large pan of the most decadent and silky cacio e pepe. I'd served a large portion of the chicken atop the pasta—like a barbarian—and had curled up on my secondhand sofa in my pajamas, prepared to watch something romantic and silly as I ate my dinner.

When I answered my phone, I could barely understand Peter over the sounds of his tears and sniffles.

It happened, Enzo. Come home. You can come home to me.

Much of the rest of the phone call I cannot remember. Other than the tears and laughter and proclamations of love and excitement. I had turned my television to the news, and well into the night, Peter and I had watched the world celebrate the United States declare that love...*really is love.* That Peter and I were as valid as any other couple.

That we were actually husbands.

The pasta and chicken had gone cold by the time Peter and I ended our phone call. It was still one of the best meals I'd ever eaten. I didn't even watch the movie I had intended to watch that evening. No romantic comedy could compare to my life at that moment.

After washing the dishes and storing the leftover food in the refrigerator for weekend meals, I shuffled through my apartment. I didn't know it then, but I was already beginning my "goodbye." And, as I paced around the five rooms that had once held so much grief and sorrow, I found that I was sad to let it go.

Home.

That word stuck in my head. Peter had told me I could come home to him.

My horrible little apartment in Montreal that was never warm enough or clean enough or quiet enough or safe enough had grown on me over time. It had served its purpose. It held ghosts in every corner. Of my mother. My sister. My brother. But it had never been home.

Peter was my home.

The United States was my home.

And I could finally go home.

Those ghosts would have to go with me and learn to appreciate their new home as well.

In the following weeks, I sold furniture and belongings to neighbors and coworkers. I threw out everything not fit to pass on to others or donate to charity shops. Other than my personal toiletries and my clothing, I stored a few sentimental items in a box, packing it carefully, before taping it shut securely.

I quit my job.

And then I went home.

We'd still have a year before I could apply for full citizenship and take my citizenship exam and pledge, but we were on our way.

"I get to pick out your underwear," Peter said, ripping me from my daydreams.

"Quoi?" I shook my head. "What?"

Peter laughed. "We'll go buy some clothes for you."

"Okay?"

"And I'm picking out your underwear," he said, winking at me as he eased the car forward a few inches with a glance through the windshield. "I'm thinking I'd like to see you in some tight little boxer briefs tonight. Black. With a gray waistband."

Even after two years of marriage—*the things Peter and I had done together and uttered during our phone calls*—he never failed to make me blush.

"And only that," Peter said. "I want an evening of leering at my husband as he walks around in nothing but his underwear."

I cleared my throat. "Is that all? Do the underwear ever come off?"

Peter growled playfully at me, making me chuckle, before he kissed the back of my hand again. Then he nibbled at it, making me laugh and yank my hand away.

"Oh," Peter said, "look at that. People learned where their gas pedals are."

I was still laughing as Peter's car began to move forward steadily, then finally, at a speed one would expect on a freeway.

"Why don't we stop for a coffee?" Peter suggested. "Sit and enjoy this moment together? Then we'll go get some clothes to get you through the next few days. Then we'll go home."

"Home," I parroted, smiling out at the road laid out before us.

"Home!" Peter howled the word like a wolf.

Of course, I laughed. My husband was ridiculous. And I loved it.

Overladen with bags from Target, along with my nearly empty to-go cup from the coffee shop, I somehow managed to shove my way through the front door of Peter's—*our*—house. Peter, behind me, his arms as full as mine, laughed as I stumbled into the house. Though Peter had suggested a trip to the store to buy enough clothes to get me through a few days until my luggage from the airport was located, he had gone overboard. I had intended to buy a few t-shirts and maybe some gym shorts and a pair of jeans, along with some underwear and socks.

Peter ended up having different ideas.

I had told Peter as we waited to check out at the gargantuan store that I felt horrible that he was buying me so many clothes when it wasn't needed. However, he once again reminded me that there was no his and mine. We only had *ours* now. So, I swallowed down my embarrassment and shame and let him have his way. Having a whole new wardrobe, even from a store such as Target, was a dream for me. Nothing was secondhand or thrifted. All of the clothes in the bags would be worn for the first time by me. Well, probably. I could easily ignore the logic that surely someone had tried the items on before.

Of course, I had let Peter go wild in the men's underwear department, picking out the underwear he most wanted to see on me. Though I had been clear that anything uncomfortable would stay in its package. Needless to say, I ended up with enough new underwear to last me for years. So, that helped me feel less awful about all of the new clothing. In fact, the way his eyes lit up with each article of clothing I selected, as though he couldn't wait to see me in it, made me feel less horrible. I began to realize that Peter's insistence on buying clothes for me was not only a kindness to me. My husband obviously had derived some sensual glee from thinking about discovering my body in all different styles of clothing.

That, too, made me feel better about everything.

Inside the front door, just far enough that we could close it, Peter and I dropped our bags and I immediately turned to wrap my arms around him. He greeted my mouth with his and moaned happily as I kissed him deeply. Peter and I stood in the entryway, kissing and holding each other tightly for several minutes, whispering "I love you's" and other sickeningly sweet things to each other, surrounded by piles of bags.

"What should we do first?" Peter asked. "We probably need to wash all of these clothes so we can hang them up, right?"

"Later," I cooed, kissing the tip of his nose. "First, we should go upstairs."

Peter stared at me for a moment before the realization of what I was suggesting registered.

"Oh, yeah?" he said with a grin.

"I thought you might like to see the underwear I arrived in," I said.

Peter chuckled warmly. "I can't believe you're here. Fuck. I'm so glad you're here."

I sighed happily.

"It seems so un-fucking-real," Peter said, his arms tightening around me. "And you're not leaving again. Ever."

"Hey," I said, "focus. Do you want to see my underwear or not?"

Peter laughed uproariously as his phone chirped. I didn't let go of him completely, but I pulled back, my arms looped around his neck lightly, as he dug his phone out of his pocket. I sighed happily and stared into Peter's face as he looked down at his phone, checking to see what had warranted the notification.

"Well," Peter groaned, "bad news."

"What?" My arms tightened around him.

"Not *bad* bad," he said with a chuckle as he slid his phone back into his pocket. "I have to run over to the office."

"Oh."

"I'm sorry, babe." Peter pulled me against him playfully and kissed me. "Just a small issue. No big deal. But I can't handle it from here. Do you want to come with me? It will only take a few hours. You can hang out in the coffee shop on the corner, and—"

"No, no." I waved him off, letting my arms fall from his neck. "It's okay. I need to wash these."

I gestured vaguely at the bags surrounding us.

"That will take a while," I said. "I can occupy myself with that."

"Are you sure?" he asked, giving me another gentle kiss. "You're not mad, right?"

"Of course, not," I said. "It's Friday. I will have you to myself for two days when you get back."

"Damn right you will." Peter sighed and kissed me again. "Okay. You know where everything is, right? For washing your clothes?"

Peter stepped over the pile of bags he had brought in as he reached for the door.

"Basement," I nodded. "I've been here before, babe. I will be okay."

"Call me if you need to, okay? I won't be so busy that I can't answer."

"Okay."

"I mean it," he said as he swung the door wide. "If you need anything or have any problems, just—"

"Go!" I demanded with a pointed jab at the door. "I'll be fine, Peter."

He stopped in the doorway, his fingers loosely gripping the knob.

"Okay," he said, sighing happily. "Husband. I love you."

"I love you, too," I said. "Husband."

"Never going to get tired of that, either."

"I'll make dinner," I said. "Let me know when you'll be home."

Home. Saying that word in my actual home hit me in the gut.

"Okay," Peter said. "I'm going, I'm going."

With that, Peter gave me a wink and blew me a kiss, then reluctantly stepped out onto the porch and closed the door. For a moment, I thought I might run after him, take him up on his offer to go with him to his office. I could sit in a café for hours, drink coffee, and read a book. Not be alone. However, as the thought entered my head, something strange happened. No one would ever believe me if I told them. Not that I would have uttered such things to anyone.

The house groaned. Like a sigh. As if exhaling a greeting of some kind.

Of course, Peter's—*our*—house was old. Renovated, but old. It was settling and the noise was purely coincidental. However, something inside of me right then told me it wasn't. I was being welcomed home.

Over the course of two years, I hadn't spent a tremendous amount of time in our house. I'd only been able to visit every few months. However, anytime I had visited our home, I'd always felt *at home*. And then, standing in the circle of Target bags in the quiet left in Peter's absence, I felt as though our home was telling me it was glad I was back.

So, I didn't chase after Peter. I lifted the paper coffee cup to my lips and took the last cold dregs in one gulp.

"Okay, house," I said after I swallowed. "Let's reacquaint ourselves."

It groaned again.

Four hours later, I was at the stove. I had washed all of my new clothes and found homes for them in the second closet in the master bedroom and on the side of Peter's dresser he had cleared out for me. I'd answered no less than twenty texts from Peter asking if I was okay and if I needed anything. Of course, with the house as company, and our need to familiarize ourselves with each other once again, I was doing fine and needed nothing.

Though having Peter race away to work on my first day home hadn't been ideal, it had maybe been for the best. Having a few hours alone with our home had been lovely. I had gotten to run my fingers along the wainscoting in the dining room. Fluff the pillows on the den sofa. Walk around the backyard in the chilly early autumn air. And I had washed the airplane smell off of me in our shower. And I had been able to decide on my own what we would have for dinner.

That was the best part of it all.

"*Babe!*" Peter called out from the front door as I poked at the contents of the pot. "*I'm home!*"

I smiled at Peter's shouted greeting. I had a husband who actually announced his arrival when he came home. Like in old television shows or movies.

"I'm in the kitchen!" I announced.

Continuing to cook, I listened as Peter made his way from the front of the house to the kitchen, making those lived-in noises that all houses possess. My husband stepped through the kitchen doorway with a wide grin on his face, prepared to announce something of obvious importance. However, when his eyes landed on me, he froze.

"Yes?" I turned to him, a grin on my face.

Peter's eyes traveled up and down my body. Obviously, the fact that I was only wearing a new pair of underwear was not lost on him.

"Well," Peter managed, "if I get to come home to this every day…"

I chuckled.

"Do you like them?" I asked, turning a bit in front of the stove.

He whistled lowly. "Those fit *just right*."

"I missed you," I said, playfully.

"I didn't realize how much I missed you until just now," he replied. "Enzo. Those underwear…"

Grinning to myself, I turned back to the stove.

"I made a chicken stew," I said, pretending I was unimpressed with Peter's obvious arousal. "It will be ready soon."

Mere seconds passed before Peter was pressed up against me and his mouth was on my neck. Laughing warmly, I poked at the stew in the pot as Peter fed at my neck like a ravenous man. Peter's hands on my hips, his fingers playing along the waistband of my underwear destroyed my concentration, but I didn't mind.

"I can't finish dinner if you do that," I said softly.

"I'm hungry for something else right now," he mumbled against my flesh.

Turning in his arms, I affected a pout. Peter froze at the look on my face, but his arms stayed around me.

"Are you saying that I spent all of this time cooking such a nice dinner for you and you are more concerned with what is in my pants?" I asked, my bottom lip sticking out.

"Oh, babe," Peter sputtered, "I didn't mean to imply that—"

I couldn't help it. I grinned.

"You little shit," Peter growled at me before pulling me tightly against him.

With a laugh, I met his mouth with mine and Peter happily returned the kiss.

"We should really eat first," I said. "It will get cold. And you will need your strength."

"Oh, really? I like the sound of that."

"It will be my first night home. For good," I said. "We must celebrate it properly. And for the appropriate amount of time."

Peter kissed me again. "I can't really argue your point."

"I got a text," I said as Peter peppered my face with kisses. "The airline found my things. It will be delivered tomorrow. All of the clothes we bought were pointless."

Peter immediately pulled back far enough to glance down at my body.

"I wouldn't say it was for nothing," he said.

I swatted at him before pulling him back into my arms to kiss him.

"How was work?" I asked.

"You know," he said, glancing down to take in my body again, "not as good as being home."

"Are you hungry?" I asked.

Peter sighed. "You know what?"

"What?"

"I always thought coming home to a husband, having dinner on a Friday night," Peter said, "would be a little boring."

"Yeah?"

"And maybe it would have been," he said. "But if you find the perfect guy—"

"I'm not perfect."

"Perfect for me."

I gave him another kiss. When I pulled back, Peter was staring at me.

"What?"

"Are you happy?" he asked. "That you married me? Moved here? You know. All that."

Looking around the kitchen, taking in the dark woods and tile and appliances fancier than anything I'd ever hoped to have in my own kitchen, I shouldn't have felt at home. I should have felt like a stranger in someone else's house. Like an intruder. With Peter in my arms and the pot of stew simmering on the stove behind me, clad only in underwear...I felt like I was at home.

"I've never been happier," I said.

"You mean it?" He smiled.

"Yes."

Peter kissed me, then whispered, "I'll keep you happy. I promise. I'll do everything to make sure you're happy. Anything."

Typically, if someone had said such a thing to me—promised to ensure my happiness—I wouldn't have believed them. However, Peter didn't say words to say them. He looked me in the eyes, stared me down, let me feel the heat of his promise. I knew that Peter would do his best to make sure I was happy. And I wanted to make sure that I did the same for him. I reached behind my back blindly, found the stove knob, and turned the burner off.

"What are you doing?" he asked.

"I suppose we have time to go upstairs before dinner," I said, biting at my lip.

"I don't mind cold stew," Peter growled, swatted my butt, and pushed me towards the back stairs.

Giggling like school children, we raced up the stairs. The stew could always be reheated. Spending our first night together in our home after two years of waiting for the day, we could focus on simply being happy.

The attic, accessible via a stairwell behind a door in the upstairs hallway, is a dark, cavernous room where dust motes dance in the beam of light that shines through the one window at the far end of the room. Floorboards that creak, boxes stacked neatly along the walls, and shadows that seemed to swallow everything they encounter to create an air of foreboding for anyone who ascends the stairs. Anyone except Peter and me. I always found the attic calm and peaceful. Too cold in the winter months and too hot in the summer months, it's still a room that induces feelings of fondness when I think of it.

Because it holds special memories. Those that belong to Peter. Those that belong to me. And those that we'd made together.

On my second day in America, I carried a box of my memories up to the attic once the airline delivered the things it had temporarily lost. I knelt in the far corner of the attic and set the box in an out-of-the-way space, deep in the shadows. Compulsively, and in a mild panic, I opened the box, and stared down into its contents, making sure the airline had returned the right box. A coat made of sugar and blue clouds. A black peacoat, fancier than any coat I'd ever owned. A bamboo wind chime. My notebooks.

It was all I had brought from Montreal besides my clothes and toiletries and a few books I'd yet to read. Because they were my favorite memories.

The attic would keep them safe for me.

Because the attic was a good room.

Is It Me? It Must Be Me.

Upon moving to the U.S., I hadn't expected that finding a job would be quick or easy. I had no expectations that I would move to the U.S. one day and I would have a job lined up the following Monday. I wasn't delusional about being an immigrant with what was essentially a green card who was seeking citizenship through marriage. Those facts alone would make me suspect to potential employers.

What happens if we hire this guy and he gets deported?

Does he only want the job to help validate his claim to citizenship?

Will he fit in with the office culture?

The potential for employers to toss my applications and résumé aside after a glance was high. I understood that. However, when a month passed, and Minneapolis was sneaking into mid-autumn, I became forlorn. Not a single company had so much as wanted to interview me for a position. Surely, within a month, it was reasonable to assume that, at the very least, I would have an interview for a position somewhere. Anywhere. Following up via phone did nothing to help my prospects. I was never spoken to rudely, but I consistently received a firm "no, thank you" to all of my inquiries about job openings.

Peter tried to be reassuring and understanding—and he was—but I was beginning to feel hopeless in my new home within a mere month. *In eleven months, you'll be a full citizen, Enzo.* Peter had said. *Things will be different then. Even if you can't find a job now, who cares? Everything will be fine. Things will change once you're a citizen, so don't worry too much.* I tried to believe Peter. I really did. There was logic to his words. But it began to feel dismissive.

Things *would* change once I received legal, federal citizenship in America. However, that did nothing to soothe my hurt feelings. Why wasn't I employable as an immigrant who was legally allowed to work, regardless? I had plenty of work experience. A degree from an accredited university. A willingness to do any job to the best of my ability. A desire to contribute to the economic power of the country I had chosen to make my home. I would be a good employee for any company.

American companies' feelings diverged on the matter.

So, I tried to focus on other important matters. I made sure that Peter had a hot, fresh breakfast each morning before he went to work each day. I cleaned the house from top to bottom, getting on my hands and knees and scrubbing with abandon every little nook and cranny. Dinner was always homemade and hot when he came home from work at the end of each long day. I did the grocery shopping, taking the bus to and from the grocery store. Any inconvenience, no matter how minor or major, I handled before it bothered Peter. I dealt with service people, did all of the laundry, met neighbors, and introduced myself. I started regularly attending services at a local Catholic church that I'd gone to numerous times while in Minneapolis when visiting. My prayers each day and services on Sunday helped ground me. Peter never wanted to attend Sunday services with me, so it was one event in my weekly routine that was mine alone, something independent from my marriage.

I tried to be a good househusband while I was forced to be one.

I worked on learning the kind of English Americans used. I studied the culture and slang and lesser-known things that make America what it is that one never hears about outside of the country.

Perfection. I strived to be the perfect partner for my new husband, even if contributing to finances was impossible.

Peter and I took weekend trips twice a month to visit his parents on the other side of the state. His mother and father, both lovely people who welcomed me with open arms, enjoyed our stays. Because I did my best to show that I was the perfect partner for their son. I did everything I could to be the best Enzo that I could be. Even as I was eaten up inside with self-doubt formed from rejection after rejection from potential employers.

Peter was happier than I'd ever seen him, reveling in our marriage and our arrangement—no matter how temporary. *Hopefully, it would prove temporary and I'd have a job within a year.* I suppose I was happy. I loved being married to Peter. I loved our breakfasts and dinners together. Our weekends at his parents' house or sequestered in bed with each other. I loved our home. I loved the city. But I found that I was not a person for whom "househusband" was a deep enough purpose in life.

I needed my own purpose. My own reason to get out of bed each morning that had nothing to do with our union.

After a while, I began to wonder if the problem was me. Was it not simply that I was an immigrant? Was my personality off-putting when I called employers? Presented myself in person? Was I not adapting and conforming to American culture well enough? Was it my accent? My obvious differentness? I had no one but Peter to ask about those things, and, of course, as my husband, he assured me that I was wonderful. However, of course, Peter thought I was wonderful—why else would he have married me? There were no friends for me to turn to and ask for their honest opinion.

It's not you, Enzo. You're wonderful. They're all just worried about your status as a citizen. That's all.

That seemed true, but one can't help to doubt even the opinions of their spouse when enough time goes by and one can't even get a job interview.

I don't have any friends here. It had slid out of my mouth over dinner one evening in early November.

I hadn't intended to be so honest with Peter, or imply that he wasn't enough to fulfill my social needs, but it happened. As I said it—as the words were leaving my mouth—I realized that what I'd said would sound rude. Maybe even cruel. I didn't want to hurt Peter's feelings, but I had to share mine. That's what husbands are supposed to do.

Silence filled the kitchen as we sat at the table and ate, Peter's eyes on his plate as his fork poked at the meal I'd prepared. For a moment, I felt that I'd offended Peter. That he might be upset with me. That I'd hurt his feelings. When he finally looked up at me, a smile on his face, he said:

That's a good point. You need a friend besides me.

I managed to smile back.

We never had a real wedding. Or a reception or anything. Why don't we throw a party?

A party?

Yeah. Peter had said. *We'll get someone to cater, I'll invite some friends and coworkers. You need to meet some people.*

Though I was nervous to meet more of Peter's friends and coworkers—I'd met so few in the month I'd lived in Minneapolis—I was ecstatic. The potential to make new friends lifted my spirits immeasurably. Even if being in a room with strangers was not within my comfort zone, I could be perfect at that, too, if I had to be.

Anything to make life better.

Lady FiFi Knobhouse, Heir to the Throne of Gang Bangs

Boxes and platters and foil pans full of food filled our kitchen. Hundreds of pork potstickers filled a few pans. Mini tortieres filled another. Meat and vegetable skewers, shrimp tartlets, sweet and savory mini meatballs on toothpicks, stuffed mushrooms, and bacon-wrapped apricots filled others. Trays of tiny dessert pastries filled others. The catering company and two waiters they'd sent along had taken over our kitchen for the evening. Trays that had been arranged beautifully by the waiters were set upon our dining room table for guests to help themselves to throughout the party.

Bottles of wine were arranged neatly on a side table. Liquor bottles containing drinks I knew nothing about filled another, and one of the waiters stayed stationed nearby, waiting to mix a cocktail for any partygoer unhappy with the wine selection. Peter had filled a cooler with ice and his favorite beers in the kitchen for guests who were not fond of wine or spirits. A selection of sodas and water was in the refrigerator for guests who were like me and did not partake in any of the offered alcohol.

Fancy little bone-white plates, tiny utensils, and linen napkins were stacked and ready by the platters of food on the dining room table. The display was far too fancy for me, but the food itself looked delectable. I'd spent the first hour of the party wishing that I could try one or two of the things the caterers had on offer. However, my stomach spent that hour grumbling quietly about being deprived of food as Peter introduced me to his friends and coworkers who arrived by the dozens. Before the first hour of the party had gone by, the front of our house was filled with people, every seat taken with people lining the walls huddled in small clusters and chatting.

Holding their fancy cocktails and stemmed glasses of wine, or possibly pawing an icy-cold bottle of beer, clad in cocktail dresses, slacks, and button-down shirts—some even wearing fancy dresses or suits—Peter's friends looked extremely chic. Our house had been turned into a set from a movie where people with fancy jobs, fancy clothes, fancy haircuts, and endless fancy things to talk about gathered. As Peter paraded me through each room, squeezing between clustered people here and there, introducing me to this person or that, I realized that Peter's friends were much different than I.

People who worked for the government or in finance or owned businesses or even weren't required to work due to the provenance of their existence were…intimidating. Though unfailingly polite, it was obvious that they were aware that I was *not one of them*. It could have been that I had nothing to add to the discussion we fell into with each group I was introduced to by Peter. It could have been that I was shy and unsure of what to say, other than "nice to meet you." It could have been that my clothes were not nearly as fancy as the rest.

Peter and I had gone and bought some nice slacks, a beautiful button-down shirt, and a tie for me to wear to the party, but it was a uniform. Anyone whose eyes landed on me at the party could easily guess that I was more suited to jeans and pullovers and sneakers. On any given day, I was not the type to prefer the glamour of a suit over comfort. For me, suits were reserved for church or weddings or funerals—not a party thrown in one's own home.

To me, throwing a party—though this might have been residual from my time at university—was bowls of chips and dips and beverages served in cans. Peter and I obviously had lived in very different worlds. Potato chips and dip that may or may not have been kept at room temperature for too long were not exactly the preferred snack for Peter or his friends.

As we entered the second hour of the party, I realized that there was no one at the party similar to me. They were all a decade older, infinitely more sophisticated, and terminally disinterested in the young French guy who had married their friend and immigrated to America. Peter held my hand and pulled me around the party anyway.

I stood by his side, nodding along and smiling as he and his friends chatted and laughed at jokes that I struggled to understand. People I'd never met were discussed. Office politics I had no interest in were talked about. American politics I didn't quite comprehend were argued about heatedly, though in a friendly manner. Insider gossip about industries flew over my head.

Finally, I had to excuse myself from Peter's side. With a smile and a whispered assurance that I needed something to drink—and hoped to visit the food table—Peter gave me a quick kiss and let me excuse myself.

Even though I did one of the things I said I would do, getting a drink from the refrigerator, I found that I couldn't force myself to return to Peter's side. I knew that I would only be subjected to more talk that I didn't understand from people who, though educated and chic, were boring. Instead,

I found a mostly empty corner by the living room and propped myself against the wall. Intermittently, I sipped at my soda as I watched Peter's friends delight themselves with each other's boring observations about uninteresting topics.

The party had done nothing to make me feel more welcome in America. And it was obvious that finding a friend amongst Peter's was a waste of time. A great sadness began to overwhelm me as I watched the clusters of guests chatting animatedly with each other, happy to ignore me.

Had I made a mistake? Coming to America?

"See that lady right there?"

The sudden sound of a voice and the feeling of someone's face close to mine nearly made me come out of my skin. Turning my head to look for the source of the voice, my face nearly collided with one that belonged to someone I had never met before. Deep brown eyes and a wicked grin met me as I found myself staring into the round face of a man standing just behind me to my right. Where he had come from, I wasn't sure, and I wasn't entirely certain that he wasn't someone who had simply wandered in off the street when he saw that a party was in progress. He was dressed for the occasion and seemed comfortable in his surroundings, so it was likely I had not met him yet. However, with as many people as Peter had already introduced me to, it seemed odd that I had not laid eyes on this man at some point throughout the early evening.

"Pardon me?" I managed to stammer.

"Frenchie." His grin widened at my reply. "You must be the man of the hour. I was pretty sure I was right."

Who was this man?

"I—"

"See that lady over there?" He cut me off, his head flicking towards the opposite side of the room. "Dark hair, the brooch that is obviously paste, and the pocketbook that she refuses to set down for fear that someone will find out it's faux instead of Fendi?"

"I—what?" I turned to look in the direction he had indicated. "Who?"

"For fuck's sake." He sighed; his mouth close to the side of my face. "Don't be so obvious. That lady. Là-bas. See? In the corner talking to the three men? Red lipstick? Audrey Hepburn little black dress that's seen the dry cleaner's far too many times?"

My eyes went to the corner across the room and finally found the target. A woman with an Anna Wintour bob, lipstick that was startlingly red, heavily-lined eyes, and the aforementioned purse, was standing in the corner, cocktail in hand, carrying on an animated—and obviously flirtatious—conversation with three men. Two of the men I knew to be married, though they seemed to have forgotten their wives for the time being.

"That's Lady FiFi Knobhouse, heir to the throne of Gang Bangs," the man behind me whispered conspiratorially. "She was here when Peter threw a Halloween party a few years ago."

"Okay." I couldn't help but grin at this ridiculous introduction.

The man moved in closer. I could practically feel his face touching mine as he looked over my shoulder.

"She came dressed as Scarlett O'Hara. Ya' know? From *Gone with the Wind?* Anyway, this other guy—*married, of* course—came as Darth Maul. From *Star Wars?* He had one of those fake two-ended light-up lightsabers—for authenticity, I guess. The face paint wasn't enough to get his point across, apparently. Well, they ended up in a room together with a few other guys, doing unspeakable things with Darth Maul's accoutrement. Apparently, they got so enthusiastic that the lightsaber broke, totally ruining it, and Lady FiFi Knobhouse spent the night in the emergency room getting treated for chemical burns on her hoo-ha."

"What?" I gasped, shocked at this stranger telling me such a lurid story.

"Yeah." He sighed, his chin coming to rest on my shoulder as though we were old friends. "It was tragic really. I hear that due to the disgrace of such an incident, Lady FiFi had to abdicate her line to the throne to her younger brother, Sir Sloppy Knobhouse. It was a bloodless change of succession—except for the vial Lady FiFi gave at the hospital to be tested for all manner of sexually transmitted diseases, of course."

"You lie." I threw a hand over my mouth to keep from laughing.

"Believe what you want," the man said. "Everyone still refers to that incident as *the night the lightsaber went out in Georgia.*"

Unable to control myself, my belly convulsed, and laughter poured from my mouth. My hand did no good in keeping my laughter from spilling forth. Obviously, someone laughing so uproariously spontaneously caused everyone in the room to turn to find the source of the noise which had disrupted their chic, yet profound conversations. With all eyes on me, most of them concerned or annoyed, I turned to my right, hoping the stranger would help me out of such an embarrassing predicament. But he was nowhere to be seen. Heat started to crawl up my face as I turned back to face all of the people who were slowly going back to their conversations, looking unsettled by what had happened. *Obviously, I was now going to be branded a crazy person.* Fortunately, Peter rescued me before my entire face turned as red as a tomato.

"Enzo." He smiled at me, obviously having seen what happened, but pretending it was of no consequence. "I've been looking for you."

"Have you?" I asked with more irritation in my tone than I had intended.

"Of course." He leaned in to give me a quick kiss on the lips. "I haven't shown my amazing husband off to everyone yet."

"Peter," I mumbled as he slid his hand into mine, trying to pull me after him.

"What is it?" He stopped to lean in to speak with me more privately.

"I am…" I began, my eyes darting around the room, "I am…"

"Need a break? Want to go get something to drink?" He smiled warmly, understanding my intent. "Maybe raid the food table?"

"Please." I breathed a sigh of relief.

Peter's fingers were laced between mine, so he gave my hand a firm yet gentle squeeze, then lifted my hand to kiss the back of it. There was no way that I couldn't smile at his effort to comfort me. Regardless of what I thought of the party and its attendants, Peter was still charming in the face of all of it.

"Come on, husband," he murmured. "Let's go to the kitchen. I'll get another drink and you can gorge on potstickers."

My stomach grumbled loudly enough that Peter noticed. He glanced at my stomach before giving me a wink and dragging me away from the living room by my hand. Making our way through the dining room, Peter was stopped by a few of his friends, whom he was then forced to reintroduce me to before he chatted with them for a few moments. I did my best to look interested, though joining in on the conversations was still nearly impossible. Everything felt as though it was happening on a level I was still trying to scratch and claw my way to—another floor in a building where I was still stuck in the basement.

Our house, for the evening, no longer felt like a sanctuary in my new homeland. That deepened the sadness swirling in my brain. When Peter and I finally managed to make our way through the house to the kitchen, I was relieved to be away from it all. However, when we entered the kitchen, we found that the refrigerator was open, and the sounds of someone rummaging around inside made my stomach drop. I wouldn't be able to let my guard down and talk to Peter in a way that was typical for us. I would have to continue to perform.

Peter squeezed my hand, picking up on my consternation, and gave me a small, comforting smile. When the person rummaging in the fridge stood and closed the door, my curiosity was piqued. The man who had told me the unbelievably salacious story in the living room was standing there, a can of beer in hand. Peter gave a sharp bark of a laugh at the sight of the man.

"When the hell did you get here?" Peter asked.

Peter's tone surprised me. The way he had spoken and conversed with his friends all night had been formal. Appropriate. Upon seeing this man, he reverted to the Peter I knew. That both brought me elation and concern.

Who was this man?

Was he an ex-boyfriend of Peter's?

"Who the hell are you trying to impress?" the man asked. "IPAs in the cooler and Pabst in the fridge? No one likes IPAs, you ginger fuck. They just want everyone else to think they like IPAs. Fucking hipsters."

Peter laughed again. My eyes darted from my husband to the man at the refrigerator, curiosity gnawing at my gut.

"Oh," the man said as he popped the tab on the can of beer, "fifteen minutes ago. *Ish*. I don't know. It's been a day. Minnesota time."

"Fair enough," Peter chuckled, then suddenly remembered me at his side. "Have you met—"

"Frenchie?" the man asked. "Of course. I'm not rude. I introduced myself as soon as I got here."

"Enzo," Peter said as I clasped his hand with both of mine. "My husband's name is Enzo."

For some reason, this uncouth man in the kitchen unnerved me more than anyone else at the party. Even the chicest of party attendees made me feel less self-conscious. It wasn't the man's aggressive speech or how self-assured he seemed—it was that he fascinated me more than anyone else. I desperately wanted to ask who he was, but I was uncertain if his sharp tongue would be turned on me.

"Nice to meet you, Enzo," the man raised the can of beer in a salute, then took a sip. "I was telling Enzo about Lady FiFi Knobhouse, and—"

"Damnit, Alex," Peter grumbled, his head rolling back on his shoulders, an amused grin stretching across his face. "Her name is Katherine."

"—but then I got thirsty," he continued, unbothered. "After scoping out the bullshit in the dining room, I knew you'd have hidden the good stuff in here."

"Pabst?" Peter asked. "That's...*the good stuff?*"

The man shrugged and took another sip.

"Yet it's in your fridge. Towards the back. Hidden from the guests so you can have it to yourself later. The food doesn't have two vultures watching over it in here, either," Alex said as he moved to the island and plucked a potsticker from one of the warming pans and popped it into his mouth. "You hungry, Frenchie?"

He grinned at me in the most mischievous way as he chewed, one cheek bulging. I found that I liked this person deeply immediately. Probably because he offered me food. Sure, it was mine and Peter's food, but he was still offering food.

"Enzo," Peter said.

"Look, *Pecker*," Alex rolled his eyes as he swallowed the bite and plucked another potsticker from the pan, "he doesn't seem to mind."

"Enzo—" Peter turned to me.

"It's fine," I mumbled and squeezed his hand, letting one of them fall from his. "Um—"

"This is Alex," Peter said, waving his arm in Alex's direction. "He's a complete piece of shit and annoyance. You'll despise him."

Alex simply grinned, bowed his head slightly, and popped the second potsticker into his mouth.

"We, unfortunately, met years ago at a bar," Peter explained as Alex sipped his beer. "He's been orbiting me ever since."

"To fuck," Alex said casually. "Anytime this guy needs to liven up a party, he calls me. He's absolutely enamored with me. In the non-Biblical sense, of course, so don't worry, Frenchie. He simply thinks I'm the best. Aside from you."

"Stop putting your fingers in the communal food," Peter said, not disputing what Alex had said.

I found that interesting.

"Life's too short to care if I give Norovirus to someone who drinks IPAs and wears alabaster pearls," Alex said before dipping into the pan once more. "Fifty cases of explosive diarrhea and three bathrooms would liven up the joint anyway."

Peter rolled his eyes, though not unamused.

"Are you hungry, Frenchie?" Alex asked again. "You look hungry. I don't bite. Come get some food."

"I'm starving." I found myself saying.

"Waddle up to the trough," he said. "Y'all paid for it."

I turned my head to look at Peter. He squeezed my hand and smiled.

"It's okay if you want to have a snack with Alex," Peter said. "I'll go back to the party. Make sure everyone knows they weren't abandoned."

"Okay," I said. "Are you sure?"

"Absolutely."

Peter leaned in and gave me a quick kiss. Then he turned his attention to Alex.

"Don't corrupt my husband," he said.

"Qui? Moi?" Alex asked.

Even more interesting, I thought. *He speaks French.*

Peter said nothing, but he laughed and gave my hand another squeeze. After another quick kiss, he slipped out of the kitchen the way we had entered. As the door slid shut behind him, I was left with the thick silence of being alone with a complete stranger. I turned my attention back to Alex to find he was sipping his beer and appraising me. For the span of a few breaths, we stared at each other.

"It was a true story," he broke the silence. "That lady in the black dress? That really happened. Though, admittedly, I sounded like I was judging her. I admire her style. Three guys and a lightsaber. That's a party."

I managed a nervous chuckle.

"People clusterfucked together, sipping dirty martinis, and talking about the health of the stock market is a corporate retreat," he said and shook his beer at me. "PBR and chemical burns on your cooch? That's a shindig."

Again, I chuckled, though it was more genuine.

"Are you going to eat?" he asked. "It's really good."

He lifted a potsticker from the pan with the tips of his fingers and shook it at me before popping it into his mouth with a grin. Hesitantly, I shuffled over to the kitchen island and peered down into the pan nearly overflowing with uneaten potstickers. Peter and I had ordered far too much food. Then again, once people were inebriated, the food might go quicker. I plucked a potsticker from the pan and stuffed it into my mouth.

Bursting with meaty juices, the dough sticking to my teeth and roof of my mouth, and spices that played along my tongue, I couldn't help but groan with pleasure at the bite. I hadn't eaten since lunch and I hadn't realized how hungry I really was. All I had needed was a bit of food to help me clear my head. Alex smiled at me and sipped his beer, watching as I shoved two more potstickers into my mouth in rapid succession.

"People who love to eat are the best people," he said suddenly. "I tend to hate the skinny ones, but I'll make an exception for you."

I couldn't help but laugh. Rotund and tall, though not quite as tall as me, Alex obviously knew what he was talking about—and I agreed with him. People who loved food were good people. I'd said so many times throughout my life. To hear those words come from Alex's mouth, I couldn't help but feel I'd been correct in assessing him as someone I'd like.

"Parlez-vous français?" I asked as I selected another potsticker.

He snorted. "Très peu. I know a few words. Just like Spanish. I can order a great meal if I'm on vacation, but I can't hold a conversation. I can make fun of your mother's vagina in Arabic. But I'm not fluent in French, no. Though, I did notice you used the formal 'vous.' I'll be a 'tu' before this party is over."

I smiled at him. He was quick. Witty. Deliciously intelligent. Self-possessed in a way that I'd always hoped to be.

"It's important to know a little bit about everything, don't you think?" he asked. "Then you're able to talk to rich assholes at house parties where the cheap, tasty beer is hidden in the kitchen so no one knows the homeowners are, actually, trash."

"I suppose," I said with a rich laugh.

"Anyway," he said, holding his hand out, "to be deserving of a 'tu,' I'm Alex."

I popped the potsticker in my mouth and used one of the caterer's cloths to wipe my hand quickly before accepting Alex's.

"I'm Enzo. Nice to meet you."

"Nice to meet you," he said. "You know this party is taking place in your house, right?"

"Um—"

"You're not an outsider here."

"Uh—"

"I saw you," he said. "Hiding in the corner. Trying to be invisible. Why?"

I shrugged.

"Look," Alex said, setting his beer on the island before reaching into the pan once more, "conversation works the same in every language. I say something. You answer. Maybe you ask something in return. Or suggest a topic. A shrug is not a response."

I laughed nervously.

"Why were you hiding?"

"I wasn't hiding," I said. "I was just—"

"Making yourself small," he said. "In your own home."

"I suppose," I said.

Alex was unlike anyone else I'd ever met. We had barely introduced ourselves and he was talking to me as though he had known me for years. He was interested to know about me of all people. And he seemed to not care how anyone perceived him. I suddenly felt I needed to know everything about him. I had no idea how to convey that to him.

With a snort and a grin, Alex leaned in from the other side of the island.

"These rich assholes just need to be validated," he said. "They don't care about you. They care what you think about them. They're the easiest to talk to at parties."

"I think they're boring," I said, then realized what had escaped my mouth, and slapped a hand over my mouth.

"Fuck yeah they are," Alex nodded. "I've been here less than twenty minutes and I already want to slip Ecstasy in the punch. Do you have a punchbowl? I didn't see one."

"No," I giggled nervously.

He waved me off. "I didn't bring any Ecstasy. I quit that shit when I woke up next to a FedEx guy in my bed and had to piece together the previous night's events using clues in concerned texts from friends. Anyway, that's another story. These rich assholes don't have to know you think that they're boring. They just want you to *believe* they're not boring. Nod, say complimentary things, ask them their opinions, congratulate them on the most basic of accomplishments, then apologize and say you *have to make sure you talk to so-and-so* and thank them once again for gracing you with their presence. You don't have to know what the hell they're talking about. That doesn't matter."

I stared at him.

"How do you know Peter?"

That was the biggest question on my mind. Crass and unrefined, though obviously not unintelligent, Alex seemed like the last person Peter would have had as a friend. Though, I found I was glad they were friends. It made me love Peter even more somehow.

"My family's from down south. Rochester? I was up visiting from Texas and Peter and I happened to be at the same dive bar one evening. I was escaping my family for a few hours. I think he was down in Rochester for business."

"Did you…"

Alex cocked his head and stared at me for a moment, as though trying to figure me out. When the realization of what I was asking hit him, he cackled.

"I'm queer but I ain't *that* queer," he managed to say through his laughter. "No offense."

I grinned.

God, I adored this person. He was so awful.

Alex was rude. However, it was apparent to anyone with half of a brain that his rudeness wasn't genuine, but a way to loosen up strangers, to ease them into conversation with him. He was making me comfortable. Alex made himself seem awful so others would feel superior and more comfortable talking to him.

I did not feel superior to Alex. But I was comfortable.

"No." He waved me off as he grabbed his beer and leaned against the island. "We both ordered the same beer and got to talking. The bar was empty so we didn't have a lot of options for conversation. He saw how charming I was and realized that I needed to be a close friend. I realized he could be interesting when he wasn't trying to impress people. Nothing more."

"Oh."

"Yeah," he said. "When he broke up with Michael I came and stayed with him for a bit while he worked himself out. We're just friends."

"Michael?"

"His ex?" Alex asked. "Oh. Maybe I shouldn't have—"

"It's fine," I said, stopping him. "I just…we haven't…"

"Gotcha. Well, anyway, that's basically it. I live in Texas. He's here. We don't get to see each other often, but I guess we're those friends that are there when they're needed."

"It's nice that you were in town for the party," I said, unsure of what else I could say.

"I'm up visiting family again," he said.

"Oh."

"So," Alex began, "how did that ginger fuck manage to convince *you* to marry him?"

I couldn't help it, I laughed uproariously.

"What?"

"He's elderly," Alex said. "Not that you didn't know that. He's not much to look at. You're young. Handsome. French. The people who essentially invented romance. How'd he sweep you off your feet?"

"How old are you?" I asked mischievously.

"That's beside the point."

We both laughed.

"Maybe I swept him off of his feet?" I found myself teasing back, suddenly comfortable as I plucked another potsticker from the pan. "And he's the most handsome man I've ever met."

A soft smile slowly bloomed on Alex's face.

"He's the kindest, smartest...I love Peter. That's how he swept me off of my feet, I suppose."

Alex smiled at me a moment longer, then his mouth fell open to utter one word blandly. "Barf."

I found myself laughing again.

"It's true."

"I believe you," he said. "It's just gross. You're a gross person, Frenchie."

I shrugged. "It's still true."

"So," Alex fluttered his hand in the air, "how's the U.S. for you?"

"I don't know," I said, averting my eyes. "It's nice."

"Yikes," Alex winced. "*Nice.* Usually, it takes people a bit longer to realize what a shithole they've stumbled into here. I knew you were smart."

"No," I said, shaking my head, hoping I hadn't offended the first friendly person I'd met at the party, "it's just that—"

"Oh," he said, leaning in again, "it's a shithole. But it has its good parts."

"I don't know if I'll...fit in?"

He nodded. "You'll figure it out. Be loud. Obnoxious. Act like you know what you're doing. Be friendly when you can. Eventually, you'll get it."

I couldn't help but smile at that assessment of American culture. Loudly be yourself and...wait.

"You're from France but Peter found you in Canada?" he asked. "What's it like riding a moose?"

Again, before I could stop it, I found myself saying the first thing that came to mind.

"You are such a strange person," I slapped my hand over my mouth again.

Finally, Alex laughed. *I had made him laugh.*

"Thanks," he saluted me with his beer again. "But you have no idea, Frenchie."

I lowered my hand from my mouth, though I knew my cheeks were red from embarrassment, and smiled down at the island. I had done all I could—unintentionally—to offend Alex, but he was laughing with me.

"Do you smoke, Enzo?" he asked.

"Um—"

"Cigarettes," he assured me. "I quit drugs around the time the FedEx guy just had to overnight his package."

"I haven't in a year," I said. "It's bad for you."

Alex stared at me.

"Do ya' smoke? Frenchie?"

I grinned at him.

The pocket of my new slacks became a depository for numerous cigarette butts as the hours passed under the pergola in the backyard. Alex and I had left the kitchen and went to sit at the table outside. Using the empty can Alex had from his drink in the kitchen, we sat and smoked under the cover of darkness. Only the stars to share in our secret. We could hear the party carrying on inside, but it didn't stop us from talking as if we were old friends.

It took me a bit to feel completely comfortable with Alex, but he had a way about him that made me want to open up to him. About everything. Within a half-hour, I was telling him everything about myself, asking him questions that were far too personal after having just met someone. But, as I had suspected, he was as open and interesting as he seemed. When he was removed from the prying ears of other people, he also became less crass. Calmer. More thoughtful and well-spoken. Still hilarious, but less manic in his conversation.

I adored him. And we'd known each other for less than two hours.

Peter hadn't come looking for us, but he had texted me to make sure that we were okay since we were no longer in the kitchen, nor were we mingling. I had been concerned that he would be cross with me for abandoning the party to talk to only one person, but he seemed delighted that I was having fun. Even if it wasn't with his other friends. That made talking to Alex even easier since I knew Peter approved.

Over the remaining cigarettes in Alex's pack, plus a fresh one he seemed to produce out of thin air, I found myself telling him everything about my life. My family. My struggles. Things I wouldn't have told any friend or even my family. It was as if I'd known Alex for my entire life and we had just found time to actually sit down and catch up.

I began to wonder if I'd finally made a friend in America.

"So," Alex asked two hours into our conversation, "where are you working? What do you do, Enzo?"

"I haven't found a job yet," I admitted.

"I'm in health care. Mostly."

"It has been difficult to find a job here," I said.

"Oh? Why? You have a degree, right?"

"I think people don't want to hire an immigrant who isn't a full citizen yet? That concerns them?"

"You want to work, right?"

"Of course! I don't want to be a househusband forever."

Alex chuckled, then thought on this for a second, watching me, as though unsure if he should speak.

"Can I be honest with you, Enzo?" he asked finally.

"Yes. Please."

I desperately needed honesty. What was I doing wrong? If Alex knew the key to unlocking the mystery as to why American employers didn't want to so much as interview me, I wanted to hear it. Even if it was painful.

"You're going to need to work in fast food, a restaurant, or custodial services," he said. "For now. Until you're a citizen."

"Oh."

"It's fucked up," he said, "but as an immigrant, it's going to be hard to find anything else right away. I wouldn't give this advice to anyone because it's not fair. But you really want to work? Apply for the custodian, waiter, or cook jobs. When you get your citizenship, you can apply somewhere else. For a job you really want. Or you can work your way up in the company. Let the assholes in charge think you *know your place*. That's how you sneak in the backdoor around here. Again…fucked up…but it is what it is. If you want the truth, there it is. An employer is going to look at your application right now and figure it's not worth risking having to replace you in a few weeks or months if you don't stick around. They can easily replace lower-paid jobs."

"That is…*fucked up*," I said with a sigh and an exhalation of smoke. "Thank you."

He chuckled. "America, man."

"It's not all that bad, is it?" I asked. "I haven't chosen poorly?"

"Coming to America?" he asked. "Nah. Well, it's no worse than any other country where white people think they're more important than everyone else. It has its good points and bad points. You just have to learn how to work with the system. Until someone fixes it, I guess. Marrying Peter? I don't know on that one, man."

I laughed raucously.

"You are so awful to him!"

Alex and I tapped our cigarettes on the mouth of the can at the same time.

"Peter's all right," Alex said, sitting back in his chair. "For an uptight ginger. I just have to give him shit. That's what you do with friends."

Looking around, as though there was anyone nearby who might hear us, I leaned in to whisper to Alex.

"I feel so out of place here," I whispered. "Peter is so…refined? When he has to be, I mean. And I'm just…I don't know? I'm just not refined. I cannot even pretend to be. I don't understand his friends or his job. I've never had money as he does. His car is fancy. Our house is huge. I don't really know how the television works because you have to push too many buttons to make it do anything. It's all…confusing."

Alex was grinning.

"I love that," he said.

"What?"

"Enzo," he said, "you're going to make him more human."

"What?"

"I think you'll make Peter better. That's what."

"He's so wonderful, and—"

"Well, yeah," Alex dismissed me with a flick of his cigarette against the can. "To you. He loves you. Wants to sex you up and shit. That's different. He wants you to think the best of him. But he's obsessed with himself and his life sometimes. I think you're going to make him a better person, Enzo. You severely underestimate your worth here."

I blushed.

"And maybe he'll make you a little more refined," Alex added. "Make you a little more elegant."

"I hope so," I mumbled, embarrassed.

With a sigh, Alex's head rolled back on his shoulders so that he could look up at the inky, star-mottled sky. I mimicked his actions and stared up at the pinpricks of light blinking down at us. Though I was no better off, as far as figuring out how to make America—my new homeland— work for me, I felt less hopeless. Alex had laid out the truth for me. It wasn't ideal, but the truth rarely is. However, once you know the truth, you know how to plan your next steps.

"I'm surprised it isn't colder tonight," Alex said. "This is nice. Or maybe it's the beer."

We laughed softly together.

"It feels," I said, once again letting words slip from my brain before I could stop them, "that the universe is inconsistent. Like…things go right. Things go wrong.

Things get worse. Then a little better…and then things just…stand still. I feel like I'm standing still."

"Hm?"

"I'm in stasis," I explained. "I can't do this for an entire year. I need a purpose."

"We all need a purpose, sure," Alex said.

"Do you believe in God?" I asked.

When I realized what I said, I crooked my head to look at Alex, prepared to apologize for such a question. However, when our eyes met, as he turned his head away from the sky to look over at me, he was smiling.

"Well, sure," he said.

That easy. That simple. No question was too personal or odd for Alex. In fact, the more personal or odd a question, the more he seemed to enjoy it.

"I just wouldn't give him a great performance review. All twos. Needs improvement," he said. "On a good day, maybe all threes. Meets expectations."

I couldn't help but smile at him. No one had ever explained how I felt, but hadn't known I felt that way, so simply before. Alex, for all of his jokes and quips, could be profound. As quickly as he'd fire off a joke, he'd be philosophical. But not pretentiously so. As I stared at him across the table, I wondered if there would ever be enough time in someone's life to learn all there was in Alex's head.

"My grandmother used to tell me to be good to the universe and it would be good back," I said softly, not really talking to Alex, but not really *not* talking to Alex. "I think that I've been good. I've tried. But I feel it's ignoring me. I don't feel like it's sending anything to me."

"Your grandmother didn't tell you shipping costs extra?"

"Huh?"

"It's not enough to be good," Alex said, tamping out his cigarette. "Sit around and be good all you want, Enzo. See what it does for you. But sometimes you have to go out and find what you want for yourself."

"Meaning what?"

"Be good, but take no shit," he said. "Where do you want to work? Show up there. Give your application to someone who matters. Tell them you will do any job they have. You just need to work. Don't let them tell you 'no' without having to look you in the eyes. Don't let them ignore you. It's okay if people tell you 'no,' but it's not okay to let them ignore you."

"Are you sure?"

"Positive."

"Okay."

Sighing again, Alex shifted in his chair, as though preparing to rise.

"Well," he said, smiling at me. I think it's time I head back down to Rochester. It's an hour and a half and it's getting late, so—"

"You've been drinking," I found myself stammering, upset that Alex was going to leave. "You shouldn't drive."

He snorted. "One Pabst two hours ago? I think I'll be fine. Besides, this is Minnesota. I could drink twelve PBRs and still be within the legal limit, I'm sure."

When Alex started to rise from his chair, I found myself desperate for him to stay.

"I don't have any friends," I said, the words slipping out effortlessly again.

Alex froze, halfway out of his chair, and stared at me.

"If you leave," I said, my eyes darting around, "I won't have anyone interesting to talk to. I'll have to go inside and make conversation with Peter's other friends. I'll essentially be alone. Please stay."

Alex stared at me a moment longer, then eased himself back into his chair.

"Okay," he said.

"Okay?"

"That was embarrassing for you," he said. "I can't leave now."

I blushed.

"But I hope you're prepared for an overnight guest," he sighed, extracting another cigarette from his pack. "I'm not driving through Minnesota in the middle of the night. I don't want to lose my virginity to some backwoods hillbilly."

I cackled, slapping my hand over my mouth at the joke.

"You're ridiculous!"

He shrugged and lit his cigarette. "Life's too ridiculous to pretend it's not."

As the night wore on, I became inseparable from Alex. I was certain that it had to be annoying for him, but he pretended otherwise. We eventually rejoined the party, only to find that half of the guests had left. Of course, it was nearly midnight when we went back inside. The two of us joined a group of people Peter was talking to, and I marveled at the way Alex fell into the conversation easily, though I was sure he didn't care about anything that was being said.

The way that he listened and responded, sometimes in a way that was obviously an insult wrapped in polite language, yet too witty for the target to catch, amused me. Peter caught the insults as well, and we exchanged furtive, amused glances each time Alex did it to yet another party guest. Of course, as hosts, we should have reigned him in, insisted that he behave. However, none of the guests seemed to notice and it made the party more interesting.

By the time everyone left, it was nearing two o'clock in the morning. Alex and I had taken up sitting on the couch for the last hour, laughing and joking about whatever came to mind as Peter saw people out. The caterers had cleaned up, stored the remaining food in our refrigerator, and left. The liquor and wine had to be dealt with, but there was no rush to do those things.

Once the last person was out the door, Peter joined Alex and me in the living room. He seemed pleased that I'd had someone to talk to during the party and hadn't been bored, though he was tired. He gave us his blessing to keep talking on the sofa and excused himself to our bedroom. As the morning hours rushed up to meet us, Alex and I eventually fell asleep, right there on the living room sofa. Him at one end and me at the other.

Like friends would do.

When morning came and the three of us rose to greet the day, Alex said he really had to go back to Rochester. When I hugged him as he was preparing to leave, he seemed unbothered by the affection. Though he hissed at Peter when he tried to hug him, which made me laugh. As Peter and I watched him drive away, waving at his car as he disappeared down the street, I couldn't remove the smile from my face. I wouldn't have been certain that I had made my first friend in America, except he had programmed his number into my phone, giving me permission to call or text anytime I needed.

I had made a friend.

And, thanks to his advice, I was forming a plan.

The Seeds We Plant

Downtown Minneapolis is packed with office buildings full of possibility. As it is with any large city, Minneapolis presented boundless possibilities to those looking for gainful employment. Unless one is an immigrant who is not yet a United States citizen. Someone such as that should take all of the possibilities, divide by one hundred, and assume that is the number of companies that would even consider hiring them. It's not fair. It's not right. However, right and fair cannot be addressed from the outside. Sometimes one has to work with the parameters set for them in order to change the parameters for those who follow behind them.

When Peter left for work on a Monday, a week after our party, I used my bus pass to go downtown. Though I had no reason to believe it would work out well for me, I had found a company during an internet search that specialized in translation and interpretation services. Though my degree wasn't necessarily meant for such a job, surely, even as an immigrant without full citizenship, the company would see the value in hiring me. I knew more than one language. I was a hard worker. I was polite and professional and willing to learn. I'd worked at a similar company in Montreal for four years before moving to the United States.

I could be perfect for any entry-level job they had to offer.

I could sit at a desk and tell a person in English what someone had said in French. Or vice versa. I could write it down for them in either language. I could do that for eight hours a day. A job and an income of my own were all that mattered. Some independence and autonomy from Peter and our marriage. To feel as though I was beginning to assimilate and join the culture of my new homeland.

The company, Source Language, Inc., had a receptionist who was pleasant enough. Nice, even. However, she merely had to glance at my application and take notice of the boxes that were checked—*and unchecked*—before handing it back to me. Though she smiled and did her best to be kind with her response, I could see in her eyes that when she said there were no jobs available, she was being dishonest. What she'd meant was that there were no jobs *for me*.

Please. I had said. *Any job is fine. I'm willing to do anything entry-level. Anything.*

Back and forth the receptionist and I went, her insisting there was nothing available—though I knew that to be false from my internet search—and me insisting that any job they had was fine. As Alex had advised, I was going to do my best to not take "no" for an answer. I'm unsure of how long the receptionist and I pushed back and forth, but it was long enough that I felt she would decide to call security if I badgered her much longer about a job.

Just as I felt that I had argued for too long, and the receptionist would have me removed from the building, a voice interrupted us. We both turned our heads to find a middle-aged man in a suit, impeccably groomed, watching us.

What's this now? he had asked.

My first thought was that this man was obviously someone of importance. He had probably heard us arguing from his office, came to find out what was disrupting his day, and would insist that I leave or be thrown out. However, the twinkle in his eye and the amused grin on his face comforted me a little.

The receptionist, before I could speak for myself, told the man—*Mr. Barton*—that I had come in looking for a job, but she had let me know that there were none available. She thought I didn't notice the pointed look she gave him, as though trying to convey information to him subliminally. Mr. Barton noticed her look but seemed to want to ignore it. He obviously wanted to know more about what was going on. Something had interested him.

I'm looking for a job. I'd said before the receptionist could say more. *I don't have full citizenship here yet. But I will in less than a year. I need a job until then. Any job.*

Mr. Barton smiled at me and held his hand out to me. Unsure of what he wanted at first, I stared at him.

Your application?

Nervously, I handed Mr. Barton my application. When he didn't merely glance over it as the receptionist had before handing it back, I felt hopeful. He actually read over what was on the forms, giving consideration to what I had to offer. However, when his eyes lifted from the paper and he held it out to me, my stomach sank.

Very impressive. You're absolutely qualified. If you want to come back when you have your citizenship, I'd be glad to consider you then, Enzo.

I didn't take the application from his hand. Instead, I swallowed hard, forcing myself to suppress my feelings; my pride.

Please, I'd said. *Any job.*

He started to speak.

I need a purpose. Please.

The receptionist coughed and I suddenly felt as though I might actually cry in front of them. I'd made an absolute fool of myself. With all of the pride I could muster, I reached out to take the application from Mr. Barton. When he pulled it away from me, I was concerned that, perhaps, he was keeping it so he could give my name to the authorities. However, he turned to the receptionist and held it out to her instead.

Forward that to Harry. By lunchtime, please, Belinda.

The receptionist shrugged and took my application from him and I had to wonder if "Harry" was the security guard they were going to call to throw me out on the sidewalk. As soon as the receptionist set about her task, Mr. Barton motioned for me to follow him. With nothing better to do, I followed him to a corner of the expansive lobby. I could have run, seen myself out before they got someone else to do it, but I was desperate. So, I did as he requested.

In the corner of the lobby, between two potted Ficus trees, Mr. Barton turned to me.

It won't be much, he said, *but do you have anything against custodial work?*

I exhaled heavily, afraid that I'd burst into tears. This man was going to offer me a job.

No. No. Not at all. Anything. I'll do any job. I've done custodial work before.

Mr. Barton smiled warmly at me, and I realized that I liked this man immediately.

I saw that on your application. Well, if you'd like, I'll see that the supervisor—Harry Martin—reaches out to you tomorrow. You can probably start on Monday, Enzo.

My stomach was flipping, but no longer from nerves.

When you get your citizenship, I'm sure there will be something open in interpretation or translation services. Sound good?

Yes. Absolutely. Thank you, Mr. Barton.

He held out his hand and I immediately took it, shaking it a little more excitedly than was necessary. Mr. Barton merely chuckled at my exuberance. He patted my shoulder and indicated that he needed to return to his office.

Make sure to be ready for Harry's call, Enzo. Mr. Barton reminded me as he walked away.

I will!

I'll see you on Monday.

I'll be here!

The receptionist wasn't any friendlier to me as I left, even though Mr. Barton had offered me a job, but she wasn't any ruder. She merely let me go about my business. When I started work the following Monday, I'd find out that Mr. Barton was the CEO of Source Language, Inc., and my arguing with the receptionist had disrupted the phone call he had been on. He'd merely come out to the lobby to see who had given his receptionist such a hard time.

He found me. And instead of kicking me out for my disruption, he'd given me a job.

Mr. Barton would quickly become one of my favorite people in America.

Since there was a whole day left before Peter would return home from work, I took the bus to the stop closest to La Croûte and bought macarons. Then I went to the grocery store and picked up a few items for dinner. A special meal with a delicious dessert was in order to celebrate my day. So, when Peter came home—I'd received a call from Harry and

been given specifics of what to expect with my new job—
I'd made cassoulet, modified to work with the ingredients I
could find that were comparable to traditional ingredients.

Over the decadent bean stew that I'd packed with
chicken thighs, local Minnesota sausages, and cubed pork
belly, I told Peter my good news. At first, he was excited at
my having found a job. When I told him what the job
entailed, he seemed to deflate. *Custodian work.* I knew it
wasn't a job that someone with a university degree should
have been excited about, but I was elated. Peter's poorly
disguised disappointment did nothing to ruin my mood,
though it made me cross with him briefly.

However, as we dug into the box of Earl Grey and
blackberry macarons I'd purchased from La Croûte, his
mood improved. He began to see the bright side of my
having secured employment. My obvious excitement and
happiness made him happy and excited for me. So, I was no
longer cross with him for his slight. Besides, I knew he was
only disappointed that I'd had to take any job offered due to
my circumstances. My value and worth were being
exploited. That was true.

I was simply glad to have a job. A purpose.

In time, my worth and value would be accepted.

All I had to do was have faith. And refuse to be ignored.

It'll Be the Death of Me

Our front room was decorated festively for Christmas. Peter and I had brought his large fake tree down from the attic and set it up in the corner of the room by the large picture window. Using box upon box of glass ornaments in reds, greens, silvers, and golds, we decorated the tree expertly. Garland and tinsel, white twinkle lights, and a light-up star completed the job. A giant snow globe depicting the nativity—another family heirloom, was placed in the middle of the coffee table. Pillows in shades to match the tree replaced the day-to-day pillows on the furniture.

The room was beautiful. Appropriate. Ready for any guests that stopped by over the holidays. It felt cold to me, though. Christmas was supposed to be warm and cozy. Familiar.

When Peter indicated that we weren't done decorating, I was disappointed. I didn't want to take any more decorations that meant nothing and dress up our home as a showpiece for the holidays. However, when he instructed me to dress warmly, and then took me to a tree farm to choose and saw down our own tree, my spirits were lifted. We drank hot coffees from a drive-through shop on our way home from the tree farm, laughing and singing along to carols on the radio.

Back at home, we took off our coats, scarves, gloves, and hats, and dragged the tree into the den. Working together, we positioned the live tree as perfectly as possible in a stand, laughing each time it nearly toppled on us. Then Peter showed me another box from the attic, full of Mica glass ornaments his grandmother had left him. All in a variety of colors, shapes, and sizes, we decorated the den tree with tinsel, bubble lights, and white lights, and the ornaments that meant so much to his family. When we were done, we waited to sweep up all of the pine needles so we could stand back and admire our work.

After cleaning up our messes, showering, and changing into pajamas, we curled up on the den sofa together and snuggled in front of a roaring fire. Under a shared blanket, we held each other in the room illuminated only by the tree's lights. Stealing kisses and whispering sweet nothings, we welcomed the season in a way that had nothing to do with the appropriateness of the living room. And again, I was reminded that the den was my favorite room in our house.

My first American Christmas flew by, events swirling around me, as though I was stuck in the middle of a hurricane. Neighbors stopped by with tins of cookies, and I found that it was an expectation that Peter and I would have gifts for them as well. No one had informed me, so I spent time when I wasn't working or taking care of the house baking treats for neighbors.

Peter's parents came for a long weekend in the middle of the month since they would be traveling on the holiday itself. For four days I cooked and cleaned and cooked and cleaned some more. Peter's mother and father, lovely as they were, were doted and doled over by Peter and I spent much of those days taking care of things behind the scenes. For the entire weekend, I felt ignored and taken advantage of, but I knew to be a good husband, sometimes partners had to work in tandem when guests were in their home. Peter entertained and I made sure things behind the scenes worked well.

Sometimes, especially around Christmas, I was happy to be out of the house at my job. Though I spent my days cleaning at work as well, it was a respite from the forced joy and frivolity of an American Christmas. The people I worked with, from the custodians, right up to Mr. Barton, were all wonderful people. Friendly and welcoming, my days at work, though physically strenuous, were a joy. Unlike any other place I'd worked, Source Language, Inc.'s culture was perfect. Everyone came in, did their jobs, were kind to each other, and then they went home. And even though I was merely a custodian, I felt I was paid well.

Mr. Barton ran the company with the expectation that everyone would work hard and do their jobs well, but he was fair and generous. He ran the company with a core belief that no one on the team was more important than anyone else. If you worked hard, had integrity, and did well, you had nothing to fear from the soft, yet well-spoken, older man. That December, even though I'd been with the company less than a month, I received a bonus. Just like everyone else. And it was incredibly generous.

All in all, my first Christmas in America wasn't terrible, even if I felt I barely had time to breathe. The way that Americans went overboard with decorations, carols, shopping, gifts, meals, and treats was extraordinary. Even when it all became overwhelming, I couldn't help but marvel at how the festivities went on, minute by minute, hour by hour, day by day. Leading up to the finish line, which was the holiday itself.

On Christmas Eve, Peter and I opened one gift a piece. A gift he had bought each of us. Matching pajamas. And our first family tradition—that was ours—was born. The following day, we opened the remaining presents under the tree in the den as *A Christmas Story* played on repeat on the television. With my job, I'd been able to buy a few gifts for Peter with the money I had earned, which meant more to me than receiving any gifts.

The rest of the day, we stayed in our pajamas, taking our meals on the den sofa, taking naps, snuggling, and enjoying the peaceful solemnity such a day requires. It was my favorite part of my first American Christmas, that peace and quiet.

Christmas didn't bring only gifts and season's greetings, however. Between Christmas and New Year's—which is the best time for it to be done—Peter's health insurance informed us that they would no longer pay for the medication I took for my seizure disorder. It was no longer "a covered medication."

Panic immediately set in when I received word. I couldn't *live* without my medication—and though the insurance at Source Language, Inc. would have paid for my medication, I hadn't been working there long enough to enroll in their health insurance program. They required all new employees work for them for a year before joining their insurance program. It was the one awful aspect of working for the company, but with Peter's insurance, it hadn't seemed so awful. Until Peter's insurance pulled the rug out from under us. After a month of paying for my medication with our own money, Peter and I were able to schedule an appointment with an American neurologist.

I told the doctor numerous times during the appointment that I'd tried other medications, even the generic version of my medication, and none of them worked as well or consistently. Or they presented unpleasant side effects. Or they were not as safe as the medication I was on. I'd lived with my condition for a quarter of a century—I knew it better than anyone else. Even a doctor. I'd been poked and prodded and sliced and consulted by doctors in two other countries—and all of them agreed with me. The medication I was on was the best chance for me to continue living well with my condition. The generic medication had different inactive ingredients that did not agree with me as well as the brand name. However, the American neurologist insisted that unless I wanted to try new medications that might present side effects that were even worse, the best I could do was switch to the generic form of my medication.

Peter and I had to make a choice. Spend thousands of dollars of our own money so that I could continue receiving the medication that worked best for me…or take a chance. Peter insisted that I make that choice—and he would be happy with whatever I chose. After a lot of thought and consideration, I decided to switch to the generic medication. Having grown up poor, suffering a few side effects was not nearly as horrible as losing thousands of dollars simply because of an unjust and uncaring insurance company.

How bad could the side effects be anyway?

Chase Connor

Leveling the Playing Field

"Could I see you in my office, Enzo?"

Having the CEO of the company you work for locate you in the men's room, while you're scrubbing toilets, and ask you for a meeting is never a good sign. Even if it's someone as wonderful as Mr. Barton. I froze, the scrub brush in my hand frozen against the inside of the toilet, and looked up to find him standing in the doorway of the bathroom, holding the door wide. He looked pleasant enough, as usual, but it was still such an odd request, all things considered.

"Okay," I finally managed to say.

Mr. Barton gave me a nod and exited the bathroom, letting the door swing shut behind him. For a moment, I stood there, hunched over the toilet, wondering if I had done something wrong. *Was I going to be fired or reprimanded?* I'd always done my best to do an exemplary job, be pleasant and professional, and do any task that was asked of me. I was never late or called in sick, even though I hadn't felt well for months.

My new medication had provided me with months of nausea and intermittent pains throughout my body that seemed to come from nowhere. However, I was managing. I wasn't having any seizures. That was all that mattered. However, the nausea had taken ten pounds from my already lithe frame. Though Peter said nothing—nor did anyone else—I knew that I looked nearly skeletal. I never mentioned the random pains to anyone except for my neurologist, and he seemed to think it was simply something I'd have to deal with if I wanted to not have seizures. So, I suffered in silence, even if there was physical proof in the form of my bony frame.

Other side effects were more difficult to deal with, however. Problems sleeping and staying asleep—which I'd dealt with my entire adult life—were exacerbated. My sex drive was diminished. My energy was reduced to such that I did all I could to conserve what little I had for work. I still managed to clean the house and cook dinners and keep up my hygiene—but asking much more of me was pointless. I was so tired and weak all of the time.

But I continued on, doing the best I could.

Peter did his best to be understanding, but I knew that the difficulties that had arisen from the debacle with his insurance company—and my medication—were making life difficult for him as well.

Shaking my head clear of thoughts, I returned the scrub brush to my custodial cart and pushed it to a corner of the bathroom, out of the way. I washed my hands thoroughly after removing my gloves, dried them, and made sure I looked as presentable as possible in the mirror.

Down in Mr. Barton's office, I found him clicking his mouse violently, a frown on his face. That did not bode well for our meeting. However, when he saw me in the doorway, he let go of the mouse, smiled at me, and waved me inside. He motioned for me to close the door, so I did, then sat down in the chair in front of his impressive desk.

"Your citizenship test is later today, isn't it?" Mr. Barton asked, surprising me.

That was not what I'd expected him to say.

"Yes," I said. "I put in a request for the afternoon off, but if—"

He chuckled and fluttered a hand at me.

"I'm sure you did everything by the rules," he said. "How are you feeling? Are you nervous?"

I thought about that.

"No," I said. "I don't think so. I've been studying a lot. I always pass the online practice quizzes. I think I will pass."

Nodding along, Mr. Barton seemed pleased with my response.

"Do you take the oath or whatever right after you pass?"

I shrugged. "If they have one scheduled, but usually it is a few weeks later. They said I might have to wait for a letter in the mail with a date and time."

Again, he nodded.

"And then you're a citizen of the U.S.?"

I nodded. Somehow, I managed a smile. Not that I had to fake being happy about finally obtaining citizenship; I was exhausted.

"Yes."

"Well," he said, "I suppose we have to talk about my promise?"

"Which promise is that?"

I was so tired.

"I told you when you applied here that once you were a citizen, you could apply for a translator job? Or an interpreter."

"Oh. I understand if there is nothing available right now."

He shook his head and laughed, obviously amused with me.

"Do you want to be an interpreter? Or a translator?"

"Of course."

"Which would you prefer?"

"Interpreter?" I said, though it came out like a question. "Translating might feel lonely. I would be grateful for either, but getting to talk to people all day would be more fun."

He chuckled. "Do you want to keep working for Source Language, Inc., Enzo?"

"Yes," I nodded vehemently. "I love it here."

That seemed to please him.

"You've been a great asset to us for these last several months," he said. "You've made me proud that I saw potential in you. Though, I don't want to take credit for your tenacity. Since you still want the job, the day you become a U.S. citizen, you'll also become an interpreter for Source Language, Inc."

I didn't know what to say. I could only smile.

"I...do I need to fill out an application?"

He waved me off as though this was the most ridiculous thing ever.

"You'll have to fill out some forms with HR for the transfer, but the job is yours if you want it. You'll go into training as soon as you're done with your citizenship."

"Yes. Please."

"Wonderful," Mr. Barton clapped his hands. "It's entry-level, but there is a lot of room for growth and many opportunities for promotions if you stick with it."

I chewed at my lip. "That sounds fine. But I suppose I should ask how much it pays?"

Mr. Barton had to find a paper on his desk, obviously with the job description and details, but he finally read a number off to me. I said nothing in response. Not because I had nothing to say, but because I was afraid to say anything.

The amount Mr. Barton had read off was more than the salaries of my two previous jobs put together.

I would be working the same number of hours every week but for double the pay. At a desk. Not hunched over a dirty toilet or getting blisters from mop handles. There were no words I could think of that could express my gratitude and excitement in a professional way to Mr. Barton. I found that I wanted to cry.

I had sent out good to the universe, and it had proved it was listening.

"Thank you."

I finally managed to croak out an acceptable response.

"Does that sound okay?" Mr. Barton looked concerned.

"Yes," I said. "Of course. I'm just…thank you."

It took a moment, but a look of recognition seemed to cross Mr. Barton's face, and he seemed to warm immediately. A soft smile graced his lips and he stretched an arm out over his desk, his hand presented to me. Without another thought, I took his hand and did my best to shake it without showing how excited I was by his offer.

When we finally let go of each other's hands, Mr. Barton clapped his hands together again.

It was a habit of his, a way to give himself time to think of what he wanted to say next.

"One final thing, Enzo," he said.

"Yes?"

"Do you know anything about Excel?" he asked, waving a frustrated hand at his computer. "This has been driving me crazy all morning."

With a laugh, I rose from my seat and rounded his desk. Over the next twenty minutes, I gave Mr. Barton a crash course in the program he was using. When I finally left his office to finish cleaning the restrooms, he told me that he knew I'd be one of his best employees, then thanked me for the help.

He said nothing, nor indicated it was true, but I felt that him pretending to not understand Excel had merely been a test. I didn't mind.

Though I was still exhausted, I felt light as a feather for the rest of the morning.

What did the Emancipation Proclamation do?

Who becomes the President if the current President and Vice President can no longer serve?

Who is the current Speaker of the House?

Who signs bills to become laws?

What did the Declaration of Independence do?

When was the Constitution written?

Who is the "Father of Our Country"?

How long is a U.S. Senator elected for?

What group of people was taken to America and sold as slaves?

What is the "rule of law"?

Name your U.S. Representative.

Who is the Governor of your state now?

There are 128 civics questions that could potentially be chosen for the oral U.S. Citizenship test. The USCIS officer asks those applying for citizenship 20 questions chosen at random. Every person who takes the test must answer sixty percent of the questions correctly, or twelve out of twenty. When I answered the first twelve questions correctly, the USCIS officer stopped. He said there was no need to continue. I had passed already.

Not to say that I wasn't relieved, but I was disappointed. For some reason, I desperately wanted to know which questions comprised the remaining eight. However, I didn't ask if he would tell me which were the remaining questions. I didn't want to do anything that seemed odd or suspicious in front of a USCIS officer, especially one who was so amenable.

So, within an hour of arriving at their offices, I was informed by the USCIS that I had proven my eligibility to be a United States citizen. All that was left was to take The Naturalization Oath of Allegiance to the United States. That would happen sometime in the following 2 to 6 weeks. Otherwise, I was free to go home and wait for the letter with a date and time.

Technically, I was a U.S. citizen. We simply hadn't gone through the formalities yet. Although, I suppose, no immigrant is officially a citizen until they take the oath that had one of the most ominous names I'd ever heard before.

Unsure of what else to do, I rose from the chair across from the officer, intending to find Peter where he was waiting out in the lobby. He had taken the afternoon off from work to accompany me to my final test. We'd already gone through all of the interviews and interrogations about our marriage. His presence for my test was merely for moral support.

As my hand touched the knob of the office door, the USCIS officer spoke up.

One last question, if you don't mind?

I turned to him.

When you think of the U.S., what comes to mind?

That's what he asked me.

Without having to think, I knew my answer: *possibility.*

The officer smiled at me.

That's the best answer anyone has ever given me. Congratulations on becoming a U.S. citizen, Mr. Barbier. Glad to have you.

He pronounced my last name wrong; I didn't care. He hadn't been intentionally mispronouncing it anyway. And I was a U.S. citizen. That was all that mattered.

"I'm done," I said, coming to a stop in front of the chair where Peter was sitting, reading a book in one of the uncomfortable, utilitarian-looking chairs in the lobby. "We can go home."

Peter started, looked up, and chuckled.

"What's the verdict?" he asked nervously. "What did they say?"

"I'm a U.S. citizen," I said with a smile.

I had to have been experiencing some type of shock. After being told that my three-plus-years quest to become a U.S. citizen had come to the preferred conclusion, I should have been bouncing around like a rabbit. Maybe it was the exhaustion. Or the fact that becoming a citizen of the United

States was met with such little fanfare. Not that I'd expected a parade and confetti upon passing my oral citizenship exam, but…maybe a certificate? Some music to play from a speaker? A chime to indicate that I had passed? *Something.* The reason for my disposition could have been a combination of things, but I wanted to go home.

After a little more than three years, I was a United States citizen. Peter and I were considered the same legally by the federal government. I'd been told by Mr. Barton that I would be given an interpreter position at Source Language, Inc. once I had taken my oath. My salary would be more than enough to make me feel as though I could contribute meaningfully to our household.

But I felt empty.

Something no one had ever explained to me—and I'm certain no one has ever had it explained to them—is that there are many arbitrary labels and characteristics that are used to define a person. Not for their good, but for others. Nationality. Race. Ethnicity. Sexual identity. Gender. Religion. Socio-economic class. Intelligence. Education. They inform other people who a person is, and, maybe, in some ways, they help us understand ourselves better, help us build a foundation of understanding of where we came from, where we're going, and who we will become.

But if one of those labels can be changed by the laws of a land and a pile of paperwork, did it ever really mean anything? Wouldn't changing something that, at one time, was so significant to someone's identity, feel like…*something?* I was French. I was Canadian. Then I was American. It meant nothing. It only informed a government that I was legally allowed to permanently live and work in the country for whose laws they enacted and oversaw.

Even if I'd failed my test—or if the USCIS officer hadn't approved my citizenship for other reasons—it wouldn't have changed my marriage. It wouldn't have changed that Mr. Barton was willing to give me a better job as an interpreter. It didn't change any of my other identities. My new citizenship was merely another box that was checked in my journey of life that moved me from one point to another.

No more; no less. I'd spent three years finding that out.

"Are you serious?" Peter leapt from the chair, his book fluttering to the ground.

He wrapped his arms around me and pulled me in, covering my mouth with his. I returned his kiss and rested my hands on his hips.

I was happy. I really was. But I had mostly been happy anyway. My citizenship didn't change that, either.

"We have to celebrate!" Peter held me at arm's length, grinning from ear to ear. "What do you want to do? We can go eat dinner anywhere. You name it. Anything."

Sighing, though I managed to smile, I said, "I think I want to go home."

Peter's smile melted from his face as if in slow motion. "Just go home?"

"Yes," I said. "I'm tired. We have the entire weekend to celebrate."

For a moment, I thought Peter would argue. Insist that we celebrate my citizenship. However, he finally forced a smile back onto his face and squeezed my arms where his hands were resting.

"Okay, babe."

He knelt and retrieved his book, put an arm gently over my shoulders, and we left.

A two-person parade out of the immigration office was the celebration for my citizenship.

The Center Cannot Hold

Two things happened four weeks later. During a dreary mid-morning ceremony on a Friday, I took The Naturalization Oath of Allegiance to the United States of America, and then Peter took me to the hospital. Though skinny to begin with, I had lost twenty pounds since starting my new medication. Thanks to the cumulative side effects of the medication over months of taking it, the constant nausea and intermittent pain made it impossible to keep down food. Sometimes even water was difficult to retain.

Joints that I'd never noticed in my body before ached, feeling as though they would crack with the smallest of movements. If I wasn't at work, I was in bed, doing my best not to cry from frustration, fear, and pain. And hunger.

I was so hungry.

And thirsty.

Peter had wanted to take me to an emergency room when we had woken up on the morning I was to take the oath. One look at my gaunt expression and the way I practically crawled to the bathroom to get ready, and he was certain I was at death's door. Unfortunately, I knew that I wasn't dying; it would have simply been preferable. I was suffering. Not dying. Not yet.

I'd refused to try and reschedule my taking of the oath for fear that it would make me look bad, thus revoking my citizenship. So, I took a shower, put on appropriate clothes for the ceremony, and let Peter put me in the car and drive me across town to take the oath. For what seemed like days, we sat through the ceremony as I did my best to sit upright and pay attention. Then I stood, followed the instructions, and took the oath.

Back in the car as soon as we were dismissed, Peter went straight to the hospital.

Unsurprisingly, Peter and I had to convince the nurses and doctors that, as his husband, I did not, in fact, have HIV. Peter heatedly explained about my tumor, my seizure disorder, and the medication that was attempting to kill me slowly.

Throughout the afternoon, evening, and into the wee hours of the morning, I was given intravenous fluids and medication for nausea and pain. Sometime around midnight, Peter fell asleep in the chair at my bedside, though I was unable to rest. Until the treatments started to do their jobs, all I could focus on was the pain, hunger, and thirst.

The sun was coming up and Peter was rousing from his sleep when the nurse entered again with a tray of soup and crackers, along with a pitcher of water and a Styrofoam cup. Now that my nausea was controlled, my fluids replenished intravenously, and my pain had been chased away, I was able to eat the soup and crackers and drink more than four cups of water.

Pleased with the results of the overnight treatment, a doctor discharged me from the emergency room in the late morning. Peter was given instructions—since I was too exhausted to pay attention—that I should follow up with my doctor as soon as possible.

The doctor who had practically insisted I take the generic medication that had caused me to end up in the emergency room to begin with.

There was nothing else to do but go home. Peter helped me into the house after the drive across town. Then up the stairs to our bedroom. He helped me shower and put on fresh, clean pajamas, and into the bed. All of Saturday and Sunday I slept, taking the medications the doctor in the emergency room had prescribed for my nausea and pain. I only woke to eat the food Peter brought to me at meal times.

On Monday morning, I got out of bed, showered, put on fresh clothes, and went to work. Mr. Barton had promised that I would have my new job as soon as I had taken my citizenship oath. I wasn't going to risk jeopardizing that, either.

And, of course, Peter was unhappy with me for risking my health further. He wanted me to stay home for at least a few days to recover. The only thing we did talk about was getting me back on the medication that didn't try to kill me—but I still could not see spending thousands of our own dollars when our insurance should have covered it. But we didn't talk about it for long. We simply ate breakfast and went our separate ways in stony silence when it was time for us both to go to work.

I became a shell of a person. All of the energy I could muster was used to focus on my training at work—to become the best employee I could be for Source Language, Inc. At work, I was engaged, enthusiastic, attentive, and cognizant. At home, I would often sit and stare at the wall and wait for an appropriate time to go to bed each day. I could no longer be perfect at everything. I only had the energy to be perfect at one thing.

For better or worse, and much to my detriment, I chose my job. Because it was the one thing I had left that defined me that was solely mine and didn't hurt.

"Your insurance will start in a few weeks," Peter said. "Is your doctor still going to switch you back to your old medication? It's covered under your insurance, right?"

We were in bed, our backs propped against the headboard and the blankets pulled up to our waists as we read before bedtime.

"Mmhm."

"Good," Peter said, managing to glance at me with a smile. "You can start feeling better."

"I hope so," I said.

"Maybe we can have Mom and Dad down," Peter suggested, "once you feel better? I know they'd be glad to see us. Spend time with us. I'd be glad to see them."

Exhaling heavily through my nose, I had to control myself so that I didn't say the thing I was thinking. Peter inviting his mother and father to visit as soon as I felt better so that I could cook and clean while he was the perfect son was not exactly what I considered a great way to celebrate getting back on my old medication. For all I knew, my old medication's efficacy would have changed after not having been on it for so long. There were no guarantees—only hope, which was harder to invest in more and more each day.

So, the suggestion annoyed me. I tried not to let it show.

"Maybe," I said. "Once I feel better."

"Sure," Peter responded quickly, placating me.

I hated that. I was tired of Peter placating me. Babying me. Treating me like a delicate piece of ornamentation, yet poking and prodding at my limitations with suggestions such as having weekend guests that would require more energy than I had.

I was...*exhausted.*

"Things are going to get better," Peter said.

He hadn't said it as a statement of fact. Or a reassurance. I don't think he was even talking to me, actually. Peter said it aloud like a mantra, as though willing better times into existence. Reassuring himself that, *if he just hung in there*, life would get easier. That all of life's little molehills which had piled up to create a mountain would be brought crumbling down by an earthquake comprised of a mythical, magical pill almost within our grasp.

A pill had done this to us.

Something smaller than the nail on my pinkie finger had upturned our lives. Decimated my health and disposition. Planted a seed of bitterness in my husband that had grown into a tree whose roots had strangled the faith we had leapt from when we married.

But it wasn't the pill that had done those things. It was Peter and me. We had allowed the power of a pill—and the inability to procure it easily and affordably—to change us. We were no longer the same two men who had spent one perfect night in Montreal together. Or had a two-week vacation of ecstasy and discovery. We were bitter. Angry. Annoyed with each other because there was nowhere else to direct it. And we were too exhausted to fix it.

I shut my book gently and laid it on my bedside table. Then I turned off my lamp and slid under the covers, pulling them up around my neck as I turned onto my side, facing away from Peter. He didn't even try to hide the annoyed sigh that escaped his mouth.

I laid there, staring at the wall across the room, no longer enamored with the sage green that the dark wainscoting met halfway up the wall. For what seemed like hours, I laid there in silence, not quite able to fall asleep, as Peter sat on his side of the bed in profound silence. Finally, I heard him close his book and lay it on his table. Then he switched off his lamp, casting the room in utter darkness.

Peter slid under the covers and inched up behind me, but he made no move to wrap an arm around me or even touch me.

"Enzo?" he asked.

I made a noise with my throat, but my eyes were wide open.

"Do you want to…you know?"

"I'm tired," I said.

Peter sighed.

"If we're ever going to start a family, we have to have sex again," he said.

It was an attempt at humor, what Peter had said. A way to make me chuckle or even crack a smile instead of staring blankly at the wall. A peace offering that maybe one day we would actually start the family I so desperately wanted for myself. However, the mere suggestion that having a child would somehow fix what was wrong with us—even if it was only implied—made my blood boil. I didn't have the energy to process it.

"I'm too tired to clean and cook for you and your parents for three days," I said. "I don't think I would be able to deal with a child, Peter. Even if they'd show more appreciation for my efforts."

Peter's reaction should have been immediate and fierce. I expected him to throw the covers off of us and scream at me. To fight. I was ready to fight, even if I knew I didn't have the energy for it. Maybe a fight would somehow drill deeply into the furthest reaches of me and bring forth a supply I didn't know I had in reserves.

But Peter said nothing. Which was worse. He simply turned over, settled into bed, and stared at the wall on his side of the room.

Mr. Barton gave me a promotion after three months as an interpreter. Actually, my supervisor, a woman named Magdalena gave me the promotion, but it was made clear that it was at the direction of Mr. Barton. Starting training three months prior to be an interpreter for the company, conveying information that could be either banal or secretive enough to require me to sign non-disclosure forms, was something I took to like a duck to water. Helping others to communicate, no matter how boring or exciting the conversations were, was a dream.

It was also something I could do even on days when my energy was so low that I felt I could crumple at my desk. Interpreting didn't require that I be enthusiastic and energic—I merely had to sound as though I was. I had learned to be great at pretending to be perfect.

Even on the days I woke up nauseated, or even vomiting, I could get to work and do my job. If my joints hurt and my head was throbbing, I could do my job. Exhaustion, pain, and stomach problems couldn't keep me from being able to tell one person what another said and vice versa. Medication that technically did its job and my employment could coexist.

My day-to-day life was another story.

Regardless, the promotion came with yet another raise. Also, more responsibilities. However, my job was so easy that a few additional responsibilities still didn't fill my work days. On most days, I struggled to look busy. Magdalena and Mr. Barton were more than pleased with my performance, though, and that was all that mattered.

Even on the days when I felt as though death was right around the corner, I was able to perform my job in such a way that seem exemplary. Because it was. I'd finally found a job that I not only could do well but set me on a course to feel more equal with Peter. The salary and eventual benefits conjured the outcome I had wanted since moving to the United States. I was not reliant on my husband for all of my needs. Independent from him, I could easily meet all of my needs.

That's what equality meant to me.

Equality does not nurture a marriage when there is inequity, however.

Though I couldn't prove it, I felt that our original arrangement when I had first moved to America had colored me a certain way in Peter's eyes. I had been dependent on him for all of my needs for those first few months. Before my medication made it difficult for me, I had met all of his needs—as far as domestic duties went.

Our roles in our marriage were not equitable.

They hadn't been since I had moved to the United States.

Our marriage had been unequitable from the first day. But it took over a year to realize it.

It's funny how those revelations creep up on a person.

Odder still, two men who had never been married before, and are trying to figure out how to make one work that has not been equitable from the beginning, will do anything but work together to figure it out.

Because communication and forming a plan requires equity.

A Wandering Eye

"How was work?"

That's the only thing Peter could think to ask me over dinner on a Friday evening.

"It was good," I'd said, and though I didn't want to, I'd returned the question. "How was your work?"

"Good."

Even though it all had seemed like a performance for months, the two of us had done our best to have dinner with each other every night. Especially on weekends. They were often silent affairs where scrapes of forks and knives against ceramic sounded thunderous. Eating as quickly as we could to end our suffering, every dinner was a race to the finish. Then we'd wash dishes in silence, one of us washing and the other drying, and go our separate ways until bedtime.

Once in bed, we'd read our books on our separate sides, creating a chasm between us on the mattress. Eventually, with nothing to say, and not knowing how to say something if there was something to say, we'd turn out our lamps and slide under the covers. Peter would turn to his side, facing away from me, I'd mirror his position. We'd drift off to sleep, listening to each other breathe in that pregnant silence, wondering why neither of us would say the thing on both of our minds.

Our marriage was in name only.

We were failing. We had failed. Our home felt empty and cavernous, every sound each of us would make would cause the other to tense, wondering if we would be forced to interact.

Bravely, we both fought to keep our marriage going. Which only emphasized the cowardliness we both displayed in never bringing up the one question we both had on our minds.

"Did you pick up your medication today?" he asked. "I can pick it up tomorrow if not."

"No," I said. "I got it. I stopped on my way home."

"Okay."

"Dr. Rollins said to start it tomorrow," I added.

My insurance with Source Language, Inc. was finally in full effect and the original medication—the one that didn't make me feel like a shell of a human being—was covered for me once again. Eventually, as long as no other surprises arose, I would begin to feel like myself again. Though I had no idea who Enzo was anymore. The old Enzo was an echo in the darkness of the cavern that my soul had become.

"Good."

I'd made roasted chicken, potatoes, and asparagus for dinner. Even though my energy was still drained, I'd gotten home before Peter and decided to cook a decent meal for us. Making dinners was one of the few ways that I still did my best to keep up appearances. And we had to eat anyway, so it didn't matter if it felt that it didn't matter.

Though rushing through dinner had become our new normal, the job I'd done in cooking the meal was such that we couldn't help but savor it. I desperately wanted dinner to be over with—just as Peter did—but the food was too good to rush through. So, we ate in silence, our utensils clattering against our plates as we fed ourselves.

It wasn't until Peter slid the last potato from the end of his fork and into his mouth that he spoke again.

"I'm tired of this, Enzo," he said.

I nodded. I didn't need an explanation to know what he meant.

"Some days I don't even want to come home."

I didn't need an explanation for that statement, either. Our house was no longer a home. It was a prison. The two of us played prisoner and guard for each other, constantly tiptoeing around each other, afraid of catching the attention of the other.

"I don't want that anymore," he said.

"Okay," I said.

There was nothing to discuss or argue about, as far as I was concerned.

"Can we please," Peter said, "stop doing this? Can we be Enzo and Peter again? I want us to be who we were."

That. That was not something I had expected. When Peter had said he was tired and didn't want what we had anymore, I thought we were coming to the inevitable conclusion to our marriage. Because after the last several months, that conclusion seemed natural. Obvious.

"Can't we just...do something like we used to?" he asked as I poked at my plate with the tines of my fork. "Leave the dishes on the table and go upstairs and fall into bed together? Fuck our brains out? Laugh and tease and just...not hate each other?"

"I don't hate you," I said, but I didn't look up at him.

"I'm starting to hate you."

I shrugged. It wasn't meant to be dismissive, though, in retrospect, anyone would have obviously taken it that way. I'd simply meant it as a gesture to indicate that I understood and couldn't give him a reason not to hate me.

"Goddamnit, Enzo," Peter pushed back from the table violently.

He didn't rise from his chair and I didn't look up.

"It has been months of this shit," he groaned angrily. "Day after day of you pushing me further and further away. Not talking to me. Not letting me in. Ignoring me. Making me feel like everything is my fault but not telling me what it is that I did."

"Nothing is your fault."

"Then tell me what it is I need to do, goddamnit," he pounded his fist on the table. "Tell me what I can do to help you with whatever you're going through. We're supposed to be in this together, Enzo. I can't be in it with you if you don't invite me in."

Peter was right. I had been pushing him away. I had no idea why. It could have been how hard it had been to adjust to America at first. It could have been all of the pain and nausea and sleeplessness. It could have been the feeling that he hadn't treated me like an equal in our marriage for so long. Or, actually, that he didn't do enough to prove he felt I was his equal in our marriage. Or, possibly, it was all of those things combined. It could have been the vague unhappiness I'd felt for months that had nothing to do with my physical health.

Or something else.

"I leave here each morning," Peter growled at me, "wondering if today is the day that I come home and you've just left. You've checked out mentally, so why should I be surprised if you completely left? Then I fantasize that I'll come home and you'll be waiting to throw your arms around me. Hug me. Kiss me. Lead me upstairs and have sex with me again. Or...*fuck*...talk to me like a normal-fucking-human-being."

I laid my fork on my plate and sat back.

"Or maybe even talk to me like you still care about me. Like I'm not invisible. Or that you don't hate me. I feel neglected all of the damn time, Enzo. But you won't tell me what I've done to deserve to be neglected like this."

I still could not figure out what it was that I wanted to say.

"You know what?" Peter asked, his voice shaky. "The other day, this guy I work with—gay guy—he was looking at me. Across the office. He was looking at me the way *you* used to look at me. And for the briefest of moments, I fantasized that—"

Our kitchen has hardwood floors. When a table is flipped—one containing two plates, silverware, a roasting pan, bowls, and glasses, it's thunderous. I didn't remember wrapping my fingers around the edge of the table, gripping it angrily, and flipping it, sending it crashing end over end, spilling the remaining contents of our dinner to the floor and splattering against the cabinets. However, it had to have happened. I was standing in front of my chair, glaring down at Peter as he sat two yards away from me, staring up at me with horror. And the table and everything it had held, was littered throughout the kitchen.

The kitchen seemed to whisper with the noise that the table and dishes had made, even after it had all settled, and the two of us stared at each other. Like a silent echo. A ghost of a memory being implanted in the walls of the room. Waiting to replay itself in the corners of our minds anytime we'd enter the kitchen in the future.

This is where our marriage came crashing to an end.

"Enzo," Peter exhaled the word.

I said nothing. I turned, silently left the kitchen, and went upstairs.

Later, well after the sun had set and I was certain that Peter would not be sharing our bed, he crept into our room. As I lay in bed and stared at the wall, as I had been doing for the hours since dinner had finished with a bang, he changed into his pajamas silently. My husband slid under the covers, curled up on his side, turned to face the wall, and fell asleep.

It was a sleepless night for me.

Like Toast Soldiers

The following morning, a Saturday, I slid out of bed as the sun peeked over the horizon and slipped into the bathroom. Peter continued to sleep as I showered and dressed, and I did my best not to wake him. I packed a bag with several changes of clothes and necessary toiletries, including my fresh bottle of medication. I stood in our bedroom doorway, the bag in hand, and stared at my husband lying in bed, curled up and sleeping peacefully. His alarm would go off in a half-hour and he would expect to start his weekend.

After saying my silent thoughts, I slipped down the back stairwell quietly to the kitchen. Peter had meticulously cleaned up the mess I had made when I'd flipped the table the night before. I set my suitcase by the backdoor and rolled up my sleeves. As quickly as I could, I soft-boiled eggs and made toast soldiers. I cut up some fruit in a bowl. Carefully, I set the kitchen table for Peter's breakfast and started the coffee. I cracked and removed the tops of Peter's eggs for him since he could never do it well. He would be awake any moment.

It was time for me to leave.

I retrieved my bottle of medication from my suitcase, tapped one out into my hand, and stuffed it in my mouth. I titled my head under the kitchen sink faucet for a drink of water and swallowed it down. The second most important part of my Saturday was complete.

I pulled my keys from my pocket, removed the house and car keys from the ring, and laid them gently on the table next to Peter's prepared plate. I lifted my suitcase, gave the kitchen one last, emotionless look, and slipped out the backdoor, making sure it locked behind me.

There was no need to leave a note. Shoot off a text.

My keys by his plate would tell Peter all he needed to know.

I'm a failed husband. I know that. Here's your life—your freedom—back.

Walking through a neighborhood such as Peter's with a suitcase would have drawn attention if it hadn't been so early on a weekend morning. The large houses passed as I stared straight ahead, making my way out of the neighborhood. I continued to walk until I got to the bus stop closest to our house, in an industrialized area of town.

I had no friends I felt close enough to call.

Can I stay at your place?

The thought actually made me laugh as I sat on a corner bench and set my suitcase down, letting it lean against my shins.

There were some work friends I could have probably called who would have taken pity on me, but I never liked mixing business and my life. I'd made a few casual friends here and there in the time I'd lived in America, but none so close that I felt comfortable reaching out to them, either. I had no family—even if I hadn't moved to America. I had no one in Minneapolis to turn to and ask to take me in now that I'd made my decision about my marriage.

So, I slid my phone from my pocket and pressed the contact for the person I'd phoned dozens or even hundreds of times in the last year.

It was too early in the morning to be bothering any friend, even a close one, but I had no other options. I'd never had close friends to know the proper protocol or what to expect when reaching out to one. Not having my call answered was what I'd expected. However, the phone only rang twice before it was picked up on the other end.

Before the *"hello?"* finished echoing through the phone, the tears trailed from my eyes and the story poured from my mouth. I'm unsure how long I sat on the city bench, crying and wailing into the phone, but my eyes could no longer produce tears when I was done. Gasping for breath and sniffling, I went silent, wondering if I'd been hung up on. However, a voice finally interrupted my thoughts.

"Are you safe?" Alex asked. *"Where you are now?"*

I looked around. Minneapolis had not come alive yet so early on a weekend morning, but there was nothing to indicate that I was in danger.

"Y-yes," I stammered.

"Give me twenty minutes."

And then he hung up. So, I pulled my knees up to my chest, resting my feet on the bench, and waited for him to call me back.

A Grocery Store
Present Day

Lifting my mask to cover my mouth and nose as I walked into the grocery store, I retrieved a shopping cart from the return area a few steps inside the front door. I didn't necessarily need the cart for the shopping I planned to do, but it kept me from having to carry my bundle all around the store. My arms were getting tired of the weight, though it wasn't that heavy, no matter how much the bundle meant to me, so it was a nice reprieve to nestle it carefully in the top part of the cart.

Greeting other customers with a nod of my head, since the way the world had changed made smiles impossible to convey a greeting, I ventured into the store. It shouldn't have been surprising, but the percentage of shoppers who still chose to forgo a mask was astounding. At one time, early in the pandemic, a maskless face was enough to send me into a rage. A scorching emotion that I was forced to push deep down so that I didn't say or do something inexcusable.

Stupidity is fed by rage, anyway. My rage would solve nothing, and only create bigger problems, so I chose to keep it to myself every time it boiled up at the sight of those toothy grins from reckless nitwits. Over time, it became easier and easier to pretend that I was not looking into the naked faces of people without regard for theirs' or others' health and well-being.

To date, something I'd rarely admit out loud, is that I had developed an unspoken philosophy about the careless unmasked:

That will eventually resolve itself if we keep wearing masks and simply wait.

Dark thoughts usually remind me to say my prayers. That was one of those thoughts I chose not to say a prayer over. God would have to look past it or condemn me later. I'd made peace with my feelings on the matter.

American grocery stores, as I'd discovered upon my inaugural visit, are an experience unlike any other. It's not only the crowds and the overwhelming selection of groceries one has to choose from down each aisle. It's not the overabundance of sugar and chemicals and salt in nearly every prepared food found on the shelves. Nor is it the overwhelming bright colors of every box and bag.

The thing that is most surprising about American grocery stores is that it's rare to find one that is *merely* a grocery store. One can buy books in the same store as one can pick up an obscenely cheap bag of apples. Prescription medication may be filled while a person is selecting their weekly groceries, and picked up before one pays for them. Hair products and televisions are a short walk from where cereals with colorful and cheerful mascots are on display. Even shoes and house slippers and t-shirts can be picked up yards away from a display of cake mixes.

Cakes. Everywhere I've lived, most of the larger grocery stores sold prepared and decorated cakes. They had nothing on what one would find in America, however. Cakes for every occasion. A plethora of colors and flavors and styles. Bakers at the ready to write a message on top of a cake you have selected. Pre-sliced cakes, tiny cakes, wedding cakes, birthday cakes, individually sized cakes—that would actually feed four people anywhere else in the world.

America is abundance. Unashamed abundance. I'm neither bothered by this nor approving. It's simply American culture.

I am impressed by it.

Though I've never felt justified buying sneakers in the same store where I select my dinner ingredients; America can have it, but I will not partake.

My favorite thing about American groceries stores is the produce section. Not because they are exceptional compared to other countries, but because one never knows what they will discover. Especially in the Midwest.

One will find standard fare that is typically available year-round, such as carrots, celery, potatoes, apples, oranges, limes, lemons, green beans, peppers, onions, garlic, and bananas. But at the beginning of each season, one will find new and exciting choices. Depending on where one is in the country, the choices can be truly exotic. However, the new things to choose from each season in middle America are fairly common for the country. They aren't exotic, but it is fresh and exciting after waiting for months to see them return to the shelves.

In the Midwest, one might occasionally see something like dragon fruit, papayas, or starfruit. I've run across daikon radishes, fiddleheads, and lotus root. A variety of mushrooms to choose from is fairly common in Middle America. Anytime I see something that is uncommon in the U.S., especially in the area in which I live, I buy it. Immediately, I rush home and Google recipes for the ingredient. Though there are many places in the world where many of the "exotic" ingredients I find are much more common, it feels special in America.

It's as though America is finally discovering the immensity and diversity of the world. Possibly accepting something new and challenging, and I had been present to witness it. The only way to celebrate such a step from a country that is typically puritanical and resistant to other cultures and ideas is to encourage it. Buy the ingredient. Make something with it. Eat it. Hopefully, it encourages the shop to continue stocking that item—and to try ordering even more exotic foods—in the future.

The sheer immensity of some produce sections—some the size of small stores themselves—is also impressive. There is room to walk down aisles, four carts wide. The display for one variety of apples may be ten feet long and five feet deep. When Halloween comes around, bins big enough to park a small car in will pop up in stores, overflowing with the orange gourds in all shapes and sizes—and it will not impact the ability to maneuver around the produce section at all.

When I say I love America, it means simply that.

It's a country that has given me plenty. It has taken from me, for certain, but much less than every other country in which I've resided.

However, it doesn't mean that I feel America is equal to or better than any other country in which I've lived. Or those that I haven't. I simply have an appreciation and affection for it. Even in all of its ridiculousness, all of its political and social strife, I love it. It struggles, in its youth as a country, to catch up with many other countries that have had centuries longer to figure things out. As far as its age goes, America is doing fairly well. It's not moving any slower towards real progress than any other country in the world when one compares their ages.

So, no more or less than the rest of the countries in the world, I love America.

Lost in my thoughts—as I often am—I made my fruit selection on auto-pilot. However, as it was spring, cherries must have seemed perfect. I found myself standing by the display, a bag half-full of the crunchy, juicy little red orbs, their stems threatening to stab through the thin plastic. At both times tart and sweet, cherries are one of my favorite fruits. They're familiar enough that most palates are accustomed to their flavor, yet they are common only through spring and early summer, so they feel exotic when they arrive in stores.

Cherries also connect me to my history. My heritage. My family. So, they also feel comforting.

It's funny how a cherry can do those things by simply being a cherry.

Part Three
Life Goes On

One Less Bell to Answer

"The view is something, isn't it?"

"I'm sorry?" I asked.

"The view," the building manager repeated. "It's beautiful, isn't it? You can see almost all of the city."

Though I'd seen the view from the floor-to-ceiling windows when I'd toured the historic apartment building, I set down the box I was cradling in my arms to join the building manager at the windows. The living room wall of the apartment I had signed a lease for was nothing but glass. From the tenth floor of the building, they provided a spectacular view of Minneapolis. Even though it was a dreary day, as we were moving into autumn once again, the view was awe-inspiring.

The Regal Building—an old gothic-inspired red brick and white limestone high-rise in downtown Minneapolis— had been remodeled into an apartment building and had been doing business as such for ten years. When I'd gone in search of a new place of my own in my new homeland, I'd intended on finding a simple studio apartment. One that was spartan and met my basic needs. Life had taught me to live with very little, so that decision had seemed logical. Why spend more money than necessary if less will do fine?

After living in the spare room of one of Alex's Minneapolis friends for two months, that lesson had been solidified. I could make do with little.

However, upon touring The Regal Building on a whim while apartment hunting, I became enamored with the stained concrete floors, gothic fixtures, industrial ductwork, and modern kitchens and bathrooms. The juxtaposition of a long-gone era meeting modern amenities was perfect—like being stuck in two different times. The floor-to-ceiling windows that made the living room glow golden in the early morning hours, then bright white and warm in the afternoon, sealed the deal.

It was like standing on a platform in heaven when I was in the living room. I could see forever. I felt close enough to the clouds to touch them. Light from the sun beating down on the glass all day warmed the living room comfortably. It was home the moment I stepped inside the apartment.

"You've already got my signature and money," I teased the woman, Bethany.

She cackled.

Pleasant, if not a bit crass, I'd also fallen in love with the building manager during my tour. I knew that she would be easy to get along with and fair. She wouldn't intrude on my privacy any more than necessary, but she wouldn't treat me like a stranger. Bethany also seemed to run a tight ship. Everything was clean and functioning as it should. Things seemed to be quickly fixed when inevitable problems arose. And she had no tolerance for problematic tenants. At least, this was all relayed to me by other renters when I had been touring the building.

So, The Regal Building had to be my home. Things were perfect at work, I was making plenty of money, and I wanted an apartment that felt like a home. That felt special. There was no reason for me not to sign a one-year lease. For once, I indulged a whim.

"Well," Bethany said with a sigh, "I hope you're happy here, Enzo. I like my tenants to be happy."

She turned, intending to make her exit, so I followed her, intending to show her out as a polite person would.

"If you have any problems, you let me know immediately, okay?" she asked. "And don't let me hear about you causing any problems, either."

I laughed. "I only work and eat dinner in front of the television."

"You'll be a perfect tenant," she laughed with me as I opened the door for her. "Have fun unpacking."

"I will."

"Welcome home again, Enzo."

With that, Bethany headed down the hallway to the elevator. So, I let the door glide gently shut, making sure it did not slam, and slowly turned around to look at the wall of windows again. I smiled at the golden light as it streamed into the barren living room. It would be a few days until I could procure living room furniture...but I was home. I had a bed and bedding. A single comfortable chair for the living room. I had clothes and toiletries. I would walk down to the corner grocery store to stock my refrigerator before the night was over. It would be enough to get me through a few nights.

After so many months as an interpreter for Source Language, Inc., I'd been given the option to work from home. Living in Alex's friend's spare room had made that impossible. Now that I had my own home, Mr. Barton had approved for me to transfer to working from home. So, that was one more thing on my to-do list. Be up bright and early the following morning for the tech guy from work to come to install my workstation. I had to have my desk set up so that he could do so, and it was disassembled in an oblong box in the bedroom.

That would need to be done.

Put the desk together.

Buy groceries.

Unpack my suitcases and put my clothes away.

Make the bed.

Be available for the company to deliver my washer and dryer.

"I need a sofa," I said aloud to no one.

The television I had purchased—though nowhere near as fancy or large as the one Peter and I had—was in a box in the corner of the living room, waiting to be used. Sitting in front of the television to eat dinner without a sofa to curl up on after I'd eaten would be a struggle for a few days. Somehow, I'd manage. I smiled to myself at the thought. The one chair I'd bought would do until I could get to a furniture store in the next few days. I wouldn't be finicky. Any decent sofa that wasn't hideous and could be delivered the same day or the next would be perfect.

Preferably something sturdy and cheap. I'd already convinced myself to splurge on my actual home, there was no need to throw money around every chance that presented itself. Green. A green sofa would be perfect. Deep with soft cushions that begged to be napped on. Nothing is more satisfying than a lazy weekend afternoon nap on a comfortable sofa as the sun shines down on you through the window. When it's a sunny day, anyhow.

Having no one to respond to my statement made my excitement for a new sofa abate.

It had been so long since I'd had no one to talk to and share my innocuous thoughts with each day. Even living with a virtual stranger—Alex's friend—I'd had someone to talk to at home. We hadn't become incredibly close, Alex's friend and me, but we were friendly. It's nearly impossible to live with someone for more than a few days and not become friendly.

Paloma, a middle-aged Hispanic woman who lived in an old Victorian house she'd inherited from her grandmother, had taken me in when I left my home with Peter. She knew nothing of me or what I would be like to live with, but at Alex's request for a favor, she had welcomed me with open arms. All alone in the three-story house, she had seemed glad to fill some of the empty space, even if it was only the guest room and spare bathroom.

Though American by birth, Paloma's family was originally from Mexico. Paloma identified herself as a "bruja" and practiced Mexican Folk Magic, though I knew nothing of such things to decide if it was all a performance or genuine. It didn't matter to me either way. When she had found out I was Catholic, I assumed she would be bothered, or at least be less open to being friendly with me while I lived with her. However, quite graciously, Paloma explained to me that folk magic in Mexico was greatly influenced by Catholic beliefs—or maybe it was the other way around—and many brujas also identified as Catholic. The fact that my French Catholicism didn't prejudice me against her beliefs endeared me to her.

We were both the "live and let live" sort of people. Do no harm and I'll leave you to it.

She made her living producing folk art which she sold online and at local art galleries and craft fairs. Additionally, she had a side business with charms, potions, and magic work for believers of her craft. For her method of making a living, she did well. I wasn't certain that I'd ever be a person who could believe in magic or mysticism of any kind, but I found it fascinating. Then again, I realized that Catholicism required a great suspension of disbelief, so maybe magic was real? Who could say for sure until the time came when we all found out?

In the short time I'd stayed with her, Paloma had invited me into her kitchen to cook with her. Teaching me more than I'd probably ever need to know about Mexican food, especially all of the varieties of peppers used in the cuisine, I loved sharing French recipes with her in return. But I could never learn enough from her. Needless to say, I ate well while staying with her. We hadn't had enough time to grow incredibly close in two months, but I found that I already missed her. I knew that if ever I wanted to visit, she wouldn't be averse.

Now, for the second time in my life, I had no one.

I loved my apartment, and it was home, but it was empty.

There was no one to talk to or cook with or bump into in the hallway. No one to cook breakfast for or wake with kisses and a "good morning." No one to share a meal with or talk about a new television show with over said meal. I had me and only me.

Instead of rushing out the door to buy groceries, find something to occupy my brain, or run an errand that wasn't incredibly important so that I wouldn't be left with my thoughts, I sat down. In the one chair I had that I'd put in the corner of the living room by the windows. Staring out at the gray, misty city below.

I wanted to cry. Not because I was sad or suddenly lonely. But because I felt that I should.

I'd left Peter, moved in with Paloma, and two months later, I was on my own in a city where I had a job and few friends. When Peter and I had decided to get married at the end of my two-week vacation those years ago, I'd envisioned a much different future. But there I was. Alone. Living in an apartment once again, with only myself to rely on for company and comfort.

It wasn't only the sudden loneliness that bothered me. It was the six years from the moment I'd met Peter, and how my life had turned into a tornado that swept me away. I didn't land in Oz where life suddenly became technicolor. I'd simply been dropped back in Kansas having only achieved financial independence and security. I'd failed at everything else.

I'd failed at my marriage.

I'd failed Peter.

I was enraged thinking of him, though I had no idea why, and I had no energy to do anything with that rage. I didn't lack energy as I had—going back to my old medication had returned me to normal within a week. Simply stated, I no longer knew what to say or do when it came to the feelings I had about the last four years of my life. The last six years. Everything that had transpired in my life since that fateful night in Montreal and a doughnut vendor tried to overcharge an American simply because he could.

I didn't know where to begin. So, I couldn't spare the energy. Until I knew where to direct it, I'd save it. The fact that I couldn't pinpoint the exact moment where things had gone askew with our marriage only made it worse. Certainly, having a doctor who didn't care to understand my condition and history pressuring me to switch medications didn't help. The medication stole my energy, my spirit, and drive for everything in my life.

That wasn't the entire problem, though. I couldn't lie well enough to myself to believe it.

Moving to a new country and finding I had no friends had been an issue.

Struggling to find a job before I received my citizenship had been demoralizing.

Realizing that I had not been equal with Peter for the first part of our marriage had been humiliating.

Feeling purposeless in my own life had been paralyzing.

American culture shock had contributed to my feelings of being lost.

Looking back, I realized that I hadn't been as dedicated to my Catholic faith as I had been when my family was alive, or when I'd been alone in Montreal. So, what did that mean for my faith?

Everything I knew about myself—or thought I knew—was upended.

I was a new version of Enzo that I did not recognize.

Why had I married Peter? Had it been love?

Of course, it had been love. I loved Peter deeply, even as the thought of him enraged me. But why did thinking of Peter set me on edge; make me heated and physically tense? What had happened that I had not paid attention to in the years since our meeting?

Ultimately, in the six years I'd met Peter, and the four years before that, my life had been guided by forces outside of my control. Death and grief had not been within my control. Immigration and the prejudice against immigrants had not been within my control. How to handle my own health needs was outside of my control. For nearly a decade, my ship had harnessed the winds that propelled it forward with no method of steering.

And here I was. What was I to do with what my life had become?

The box containing my favorite memories, nestled against the wall in the living got picked up and placed gently in the back corner closet in my bedroom. Back in the living room, I was left with my emptiness again.

Sliding my phone from my pocket, I clicked on a contact that had been my lifeline for longer than I deserved.

When Alex's face popped up on the screen—after merely two rings—I couldn't help but smile. Something inside of me told me that I'd never understand why I loved Alex so much, why his friendship meant so much to me. For all of his openness and willingness to answer any questions posed, he was also a steel trap. Anyone could get answers from Alex, but not the underlying stories that had led him to have those answers. Ever since I'd met him, I wondered if anyone would ever truly know who he was; but he was my lifeline. He was a great friend.

What more can one ask?

"*Well,*" he said, not waiting for a greeting, nor pausing to give one, "*you look like you've actually had a few meals.*"

I laughed. "*I'm getting better. I am better.*"

He set his phone down so he could be on screen, but also continue with some task he was in the middle of completing.

"*How's the new place?*"

"It's good," I said. "I don't have living room furniture yet, but it's good."

"The utter suffering!"

Again, I laughed.

"Whatever will you do?"

"Smartass," I said.

I couldn't help but laugh at my own statement. There was nothing like speaking with Alex to bring out vulgarity. He ignored the jibe.

"Are you going to be okay there? All by yourself? I talked to Paloma earlier. She said you were welcome to keep staying with her, but you insisted on getting your own place. Are my friends not good enough for you, Frenchie?"

"I have to be a grown-up, don't I?"

"What the fuck does that even mean? Was she swaddling you and changing your diapers?"

Cackling at him, I couldn't form an answer for a moment.

"And I'm one of your friends."

"That's assuming a lot," he said, his tone shifting suddenly. *"But seriously, are you doing okay?"*

"I'm well," I said. "I'm fine."

Alex stopped whatever task he was working on to stare at me through the phone.

"I'm lonely. And sad," I said. "Alex. I failed."

He simply stared at me for the space of several breaths.

"Do you actually believe that? That you hold all responsibility for everything that's gone wrong in your life?"

"Well, I—"

"Did you ever consider therapy?"

"Don't be rude," I said, chuckling nervously. "I'm feeling sensitive."

"*It was a serious question,*" Alex said, continuing to focus solely on me. "*You have that good insurance now. Why not actually use it for something besides simply surviving?*"

I stared back.

"*I'm not great with beating around the bush or being delicate,*" Alex shrugged. "*I don't have that kind of time. And if I did, I wouldn't waste it on people's delicate dispositions. So, I think therapy would help you.*"

"Therapy?" I frowned.

"*I've been to therapy,*" Alex said. "*Don't make that face. I still go every now and again for a tune-up because the nuts and bolts get loose every now and then.*"

That made me laugh again.

"Therapy."

"*Therapy.*"

"Can't I just tell you my problems?"

"*Sure. If you want to stay crazy.*"

"I'm not crazy, I'm—"

"*Call it what you want,*" he cut me off, "*but therapy will help. Stop dicking around trying to define what it is and go get it fixed. You can sit around being gloomy and, well,* fucking French, *or you can take the first step. The sooner you take it, the sooner you can start fixing it. Or learning to cope with it.*"

I sighed. "I know you're right, but—"

"*Great!*" he said. "*Then there's no 'but.' Call your insurance, find a therapist who is covered, and start figuring your shit out.*"

I hesitated. "Will you help me?"

Alex smiled. *"That's very brave of you, Frenchie. But you need to do this. I'm here for moral support, but you need to make those phone calls. You're not helpless. You're not weak. You're not useless. You can find a therapist. You have to be a grown-up, right?"*

With a groan, I said, "Why must you throw that back in my face?"

"You loaded the gun, I just pulled the trigger," he said. *"Call me back after you've called around."*

"Now?" I gasped.

"What else do you have going on? Aren't you just sitting in your apartment, staring off into space and feeling sorry for yourself like a character in some Cocteau film?"

I laughed uproariously.

And Alex disappeared from my screen.

He wasn't going to have pity on me, and he didn't want me to have pity on myself.

So, I made some other phone calls.

Horsey and Saddley

"I have a friend," Sheila said at the end of our meeting. "Brandon. And he—"

"You told me about him last time," I chuckled, not really looking at my computer screen, where Sheila's face was front and center, as I shuffled papers. "You do not give up."

Sheila was unbothered. "He's fresh out of a relationship. You're…well, I don't know what you are. But you could stand to get back in the game."

"I'm still married," I said.

"Separated. All's fair in love and war."

I laughed. I should have been angry with Sheila, one of my teammates at Source Language, Inc., for always trying to set me up on dates with her gay male friends. Everyone who had tried to set me up on dates since I had moved into my own apartment should have drawn my ire. Two things stopped me from being angry with them. One, it was nice that so many people were trying to be my friend. Since I'd moved out of Paloma's and into my apartment, there had been several Friday nights where new friends would gather for conversation, food, and drinks. I was making more friends each day. Maybe not close friendships, but friends.

Two, Peter and I had been separated for months. It wasn't as if anyone was trying to ruin any current relationship I was in. I suppose I also refused to get angry at the incessant suggestions that I try dating because it showed people were concerned for me. They wanted me to be happy.

It's hard to be mad at people who simply want you to be happy.

"This sounds wonderful," I said. "Two heartbroken men using each other to get over other people, but—"

"It's just a date," Sheila said. "You don't have to commit to anything else."

"Are we done?" I asked. "Is this meeting over?"

Sheila cackled, her already witch-like laugh exacerbated by the imperfect sound of the video link. I couldn't help but smile along at her amusement. However, we both still had hours left in our work days. Talking about me going on a date with someone when I had absolutely no intention of doing so was a waste of our productive hours.

"I heard some gossip today," Sheila switched tack quickly.

"You always hear gossip." I shuffled more papers. "I think you start the gossip since you're always the first to hear it."

Rude," she gasped. "Well, okay. Sometimes I do. But I'm usually right."

"Sure."

"But this time I heard that I might be calling you 'boss' soon," Sheila said.

I rolled my eyes. "Mr. Barton is always talking about promotions. That's what he does. If you do well, he gives you more responsibilities and money. He's a great boss."

Sheila took her turn to roll her eyes.

"Yeah, yeah," she said. "He's great. Lick boots some more."

"He is."

"I know," she said. "But you can't say that out loud. It sounds so brown-nosy. Anyway, I hear that since Luc is leaving for other opportunities, that you are going to take his place."

I shrugged. "Then you are the first out of the two of us to know."

"Would you tell me if you actually had been asked to take his spot?" Sheila asked.

"Well, no," I said with a laugh. "But Mr. Barton has said nothing to me. I'm just a lowly interpreter listening in on conversations and speaking up when needed. Just like you."

"Fine," she groaned. "But if you hear anything, you have to tell me immediately."

I don't have to tell you anything, you nosy bitch. The thought made me chuckle. I loved Sheila—but it was ridiculous for her to think I'd trust her with a secret.

"Definitely not," I said.

Sheila made a noise between a groan and a hiss and she disappeared from my computer monitor. Laughing, I closed the app and went back to my main software program to finish typing up notes about my last call. Though it had been like many other calls—exciting information that I was legally and contractually obligated to tell *absolutely no one*—it was also boring. I liked boring, though. Working for Source Language, Inc. as an interpreter was boring and easy. And it paid exceptionally well.

There was absolutely nothing to complain about as far as my job was concerned.

Over the previous months, living in my new apartment, and working as an interpreter from home, I'd made several new friends. None of them were close friends yet, but I always had something to do on any given night of the week if I wanted. I was invited to dinners at people's homes, out to movies with groups, and even offered up guys on a platter if I wanted to date.

Life was good.

Peter texted me every day. That was one thing that made my life difficult. He wanted to know if we could work through things. If we could at least talk. He wanted to know what he'd done wrong. He wanted to know why I'd left. He wanted to still be involved in my life however that made sense for us. Somehow, even though I knew I'd made the right decision—*our marriage was not working out*—I couldn't bring myself to answer most of his texts.

I didn't have the answers he was looking for and I didn't even know where to begin explaining how I felt about our failed marriage. Did I still even love Peter? I found myself asking that question at least a hundred times a day. While on calls. Out with friends. Eating dinner. Watching television. Trying to read before falling asleep in bed.

Yes. I desperately loved Peter.

But when is love enough?

If a relationship is not equitable, if two people don't know how to communicate and combine their lives into one, love doesn't matter. It's a nice little condiment on top of the platter of life, but it doesn't hold the dish together. It merely completes it once every other ingredient is in place.

Love is like gravy or a sauce. It hides a lot of sin.

After checking my notes to make sure they were clear, concise, and precise, I hit the button to save and file them. It was almost five o'clock, so I automatically tapped my phone to bring up a video call. A routine I'd fallen into nearly every day when my work was almost over.

Alex appeared on the screen after a few rings, and like always, he looked bothered.

"*What, Frenchie?*"

I laughed and shrugged. "I don't know. Isn't this what we do?"

"*Get a fuckin' life, bro,*" he said. "*Don't you have any* real *friends?*"

That was so Alex. Pretending that he was above actually claiming someone was his friend. Over time, I came to realize it wasn't a joke to him. It was a defense mechanism. It was his way of making sure if a relationship ended it didn't feel like an actual relationship, to begin with, so it wasn't as devastating. However, as long as he kept answering my calls, I'd keep making them. It proved he was interested in staying friends.

For months I'd been video calling him nearly every day. I'd called him on the first Christmas that I spent alone in my new apartment. It had been a lot of me to ask—that he spend time talking to me on such an important holiday that should be spent with family—but he had talked to me without complaint for hours. I called him on New Year's Eve so I didn't ring in the new year on my own. He talked to me for hours then, too.

I could talk to him about anything. He was a great friend. Even when he was pretending he didn't care if we were friends.

One topic I never broached with him—at least not in a direct way—was Peter. They had been friends for years before Alex and I had even met. I was certain they were still friends. However, Alex and I were really good friends, too. I didn't want to do anything to endanger that by saying the wrong thing about Peter. Alex never brought up Peter, either. Of course, he didn't want to say the wrong thing to me. So, Peter was a taboo subject. It's difficult to grow closer to someone when such an important chapter of your life is sealed, never to be read by them. Of course, I spent every interaction with Alex worrying that he'd tell me we couldn't be friends any longer due to the tension it might be causing between Peter and him. If it happened, I'd be understanding. But I hoped that the one true friend I'd made since moving to America wouldn't be lost.

"I have a life," I snapped. "Kind of. I mean, I suppose."

"Lightning quick wit you have there. I'm absolutely devastated by your rebuttal."

"Oh, shush," I said. "How are you, my friend?"

Sighing, Alex stared into the phone screen.

"I didn't ask to be born, you know? But what's done is done, so I'm going to fuck up as much shit as I can while I'm here. You?"

Laughing, I said: "I suppose the same. Work is good. I love my apartment. Yeah. Life is okay."

"Just okay?"

I shrugged.

"Look," Alex said, *"I'm not an incredibly busy man, but I only have so much patience. What's on your mind?"*

"Do you think I should move back to France? Or even Canada?"

I'd barely finished the question when Alex began to laugh.

"Because your life was so great then?" he asked.

Alex's question gave me pause. We had never discussed my life in great detail, but we'd had enough deep conversations over the time we'd known each other that he could put the pieces together. One day, maybe we'd fill in the gaps, but knowing enough was sufficient for a friendship.

"Well, no, but—"

"*You know,*" Alex cut me off, "*if you don't know where you're going, it's usually best to stay where you are.*"

"Huh?"

"*Stop creating the storm, man,*" he said. "*It doesn't have to rain every fucking day. Even if that's what you're used to. Maybe, I don't know, enjoy the fucking sun when it's out.*"

"You don't understand. I—"

"*Enzo,*" he said, and I knew he was being serious since he used my actual name, "*get out of your own damn way.*"

I sat there.

"*And look, I've gotta go. Not that I'm not enjoying watching a friend try to constantly sabotage their own life, but I've got a meeting in three minutes before I can call this day done.*"

"I'm sorry," I slumped in my seat.

"*It's just advice, man,*" he said. "*Not an admonishment.*"

"Talk soon?"

"*Talk soon.*"

Then he disappeared from my screen. Alex's words rang in my ears as I sat there, wondering how many times I'd done something to sabotage my happiness. Obviously, not everything that happens to a person is their fault. How one deals with the events of their life, and what they do to cope with it is. Knowing that still didn't help me pull myself out of the depths of despair I'd found myself in, even if I was pretending everything was okay.

I'd need to make another therapy appointment. We'd gotten nowhere quickly, my therapist and I, but eventually we'd have to stumble upon something.

Something important had happened though, which I didn't realize until I had called my therapist's office and set up an appointment. Alex had referred to me as a friend. Without making a joke about it.

We didn't have to talk about Peter. He'd made himself clear.

That was the thing about Alex. Sometimes you had to pay close attention, but there was a plethora of answers in everything he said.

Paris Is Burning

Cathédrale Notre-Dame de Paris was ablaze.

Typically, I'd take my mid-morning break at my little office space in my apartment at my desk. I'd flip through web pages and snack on hummus and veggies or a snack that was decidedly less healthy. *What kind of breakfast food are you?* Take a quiz to find that out. *The ten things you never knew about jellyfish.* That's something I definitely had to check out. The news. That's where the headline got my attention.

Shuffling like a zombie from my office space, down the hall, and into the living room, I turned on the television. In real-time, I watched a symbol of my religion burn.

It must be saved!

What a tragedy!

This happened because of the sinners.

Those sinners were listed.

Straight white men were not on the list.

I watched as cardinals and priests pleaded with...*the world*...to do better. To care about what was happening in Paris. To realize this was all of the heathens' fault.

They begged people to care about a building more than I'd ever heard them plead with people to care for the sick. Feed and clothe the homeless. Stop wars and violence. To love instead of hate. Their pleas for a building were greater than any they'd made for people to help them identify the perverts within their own ranks who preyed on children.

Their pleas over something that was no more than a pile of stones, steel, and glass fell on deaf ears in my living room.

Catholicism, I suddenly realized, meant nothing to me. Cathédrale Notre-Dame de Paris meant less to me. It was a beautiful building. Beautiful buildings don't last forever.

Without my family, a religion I'd been tied to simply by birth, felt no more significant to me than a thread I plucked from the cuff of my shirt and tossed away.

What had Catholicism done for me—Enzo? Had it protected my family from disease and pain? From death? Had it comforted me when I grieved, weeping and sobbing alone in my Montreal apartment at night? Had it protected my brother and sister when the world was cruel to them? Did it guide the hearts and souls of its holy men who told me that I was sick for being gay? Or their flock who found Noe and Ila intolerable during services?

Had it put food on my table?

Had it kept me warm when winter came?

Had it provided me with a coat?

Decent shoes?

Guidance when my marriage was falling apart because something so big was going on inside of me that I couldn't even begin to understand it?

My marriage was an abomination to the Catholic church.

Nothing. Catholicism had done nothing. Except ask for money so that a building could be rebuilt so the church's coffers could go undisturbed.

At one time, even when there was no food in my pantry, I had no coat, and my shoes had holes in the soles, I would have given what I could to help.

I was not that Enzo anymore.

Since I'd moved to America, my daily prayers had turned into weekly prayers. Then monthly prayers. Then I was only going to church on high holy days if at all. Somehow, somewhere, I had unconsciously separated myself from something that connected me to my family, history, and culture. And it had been so insignificant I hadn't even noticed.

Until a building burned down.

And I found I didn't care.

That night, for the first time in months, I stepped into a church. One I had never been to before. After several minutes of sitting in a pew at the back of the nearly empty church, I lowered myself to the kneeler.

I talked to God.

A prayer I'd said for many years echoed through my head:

Why?

I want to know why, God.

And I will ask every day in every prayer—in every language if I have to—I will learn every language to make sure you understand me if I have to—until I feel you have answered me.

I have always trusted in you, God.

But this I cannot trust.

I am a forgiving person, God.

But this I have not been able to abide.

And I will no longer try.

Please tell Mamie, Papa, Maman, Noe, and Ila that I love them and miss them every day.

Thank you for Peter. Please watch over him and guide him and surround him with your love.

In the name of the Father and of the Son, and of the Holy Spirit.

Amen.

I still loved God.
But I loved myself more.

That night, I dreamt of my grandmother. I was entering Basilique Notre-Dame de Montreal, the stained-glass windows alight with the mid-morning sun. Brilliant sunbeams, the color of gems, shot through the church at odd angles, landing and forming puddles of glitter upon freshly waxed wood and brass fixtures. My feet, bare flesh slapping against the floor, sounded like a frog hopping from one lily pad to another, which made me smile.

Mamie was sitting in a pew, her back to me, though I recognized her immediately.

Wanting to race to her, I was somehow held back, forced to walk calmly down the aisle to stand beside her at the end of the pew. As though, even in dreams, the basilica required reverence. When I found myself beside her, looking down as I stood in the aisle, her head turned and she lifted her chin to meet my eyes. Her pendulous, glittering earrings caught the light, casting a halo around her face. Her cotton candy hair was coifed immaculately as always.

She smiled up at me.

"You know," she said, gesturing for me to join her, so I slipped in and sat down in the pew next to her, "I don't even think God is in this church."

I wanted to say so many things to her. To ask how mother, father, Noe, and Ila were. To tell her I loved her. That I missed her.

"Oh?" I asked.

"No," she said, pulling me so that I slumped happily against her, crooking my back so that I could lay my head on her shoulder.

In my dream, she smelled as she always had. Flowery, sweet, spicy, a touch of vanilla. Home. Memories of a home that no longer existed.

She laid her hand on my knee and patted it gently.

"So, why are you? In this church?" she asked.

I didn't have an answer for that. I wrapped my arms around her and buried my face into her neck, inhaling deeply, hoping I would never forget her smell.

"I've tried talking to God, Mamie," I said, a single tear sliding down my cheek. "He never answers."

"Are you sure you're listening?" she asked.

I didn't want to answer that question.

"I've been good to the universe," I said. "It doesn't listen, either."

We sat there, me holding her and trying to memorize her scent as her hand patted my knee. Finally, she spoke again.

"But are you being good to yourself?" she asked.

I had an answer for that, but the dream ended before I could share it with her.

Somehow, I was certain she already knew the answer.

When God Closes a Door, Jump Out the Window

Source Language, Inc. had been my employer for almost three years before I had even considered taking a vacation. Mr. Barton's policies made it so any vacation days simply compounded year after year until you hit the limit you were allowed to "bank." Unless a person was getting close to their limit, no one bothered you about needing to use some of your available vacation days. Since it took nearly five years for a person to fill up their "bank," no one had bothered me yet. They probably assumed I was saving up for a big vacation, anyway. Where would I have gone, though? Who would I travel with if I did go somewhere? Vacation was the furthest thing from my mind. My life was comprised of work, sleeping, eating, spending time with friends, and trying to figure out who Enzo was.

Like most things when you're not thinking about them, an opportunity presents itself when you least expect it. In the case of my vacation time, an opportunity showed up out of the blue and laid out a destination I never would have expected. That's how opportunity knocks—in a tune you're not quite familiar with, yet compelling enough that you have to answer the door.

I'd finished work on a Monday afternoon and, per usual, I was about to place a video call to Alex. My daily informal therapy session with my best friend—whether he would admit to holding that position or not. However, before I could press the icon to place the call, his face appeared on the screen, a call from him incoming. Laughing at the coincidence—though, after-work calls were typical for us, so not that surprising, I supposed—I answered the call.

"*I need you to come to Texas,*" he said, not waiting for a greeting, nor giving one.

"Um, what?"

"*I have someone I want you to meet,*" he said. "*So, we need for you to plan to come to Texas.*"

Rolling my eyes, I said: "I'm not ready to date. Peter and I are still married—"

I'd brought up Peter, but didn't realize it until I had said his name. Fortunately, Alex didn't care. He interrupted me before I could continue.

"*Well,*" he said, "*he's a dude, but he doesn't want to have sex with you. I don't think. Honestly, I don't know. You haven't met him and I'm not certain if he likes other dudes. He's married, but what does that mean anymore, you know?*"

Ouch, I thought. I knew Alex meant nothing by the comment, but it struck me in the gut. *What* did *marriage mean anymore?*

"What?"

"*I want you to meet a doctor friend of mine,*" Alex said, his hand reaching off-screen, then returning full of popcorn, which he popped in his mouth before continuing. "*He's a neurologist.*"

I simply stared at Alex.

"*I was telling him about you,*" Alex said. "*He wants to talk to you. See your medical records.*"

"Why?" I asked.

"The little evil unborn twin in your head," Alex tapped his forehead. *"He wants to know why all of your surgeries have been unsuccessful."*

Alex knowing my medical history from all of our talks over the last few years had been forgotten. Over time the things we share with friends become threads in a woven tapestry that is a friendship. You can't possibly remember everything you've shared with each other, and no thread is more important than another. Each thread works to hold the entire tapestry together, so some are ignored or forgotten. With Alex mentioning my medical history and a neurologist, I realized how much I had actually shared with Alex about my life's biggest mystery.

"But...why?"

Alex shrugged. *"He likes a challenge. He hasn't met a tumor yet he couldn't find a treatment for."*

"I'm not someone's experiment," I grumbled.

"It's not an experiment," Alex said firmly. *"It's hope."*

I had to pause and collect my thoughts.

"Alex," I whispered, controlling my emotions, "I cannot be disappointed again. Especially not about that."

"Well," Alex said, nonchalantly, *"I also assumed you'd want to hang out with me for a few days. Take a break from life. And I'd like to see you, too."*

I couldn't help it. I smiled. Still unsure about the suggestion to see his doctor friend, my gut flipped at the thought of getting to spend time with my best friend. We hadn't gotten to spend time together in person since the party Peter had thrown.

"And if you tell anyone I said that I'll tell them you're lying so don't even think it."

I laughed.

"Alex," I said, "I'd love to visit you. I just…the doctor…I don't know."

"*Enzo—*"

"It's just part of who I am now," I said, sighing. "It's better to accept that than to get my hopes up because some doctor thinks they're better than every other doctor I've seen."

"*Look,*" Alex said, "*you don't have to commit to anything except meeting with him. If you don't like what he says or think it's a waste of time, get up and walk out. Try to be nice—he's my friend after all—but give him half an hour to talk to you. What have you got to lose?*"

Hope, I thought.

I could lose hope.

Then again…I'd lost hope ten years prior. At least as far as my tumor went. I'd given up after the last surgery had done nothing but left me with another scar, a bald patch on my head that took months to grow back fully, and disappointment. The tumor wasn't cancerous. As long as I took my medication, it was plausible that I could live for an average length of time for a human. If an exceptionally bad seizure didn't surprise me and ruin that plan.

Why would I want to put myself through more disappointment and more doctors?

Because even I wasn't dumb enough to believe that I'd given up.

"A half-hour?" I asked, considering it. "That is all I have to promise? And I can leave if I don't care for what he says?"

"*Well, yeah.*" Alex stuffed more popcorn into his mouth. "*It's just a chance. No one is expecting a miracle here.*"

For some reason, Alex pointing out that both he and the doctor had realistic expectations set my mind at ease. I didn't want more people promising things they couldn't deliver. I wanted honesty. *There's a chance it could work, but we're not going to be ridiculous about it.* That's all I had needed.

"Okay," I said. "I'll meet him."

"*Great,*" Alex said. "*Find out when you can fly down. Let me know, and I'll set up an appointment with him. Plan to stay for at least a few days after. There's too much food to introduce you to here in just a day.*"

Then he hung up.

Puke Green is the Color of Hope

"What the fuck?"

Dr. Bradley had muttered that phrase in my ear. His actual name was Dr. Carlson, but he preferred "Dr. Bradley" because he was technically a pediatric neurologist. I was sitting on the paper-lined table in an examination room of a pediatric neurologist's office. He was picking through my hair with his fingertips, examining my scalp as I sat patiently, waiting to hear anything he had to say. Curses under his breath was not what I'd expected.

Of course, I hadn't expected, after Alex had picked me up at the airport on a Tuesday afternoon, to be driven directly to Dr. Bradley's office. Nor had I expected to sit in a bright waiting room full of primary colors and children's toys for an appointment to see a doctor for patients much younger than I. Watching children play on the floor as their parents eyed Alex and me warily had been unnerving. The fact that I love children and enjoy watching them play—*watching them simply be children*—did not help the parents feel I was not dangerous.

Fortunately, Dr. Bradley had been expecting us, so we only had to sit and be stared at in the waiting room for five minutes before a nurse ushered me back to a room. Alex had said he'd wait in the car, obviously so that I could have privacy. I appreciated that, but I also had hoped he would go into the exam room with me. Seeing Dr. Bradley had made me nervous already, but seeing him so suddenly after arriving in Texas had compounded that anxious feeling tenfold.

However, when the middle-aged man with a kind smile on his face entered the room, introduced himself, and shook my hand, I felt at ease almost immediately. It could have been the fact that he had a funky, multi-colored lab coat on over his puke green scrubs. Or it could have been that he went by his first name instead of his last with his patients. Whatever it was, I realized that I would feel comfortable giving this man thirty minutes of my time.

"Pardon me?" I asked.

"How many times have they cut your skull open?" he asked, his fingers digging through my hair.

Other than Peter, I had never liked for people to play with my hair. Because then they would see the network of scars that zig-zag along the top and side of my scalp. It's one of the reasons I like to keep my hair longer than I should. Hair hides the evidence of that which I'm ashamed, though the shame is not of my doing.

"Um," I said, mumbling, "I'm not certain."

"Why did they go in through your skull instead of up your nose?"

"I...don't know," I said. "I think they went through my nose once. I think. Most of my surgeries were done when I was very young."

He sighed and continued tracing my scars with his fingertips as he picked through my hair. For what seemed like forever, Dr. Bradley obsessed over the scars. I was on the verge of either shoving him away or simply, yet firmly, asking him to stop. There was nothing on my scalp that would change the more he looked at it. Before I had a chance, Dr. Bradley sighed again and stepped back to look at me.

He started to speak, stopped himself, and walked over to retrieve the little stool on wheels that all doctors keep in examination rooms. Sitting down, he wheeled himself over until he was a few feet away, nearly eye-level with me since the table I was sitting upon had been built for shorter patients.

"What you have is a meningioma, Enzo," Dr. Bradley said. "Which isn't technically a tumor, but they get classified that way."

"You can tell from my scars?"

He laughed. "No. I've studied the medical records your doctors forwarded to me."

"Okay," I shrugged.

"That's why I took an interest in you, Enzo. The fact that you've had a meningioma since you were a child."

"A baby," I said. "I've had it my whole life. I think."

He nodded, unconcerned.

"Meningiomas in children make up five percent or less of all meningiomas," he said. "It's super rare."

"Yay," I said, giving jazz hands.

Dr. Bradley laughed.

"They're almost always benign—as you know—and often present no symptoms. Many people with meningioma simply need to be monitored once a year to make sure nothing changes and they live normal lives," he said. "Meningiomas tend to grow—*very slowly usually*—but they do grow, and can present problems further on in life. If they start growing too much, they can press on parts of the brain and cause seizures—"

We exchanged a pointed look.

"—they can lead to dementia, headaches, other neurologic symptoms…you get the idea."

"Sure, yeah."

"Since you've had this since you were born, it's particularly interesting to me since all of my patients are children. The fact that yours has grown hardly at all since then—if at all—is also interesting. Medication usually isn't used to treat patients with a meningioma, but I suppose if you want to try and control seizures, that is one way to go about it."

"Okay?"

"It's also interesting to me because you're one of the patients with meningioma who is *not* asymptomatic, so treatment through surgery would be ideal."

I tapped my head. "And they've tried. They failed. I take medication."

He nodded. "What's confusing to me is that from the scans I've seen and notes I've read, yours is a meningioma that should have been easily solved through surgery. How they've failed time and time again, is infuriating to me, considering what I've read in your medical history compiled from all of your doctors. The French ones took some deciphering."

We both chuckled.

With nothing useful to help Dr. Bradley figure out the puzzle that was my tumor, I stayed silent.

"I assume that once they got in there, they got nervous that they would do more damage by removing it—but that's not what I'm seeing in the records I've received."

"I don't know," I said. "I wish that I did. That has always been my assumption, but I don't think I have ever been told that explicitly."

"Enzo," he said, frowning again as though unsure if he should say what he was thinking, "I want to tell you something, but I don't know if it will ease some of your lifelong concern over your tumor…or it will upset you further."

Holding my hands out limply, I replied.

"What more could someone say that will make a lifelong medical condition worse?"

He blinked a few times, staring at me.

"There is no possible way that your tumor could have been removed by cutting into the side or top of your skull," he said evenly. "They would have had to lift your whole brain out to get to it because of where it's positioned. They…they should have known that. *All of those surgeons* should have known that."

My mind went numb.

"I wondered how so many surgeons could have made the mistake of trying this method for surgically treating your tumor and I just couldn't understand it," he said. "It was bad medicine at best, negligence at worst. However, I noted that in your earliest medical records—that I have access to—that a doctor incorrectly indicated the position and location of your tumor."

What does one say to that? If, after a lifetime of living with a tumor, you find out that it was due to one doctor's incorrect notes, and then every doctor after not correcting those notes…what can you say?

I knew how I felt.

"I don't have an answer for you as to why all of your doctors so far didn't change the notes. Or realize the error from looking at all of your scans before opening your skull, but...here we are. All I can do is apologize for the lack of appropriate care you've received from my peers."

I licked my lips. Willed my eyes dry.

"So, what now?" I said, trying to shrug; pretend I was unbothered.

I had to be unbothered. Fury would solve nothing; change nothing.

Dr. Bradley frowned deeply, his brow like a canyon.

"Are you happy with taking medication for the rest of your life, Enzo?" he asked.

My mouth opened to tell Dr. Bradley that the medication was fine. It kept me alive. Taking medication was simply the lot I'd been dealt in life. What other option was there now? That's not what came out of my mouth, though.

"No," I said, strongly emotional, though I controlled myself. "I hate the medication. Even the medication that doesn't give me joint pain and headaches and nausea and sap all of my energy."

Dr. Bradley watched me.

"I'm so exhausted with the medication," I said. "I'm exhausted with worrying that one day I will have a seizure that kills me because I became careless with my medication routine. Or, I don't know, a seizure that causes some type of brain damage so severe that I will be forced to live in a facility for the rest of my life. I'm...exhausted, Dr. Bradley."

Somehow, I managed to not cry. Admitting that truth had made my eyes want to well up, but I had refused. I wouldn't cry about my tumor ever again. Not if I could help it.

"I figured as much," he said, giving a single nod. "I could be wrong, Enzo. Maybe I'm as useless as your other doctors seem to have been, but I think I'm right. A proper surgeon—an experienced, competent surgeon—should be able to remove your meningioma easily."

I shrugged. "But they can't."

He nudged my knee. "None of your surgeons seem to have been what I would call experienced or competent."

I stared at him.

"The fact that they've opened up your skull that many times tells me all I need to believe I'm right about that."

Again, I had nothing helpful to say.

"So," Dr. Bradley pushed against the floor with his feet, sending him sailing on the stool across the floor to the counter next to the door, "I have a neurosurgeon buddy who practices in Chicago—"

"I don't know—"

"You gave me time," Dr. Bradley said, writing a note in a file, "And I haven't hurt you. I just want you to give him some of your time, too. He won't hurt you, either. That's all I ask."

"Just time?"

"Yes," he said, dropping his pen to turn and look at me. "I think if you meet with him, you'll find he agrees with me. And I think he might convince you that one last surgery will bring you the results you've been looking for your whole life."

"I've used up all of my hope," I said.

"That's okay," Dr. Bradley smiled. "You can have some of mine."

Alex was waiting for me in the car, as he had promised. He had the window all the way down on the driver's side, his arm laid on the sill, a cigarette dangling from his fingertips. Music was playing softly on the car stereo and he had his head laid back against the headrest, sunglasses on his face. How he was able to sit in the oppressive Texas summer heat in a hot car was lost on me, but he seemed perfectly content with his decision to wait in the car. I hadn't been in Dr. Bradley's office for more than thirty minutes after Alex had stepped out, but that was still too long for the summer heat. Possibly, if one lives in such a climate for long enough, one becomes desensitized to it.

When I'd arrived at the airport, an hour before my appointment with Dr. Bradley, I had immediately been struck by how hot Texas in July could be. In North Central Texas it wasn't a dry heat, either. Thick and humid, the air was like a weighted blanket. Or an anchor. If the concrete wouldn't scald one's skin, it would be tempting to merely lie down and wait for autumn. Stare at the world through the haze that rose from every surface that the sun's light touched. The sun, blazing and white-yellow, was high in the noon-time sky. Everything was so bright and hot and disorienting. I could barely think from the heat and light.

But maybe that was a blessing. The heat and blinding light distracted me from thinking about all that Dr. Bradley had to say. The bombs he had dropped in my lap about my medical history.

The hope.

Alex didn't even move when I opened the passenger side door and slid into the seat beside him. It wasn't until I had shut my door that he brought his hand to his face and took a puff off of his cigarette. Without prompting—as if he could read my mind—Alex turned on the car, pushed a button to roll up his window, and blasted the air conditioning.

Relief.

The walk from the front door of the doctor's office to the car had been a mere six yards. Every step had felt like death was waiting.

"Well?" Alex asked. "Good news?"

I shrugged. "I suppose. Yes. And no. But yes."

"That's clear then."

We both chuckled.

"Everything I knew was wrong," I said. "About my life. And now I...how I see the future has changed."

Alex watched me for a moment as he tamped out his cigarette in a portable ashtray in the cupholder on his side. He cracked his window and waved his hand rapidly to assist the vents in dispersing the smoke. It has always amused me how smokers—myself included—feel we can hide the evidence of our crime.

"In a good way or bad way?" he asked.

"I think good."

"Good," he said. "What now?"

For a moment, I had no answer to that question. *What now?* What now, indeed. Certainly, I'd meet with the neurosurgeon in Chicago at some point. I had promised Dr. Bradley that I would. However, this would be a journey with an incomplete map. I knew the next step, but I had no idea of the destination.

"I promised to meet a neurosurgeon in Chicago."

"That's good, right? Promising?"

I turned my head to meet Alex's eyes.

"Hope isn't something that I know how to deal with anymore."

Alex watched me for a moment, then turned his head to lay it against the headrest once more. So, I turned my head to stare out the windshield as well. We sat there, the wonderfully icy air from the vents slapping against our faces. Gooseflesh rose on my arms, and a chill ran up my spine. For once, being cold didn't bother me.

"Hope is," Alex's face was screwed up in thought when I looked over at him, "the belief that some course of action we take—*some decision*—will make our lives better. You know, we'll say or do the right thing that fixes everything. But that's not really what hope is."

I watched him for a moment before answering. "What is it?"

"It's the resolve to see everything through to its end. To keep trying. Because at the end of life, what matters isn't that one thing we said or did—it's all of the things we said and did. Hope doesn't work on a timetable—and if it did, it's not ours. So, hope is continuing to do what you think is best, based on the information you have, believing that, in the end, things will work out. Having hope that talking to Dr. Bradley will fix everything is stupid. Believing that if you take the next step, and the next, and the next, that it will lead to an improvement, is wise."

"What if it doesn't?" I asked quietly.

Alex turned to me. "Don't you already know what the result of doing nothing will be? Or, I guess, the result from continuing to do what you've been doing?"

I took a breath. "Yes."

"Do you like that result?"

Once or twice in a lifetime, if you are so blessed, you will meet someone to whom you feel immediately bound. If not by blood, and maybe not be something as banal as simple friendship, then by some secret force that only the universe understands. The second time this happened to me, it came in the form of Alex. Understandably, this is a momentous occasion in what is a small life—because that's all we have. Lives that are small compared to the enormity of the universe—for you have found a soulmate.

If you should ever discover a soulmate, and as time goes by, you realize you will never know much of anything about this person, it will either sour your feelings about the relationship, or it will become intoxicating. Intoxicating in that you must desperately discover the center of the universe contained within this creature who is simultaneously everything you needed in life, yet the one thing you know you will never understand. That was Alex for me at that moment. Maybe forever.

While affable and witty, intelligent and crass—all things rolled into one—these things produced an enigma. The things that drew me to him were the things that kept me from fully knowing him. Whether it was in the way he could become deathly silent while staring off at nothing when he thought no one was paying attention—because silence seemed to be his default—or the way that his smiles and laughter never reached his eyes, or the way he would say something profoundly insightful a moment before raucous, yet soulless laughter burst from his throat, something drew me to him.

After so much time, I realized it wasn't my desire to figure out the mystery of what lurked beyond the walls he had meticulously built around his truest self. It wasn't my amusement at his wry sarcasm and sometimes jarringly morbid humor. Nor was it the way that he had all of the confidence in the world. Because none of these things were true. My irrevocably damaged soul recognized his irrevocably damaged soul. People like us find each other eventually. We could understand each other with a look or a single word. Soulmates are rare—if you believe such things. People with souls which your soul recognizes at a glance are even rarer.

I didn't know if it was hope that made me feel that way about Alex. Hope that I had found one person in the whole wide world that, even if they weren't clear about it, understood me completely. Who didn't judge me for being me? Someone who, presented with the need, would help me when it was needed, for no other reason than our souls recognized each other's. I desperately wanted Alex's help. So far, his help had been invaluable.

"So," I asked. "What do I do?"

Alex smiled. "Easy. Decide if you would like to try Animal Fries or genuine Texas barbecue for lunch."

Gin-you-wine. His exaggerated Texas accent was comical. I couldn't help it. I laughed.

"Why not both?" I shrugged.

"See," Alex said, putting on his seatbelt, an action I mirrored, "hope is easy. You just made a decision that will probably lead to heartburn, but we'll hope for the best."

Chase Connor

You Really Got a Hold on Me

Traveling to Texas, I wasn't sure what to expect during my visit. I certainly hadn't expected the overwhelming heat. I hadn't expected to find out that Texas wasn't gunslingers and saloons and people on horses corralling cows everywhere. Ten-gallon cowboy hats were also rare. The most common accents were not nearly as pronounced as I'd heard in movies or television shows. It wasn't as laid back as I'd been led to believe, either. The traffic, near one of the largest cities in the enormous state, was intense. The cultural, ethnic, and racial diversity in the area surrounding Dallas was also surprising—though in a good way.

As had been proven to me time and time again throughout my life, what one learns from the media is rarely an accurate and complete depiction of what a culture is actually like.

Texas was a pleasant surprise, the heat of summer aside.

Indian food could be found as easily as Mexican cuisine or barbecue. Chinese and other Asian foods were popular. However, Texans were as proud of regional cuisine and homestyle meals in their restaurants. They loved variety and choice. Imperfect, certainly, Texans seemed to be the Americans who valued freedom above all things, regardless of the repercussions, because pride seemed to be endemic. For better or worse, I found I generally loved the state and its people. Of course, a few days of vacation does not give one a whole and complete picture of what it is like to live in a state.

Since it was merely a vacation, I chose to be willfully ignorant. To enjoy my time somewhere new with a great friend.

Another thing I hadn't expected when visiting Alex was that he had planned to take me to a party on the first night. After leaving Dr. Bradley's office, Alex took me to the drive-through hamburger place—In-N-Out Burger. Expertly navigating the line of cars that seemed to stretch for miles, he placed an order for two "Animal Fries." I was confused by the term but decided that Alex knew what he was talking about when it came to food.

Once the food was in our possession, he drove us a few blocks to a barbecue place that he proclaimed would change my life. Also available to drive through, I let Alex order the food for us through the tiny window in the building that was little more than a shack. An older Black man, who seemed to recognize Alex—they asked each other about their lives— took our order. Working faster than anyone I'd ever seen before, the man produced a large Styrofoam container full of a variety of meats, two large Styrofoam cups with opaque plastic lids, and two bucket-like covered cups that contained sweet tea.

After a few more friendly words with the man, Alex drove us to a mostly empty parking lot next to a park with a large pond. At the center of the pond, a fountain spout shot water fifteen feet in the air. Ducks sped across the pond, giving chase, diving for food, playful and ebullient. Alex and I grabbed the food we'd procured and walked down to a picnic table under a large Weeping Willow not far from the pond's edge and laid everything out.

With no plates and only plastic sporks and thin napkins, we simply ate from the containers communally. Buttery, melt-in-your-mouth brisket and pulled pork, creamy, crisp coleslaw, French fries covered in onions, cheese, and Italian dressing, ribs whose meat fell from the bone at the slightest touch. A deep red, nearly maroon barbecue sauce, tangy and spicy. Everything was delicious. I simply could not stop eating, which we did in silence, enjoying the shade from the tree that made the world seem twenty degrees cooler.

After we ate, nearly all of the food gone, Alex and I sat there, sipping the cloyingly sweet, yet delicious tea, catching each other up on our lives. We didn't speak of work or inconsequential things such as that. We talked about hobbies and interests. Things we did in our free time. Politics. Things that actually had an impact on our lives. We talked about what we hoped for in our futures. And we talked about the food. Neither of us could stop raving about the meal we'd shared. Of course, we had to plan the future meals we'd have over the course of the rest of my visit.

Alex chose to end our lunch discussion with the announcement that a friend of his was throwing a cookout in their backyard that evening. He wanted to take me if I was amenable. With the knowledge that it was a cookout—and I would get to try more regional foods—I was more than agreeable to the suggestion. The opportunity to meet new people was another benefit of going to the cookout.

You won't regret it, Alex had said. *There'll be so much food. And music. And they have a pool.*

Will everyone be swimming?

Some people will be, Alex had said, cryptically.

The party was shocking, but not in a way that unnerved me. In a state that I'd been led to believe was terminally conservative, possibly racist, and not exactly welcoming to the LGBTQIA+ community, the group of people at the cookout was the most diverse group of people I'd ever seen. Indigenous peoples, people of other Native and Latino heritage, Black people, white people, queer people, old and young, comprised the partygoers. I was surprised to find that a large group of people, all so different from each other, had gathered in one place…and it seemed so normal to them.

Of course, it should have been normal. It should always be normal.

However, my experience with the world had left me with the belief that people everywhere were committed to tribalism.

My vacation was leading me to rethink my views of the world.

But there, a half-hour drive outside of a small Texas town, in a gated suburban neighborhood, behind a beautiful, sprawling brick home with a giant saltwater pool in the backyard, these people had found their diverse community. A community where people could simply be themselves. *I'll accept you; you accept me.* It was overwhelming.

Alex introduced me around—not to everyone, as there were far too many people—but he introduced me to a Hispanic couple, a man and woman, who owned the beautiful home. As the hosts, they'd set up grills around the pool area, a safe distance from the water, for guests to grill any food they had chosen to bring. Coolers full of every drink imaginable—alcoholic and not—lined the back of the house. The hosts had set up what looked like a giant round griddle—which I later learned was called a "comal"—and were cooking food as quickly as people could eat it.

Balls of dough made on the spot with masa flour, water, and salt, were quickly flattened out with a tortilla press and cooked in under a minute on the griddle. They were then filled with shaved meats, chunks of meat, peppers, onions, vegetables I'd never even heard of, drizzled with red and green salsas, cilantro, diced onions, and crema. No one bothered with plates. As soon as one of the tacos was handed to them, they ate it right there beside the comal, then, laughing, held their hands out for another.

Another couple was operating a table full of blenders. Chunks of freshly chopped fruit, water, salt, lime juice, and sugar were blended to make agua frescas for anyone interested. Some drank them as is; others added their choice of alcohol. Watermelon, pineapple, and strawberry seemed to be the preferred flavors.

Sodas and beers and wines and other spirits were liberally consumed, though laughter, not angry, drunken outbursts, was the result. Music played loudly and people danced as the sun went down and Christmas lights that had been strung up in the backyard twinkled above us. A bonfire was lit, which led to more raucous, but appropriate, dancing. Alex and I laughed and ate and drank—though we both avoided alcohol—rushing from one group to another, not wanting to miss any of the festivities.

Late in the evening, as the sky turned velvety black and the stars twinkled down from above—*the stars really are big and bright deep in the heart of Texas*—the music was shut off. One of the attendees, a man who couldn't have been much older than me, brought out a guitar. A game began where he would play a song and someone was chosen at random by a spinning bottle. Instead of having to kiss the person it landed on, the person it pointed at had to sing along.

Some of the partygoers, though highly intoxicated, sang along well to the songs the man played on his guitar. Some were dreadful, but the crowd cheered them on the most, bolstering their confidence, encouraging them to sing simply for the joy of singing. I cheered along with the crowd loudly, joyful from the happy and carefree vibe.

It had never occurred to me that the bottle might actually stop spinning and have its mouth point at me. Of course, it did happen, and I found that I had never experienced a fear so profound in my life. I knew the song, *You Really Got A Hold On Me*, that the man started playing on his guitar, but I couldn't make myself sing. The crowd began to cheer, realizing how terrified I was, but I simply could not make myself sing.

So, as a true friend would do, Alex began singing for me. Loudly enough to draw attention to himself and to make the crowd forget that I had actually been the chosen singer, Alex sang the song. He wasn't half bad. Alex himself would tell anyone that he would never have a career in music, but for a backyard cookout, his singing was perfect. The crowd cheered for him, encouraging his singing. I cheered simply because I was grateful he had taken the attention from me.

When the song was over, and he was given his applause, Alex comically stood and bowed, as though he had been the best singer all night. Which only made the crowd laugh and hoot louder. As soon as it was polite, the two of us ducked away from the group of people surrounding the man and his guitar, not wanting to risk being chosen again. We could listen from a distance.

Do you have your phone? Alex had asked as we walked away, along the pool's edge.

Yes, I said, pulling it from my pocket to show him. *It's right here.*

Alex took it from me with a nod, pulled his from his pocket, and laid them both on a table nearby.

Why did you need my—

The next thing I knew, Alex had wrapped his arms around me. And then we were both falling back into the pool.

Salt water rushed up around us, filled my ears, jetted up my nose, and blinded me. Fortunately, salt water doesn't burn the way that chlorinated water does, so being pulled into the pool was shocking, but not painful. Grasping at the water, as though I would find purchase, I flapped my arms and kicked my legs, fighting for the surface.

Laughing and coughing the water from my throat, I spun at the water's surface, looking for Alex. He was already floating there, kicking his legs and flapping his arms lazily, smiling wickedly at me. I cleared my throat, coughing and laughing still, glaring at him.

That's for forcing me to sing, he said.

I didn't make you! I laughed, still sputtering water.

Someone had to come to your rescue, Frenchie.

Someone still does! To protect me from you!

Laughing, the two of us swam to the stairs and climbed from the pool, our clothes stuck to our flesh, dripping water like drowned rats. The crowd cheered and laughed, seeing that we were okay. So, Alex and I gave them another bow.

"How can people party for this long?" I asked, smiling down at the backyard.

Alex and I were lying on the hill behind the house, looking down on the remaining partygoers who were dancing, drinking, and enjoying the mercifully cool night. Midnight had come and gone, and many of the people had followed, but the party had not died off by more than half. Once we had climbed from the pool and bowed graciously for our audience, Alex and I had climbed the grassy hill to lay down and dry off. We didn't want to soak and potentially destroy any of the furniture that belonged to our hosts.

So, we laid on the hill as the night wore on, and even as our clothes dried, scratchy with salt against our flesh, we continued to lay there.

"This has been a perfect day," I said.

I wasn't not talking to Alex, but I wasn't talking to him, either. Looking up at the stars stuck in the inky, viscous swamp of the universe, I found that's who I was addressing. *The Universe.*

The universe didn't respond. Because the universe doesn't have a mouth, I suppose. Alex didn't respond. Because Alex seemed to understand that my statement needed no response.

It's a funny thing, what our mind will bring forth from the deepest recesses of our subconscious when we're afforded the luxury of being still. Being quiet. When nothing in the world is weighing heavy on our minds. When we're having a perfect day. My mind decided that while I was sitting on that hillside, looking down on the remaining partiers still having fun, was a great time to speak up.

Why had I married Peter?

Why had I moved to America?

Why had I not nurtured my marriage?

Why had I not tried harder to nurture a wonderful life?

Why? Why? Why?

Why was I so angry and sad and happy and confused and determined and…I suppose, why was I unsure of my next step?

It was laid out before me. So…why?

"My therapist has told me that I was suffering from depression," I said softly.

Alex didn't physically react to my sudden statement, but I could tell he was listening.

"That I didn't care if my marriage worked out or life was going okay…because I was suffering depression," I added.

Alex still didn't speak.

"She thinks I'm starting to come out of it," I added. "But it will still be a process. I guess that sounds true. I felt depressed. Maybe I didn't care enough because of it. I don't know. But that's what she thinks."

Talking about what my therapist had said, there on the hillside, after such a perfect day, I wasn't saddened at the mention of my troubles. I felt safe talking about it. I felt safe with Alex beside me, listening to my deepest thoughts.

"I suppose it makes sense," I said. "I was depressed before I met Peter. Or...I guess I was really sad. After losing...*everyone*...I loved, how could I not be?"

The universe continued to blink lazily down at us. Talking about Peter was not something I would have ever tried to do with Alex, but something inside of me was compelling me to take this moment—this perfect day—to find out how good our friendship was. If it would survive the thing that had tied us together being ripped apart, maybe that would be a good sign.

"So," I sighed, "I suppose that is the answer. I was...*I am*...depressed. Marrying Peter had been selfish of me. I needed to fix me first."

"Is that so?" Alex finally asked.

I shrugged. "I suppose."

Alex and I sat in silence for a few moments, the music from down at the house drifting up the hill like a wave toward us. I rose to sit cross-legged alongside Alex, wondering what else could be said. It was obvious that Peter was a topic I shouldn't have brought up.

"You know," Alex said, "I wasn't invited to your little post-wedding party."

Slowly, confused, I turned my head to look at him.

"Initially, I mean," Alex smiled at me.

"Oh?"

"Peter invited me at the last minute when he found out I'd be in Rochester."

"Why?"

"He said you would be bored around his other friends. He wanted you to have a good time," Alex said. "He said I'd be good for you."

I frowned.

"I'm assuming that meant that since I'm such an obnoxious jackass, he felt I might bring you out of your shell a bit." Alex shrugged, moving to prop himself up with his elbows. "He wanted you to enjoy the party and maybe find someone to be your first American friend. I guess he figured—and he was right—that there wouldn't be anyone else at the party who would fit the bill."

A soft smile grew on my face.

"He wanted you to find a true friend," Alex said. "And, I guess it didn't work."

I was suddenly frowning again.

"You found a brother instead," Alex reached over and jabbed me in the side.

My smile was back and my eyes were suddenly brimming with unshed tears.

"Don't get all emotional and shit," Alex said. "You just need to know, right now, that I'm Peter's friend. And I'm your brother. I can be both. That's all."

Alex laid back, his head resting in the scratchy late-summer grass, and stared up at the stars once again. I turned my head so that I could wipe my eyes without him seeing. Not for my benefit, but for his.

"You were probably depressed." Alex's voice rang out again. "You probably still are. But that's probably just a pebble on the pile."

"Meaning what?"

I didn't turned to look at him.

"Well, why wouldn't you be depressed after what you went through with your family, yeah?" he asked. "Depression is obvious."

"Sure."

"But why would you feel you deserved the life you built after they were gone?"

I turn to frown at him.

"Survivor's guilt," he said. "All of your family members are dead. They were fucked over by…whoever you think is up there."

Alex pointed lazily up at the night sky. I followed his finger to stare at the inky blackness.

"But there you were," he continued. "Pulling yourself together against all odds, scratching and clawing and doing everything you could to make a life for yourself. And you found it. You found happiness. With someone you love. Someone who was good to you. You built a life when everyone in your family had been denied that privilege. Why would you feel worthy of it?"

Caught in my throat, my breath threatened to strangle me.

How had it not been obvious to me?

Pushing Peter away during our marriage because of depression was plausible. However, when one considers they also felt guilty for surviving what their family could not—and they were going through a difficult time with their health—how could one not act in such a way?

"When someone experiences trauma—no—when trauma becomes the default," Alex said, "they go a little batshit crazy when life turns out okay. They don't know how to live if they are not constantly facing trauma."

314

How could one respond to that? I continued to stare at him.

"You missed the storm, because it was all you knew, so you created a fucking hurricane," Alex chuckled, looking up at me.

I took a breath. "My medication was also—"

"People go through health shit all the time," Alex waved me off. "And they choose to rally the troops—pull those they love in around them for help and protection—or they suffer in silence, pretending no one could possibly understand their plight. You chose to suffer in silence. And Peter had to suffer because of it."

Swallowing hard, I said, "You must hate me. Peter must hate me."

"I don't hate you, Frenchie," he chuckled. "I don't pity you. I simply understand you."

That brought me a bit of comfort. It also brought up a million questions I had for Alex—about his life—but I knew I had not been invited to ask them.

"What about Peter? He must hate me."

"When's the last time you talked to him?"

"I haven't really talked to him in months," I said. "But he still texts me every morning when he wakes up. And before he goes to bed."

"I don't think he hates you," Alex said, amused.

"Maybe."

"Stop hating yourself," Alex said, "for surviving. Stop hating yourself for struggling. Stop hating yourself for being human and not always knowing how to handle your shit. None of the shit you went through that made you act that way was your fault anyway."

Looking up at the stars, I sighed.

"I have never told anyone this," I said. "Not even Peter. After my grandmother died, I planned to run away. I was going to leave my brother and sister with my parents. I wanted my life to be easy. I was so young, but I...I wanted my life to be easier."

"Why didn't you?"

"Then my father got really sick and died. I stayed."

"I asked you—why didn't you?"

"Then my sister, and—"

"Enzo," Alex stopped me, "why didn't you leave?"

"I—I don't know. Each morning, I woke up, ready to leave. I had a plan and a bag with a few things, but..."

"What?"

"Then Noe would say 'good morning.' And 'good morning' might be the only thing he'd say all day. But he'd always say it...and...I couldn't leave."

"I see."

"He was my baby brother. My best friend. Ila was my little sister, too—even though she was older—and she was my other best friend. I couldn't leave them. Who would watch over them?"

Alex and I stayed there, him lying in the grass, me sitting next to him, staring up at the sky together.

"When we're young, we all want an easier life," Alex said. "We want what is best for ourselves. What's more convenient. Then it goes away for a while. We learn to be mature adults and a little more selfless—to care about people other than ourselves. It comes back when you're close to forty—the wanting what's easiest and most convenient. Plus, you're really fucking tired, so that exacerbates it a bit."

"What do you do? To make those thoughts stop?" I asked.

Alex sat up with a grunt, his knee against mine as he crossed his legs, but he didn't move away at the touch.

"You straighten your back. You clear your throat. Hold your head up high. And you tell the universe who the fuck you are. Let it know who it's dealing with. That's what you do. You're not a bad person, Enzo. You have bad thoughts. You're just like the rest of us who could run away, but chose to plant our feet," he said. "You know you're allowed your thoughts, right? No one can take that from you or keep you from having any thoughts you want. It's when you act on those thoughts that judgment is fair."

"Do you think my bad thoughts make me a bad person?"

"I think your bad thoughts took some of the pressure off at the time. They reminded you that you *could* leave. But you chose not to. I think the fact that you had bad thoughts and ignored them makes you a great person."

I took a breath.

"Do you have bad thoughts?"

"All the time. I haven't always been as stubborn as you."

"Tell me one."

"No," he said.

The word was like a lock to a door.

"But I will tell you this," he continued. "The bad thoughts usually don't have your best interests in mind. We all have two voices in our heads. The first voice that speaks up is usually the one that lies. Wait until you hear the second voice."

"The second voice?"

"The first voice is usually the one we've learned from society. What we've been trained to think," Alex explained. "The second voice that comes after the bad thoughts is usually the one telling the truth. It starts as a whisper, but the more you practice listening, it eventually sounds like the voice of God. You can't miss it."

I stared at him.

"Does the first voice ever go away?" I asked.

"Well, right now, I'm being told that we need more food. So...take that as you will."

I laughed uproariously.

"And," he said, "I suggest that just this once, we don't listen for the second voice. What do you say?"

I nodded and the two of us pulled ourselves up together.

"I'll try to keep listening for the second voice before I act," I said before we took a single step to walk back down the hill. "I really will."

"Good," Alex patted my shoulder. "But if it literally starts feeling like someone's talking in your ear—go see a psychiatrist. This is all metaphorical, to be clear."

Laughing, we walked down the hill together, back towards the party that was still, somehow, going on.

"Alex," I asked as we trudged down the hill. "What do you think the meaning of life is?"

He laughed.

"What?" I chuckled nervously.

"There's no meaning to life."

"What?" I gasped.

"That's what makes it so great," he said, lacing his arm through mine. "If there's no meaning, you get to make your own. And there are so many possibilities. I love possibility."

What Could Go Wrong?

Dr. Berger was a middle-aged man with kind eyes and soft hands with nimble fingers, thick around the middle, and had an easy, comforting laugh. The moment he'd walked into the examination room where I'd been waiting inside his office in Chicago, I knew that I liked him. It was odd, traveling to a new city all by myself yet again, navigating the public transportation, and checking into a hotel as a single. Finding his office in the same fashion had been an arduous task as well, but one that I managed. After living in Montreal, there wasn't a city whose culture I couldn't figure out one way or another.

All glass and metal—sterile and cold—I was concerned that Dr. Berger would be a stern man who would convince me to give up. To run from his offices, deciding that all doctors were my enemy, once and for all. However, his bedside manner was warm and kind, though professional. Immediately upon meeting him, I felt that, at the very least, the trip I'd promised Dr. Bradley I'd take to Chicago, would not be a complete waste.

"So," Dr. Berger sat before me on his little stool after examining me, "you've been living with this for—"

"My whole life," I said, looking down at him from my perch on the paper-lined exam table.

Unlike Dr. Bradley's shorter exam tables built with children in mind, Dr. Berger's office had adult-sized furniture.

"How's that going for you?" he asked.

"I suppose it is just what it is?" I shrugged. "C'est la vie?"

Laughing, he reached into his lab pocket. When his hand was pulled out, he was holding two lollipops. One red; one green. He held them up.

"Cherry or apple?" he asked.

I gave him a confused smile.

He jiggled them at me. "I keep them on hand for patients who have their kids with them. Sometimes I treat myself to one."

Cautiously, I reached out and took the red one.

"Cherry," Dr. Berger nodded. "Wise choice."

He unwrapped his lollipop and stuffed it into his cheek. I followed his lead. If he was going to have a lollipop, I wouldn't feel odd having one, too.

"Enzo," Dr. Berger frowned, "you shouldn't have your tumor."

"I know," I said around the lollipop in my mouth. "It's just something I was unlucky enough to be born with."

"No." He shook his head. "I'm not making some philosophical statement here. People get sick, have tumors, die—it's just how life is. You were supposed to have the tumor. That was just how you were meant to be born, I suppose. If we were being philosophical, I mean."

"Okay?"

"What my meaning was is that your very first surgery should have solved your problem," he said. "This is a highly operable meningioma. One of the best placements and sizes I've seen to be plucked right out."

I stared at him, my tongue resting against the lollipop.

"You shouldn't have this tumor now."

"Then why do I?" I asked, suddenly angry. "Tell me why."

Dr. Berger stared at me.

"I ask everyone 'why' all of the time," I growled. "I've asked doctors and my parents, and even...*fuck*...God. No one will tell me why! I'm tired of being told this shouldn't be but no one will give me one fucking reason why it is. And I'm so tired of asking why. Wondering why. I'm tired of asking a simple question and only becoming more exhausted."

My sudden outburst was shocking to us both. Even though I am in control of my emotions and what comes out of my mouth, I hadn't anticipated the frustration and anger that flowed forth. Immediately, I lowered my eyes, looking at the exam room floor as I folded my hands in my lap. The lollipop was still stuck in my cheek.

Dr. Berger waited a moment, then cautiously reached out and laid a hand on my knee.

"Because my profession has failed you," he said. "It's not the answer you want, I know. But that is the answer."

I nodded, my eyes still down.

"It's not a good answer, but it is the answer," he said.

"Okay."

"Don't be mad at anyone but your doctors," he said softly. "But especially, don't be mad at God. God had nothing to do with this."

That...*that* surprised me. This man of medicine and science didn't mock me for my belief in God. My head rose to meet his eyes.

"But I would like to atone for them," Dr. Berger said. "I want to ask you to trust me to do one last surgery. I want to remove your meningioma for you."

"Why should I trust *you*?" I asked.

It was a dumb question. I already trusted him.

"Because I will not agree to do this surgery unless I feel I have your trust," he said.

That made perfect sense. I took a deep breath. Not because I had a decision to make, but because I knew I had to ask the thing that I'd never had the opportunity to ask as an adult with my own agency. An adult in full control of their own health care. Someone who got to make the decision that will, possibly, change their entire life.

"What could go wrong?"

Dr. Berger smiled. "The surgery has to be aborted and nothing changes for you. The surgery goes well and your tumor grows back—there's a twenty-percent chance. The surgery doesn't go well and cognitive and neurological function is lost. Brain damage. Death."

I nodded slowly.

"Do you want to know what could go right?" he asked.

"Yes."

I knew what could go right. I simply wanted to hear Dr. Berger say it.

"You no longer have a meningioma pushing on your brain," he said. "You get to stop taking your medication and never take it again. You lead a normal life."

"What is normal?" I scoffed.

"Good question," he chuckled. "I suppose it is whatever you want normal to be. Because you'll be in control of that for once."

"What if it grows back?" I asked.

"Well," Dr. Berger patted my knee and let go of it so he could sit back, "after a successful surgery, we get you scanned six months after, and then after another six months. If they come back clear, you get scanned after another year. Then three. Then five. Eventually, we give up on the scans if they keep coming back clear—unless you begin having problems. You go on with your life. If they show growth, we can try surgery again. Radiation. Chemo. There are options. Or you may decide that you don't want to go through any of that and go back to living with your new tumor."

"What are the odds it will grow back? How quickly will we know?"

"Well," he said, "meningiomas, if all of the cells are not removed, they tend to grow back within ten to twenty years without fail. Though evidence of them starting to grow back can be seen fairly soon after the surgery. Within months. That's the reason for the scans so soon after the surgery."

"Do you think it will grow back?" I asked.

"I can't—"

"Please?"

He sighed, thought it over, and set his face sternly decisive. "I'm hopeful—considering your tumor hasn't grown any since you were a child, its placement and size—that once it's removed, it won't grow back. I can't promise anything, but that's my hope."

"Did you know that hope is not the belief that one decision or action will fix everything? Hope is the resolve to take one step after another, seeing things through to the end. Because you believe that, in the end, everything will be okay. Hope is, actually, possibility."

Dr. Berger cocked his head to the side with a smile.

"I like that," he said. "Yes. That's what hope is."

I sighed and straightened my back.

"I want to keep taking steps," I said.

Dr. Berger patted my knee once more with a smile.

"I'll take that step with you."

At the end of summer, I found myself in Chicago at a surgical hospital. But I wasn't alone. Alex had traveled from Texas to be with me for the surgery and to stay with me for the first two weeks of my recovery. We had checked into a hotel the night before my surgery, slept as best we could, all things considered, then checked out in the morning before the run had risen. We were checking in at the surgical hospital as it peeked over the horizon.

Over the next two hours, I was prepped. Removing my everyday clothes, I was given a backless paper robe to wear. Needles were stuck in my arm. My hair was covered with a cap. And I waited for Dr. Berger and his surgical team to take me into the surgical room. Alex stayed with me until the very last moment, holding my hand, telling jokes, and distracting me from what was to come. He did his best to keep me from being nervous.

However, I wasn't nervous. I was determined.

I had made the decision to take a step, and I was going to take it.

As I looked up into my best friend's eyes—*my brother*—as the nurses came to wheel me into surgery, I was struck with a thought. Until I had met Alex, I had resigned myself to living with my tumor until I had died. Whenever that would be. Alex had renewed my hope. Simply by being Alex. I didn't know how to thank him at that moment. So, I squeezed his hand and stared into his eyes until he laughed and pried his hand from mine so that the nurses could wheel me away.

I know he thought anxiety was the reason I'd held onto his hand. And I never told him differently. However, it had been the only way I could think of to express my gratitude at that moment.

Inside the surgical room, everything seemed blindingly white. Cold. Sterile. Alien. Vaguely, I can recall Dr. Berger greeting me from behind a surgical mask and face shield. His hair was in a surgical cap and he was garbed in those horrible puke green scrubs that surgeons tend to wear. I'd barely had a chance to respond to his greeting before anesthesia was beginning to be administered.

Surely, that is not the truth. There had to have been time between being greeted and being put under, but that's how it felt. Sudden.

I was thinking about how grateful I was for the hope Alex had extracted from me and how Dr. Berger was wearing those awful scrubs.

Peter entered my mind. I wondered if he was okay. If he knew what I was doing. The compulsion to tell him how much I loved him flooded my mind. Just in case.

Then the world was black.

Only the Weak Survive

Alex was annoyed with me. Again. It wasn't my frustration, but how I reacted to that frustration, that was getting on his nerves. Of course, when a person kicks a butcher knife across the kitchen, nearly hitting another person's bare foot, it's bound to cause consternation. Sharp knives and bare flesh are often enemies.

When I had tried to chop the carrots for our dinner, my hand had twitched, the knife had slipped, and I'd nearly cut my thumb. Aggravated at yet another slip of my hand, I'd let the knife fall to the floor. Before it had even finished clattering against the cement floor in my apartment kitchen, I'd kicked it, sending it sailing across the kitchen. Alex had been walking in to see what had happened and the knife missed his foot by inches.

Alex knew that my fine motor skills were a bit off-kilter since my surgery, and that was frustrating for me. However, after nine days of dealing with my outbursts, he was obviously tired of them. Almost getting sliced by a speeding knife was the straw that broke the proverbial camel's back. As soon as I looked up from the floor and saw the expression on his face, I was sorry.

"You know," Alex said, his voice intentionally controlled, "stabbing me won't make things better faster."

"I'm sorry," I said quickly.

Alex stared at me for several moments. The sliced meat in the wok was sizzling behind me. A stir fry for dinner had been my idea. Alex had wanted to help, but I knew that I needed to learn to do things on my own. He'd been with me

327

for the day of the surgery and the nine days that followed. Making sure that I was safe during my recovery was not an easy thing to ask of anyone. Alex, like me, was doing the best he could.

"I can make the dinner," he said. "This was your idea."

"I know." I looked down at the floor.

Alex retrieved the knife from the other side of the kitchen, picking it up gently and walking it back over to me. He didn't hand it to me, though. He set it in the sink carefully. Then he withdrew another knife from the block—a much smaller one—and handed it to me.

"Smaller, chunkier handle," he said. "You aren't a superhero. Start small."

I slid the knife from his hand carefully, making sure I didn't twitch and nick him with it.

"You can do it," he said, flicking a finger at the carrots still waiting on the cutting board. "Just go slower."

Taking a deep breath, then exhaling with intention, I turned and brought my nervously shaky hand up to hold one of the carrots on the board. I raised the hand with the knife and positioned it over the carrot. Slowly, I brought it down, cutting off a slice of the carrot. Not an even slice, but a slice. Then another. On the third slice, the knife slipped again, and I barely avoided cutting myself once more. Without a word, I shoved the cutting board, knife, and carrots into the sink.

Clattering loudly, my kitchen tools and the carrots came to rest at the bottom of the sink and I sat down. Right there in the kitchen. Turning to put my back against the cabinet under the sink, I pulled my knees up to my chest and glared at the stove across from me, but not really seeing anything but red. *The color of my frustration.*

Alex stood beside me for the longest time, watching me sit there and feel sorry for myself. Finally, with a sigh, he stepped over and turned off the stove burner so that the meat in the wok wouldn't burn. He lowered himself to the floor with a grunt, sitting cross-legged in front of me, his back to the oven. I didn't want to look up and meet his eyes, but I knew he would stay there until I did.

"Okay, fucker," he said once our eyes met. "Let's have a talk."

The tears fell from my eyes immediately.

"It has been nearly two weeks," I managed.

"And it might be two more," he said, nodding. "And maybe two more after that. You know that."

"I—"

"When a tumor gets cut out of someone's brain," Alex said, stopping me, "things aren't just la-di-da perfect immediately. You just had people poking around in your brain. Time is needed for everything to settle and for your body to readjust. You need time to heal."

"Alex—"

"We're done with this," he said, jabbing a finger at me. "I've given you nine days to feel sorry for yourself. That's over. We're done with that. Tough love time."

I looked down at the floor again.

"Today is a new day, Enzo," he said firmly. "You're a new man. You have been for nine days. New men need to get used to having new lives. Your motor skills are not going to be perfect for a while. You're going to drop things. Your handwriting is going to be wonky. Your knife skills are going to be imperfect. You might spill a spoonful of soup on yourself or dribble coffee down your chin. Maybe you'll go to take a leak, twitch, and pee all over the shower door."

I couldn't help but give a small smile at that.

"So," he growled, "you slow down and write with purpose. You're extra careful while chopping vegetables and use a knife that won't slice your finger off if you slip. You dab your shirt and chin clean—or wear a bib. Sit down to piss."

I looked up at him.

"You fucking cope," he said. "Just like you did while you had the fucking tumor. But there's a big difference you're ignoring here."

"What?"

"Your tumor was never going to go away on its own. You *were* going to have to take medication forever," he said. "Now...now you just have to wait. Eventually, your motor skills will be back to what they were. You'll eventually get weaned off of your medication. All you have to do is be patient and wait—adjust to cope with the difficulties until that happens. That's all that you fucking need to do. Because there's finally an end in sight. I don't think that's too much for one person to cope with, Enzo."

He was right.

"Being angry because things aren't perfect—"

"That's not why I'm angry!" I demanded.

As soon as I found myself shouting back, I shut my mouth and lowered my head. I didn't want to scream at Alex. I didn't want to scream at anyone. But if I was going to scream, I didn't want Alex to be the target.

Alex had been at my bedside in recovery at the hospital. At least, he was there when my memory picked back up. He was there when Dr. Berger had come in to let me know that he considered the surgery a complete success and that my tumor had been cut out using a scope they had sent up to my brain through my nose. Then it had been extracted. Completely. They believed that no cells had been left behind that would cause it to grow back. Absolute certainty can never be had in a situation like mine, but Dr. Berger said he was as hopeful as he'd ever been after a surgery such as mine.

All I had to do was wait for my jostled brain to start shooting off the proper signals at the proper times so that my motor skills were as they had been before.

A night of observation in the hospital after the surgery was all that was needed. Then Alex drove me back to my apartment in Minneapolis. It had all been…nothing.

I no longer had a tumor.

Eventually, I would no longer need to take the medication I had been dependent on for my entire life.

I would soon be normal. Whatever I wanted "normal" to be.

That choice had been given back to me.

"Why are you angry?" Alex asked, speaking through gritted teeth, doing his best to control his frustration with me.

"Because," I said, choking back tears, "nine days ago I couldn't even hold a pen for more than a few seconds. Now I am chopping vegetables."

"Poorly," Alex said softly.

I chuckled wetly and nodded. "Poorly. But I am doing it. In a few days, maybe I won't slip at all. Maybe it will be a few weeks—but it will happen. I will chop carrots. I will be fine."

"And?"

I looked over at him. "Why me?"

He frowned, his head tilting to the side.

"Why not my brother? My sister? Anyone in my family? Why are they not here chopping vegetables—*poorly*—and I'm dead? Why am I special?"

Alex's expression softened.

"What did I do to deserve this?" I asked, sniffling. "Leukemia. Embolisms. Cancer. Why is a brain tumor the easiest to fix?"

"Was this easy?" he asked. "The last few decades? Your life?"

"Well, no," I said. "Nothing ever was. For any of us. But I am here. They are not. Why?"

Alex said nothing as he scooted across the floor and turned so that he was sitting beside me under the sink, our sides touching. He took my hand in his, our fingers intertwining, and rested them upon his knee. He squeezed my hand firmly and leaned into me, pushing our shoulders together. And he stayed silent.

"What?" I asked, chuckling wetly as tears dripped down my face softly. "You aren't going to tell me what to do? How to get through this?"

He laid his head on my shoulder and squeezed my hand again.

"Life isn't fair. In fact, it sucks," he said.

"But?"

"That's it, Enzo," he said. "There is no 'but.' Life sucks. It isn't fair. There is no answer to that one. There's nothing I can say that will take away your grief. And even if there was, I'm not sure I would say it."

"But why?"

"Because I hope your grief—when you think about how much you wish your family hadn't suffered the way they did—will remind you that they wouldn't want you to suffer now," he whispered. "I hope your guilt over surviving will be softened when you finally get your head out of your ass and realize how happy they would be for you."

I said nothing.

"Don't hate yourself when so many people would be happy for you—are happy for you," he said. "That's not really honoring your family, is it?"

"I…I know. I'm sorry."

"Don't be sorry. Just be you. Live, fucker."

We both laughed softly. I had asked God many times "why," and I had never gotten a response. So, I whispered the question to Alex.

"Why did my family have to die?"

I didn't expect an answer, but I needed to see if someone could explain it to me.

"Illness. Disease. I don't—"

"Why?" I demanded.

Alex sighed. "Because life means nothing without death. More specifically, life means nothing if every life—and every death—is the same."

Sitting there, my eyes focused on the oven door, I couldn't speak.

"Whatever the reason for your family's deaths—when they died, how they died—brought meaning to their lives. To your life. To everyone's life," Alex said. "Because life means nothing if it doesn't end. And it means even less if we all have the same life and death."

'Then…what?" I sniffled. "What now?"

"You live, Enzo," he said. "You figure out what your life means."

"You told me that life has no meaning," I grumbled.

"I told you life had no meaning so you get to make your own," he said softly. "That's also what gives life meaning, Enzo. Possibility."

"What was the meaning of my family's life then?" I asked angrily as tears slid down my cheeks. "My brother's? My sister's?"

"I told you," he said, "we all make our own meaning. I can't tell you what they thought the meaning of their lives was. You'll have to ask them when the time comes."

I sighed. "Do you really believe that? That I will see them one day?"

"Are you calling me a godless heathen?"

I chuckled, still a bit angry.

"You don't seem religious. That's all."

"Enzo," he said, "I believe that this isn't all there is. I don't know what else there is. But this isn't all of it. But I guess that gives life meaning, too."

"What?"

"I could be full of shit and my belief that there's something bigger waiting could be bullshit," he explained. "But living our lives, waiting for the big reveal at the end of it, kind of gives it meaning. At least a purpose. Don't you think?"

"I suppose."

"What do you want the meaning of your life to be, Enzo?" he asked, his head still on my shoulder. "What purpose do you want to give your life? What's possible for you?"

I took a breath.

"Does it have to be grand?"

"Definitely not."

"I want to be happy. That's all I've ever wanted."

Alex didn't say anything for the longest time.

"You know what makes me happy?" he asked.

"What?"

"Being lazy, not cooking dinner, and ordering in," he said.

He lifted his head from my shoulder to look at me and we both laughed.

"Give your hands a break for a night," he suggested, sliding his hand from mine. "Let's just be happy tonight."

I nodded. "Okay."

Slowly, the two of us rose from the floor, coming to stand beside the sink.

"Also," Alex said, not looking away, but not quite looking at me, "your entire family isn't dead, Enzo. I'm still here. I'm your family, too."

"Of course, you are."

He nodded. Started to step away. Turned back to me.

"So is Peter," he said softly, his eyes meeting mine briefly. "Still. You're not alone."

Then he walked away.

"I'll order pizza," he said over his shoulder before disappearing down the hallway.

And I was left to clean up the mess I'd made in the kitchen. Shuddering with a shaky breath, I was stunned by what Alex had said to me. But I flexed my hands a few times, took a deep breath, and set about cleaning up the kitchen.

I could do that.

No matter how long it took.

No matter how many things I dropped.

Because, eventually…one day soon…cleaning the kitchen would be easy again.

My temporarily messed-up motor skills gave that meaning.

Repainting the Universe

Alex left on a Friday. We barely exchanged any words as we said "goodbye" to each other. We had hugged, holding on tightly, a wordless understanding passing between us. My hands were still not entirely reliable; I knew that I still had weeks of recovery ahead of me. However, Alex had seen me through the worst part of it all. There weren't words to express my gratitude—or my love for my found brother. So, a hug would have to suffice.

Alone in my apartment once again, I sat for an inordinate amount of time on my sofa, staring out at another gloomy day in Minneapolis. My hands lay limply in my lap. Summer would be gone soon—in fact, in Minneapolis, it may as well have never come—and autumn would rush up to meet us. Winter wouldn't be far behind, bringing in the cold and snow, putting the world to sleep; a slumber to prepare it for a new life.

My winter had finally passed. I was waiting for spring.

I needed to say "goodbye" to winter and welcome a fresh spring.

It was a funny thing, waiting to come alive as the world was slowly going to sleep.

For most of my life, I'd always felt like I was a step behind. Waiting to catch up to the rest of the world. I'd spent so many years without enough friends, without enough money, without romance, without enough food, without family. Now I was ahead of it all. My future was opening up wide, waiting for me to decide how to give myself a purpose.

To find the meaning of my life. To live with a belief in possibility.

Though I'd expected that my life after the surgery—however it turned out—would be different, I hadn't expected to be confused by my emotions. If the surgery went well, I expected to be elated. Joyful even. If it went poorly, I'd be disappointed. Or angry. Or maybe even unbothered. I'd gotten so used to being disappointed by doctors and health care in general that a poor outcome would not have seemed that upsetting. The fact that I wasn't simply happy that things had gone so well was the most confusing part.

Things hadn't simply "gone well" with my surgery, however. What had happened was a miracle. Not because the surgery was a miracle. According to my American doctors, one surgery when I was a child should have fixed my problem. I never should have led the life I had. My history should have been different. My life, essentially, had been a lie. The miracle was that after so many years, so many disappointments, I had found someone who had given me hope. A hope strong enough that I had put trust in them.

And that it had paid off.

So, why wasn't I simply happy?

Sitting there, confused by my previous life, I found that I hated myself. I had spent so many years angry, confused, and pitying myself. I was tired of pitying myself. If I was tired of my pity, I knew that everyone around me had to be tired of it, too. Even if they were too nice to say so. I'd been morose; a fatalist. I had been existing—even when I thought I was living.

Even as I'd moved to America and married Peter, giving myself over to possibility, I hadn't allowed myself to believe it. I couldn't even force myself to believe that my life was getting better. Or, even if I had, I refused to allow myself to enjoy it. Because I felt guilty for it.

Guilt is a funny thing. A person doesn't have to do anything wrong to feel guilty. Guilt only requires that a person exists. And I had been doing a lot of existing.

I didn't want to pity myself anymore, but I didn't know how to do that quite yet.

So, I decided to stop hating myself.

That was a step I could take.

Learning to stop pitying myself would come eventually.

Watching through the living room windows, the clouds parted—only briefly—and a beam of sunlight managed to sneak through. It shone through the wall of glass and landed on my hand as it lay on the arm of the sofa. Warm and golden, the light reminded me that summer wasn't quite over. Winter had yet to arrive. And even when it did, it never lasted forever.

Minutes later, I found myself kneeling at the back of my closet, a simple cardboard box in front of me. It took some effort, but I finally forced my hands and fingers into action, pulling back the flimsy flaps to reveal its contents.

Gently, I removed Noe's coat made of sugar and blue clouds. I held it by the shoulders in front of me, staring at the polyester fabric, stuffed to a puffy comfortableness. Bringing it to my face, I inhaled deeply. Pressed it against my flesh. It no longer smelled like warm sugar. It smelled like dust and the inside of a cardboard box. But it still felt like it was made of clouds.

I smiled. Folded my brother's coat and set it to the side.

Next, I removed Peter's fancy black peacoat and folded it before laying it on top of Noe's coat. I removed Ila's windchimes and set them on top of the bundle, smiling as they made their distinct "bonk" sounds. Then I reached inside and removed my notebooks, setting them on the other side of the box. Once I had carefully returned the stack of coats and windchimes to the box, closed the flaps, and pushed it back into the corner of the closet, I gathered up the notebooks.

Back at my desk in the corner of my bedroom, I stared at the stack of notebooks I had written my thoughts and stories in for as long as I could remember. Since I was a young teen.

In the past, when I didn't have the tools to deal with my feelings, I wrote them down. Sometimes they were like journal entries—an indecipherable cluster of words and run-on sentences. Sometimes, when I had a better grasp of how I felt, those thoughts were laid out like stories. And, even other times, with clarity, I wrote fully formed stories based on my life and my feelings.

Now, as an adult man, with a new life, maybe my notebooks would help me understand my feelings. So, I flipped the top notebook open to a blank page, flexed my fingers, picked up a pen, and put it to paper.

I couldn't change my past—that lie of a life that I never should have had to live. But I could decide my future.

I didn't know what was possible. Or where I was going. But I'd been told that if one doesn't know where they're going, it's best to stay where they are. So, I sat at my desk, writing in my notebook until the sun had set and I had to work in a pool of light from my desk lamp. I worked until my hand was aching. Until my eyes felt so heavy that I could barely stay upright. Somewhere, in the brain that had been poked and prodded—and refurbished—was possibility.

I was determined to find it.

Because what is a life without possibility?

A Neighborhood
Present Day

There's something comforting about walking in a peaceful neighborhood in the early afternoon hours when everyone is at school or work. Especially in spring or autumn when it's cool outside and you can enjoy the weather. With no rush to hurry inside to escape the cold or heat, a person can take time to get lost in their thoughts, think about life. A neighborhood is full of life. Many different lives. So many different lives.

So many different possibilities.

Walking through a neighborhood in spring, the trees that lined the street with their branches beginning to bud, the mist from the gloomy day dripping from the skeletal limbs waiting to be dressed by the season, I thought a lot about life.

Not necessarily mine, but life in an abstract way.

What *was* life? The purpose? Its meaning?

Ambling through shallow puddles left on the sidewalk by the lazy, uncommitted rain, I wondered if I'd finally come to a conclusion.

In my three decades of life, maybe I hadn't had enough time to discover the correct conclusion about life. Maybe no one was ever afforded enough time for such a thing. It was possible that one could live to be the oldest human alive and still draw the wrong conclusion about life. However, it was possible that I had figured out life in a way that made sense for me, and thus, came to a conclusion that was as good as I needed it to be.

The meaning of a person's life does not have to be correct. It doesn't have to make sense for everyone or align with what they feel is correct. It simply has to be true for the person who is living the life in question.

Stopping in the middle of the sidewalk, I held the bundle against my chest tightly, the plastic bag of cherries dangling from the fist in which it was clenched. I turned my face up to the sky, letting the mist tickle my cheeks and forehead, dampen my eyebrows and hair. I had nowhere important to be, so a little mist would hurt nothing.

Many people think—and I had been told—that death gave life meaning. Without death, life means nothing.

I don't feel that is true. Death is merely a stopwatch. A timer. The endpoint where a person's possibilities run out. If you haven't found your meaning by that point, well…you're shit out of luck, I suppose. Yet, it's not death that provides meaning at the end of a life. It's everything that happened before that moment. Death was simply the stopping point so that those events could be considered as a whole.

Here is the entirety of your life.

Let's figure out its worth. If it has any.

In that way, I suppose purpose and meaning cannot be calculated without death, but death is not what provides either.

It's possible that there is something after life, something greater. And we can discover our purpose and meaning there.

I've come to love possibility, but I'm a bit petulant. I'm impatient.

An afterlife is not something I can wait for when I'm uncertain if it even exists. And, if I'm honest, even if I knew for certain that there was an afterlife I simply have to wait for, that would not solve my impatience. I'm not alive so that I can wait.

To wait is not a purpose in which I'm interested.

People seem to think that the opposite of life is death. If you're not alive, you are dead. So, they must be the antithesis of each other. That's not true either. They are the starting and stopping points on a timeline that is not linear, even if that is how human perception works. If you believe in an afterlife, they are not even the beginning and end points. They're simply points. They become wholly insignificant, especially in the search for purpose and meaning.

So, I suppose, to figure out what gives life meaning, if it's not death, one has a conundrum. Certainly, death cancels out life. At the end, death is the stopping point for all life as we know it. A person can no longer add to the history of their life when death comes. That's it. Death is final. Maybe. No one knows until that moment comes.

So, what cancels out death?

If life and death are not opposites, surely at least one of them has an opposite.

What is the opposite of death?

What is a life without possibility? And how does a person find possibility?

Creation.

We create. The things a person creates, what they bring forth into the world, the things that will remain after they are gone, when death comes, are what give life meaning. It's what gives humans purpose—the things they create.

It could be art. Machinery. Technology. The discovery of fire. A working postal system. A well dug for a village to grow crops and nourish its people for generations to come. A needed kindness. A teacher explaining why two-plus-two equals four to a child. Having a child.

These things live on, in some way, when a life ends. They are there to contribute to humanity. To life. Their creation gave meaning and purpose to another and created possibility for numerous others. Some creations—such as the discovery of fire—haven't only given meaning and purpose and created possibility—they changed the course of human history.

So…creation is the opposite of death. With creation, death is never truly final. Even if there is no afterlife and at the end of our days our vision simply goes black and we cease to perceive the world ever again—we're simply a shell in the ground or ashes in an urn—we still exist.

Because we created. We raged against death and insignificance. And won.

A victory that can never be taken away until everything ceases to exist.

The only thing left in the whole wide world to decide, if one accepts this proposition, is what to create.

The possibilities are infinite.

Something, once created, can alter a life forever.

Meanings and purpose can change as one creates. If a person is exceptionally prolific with their creating, their life purpose and meaning may change dozens of times throughout their life.

The happiest people learn to go along with those changes. Lean into them. And keep creating. Keep living. Keep believing in possibility.

The Warmth of Our Closest Star

Finding myself standing on the sidewalk at the edge of the street in front of the two-story Craftsman-style home, I hugged my bundle to my chest. Pulled my arms tightly around it to protect it from the mist that was still sputtering lazily from the sky. Minneapolis loved its gloom—and it had grown on me over the years. Gloomy doesn't have to be bad.

It gives the sunny, warm days meaning. And the warmth of our closest star gives the gloominess meaning, too. Though, like life and death, they are not opposites. Opposites are rare.

Smiling, I strolled up the walkway towards the house.

Part Four

Here You Come Again

Why'd You Come in Here Lookin' Like That?

"Are…are you drunk?"

Pounding at my front door in the late evening hours was something to which I was unaccustomed—especially in America. Maybe it wouldn't have seemed so odd at my apartment in Montreal since I hadn't lived in the best of neighborhoods. But The Regal Building, my beautiful high-rise apartment, didn't have many troublemakers. Most of the people who lived there were middle-aged or had families. Peace and quiet was the unspoken rule, and those going against it were socially shunned. At least for a few days. Until amends were made.

So far, I'd managed to avoid upsetting my neighbors with the sounds from my television or music. None of the friends I had invited over on Friday evenings after work were disrespectful to my home or the building's residents. I always made sure to let my front door shut gently and I never slammed things in my apartment. Not that I was prone to such behaviors—aside from occasionally kicking a knife across the kitchen out of frustration. One evening, early in autumn, it looked as though my neighbors' belief that I was boring would change.

"You are drunk," I said. "Jésus Christ."

"Oh," Peter clutched the doorframe with one hand as his feet struggled to keep him upright, "so now we're just taking the lord's name in vain all willy nilly?"

He actually hiccupped. His feet did a little dance and it seemed as though Peter would tip over right there at my threshold. Somehow, his feet managed to find purchase, and his hand gripping the doorframe kept him upright.

"You'll go to hell for that, you know," he said, laughing.

After I had walked out of our home, Peter had texted me dozens of times a day. At least for the first few months. He never stopped completely, though. He started texting five or six times a day. Then he was texting when he woke up in the morning and before he went to bed each night. He had been following that routine for months, obviously still upset, but trying to give me space. I had appreciated it.

I still had not figured out everything in my head, so giving me time to do that had been kind of him.

Showing up drunk on my doorstep when it was nearly bedtime was something I did not appreciate. He hadn't even texted or called first to indicate he had such a dumb idea in mind. It also occurred to me that I had never seen Peter drunk. Not *really* drunk. As he was as he stood there and held onto the doorframe like it was his only lifeline.

Sighing, I leaned against the door and said, "What are you doing here, Peter?"

"I am here…to bring you home," he said resolutely, his mouth setting sternly.

"Is that so?" I asked. "You didn't drive, did you?"

"I took an Uber. Because I am drunk. Not dumb."

He wobbled precariously.

Peter's attempt at pronouncing "Uber" while drunk was admirable but hilarious. Well, it would have been if he hadn't been causing a scene.

"You should not have gotten out in your condition, Peter," I said. "You could have gotten hurt. Or hurt someone else."

"Aw," Peter pretended to swoon, nearly toppling over in the process, "Enzo cares if I'm hurt. My husband—*my husband*—still gives a shit. Did everyone hear that?"

I shushed him. "They will if you don't keep your voice down."

"I don't give a fu—"

Across the hall, I heard my neighbor unlocking their door. I grabbed a fist full of the front of Peter's shirt and pulled him into my apartment. Quickly, yet quietly, I shut the door. Fortunately, I had kept my grip on Peter's shirt, because when I turned to him after the door was securely shut, he was wobbling on his feet, trying to find his balance.

I waited until I was sure he wouldn't topple over, then let go of his shirt.

Peter snatched my hand into both of his before I could pull it away.

"My husband cares about me!" he said sarcastically, batting his eyes at me. "Who would have thought such a thing?"

He held my hand in his as though it was precious, staring into my eyes like a baby deer.

"Don't be a jackass," I said.

Snorting, he gripped my hand tighter, as though afraid I would yank it away.

"That's the pot calling the kettle black," he said. "At least you knew where I was."

"You knew where I was," I said gruffly. "I've told you in our texts."

"You've parceled out information like you were protecting government secrets," Peter spat. "Well, I'm sick of it. I'm here to bring you home."

I yanked my hand out of his grasp.

"I'm not going anywhere with you," I said. "You're drunk, Peter. You shouldn't have gone anywhere in your condition."

"I know!" He groaned dramatically and leaned toward me. "I could've gotten hurt. So tragic. You'd have no marriage to neglect. No husband to torture. Poor Enzo. Whatever would you have done then?"

I waved a hand between our faces. "What have you been drinking, Peter? Gasoline?"

"Whiskey."

He burped.

It didn't help the smell.

"I'm not going anywhere with you," I repeated. "I can't think of anything less safe right now."

Peter opened his mouth, as if to argue, or say something sarcastic, but then he stopped, his eyes darting around. It had dawned on him that he was inside my apartment for the first time. Since I had walked out of our shared home with little more than a suitcase, we hadn't seen each other in person. We'd barely had a single conversation that was more than a few sentences. We certainly hadn't stepped inside each other's homes.

Peter gave a low whistle as he spun slowly in place, unsteady on his feet. The compulsion to reach out and steady him rose in my gut, but I ignored it. Touching him more than necessary would only send the wrong message. *Though I didn't know what the wrong message was, actually.*

"Look at you," Peter said. "You're moving up in the world. *Husband.*"

Peter was facing away, staring at the wall of windows that looked out over Minneapolis and the night skyline. It was impressive and beautiful. Even I couldn't argue that. But my apartment, for its size and trappings, was relatively humble, all things considered. It was nothing like Peter's home.

"It's just an apartment," I said. "The view is nice."

"I should say so," Peter said, stumbling towards the windows.

Tripping over his feet, Peter seemed as though he would tumble across the living and fall through the glass. His body would plummet to the street below. Scared out of my mind, I raced forward and grabbed a handful of the back of his shirt, walking with him as he made his way to the windows. He didn't even notice that I was holding onto him. That's how drunk he was.

"I bet you could see the house from here," Peter whistled again as he stood a foot away from the windows. "*Our house.*"

I said nothing.

"You know," Peter asked, "our home where we live together and we're husbands and you didn't walk out without saying a word or giving me any idea what the fuck was wrong? That place?"

Sighing, I said, "What are you doing here, Peter? Really?"

He spun around, ripping his shirt from my grip, and faced me.

"I'm here to bring you home."

"You know I'm not leaving here with you," I slowly shook my head. "You knew that before you got here. *You're drunk, not dumb.* You've never been dumb. So, what are you doing here?"

Peter's bottom lip jutted out, and for a moment, I thought he might start crying. As quickly as his eyes turned sad, they turned angry.

"I'm taking you home, Enzo," he said. "This has all been—whatever you needed it to be—but it's time for you to come home."

"I am home."

"This is not your home."

"It is."

"It isn't. *Stop fucking saying that.*"

"You shouldn't have come here. Especially in your condition."

"Then tell me to leave," he shrugged, his body swaying.

I stared at him. Could I tell Peter to leave? Even if he wasn't drunk and a danger to himself?

"Tell me to leave, Enzo," Peter said, drawing out the last syllable of my name. "Tell me to leave."

The ice machine in the freezer clicked, dumping fresh ice into the tray waiting for the cubes. Someone was walking down the hallway, coughing as they made their way to their apartment. Lights from all of the buildings in Minneapolis twinkled in the sky beyond the windows. And I had no idea what I wanted to say to Peter. I didn't want to tell him to leave, though I had no idea why.

I wasn't mad at Peter. I'd never truly been mad at Peter.

Things had gotten complicated. At least in my head, they were complicated. And I hadn't had the tools to figure things out for myself. Especially when my brain was doing all it could to keep me going day after day, fighting against medication that fought against its efforts. As I stood there, staring at Peter, I realized that I still had no idea what had happened between us, or why I had felt that simply walking out was the best course of action.

I had no idea how to fix that, either.

"Peter—"

"I'm not leaving."

I hadn't been about to ask him to leave, but his statement made heat crawl up my neck.

"You'd leave if I told you to."

Peter started to speak but stopped himself. It was as if he was going to argue, but even in his drunken state, the real Peter was still there, somewhere in his brain.

"I would," he said, finally. "But I'd call you an asshole first."

I squinted at him, half-angry, half knowing I'd deserved it. Kind of.

"You're an asshole, Enzo," he said, then lazily jabbed a finger in my direction. "That's what you are. Asshole."

"And you're perfect?" I snapped before I knew I would say anything.

"Hell no," he barked. "But I haven't been giving you the silent treatment, have I?"

"Maybe you weren't quiet," I bellowed, not caring if any neighbors heard, "but you weren't talking to me!"

Peter's head cocked to the side.

"Who talks about anything important with the window dressing, Peter?" I asked, stepping up to him. *Give it time, Enzo. You'll figure things out. Who cares if you have a job*

now? You will one day! We'll get through this. Don't worry!
You had a lot to say, Peter. But you didn't give a shit what I
thought most of the time."

"That's not fair," he said.

"Is it not?" I asked. "How long after I got off the plane
was it before you stopped asking for my help in making
decisions? Before you stopped asking how I felt? Or what I
needed out of our marriage?"

"That is not—"

"You have a job." I stopped him. "A great job. You had
a husband. A house."

"*We* had—*have*—a house."

"Your life was great. So, it never occurred to you that
maybe...*maybe*...I was struggling."

Peter stared at me.

"I was struggling every day and all I got from you was
'wait' and 'it will work out' and 'don't worry' and shit that
didn't take my feelings into consideration, Peter. Maybe I
wasn't talking—but you weren't asking, either."

"That is so unfair, Enzo," Peter was obviously still
drunk, but he seemed a bit soberer. "You're a goddamn
adult. If something is wrong, I expect that you'll tell me. Not
just shut me out and not say a word. Not expect me to read
your mind. Give me a goddamn clue."

"You'll go to hell for that," I snapped.

"You are so fucking insufferable," he growled.

I shrugged.

"Get your things," he said, reaching for my arm. "We're
going home."

Snatching my arm away, I stepped back.

"This—*all of this*—is my *things*, Peter," I said. "All of this shit. It's mine. My life isn't so small anymore that I can throw some clothes and a toothbrush in a bag and move. I've made a life here. This couch? That's mine. That television? It's mine. The pots, pans, bed, desk—*the goddamn half-empty bottle of soy sauce in the refrigerator*—is all mine. So, I can't just *grab my things* and follow your orders, can I?"

"Where is this anger coming from?" Peter asked. "It's like you hate me."

"*I don't hate you, Peter,*" I snapped.

"I've put up with this shit—whatever it is you're going through, not talking to me, not answering texts, refusing to have a discussion—for far too long, Enzo," he said, stumbling slightly. "And I'm done with it. You're coming home."

"I'm not going to do shit," I tilted my head back and forth sassily with each word.

Peter, his face starting to turn red, stepped up, as if to argue, then he stopped. He took a breath, turned his head to the side, and grinned. Turning further so that I couldn't see his face, I could tell he was doing his best to hide his widening smile. Licking my lips, I did my best not to smile along with him. Our argument had turned ridiculous. Honestly, I wasn't even certain what we were arguing about.

Of course, there was the dispute about whether or not I'd leave right then to go back home with Peter. That was obviously something that was causing friction. However, I had no idea why Peter had decided on that night—after so long—to give up on waiting for me to make the first move. Why he had decided that night that he was done giving me my space? I didn't know why that night was the night he decided we should have it out.

"*I'm not going to do shit,*" Peter mumbled.

He chuckled. I licked my teeth again, willing myself to stay steely-faced.

"You've changed, Enzo," he said.

"So what?" I snarled. "I can't be perfect for you, so—"

He sighed. "I didn't mean it as an insult. I didn't mean it was bad."

Peter and I found ourselves standing there, an arm's length away from each other, simply staring into each other's eyes. What did we really have to say? There was plenty. But where did we start? After so long apart, not communicating, how did we begin again? Did we both want to begin again? There was so much, how did we do that?

In my heart of hearts, I realized that even before Peter showed up on my doorstep, I would eventually want to talk things out with Peter. I knew our story wasn't over. One day, I would figure myself out—the storm I'd created in my head—and talk to him about it. Help him understand so that he would understand what I needed. After so long, how to do that had gotten hazier. With Peter standing before me, I was even fuzzier.

All I could focus on was the fact that we were in the same room after such a long time.

I'd missed him. Somewhere along the way, I'd convinced myself to believe otherwise. However, if you think you don't miss someone, but the moment you see them again your heart starts to ache, you're simply full of shit.

"You seem more confident," he swayed on his feet. "You're…not meek."

"I've never been meek," I said gently so he would know I wasn't starting another argument. "I've been terrified."

"There is a difference," he said, his head nodding once.

Slumping, I held my hands out as if offering something to Peter.

"What do you want, Peter?" I asked. "Why did you come here tonight?"

"I told you," he said. "I want you to come home."

"Why tonight?" I asked again. "We haven't talked in…a long time."

"I'm done with that shit, too," he said, but he wasn't trying to be crass. "Talk to me, goddamnit. Stop treating me like I'm the enemy when I don't even know what I did."

There is at least one moment in everyone's life where they are presented with an opportunity to swallow their pride and own up to their own bullshit. Or they can double down. The second choice always leads to trouble…but it's the easiest. Of course, I'd never taken the easy option regardless of what strife it might cause.

"I don't know what to say," I said, looking away. "Actually, I know a lot of things to say but I can't put them into words."

"Well, say something," Peter grumbled. "Say one goddamn thing that matters for once. Don't just—"

"I hated myself for being alive," I said. "Because my family wasn't. Specifically, I hated myself for having a good life. With you."

Peter said nothing, so I shrugged.

"That's something, Peter," I said. "I didn't know it then, but that was…that was something I was going through."

Peter visibly swallowed, and it took him a few tries to get out what he wanted to say.

"Weren't we happy, Enzo?" he asked. "Wasn't our marriage happy?"

"No," I said. "Well, you were happy. I wasn't. Not those last few months."

He closed his eyes.

"Is that my fault? Did I do that to you somehow? Was it our marriage?"

"No," I said. "I haven't allowed myself to be happy. For a long time, Peter. You ignoring my needs and, I don't know, uh, brushing off my concerns, didn't help. But, no. It wasn't your fault. But I am glad that you were happy."

When Peter's eyes opened, a tear leaked from his right eye.

"I'd never been happier in my life," he said angrily, though his voice didn't match the heat of his words. "And I haven't been happy since."

"I'm sorry."

Peter rolled his eyes, but I knew he wasn't mocking me. He was frustrated, and I couldn't blame him. I was frustrated with myself, too. Somewhere, deep inside of me, I knew that the majority of the blame was to be put on my shoulders. Peter was imperfect, but he was collateral damage in the tornado I'd created in my head to try and understand my life.

Motioning at the couch, he wobbled slightly. I nodded, so Peter sat down on the sofa with a grunt. His elbows went to his knees and his head went to his hands. He sat there, holding his head, covering his eyes with the palms of his hands, saying nothing. So, I shuffled over cautiously and eased myself down to sit on the sofa a few feet away from him. I didn't know what else to say—not that night—so I let him have silence.

Finally, Peter sniffed heavily and drew in a ragged breath. When he lifted his head from his hands, his eyes were red. He looked around, as though suddenly aware of where he was, then his head turned so he could look at me.

"I like your sofa," he said. "Good choice."

"Thank you," I said. "It's new but it was—"

Peter waited.

"—on sale," I smiled and looked away.

He chuckled softly. "My little money-conscious guy."

I smiled. "You smell like a bar, Peter."

"I'm sorry," he sighed. "I shouldn't have come over here. I guess. I mean, I'm glad I came over here. I'm done with all of this, Enzo."

"Meaning?"

"I want you to come home," he reiterated. "I'm done with the no talking or seeing each other. I'm tired of being patient and understanding. *You're my husband.*"

"I'm not coming home with you," I said.

"Ever?" He croaked. "Is this it, then?"

I took a breath. I knew the answer, but saying it out loud would open a line of questions from Peter that I wasn't prepared to answer. Additionally, it would be admitting that my leaving—my staying gone and not talking to him—had been a selfish, immature act.

"Tonight. I'm not going anywhere with you tonight."

Peter didn't speak for several moments. When he did, his voice was measured. Less desperate. Hopeful.

"Okay. I can live with that. I guess I have to."

"I'm sorry."

"I should leave," Peter said softly.

Rolling my eyes, I rose from the sofa.

"I'll get you a pillow and a blanket," I said. "You'll hurt yourself if you try to go home, Peter."

"I'm perfectly fine to—"

"Take your coat and shoes off," I said, ignoring him as I walked towards the hallway. "I don't want your dirty shoes on my sofa. And you won't sleep well with your coat on."

Peter didn't make any sound as I walked down the hallway to my bedroom and got a warm blanket and an extra pillow from the closet. When I got back to the living room, cradling his bedding in my arms, he had managed to remove his shoes. He had kicked them off haphazardly so that they were laying on their sides, a few feet away from him. He looked exhausted—and drunk—as though the small act of taking off his shoes had taken the last bit of his energy.

I set the blanket and pillow on the end of the sofa and sat down next to Peter. He didn't resist me as I slowly slid his jacket off and tossed it onto the easy chair. Peter simply stared into my eyes, watching me as I helped him. Finally, I rose from the sofa and grabbed the pillow. I gestured for Peter to lay down as I slipped the pillow under his head, with him still staring at me. Then I shook the blanket out and laid it atop him, making sure he was covered well. Even though I ran the heat at a reasonable temperature, my apartment could get cold at night.

As my hands brought the blanket down, making sure it was tucked under his chin, Peter snaked a hand out from under it and grabbed my wrist. I froze, wondering if he was going to do something regrettable, something that would start another fight. Instead, he stared up into my eyes as I stayed there, frozen and bent over him. When his other arm snuck out from under the blanket and went out to cup the back of my neck, I didn't resist.

Peter brought my face down to his. When his lips pressed against mine, I returned the kiss. Because I did miss Peter's kisses. I wasn't prepared to do more than that, but I desperately wanted the kiss he obviously desired. When we separated, Peter held my face close to his for a moment, staring into my eyes.

"*I love you*," he whispered. "*I won't stop loving you.*"

I cleared my throat. I knew that if I spoke immediately, I would sound gruff. Throaty. Too warm.

"You taste like whiskey," I said softly, pulling away gently.

Peter groaned and let go of my head, his arms falling to either side of him on the sofa. He was so annoyed. I didn't blame him. I rose from my bent position and headed back to the hallway, intending to go to my room. To put space between Peter and me. When I laid my hand on the light switch, I looked over my shoulder at my husband on the sofa, drunk and annoyed. It didn't make me feel differently about it, seeing him in that state. Drunk. Annoyed with me.

"I love you, too, Peter," I said.

Then I flipped the lights off, leaving the room to the soft glow of the lights of Minneapolis beyond the windows. And I went to bed.

God Had Butterfingers

Peter was still asleep the following morning, curled up in a tight ball on his side with the blanket wrapped around him. Tiptoeing into the kitchen, I somehow managed to make a pot of coffee without waking him. The sound of the beans grinding didn't even rouse him. Of course, he had shown up on my doorstep drunk, demanding I come home with him, and unreasonable for a good part of his visit. I shouldn't have cared if I woke him from his drunken slumber. For some reason, I did.

I knew that reason. Anyone with half a brain would have known the reason. It wasn't something I wanted to think about so early in the morning.

With a fresh cup of coffee to start my Saturday, along with a plate containing a bagel I had toasted and spread liberally with cream cheese, I slunk back down the hallway towards my room. Taking up the seat at my desk, I pulled out the notebook in which I'd last written and flipped to my last stopping point.

I sipped my coffee and ate the bagel slowly as I read over the pages I'd last written. I'd started in one notebook a month before, and I was already halfway through another. With no idea what I was writing, where it would lead, or what the point was, I'd written a lot of words. It was as I'd done when I was a teenager with so many things going on in my head that I had to get them out of me somehow. Sipping my coffee, eating my breakfast, and reading what I'd last written took me back to that time.

Except now, my life was peaceful. Quiet. My days were not filled with xenophobia or homophobia or illness, sickness, and death. I wasn't worried about where my next meal would be coming from. There was chicken thawing in the refrigerator for a lazy Saturday lunch. Later, I planned to go to La Croûte and pick out something for dessert after dinner. Maybe something to nibble on while I watched a movie before bed. I'd be curled up with a warm blanket on my comfortable, yet reasonably priced, sofa, watching a movie on my television that I hadn't bought from a neighbor who was moving.

I wasn't as unnerved as I'd once been, thinking about the mundane, easy tasks I planned to complete during my weekend. Finding that the sun had come out, and there was no storm on the horizon, didn't bother me. In fact, I was looking forward to lunch, dinner, dessert, and some silly movie while I ate a snack and lay on my sofa in my pajamas. Even on a Saturday night. It was a small life, but it was mine. Every decision was mine.

At what point in my life had I relied on trauma to feel alive?

I thought that over as I picked up my pen, set down my coffee mug, and began to write again. Though it would be impossible to pinpoint such a thing, it was obvious that at some point in my past, I had needed trauma every day to feel as though I was alive. It had become as though life didn't feel real if I wasn't constantly struggling against or for something. Alex had told me that I had missed the storm so I created a hurricane. He had been right. As he always was.

Well, almost always.

As a young teen, I had experienced the death of one of the most important people in my life. My grandmother. Then I lost my father. My sister. My mother. And, finally, my brother. All within the first two decades of my life. The storms were my only constant—the trauma and grief. They were the only things on which I could rely.

How does one not become accustomed—even fond—of it?

Trauma demands that a person sink or swim. There is no other option. If you are forced to swim for long enough, if you ever stop paddling, kicking your legs, and flailing your arms, it feels as though you are sinking.

During the first few years in America, I'd felt as though I was sinking.

It wasn't my fault, but it was my responsibility. It had been up to me to seek out help in dealing with what I was going through. Instead, I created another storm. Some of the damage done by that storm was sleeping on my sofa. The sofa I'd bought with my own money from an actual store that was one of the building blocks of my small life.

It is my belief that if you ask anyone when they are young—a teenager, maybe—what they want to do with their life, you will get big answers. They want fame, fortune, adventure, fast cars, exotic foods, and for everyone to envy the life they lead. I had never been like that. Trauma had made me suspicious of a small life. Made me afraid of peace. Of simple things.

I'd never feared leading a small life. A modest home. A sofa. A husband. Lazy weekend dinners followed by walks to the bakery. I didn't need my name in flashing lights or more money than I could possibly spend in my lifetime. I wanted happiness. Peace. Quiet. Love.

If a part of my life ended up being bigger than I had imagined, that would be fine. But it was unneeded for me to feel fulfilled.

I hated myself for letting trauma turn me from the things—the small life—that would have made me the happiest. I hated myself for fearing happiness when it was what I desperately wanted more than anything else in the world.

"You work at home now?" Peter's voice startled me.

Spinning in my chair, I found him standing in my bedroom doorway. His hair was sticking up in a million different directions, his clothes were rumpled, and though he had slept well, he didn't look well-rested. I couldn't help but grin at his appearance.

"Hard night?" I asked, reaching for my coffee mug.

He chuckled and reached up to scratch his head. Finding his hair sticking up, he began to pat it down, finally giving up when it was obvious it had a mind of its own after a night on the sofa.

"You could say that," he said, finally.

"There's a pot of coffee," I said. "I made it fresh."

"I could use a cup."

"Help yourself. The mugs are in the cabinet next to the refrigerator."

"Okay," he said, then stared at me.

I simply returned his gaze and sipped my coffee.

"You work at home now?" he asked again.

"Oh. Yes."

"You work on Saturdays?"

"No," I said. "I was just writing. I've...I've been writing. To understand the things in my head."

The smallest of smiles played at the corner of his mouth. "Like when you were a kid."

Peter never failed to amaze me with how he could remember the smallest details of my life that I had maybe mentioned to him once in a casual conversation.

"Yes."

"What are you writing?"

"I don't actually know," I said. "Probably nonsense."

"Is...is it helping?"

"I think so, yes."

Peter nodded slowly, looking around the room. Fortunately, I had made my bed upon waking so that everything seemed put together. I always made my bed each day, but sometimes I waited until after breakfast. I was glad that Peter had not seen one of those days.

"Look," Peter said, "Enzo—"

He stopped and motioned at the side of the bed. I gave him a nod as I sipped my coffee, so he shuffled over in his socked feet and sat down gently on the side nearest my desk. A mere few feet apart, we were able to look at each other as we talked. Somehow, even after everything, it didn't feel uncomfortable having him on my bed, sitting so close to me.

"I'm sorry that I was a jackass last night," he said. "That wasn't what I meant to do."

"Forgiven," I said.

There was really nothing to forgive, because Peter had not done anything unforgivable, so I said what he needed to hear from me.

"Good," he said. "But I do want you to come home. That's why I came here. I'm just sorry I did it while drunk and upset."

"I am home, Peter."

Sighing, he rubbed his hands on his knees.

"You're going to be impossible, aren't you?" he asked gruffly.

"I'm not trying to be," I said. "But…being alone…it has shown me that before I can be part of *us*, I need to be Enzo. For a while. So I can know who Enzo really is. I've hardly ever had the chance to just be Enzo. At least, not when life was good."

Peter's bottom lip quivered.

"Are you going to divorce me?"

I had to keep myself from looking shocked. Of course, acting shocked would have been incredibly insensitive of me. Peter's assumption that I was considering divorcing him was reasonable. After my decisions and actions, who wouldn't come to that conclusion? I suddenly hated myself even more for doing that to Peter—especially since it had never occurred to me that might be a side effect of what I'd done.

"Wouldn't I have done that by now?" I asked evenly.

"That's not a 'no.'" Peter was gripping his knees tightly, as though trying to comfort himself.

"No. I have no plan to divorce you, Peter," I said.

"But you won't come home?"

Sighing, I realized it was a terrible time to repeat my 'I am home' mantra.

"I want to be here," I said. "For now."

"But I'm not the problem? Our marriage isn't the problem?"

Mumbling, I said, "I'm waiting for the storm to pass."

"Huh?"

"I'm waiting for the storm to pass, Peter," I said. "I'm the biggest problem."

Peter reached out tentatively, so I offered the hand that wasn't holding my coffee.

"Why can't I weather it with you?" he asked.

"It's not your storm, Peter."

"We're supposed to be a team. Your storms are supposed to be my storms."

"Please," I whispered. "This is what I need. I need you to not hate me for that. Please don't hate me."

"It's impossible to hate you, Enzo," he said, shaking his head, his hand gripping mine. "I know I said before I was starting to hate you, but I never could. I couldn't even *force* myself. I guess…I don't understand…but I'll support you. If that's what you need."

"Thank you."

Peter sighed, grumbled something under his breath, then smiled. I didn't ask him what he had been grumbling about. If he was going to have more patience with me, I would let him grumble. He gave my hand a squeeze and slid his from mine. My fingers immediately missed the warmth of his hand, so I brought my hand up to join the other holding my mug.

"Can I still have some of your coffee?" he asked. "I'll need it before I go home."

Chuckling, I started to stand. Peter attempted to stand at the same moment and we were brought face to face, our chests nearly touching. Being so close to Peter, so close I could feel his breath, after so long, I shouldn't have been as affected as I was. But my breath was caught in my throat and all I could do was stare into his eyes to keep from stuttering or saying something utterly stupid. Peter, like me, seemed to be forcing himself not to speak.

For the longest of moments, we stood there, face to face, so close barely a hand could fit between us, neither of us speaking. Neither of us moved. I realized that if we were to break the spell we were suddenly under, one of us would have to speak.

"Peter—"

Then his hands were in my hair, his fingers twisting through it, and he was pulling my mouth down to his. I did nothing to stop him. My arms went around him, pulling him into me violently as our mouths met; we immediately started to devour each other. Pulling Peter into me as though trying to crush our bodies together, I realized how much I'd missed his body. There was no one in the universe who could make such feelings well up inside me, demanding to be released.

The night before, when Peter was drunk and vulnerable—and I was annoyed—it had been easier to ignore my feelings while having him in close proximity. Now that he was sober and I wasn't annoyed, it was impossible.

Was that another reason I'd left?

I knew I couldn't ignore those feelings for much longer and I needed to in order to figure out what was going on inside my head?

I pushed that thought aside; other thoughts demanded my attention.

Peter's hands were firm, maybe even rough—our mouths against each other felt violent but in an utterly arousing, desperate way. My hands dug into his sides as I fed at his mouth, frantically kissing him, overwhelmed at having his body against mine after so long. Racing with thoughts, my mind tried to explain to me why I had deprived myself— and my husband—of this for so long. Why I had been so stupid. So petty. *And for what?*

When Peter's hands went to the waist of my pajama pants, he paused, nearly breaking our kiss, as though concerned he had gone too far. When my hands shot to the button on his pants, he urgently continued his actions. Peter's hands worked to unfasten my pants as mine did the same to his. Moments, later, our pants and underwear shoved to our ankles, we fell onto the bed together.

Sex with Peter—though never less than incredible— always seemed to fly by. It wasn't that it was quick—unless we wanted it to be—it could simply never last long enough, no matter how long it lasted. So, when our orgasms had subsided, and I was still on top of him, his legs locked around me, and my hand was still gripping him between us, I felt empty. Not emotionally empty, but as though once with Peter was never enough.

It was never enough.

Shuddering as I let go of him and extracted my arm from between us, Peter twined his fingers in my hair again, pulling me down to kiss him once more. Panting and shivering, the two of us kissed for what seemed like forever. Finally, I knew that I had to slide off of and out of Peter, though it was difficult to convince myself. I pulled back enough so that we were no longer connected, but our eyes stayed locked.

Peter, breathing heavy, his fingers still twisted in my hair as I gazed down at him, said one word. My name.

So, I had to kiss him again.

And again.

Finally, once we had settled down and were sitting on the edge of the bed together, our pants in a heap on the floor, I looked over at him.

"I miss that."

"But you won't come home?"

"You said I could have time," I whispered.

Peter frowned, then nodded, and forced a small smile to his lips.

"Okay," he said. "Okay."

He was convincing himself to be patient.

"I'm going to take my coffee to go," he said. "I...that's best, right?"

"Okay."

Peter nodded and stood, then bent and pulled his pants up, zipping and buttoning them as he looked down at me.

"Can I bring the mug back tomorrow morning?" he asked. "Would that be okay?"

Peter was asking if he could visit again. Who gives a shit about a coffee mug?

I inhaled softly, calming myself. "Okay."

The next morning, I had barely finished making my breakfast when the knock came at my door. Looking down at the meal I'd prepared, I realized I had made enough for two people. It had been a subconscious thing, making two portions. I'd told myself I would not be excited for Peter to return so that he could give back my coffee mug. My brain had told that idea to go fuck itself and led me to make enough food to share with Peter. I didn't know if he'd even be hungry, but if he was, I wanted something to offer.

I wanted to share my breakfast with him.

Opening the front door to find him standing there shouldn't have been an event that made me nervous, giddy in a way that I had to force myself to hide my excitement. But it did. I wanted to hate myself for it, but why shouldn't I be excited to see my husband? The fact that a smile immediately bloomed on Peter's face made it easy to not hate myself. I wasn't the only person who was happy to see the person on the other side of the door.

"I brought your mug back," Peter said, holding it out, cupped in the palm of his hand.

Wordlessly, I held the door wide, and crooked my head, inviting him inside. Peter entered my apartment and I closed the door gently behind us before taking the mug from his hand. I made sure that my fingers played along his as the mug slid from his hand to mine. Peter noticed, gazing into my eyes as my skin brushed along his. His hand was cold from having just been outside, and I was compelled to take his hands in mine to warm them.

Maybe let him put them in places that would warm them quickly.

Instead, I stepped away, carrying the mug over to the kitchen. Peter followed silently and watched as I opened the dishwasher and put the mug in the top rack before closing it again. When I looked up at him, he was shaking his head with a grin.

"I washed it."

"I've seen you wash dishes," I said.

Peter chuckled. "I'm not that bad. I was never that bad."

I grinned at him.

"Fine," he said. "I'm not as good at kitchen duties as you."

"Thank you," I teased.

It was then that I noticed what he was wearing. Peter had put on one of his suits and had his beautiful navy coat that he'd bought in Montreal years before on over it.

"You look overdressed," I said. "To return a coffee mug, I mean."

Peter looked me up and down, taking in my bare feet, my loose jeans barely hanging onto my hips, and the silly vintage t-shirt I'd bought at a thrift store that I'd thrown on after my shower.

"You look underdressed," he replied. "To have a coffee mug returned."

I glowered at him, but it was playful. Peter chuckled.

"I thought," he said, looking around nervously, "that I'd go to church with you today."

"Oh."

"Yeah," he said with a small shrug. "I never really went with you before. When you'd go. So, I thought maybe today…it's Sunday. Yeah."

My hands found my pockets and I sighed.

"I quit going to church," I said. "Earlier this year."

"You quit going to church," he parroted, his face blank.

"I haven't been in months," I said. "I...guess I fell from grace."

I tried a joke, though it wasn't my best.

"God didn't catch you?" Peter asked.

"Butterfingers," I said with a small shrug.

Peter snorted, amused, but he looked concerned.

"It's not God," I said. "It's just the church."

He nodded along slowly before quietly responding. "It meant so much to you, Enzo."

Shaking my head softly, I tried to figure out the words to explain myself.

"What it represented meant so much to me," I said. "But I can honor those things without the church."

"Okay," he said simply. "Okay."

We stood there for a moment, not really looking at each other, but not necessarily avoiding looking at each other. I felt, momentarily, that I had somehow disappointed Peter. He should not have had any say so in my religious or spiritual path—especially one in which he was never involved—but I found I still cared what he thought. Of course, I wanted to be sure that he knew his opinions about that would not change my mind. I didn't have to ask, though.

"I'm proud of you, Enzo," he said.

"What?"

"For having the courage to make that decision," he said. "It must have been difficult."

I shrugged. "A bit."

He smiled again. "A bit, huh?"

Chuckling, I said, "It seems so...nothing now."

"Okay," he said, shaking his thoughts away. "I'm glad it worked out well for you. But I got gussied up for nothing."

I laughed at his choice of words. "Not for nothing. You…you look very handsome. I made breakfast. I made enough for you, too."

"What did you make?"

I gave him a look that let him know that I knew he was not nearly as picky as he tried to pretend to be at times. He grinned.

"A frittata. I have buttered toast."

"Sounds good," Peter said and slipped his coat and suit jacket off before laying them across the arm of the sofa. "Coffee?"

"Of course."

"Well," he said, "let's eat. You probably need to take your medication anyway, right?"

I didn't respond as I set about getting two plates from the cabinet.

"They haven't made you try anything new, have they?" he asked as he sat down at the small dining set I had in the corner of the kitchen. A round table, two chairs, no more than I needed. "No more experiments with your health?"

He chuckled as I set about cutting into the frittata so that I could put a piece on each plate.

"I don't take it anymore," I said.

Peter frowned at me.

"That's not more dangerous?" he asked.

"It's nothing," I said.

"Okay. It's not my business, but that seems unwise is all. Your doctor was sure that was okay for you to do? You did ask before you stopped taking it, right?"

With a sigh, I stopped dealing with the breakfast and looked out at nothing. I wasn't upset with Peter or annoyed by his questions. I was mad at myself because I hadn't told Peter about my surgery in Chicago. About my new life. He was going to be upset with me. However, I knew that if I waited longer to tell him, he would be even more upset. And I wouldn't be able to blame him. Especially since it was all my fault for not keeping him informed about my life as I tried to figure it out.

I turned to Peter and he winced.

"Sorry," he said. "I know that's none of my—"

"A neurosurgeon in Chicago removed my tumor," I said simply. "And then a few weeks ago I finally was weaned off of the medication."

Peter stared at me blankly; he said nothing.

"Alex introduced me to a wonderful neurologist in Dallas—Dr. Carson. He referred me to Dr. Berger in Chicago. I…he removed it. I get scanned early next year to make sure it hasn't started growing back. But…yeah. It's gone."

Seconds ticked by as the two of us stared at each other. I was waiting for the explosion.

Peter finally answered, his voice a whisper, "You didn't tell me you were going to have surgery? *Brain surgery*?"

"I didn't—"

"What if you died, Enzo?" he asked, his voice the same dangerous whisper. "What if you died during the surgery and I didn't even know you were going to have surgery?"

"I'm sorry," I said. "I didn't think."

Peter stared at me for the longest time.

"I—" he stood. "I don't—"

I watched him as he stood by the table and stared at me in shock.

"I—"

Peter couldn't finish a sentence. He kept repeating the same word and staring at me as if he'd never seen me before.

"You what?" My voice was tentative.

Not responding, Peter marched over to the couch angrily and violently ripped his coat and suit jacket from the arm. Before I could say anything, he had marched out the front door, slamming it behind him. With a sigh—and the hope my neighbors wouldn't complain—I slumped against the counter, bracing myself with my hands. I'd barely had a second to think before the door swung open and Peter marched back in, his coat and jacket in his fist.

Peter closed the door—a little less violently, but not much—and glared at me.

"I'm so mad I don't even know what to say to you," he barked.

"I'm sorry," I repeated.

"I feel like I'm going to have a fucking stroke, Enzo," he glowered at me. "That's how pissed I am right now."

All I could do was repeat my apology mantra, so I did. Peter glared at me, then looked up at the ceiling as if praying.

"This is it," he said. "This is how I'm going to die. Stroking out because you pissed me off so much that my head exploded."

Telling Peter to calm down or insisting that he do anything at that moment was a bad idea, so I didn't suggest he do anything in particular. Instead, I stayed quiet, making sure that I looked as sorry as I felt. Desperately, I wanted to explain to Peter that I hadn't intentionally done anything to upset him—that I was simply too consumed with my own feelings to have considered his at the time—but I knew that wouldn't make things better.

It also occurred to me that, as mad as Peter obviously was, I never felt unsafe or in danger around Peter. Never once in the years I'd known him and then been married to him. In fact, his anger made me feel closer to him. Knowing that he could be so upset at the thought of losing me before he even knew there was a chance it might happen, further endeared me to him. Even at his angriest, Peter was never violent or irrational. If I ever had to fight with a partner—this was how I would want to fight. With words. His over-the-top anger was also humorous—his dramatic display—but I didn't allow myself so much as a smile.

"Why would you do that to me?" Peter barked. "I get that you needed time to yourself. Maybe I don't like it—or even understand it—but I can try to be patient. I will be patient. I want you to figure out what's going on in your head so that we can be the team we were supposed to be all along, Enzo. But how could you not tell me something so important?"

"I—"

"How?" he demanded.

"I'm trying to tell you," I said. "If you'll just—"

"I just—"

"Peter!" I yelled, not in anger, but to get his attention. I struggled to not chuckle. "I can't answer you if you keep interrupting me."

"Then tell me!"

"I don't know," I said, almost pleading with him. "That is the answer. I'm sorry. But I don't know. I have been so in my own head, trying to figure out why I am still dealing with…things from my past. It didn't occur to me how much it would matter to you. It was selfish. I hurt you. And I'm sorry."

"Well, that's fucking rude," Peter growled. "You're fucking rude, Enzo."

Then, he tossed his coat and jacket back on the arm of the couch, stomped over to the kitchen table, and sat down. Sighing, I once again ignored the breakfast and shuffled over to stand beside Peter. He didn't even acknowledge me next to him for several moments, so I simply stood there. However, when he finally stopped pretending that I wasn't standing beside him, he did so by spinning violently in his chair and wrapping his arms around my middle.

Peter buried his face in my stomach, and though he did his best to cover the sounds, I could tell he was crying. Startled, it took a moment for me to respond. Finally, I brought my hands up and ran my fingers through his hair, trying to comfort him as he held me tightly and cried against my stomach. I had to force myself to not immediately switch to hating myself for yet another thing I had done wrong. I didn't want to hate myself. But I wanted to take back what I'd done to hurt Peter. If I could have gone back and told him, I would've.

I'd been honest when I said I didn't know why I hadn't told him. Because it hadn't even been a thought. I'd simply been selfish and had only been thinking of myself and how I felt and what I needed and wanted at the time. I'd let myself forget that I had my own family now. A man—my husband—I loved deeply who cared if I lived or died.

I wouldn't hate myself. Atonement was required, however.

"I'm sorry I hurt you, Peter," I said.

Peter somehow mumbled "okay" over his tears.

"I left the church before I met the doctors and had my surgery," I said.

I knew Peter would understand what that meant. When his grip on me tightened, he confirmed that he did. It was quite a while before he stopped crying and released me from his arms, as though afraid to let me go.

Home Is Wherever I'm With You

Peter and I fell back into an easy routine with each other. As was typical of us before I had started dealing with the whispers of traumatic memories in my head. Of course, I had my apartment and he had our old house, but we saw each other every day. Still unsure of how to go home—and not knowing why—Peter would come to my apartment at the end of each work day.

Sometimes, I had finished work earlier than him, and I would be cooking dinner when he arrived. Other times, I would still be working when he showed up, and he would cook. Each evening we had dinner in my little kitchen. Sometimes we'd talk nonstop—serious topics, political news, gossip, or simply silly stories that made us laugh.

After dinner, we'd wash dishes together and then fall into the sofa to watch television, or use it as background noise while we, inevitably, kissed like teenagers. Many nights, we fell into my bed together, ripping and tearing at each other's clothes as though it was the first time every time. Our hands, fingers, and mouths explored each other every time as though discovering a new land—one we hadn't visited thousands of times before. And each time was as exciting as the last.

Some nights we would visit our favorite restaurants, though we took turns paying for once. Making sure Peter knew it was important to me that I paid as much for our dates as he did, I refused to let him pay every time. Peter's career had been longer than mine and had more time to develop and grow, so it was likely I would never match him in salary. But

I made plenty of money to support myself, have spending money, *and* take him out on dates every once in a while. He needed to know that. I needed confirmation that we were equals.

Peter didn't argue; so, he had obviously figured out one of the problems we had in our marriage. It endeared me to him further to know that he was willing to pay attention and see the things I needed to feel as though we were in an equal partnership. The nights out at restaurants also ended back at my apartment in bed.

Night after night, however, in an unspoken agreement, Peter would leave and go back home to sleep. Kissing at the door, telling each other "I love you," Peter showed he was willing to compromise. And it broke my heart each time.

I wanted whatever was going on in my head—the thing I was trying to figure out—to release me from its grip. Though I knew Peter would go along with our living arrangement as long as I needed, I was tired of seeing the sad look on his face each evening when he left. Something inside of me wouldn't let me be ready to return home.

Hating myself was no longer a choice. Every day I hated myself for not being able to figure out what was going on inside of my head and causing Peter more heartache. Of course, I knew that Peter hadn't been perfect, though he hadn't been horrible to me in any way. However, dismissing my concerns and making them seem less important than I felt they were was an issue—but it could be resolved. It was something we could figure out because it wasn't an egregious sin.

Even if it wasn't his intention, Peter had made me feel as though my sole worth was as his husband. I could cook and clean and do the errands and chores that needed doing each day while he was at work. When he came home to a clean house and dinner being made and a husband who loved sex as much as he did, he was happy. When my medication had to be changed and it nearly physically destroyed me—and I could no longer be a perfect husband—he made me feel...I didn't know how I had felt.

Like a failure?

Worthless?

As though he didn't love me the same amount?

That, if I couldn't be all of the things I'd been, I was of no use to him?

Or had it all been in my head?

It wasn't like Peter and I had sat down and discussed our feelings or what was going on in our lives. We had faced our first big enemy as a married couple, and we hadn't pulled together and worked to defeat it. Closing ourselves off from each other, treating our feelings as secrets we couldn't share, we had pushed each other away. Certainly, I had been worse, but Peter wasn't without his faults. But if we could discuss them, we could get past them.

If only I could understand what was anchoring me in place, making it impossible to continue on into the next chapter of my life.

I needed to put my past, my trauma, and my old family to rest. I could keep them in my heart, but I had a new family now.

I wanted to have my own family.

Figuring out how to make that happen was nearly impossible.

After weeks of our arrangement—dinners and snuggles and television programs and sex after work each night, with more of the same on the weekends—I could feel Peter growing tired of it. Not that I expected Peter to heave a great sigh one day and proclaim that he was tired of waiting for me to move back home—to do as he wanted—but I knew he was tired. Regardless, I didn't have to wait for a great sigh or for his frustrations to bubble over in some other way.

On a Saturday, the one before Thanksgiving, we were sitting in my living room. We were next to each other on the couch, our feet propped up on two cushions. I was reading a book and Peter was scrolling through the news. Minneapolis was gloomy again, the city barely visible through the giant windows due to the fog and mist. Peter had draped a throw blanket over us to fight off the chill of the day.

"I'd like you to be back home before Christmas," Peter said out of the blue, not looking up from his phone. "Mom and Dad are coming to visit. It would be nice if I didn't have to explain your absence another year."

It was cruel of me. A bit petty, what I said next.

"Is that why you want me back home?" I asked. "So your parents don't think your life is imperfect?"

I had said it on a whim. Not necessarily to be cruel, or to start a fight, but it was something that I wondered. Peter had always been concerned with the enjoyment his parents experienced while visiting. He had never been concerned with my needs when they were staying at our home. So…while cruel…it was a valid question. Peter visibly tensed, but surprisingly, he didn't lash out at me like I'd done to him.

"Maybe I said it wrong," he said, his voice tight, "but that's not what I meant. I want you back home because I love you and you're my husband. You're part of my family. Like my parents. So…it would be nice to not have to tell one part of the family that the other part didn't show up for some unknown reason."

I chewed at my lip.

"I'm sorry," I said.

Peter sighed. "Forgiven."

"Do you think," I said, laying my book down, "that maybe we're just too…opposite? Maybe that's part of the problem?"

Peter put his phone to sleep and laid it on the arm of the sofa.

"That's the dumbest thing I've ever heard," he said, turning on the sofa to face me.

"Now who's rude?"

"I'm not trying to be rude," he said. "But you're grasping at straws, Enzo."

"Am I?" I asked. "You're older, I'm younger. Your friends are not like my friends. You read the news. I read novels."

"I read books."

I chuckled. "You know what I mean. You like weird television shows and don't care about the movies I love."

Peter rolled his eyes.

"I'm serious, Peter. Don't make fun."

"I'm not making fun," he said. "But this is ridiculous. You're just listing off arbitrary things about us."

"Things that help define who we are."

"Well," Peter said, "how about…our feelings about family? How we feel about our careers? How we want our home life to be? The way we view the world and how we hate injustice and inequity? The fact that we love having sex with each other and can't get enough? How we love to snuggle and say nothing and watch the weather? How we can be silent with each other and it doesn't feel awkward? How even if we don't understand the things the other person loves or the things they want to accomplish, we support and encourage each other? We're each other's biggest cheerleaders. How about those things?"

I stared at him.

"Our tastes in movies and television shows?" He snorted. "That's stupid. It doesn't matter what you like, Enzo. As long as I can do it with you and enjoy doing it because I'm with you is all that matters. Or, if we don't feel like doing the same thing, we can go our separate ways, do the things we love, then come back and tell each other about our days. And be happy for each other. I'm genuinely happy for you when you have a good day. And you're genuinely happy for me when I have a good day. We're not opposites. We're the same where it matters—*we align where it matters*—the things we love doing are sometimes different."

I thought about that.

"We just have to learn how to be there for each other on the bad days," he added. "Instead of pretending things are fine. Instead of shutting each other out."

Looking down at my feet, I knew Peter was right. I knew that a lot of the things going on in my head—the things that were not leftover trauma from my previous life—were problems of my own making. How does one explain their own mental health issues to themselves? Can a person ever fully understand the synaptic misfires and chemical imbalances enough to work around them? To learn and manage them so that their life can be relatively peaceful?

"You know," Peter said, "Alex told me to give you a break. That you'd had a difficult life and you had things to work through. That I needed to be understanding."

My eyes shot up to Peter.

"Yeah," he said, sitting forward on the couch. "I screamed at him for taking your side in all of this—"

"He didn't take my side."

"I know that," Peter said. "Now. But he told me to give you space to figure things out. To have patience. But when you say things like '*maybe we're opposites*,' I have to wonder if you're not just looking for reasons to not be with me, Enzo."

"That's not it," I stammered. "That's not fair."

"Who cares?" Peter stood, the blanket falling from his legs. "Life's not fair, Enzo. You know that better than anyone."

I stood from the sofa to glare at him.

"You blame me for everything!" I shouted. "I'm not perfect, Peter—no matter how much you want me to be— but you refuse to realize not everyone is perfect. Nothing is perfect. You just ignore the problems and close yourself off!"

"I never asked you to be perfect!" he shouted back.

"Fine," I said, throwing my hands up. "Whatever. But you still refused to communicate when you knew things weren't right."

Peter shoved his face in mine. *"Because you wouldn't say what the fuck was bothering you, Enzo.* You just moped around, slept, kept to yourself, and suffered in silence instead of treating me like part of the team!"

"And we both know who the owner of the team is, don't we?" I barked.

"What does that even mean?" Peter took his turn throwing his hands in the air.

"You wanted everything to go the way you imagined it would," I said. "But you obviously could tell I wasn't doing well—that I was struggling—but you ignored it!"

"You're an adult, Enzo! Why do I have to pry things out of you?"

"Why can't you just—"

"Maybe I was fucking scared that you were thinking about leaving me and I didn't want to ask because then I would know for certain!" Redness was crawling up Peter's neck.

I stopped. *Peter had been scared?*

Clearing his throat, Peter growled, "Because I knew something wasn't right, Enzo. But you weren't talking or even giving me one damn clue what was going on with you. I knew I wasn't perfect. I know I'm never going to be perfect. But I was scared that you were going to tell me you couldn't be my husband anymore. That you'd made a mistake. I was fucking terrified to hear those words. I was scared to even consider it a possibility."

"That's not what was going on, though," I managed. "I don't want to divorce, Peter. I love you."

"I love you, too," Peter threw his hands up again. "When are you going to come home?"

"I don't want to commit to a timeframe right now," I mumbled.

"That's it, then?" Peter asked. "This is it? That's your answer? You'll just risk throwing me and anything we had away—*that we might have had*—because I fucked up? No. Because *I* wasn't perfect either?"

"I didn't—"

"That's not what love is, Enzo! Love is—"

"*What is love, Peter?*" I demanded. "*Tell me what it is!* You said you loved me—you're standing here telling me you love me now—but at the first sign that something was wrong you got scared and blocked yourself off from me emotionally. You tried to pretend everything was fine when it clearly was not. You wouldn't talk to me about your concerns. Or mine. You just…became a robot. Because you were afraid you were losing me? That's ridiculous. Love isn't about fear, Peter!"

"*Of course, love is fear!*" Peter rushed forward, putting his face dangerously close to mine again. I refused to be moved. "Maybe it's not just fear, but fear is a big part of love."

"That's the dumbest—"

"How can you love someone if you don't fear that you'll lose them every day, damnit?" Peter spat.

As if struck, I recoiled.

"I spent months—*months*—wondering what I did to you, Enzo. Wondering why you wouldn't tell me what was wrong. Why you wouldn't just talk to me. Why you wouldn't open up to me—the man who is supposed to be the most important person in your life, aside from yourself. And you just…you cut me out. Of everything. You suffered alone and pushed me away. You suffered more and pushed me away harder. For what? Pride? Your ego? Embarrassment? I spent *months* in fear that I was losing you. Because I loved you. I *love* you. And then you just walked out on me without a word."

My eyes were suddenly on my feet.

"If I didn't love you—if I hadn't loved you—I wouldn't have been afraid when you stopped talking to me." Peter sighed and his whole body seemed to deflate. He shook his head and took a step back, removing himself from my space. "Two things I know to be true in this world, Enzo. I love you and it scares the shit out of me every day."

I stared at my feet and listened as Peter sighed, his shoulders rising and falling. When I said nothing, he stepped back again.

"So," he said, the fight gone from his voice, "maybe my love isn't perfect to you. But you don't understand love like you think you do. If you think I can love you and not also be afraid of losing your love, you're insane."

Peter turned and shuffled to the front door, shaking his head. His hand rested on the knob but it wasn't the thing that turned.

"I guess I know three things to be true in this world," Peter said, turning his head as I lifted mine, and our eyes met. "I love you. It scares me. And I know that you didn't marry me because you thought it would be an easy life."

"Peter—"

"The moment I laid eyes on you, Enzo," Peter stopped me, "I saw you shout at some asshole vendor under the glow of those paper lanterns—the ones they had hung everywhere at the Autumn festival?"

I nodded my head.

"I hadn't said a word to you. I didn't know your name. I knew shit all about you. But I knew at that exact moment that I loved you. It scared me then. Because I knew I was looking at my life. The decades that were laid out ahead of me. And you were in every fucking scene. It was like looking into some psychic's crystal ball and seeing your future play out in front of you. I saw the minutiae of a boring married life—something I had never been brave enough to dream up before—play out in front of me. And it scared me."

I stared at him.

"Because I knew if I did anything to lose that vision, to not make it real, I would be making the biggest mistake of my life," Peter finished. "So...I can't love you without fear, Enzo. Everything about you scares me because life is tenuous, so every moment of every day there is a chance I'll lose you."

"I—"

"You married me because you knew, just as I do, that we met for a reason," Peter said. "And we both know how much I hate this kind of shit, and I don't believe in it ninety-nine-point-nine percent of the time, but you were put here to be mine and I was put here to be yours. Against all reasoning, all of the obstacles that tried to convince us that we should take the easier road, we chose to go through Hell to be together. Because the fear of what we might find was a shit less scary than the fear of losing each other."

Peter shook his head in frustration.

He sighed. "So, fourth thing I know," he gave a bitter laugh, "I'll leave you be, Enzo. I'm not going to try and force you to be with me. I know *that* isn't love. But I know that if you ever get your head out of your ass, and stop being so goddamn stubborn, I'll still love you. And I'll be waiting. I'll love you and wait until…well, I guess until I die."

I snorted, a small, amused laugh escaping my mouth.

"And as I'm a bit older than you, if you could do me a favor and not waste any more fucking time than is absolutely necessary, I'd appreciate it."

Peter turned and twisted the knob.

"Peter," I sighed.

"What?" he barked, not bothering to turn back.

Nothing but air whispered between us. After a few moments, Peter let go of the doorknob and turned to me, concern on his face. With no idea of what I wanted to say to him, or how I wanted to say it, I was left staring at Peter's face. Regardless of what came out of my mouth, I knew I didn't want him to open the door.

"I still don't have the words," I said, "for what I was going through."

A soft happiness, mixed with sadness, crossed his face.

"For now, I only need three," Peter said.

"Of course, I love you," I said.

"That's four. Or five," he said. "I'm not sure."

I laughed. Sniffled. A single tear rolled down my cheek. Peter made "shushing" noises and stepped over to me. He reached up and wiped the tear off my cheek. Cupping my chin, he made me look up from my feet so that our eyes could meet.

"I still don't know how to not push you away from what I was going through then, Peter," I said. "I've tried to think of how to explain it to you. Or, I suppose, I've tried to figure out how to explain it to myself so that I could begin to explain it to you...but I feel...I feel like someone has cut me open and I'm just...life has been hard."

Peter stroked my cheek.

"My life, when you met me, was a battlefield after a war. Hundreds of little bombs had gone off. Each one had blown a hole right through important parts of me, and I haven't figured out how to fill them back up. I tried filling them with my love for you and our marriage and our home and our new life and a job and...some days I feel like more and more of me is just...falling out of those holes. Sometimes it's not the bombs that kill you but the wounds that refuse to heal."

"Well," Peter said, his voice wet, "it doesn't help if someone keeps poking new holes, either."

"It wasn't you," I said. "Well, maybe some of it was—"

Peter chuckled.

"—because you tell me that you are scared of losing me from your life but I feel like I've never been a part of it. I've been a satellite caught in your orbit, mindlessly circling, waiting to be given a purpose. Maybe I have pushed you away, but sometimes I feel like you've never...*pulled me in?*"

Peter frowned and cupped my cheek, looking into my eyes as he listened.

"I've felt superfluous to my own existence," I said. "You made me feel like you wanted a husband in name, but I've felt—for a long time—as if I'm simply playing a role for you. I haven't felt like I'm a partner."

"Of course, you're my partner," he said, both of his hands suddenly on my face as he stared into my eyes. "You've been the best partner, Enzo."

"I have not felt that way. Maybe that is part of why I didn't invite you in when I began to have troubles?"

He nodded.

"We're a pair, aren't we?" he asked.

"A pair of what?"

He chuckled.

"I'll try harder, Enzo. I'll try as hard as I can. I can't promise you perfection, but I can promise you that. I just...I need you to not shut me out."

"Okay."

Peter ran his thumbs under my eyes, clearing away barely shed tears.

"I'm sorry," I said.

"I'm sorry, too," Peter replied. "I'll probably be sorry for a long time."

"I don't want you to be sorry for a long time," I said. "I want...I want this all to be a memory. Can we do that?"

He smiled. "I think we probably need to talk it out. Resolve things. Put things to bed. That would be healthier than pretending it didn't happen."

"I know," I said, sniffling again. "I mean that I want the day that we've done all of that to come."

Peter shook his head slowly. "I don't wish the seconds away with you, Enzo. Even the difficult ones."

"Oh, shut up," I laughed wetly and shoved at his shoulder.

Peter caught my hand and held it; his eyes locked onto mine. The laughter that had been upon my lips slid back down my throat.

"Home isn't home without you, Enzo," he said. "Now that I've known what a home is like with you in it, nothing else will do."

"I'm not ready to come home," I said, shaking my head.

Peter slumped a little, but he smiled. "But you called it 'home.'"

I nodded.

"Give me a little more time?" I asked.

"Okay," Peter nodded. "I can do that. As long as I'm with you, I'm home anyway."

I cleared my throat, trying to chase away the emotion he had brought up in me.

"But," I said, "maybe...maybe you should stay here tonight?"

Peter looked up into my eyes, his face a blank slate.

"Yes," I said. "That's what I mean."

Peter stared at me for the longest of moments.

"You still sleep on the right side?" he asked.

"I'll sleep on whichever side you want me to," I said.

Peter pulled my face down and his lips met mine. It was likely the most chaste kiss we'd ever shared, but it was the kiss we needed to share at that moment.

I whispered, *"That means I get the right side."*

Peter pulled me in, wrapping his arms around me.

"After Christmas," I said. "We'll figure things out then. Okay?"

"Okay."

"I'll stay at home while your parents are here," I added. "If that will make you happy."

Peter sighed, smiled, and kissed me gently on the lips.

"Thank you. I love you."

"I love you, too," I said.

Peter stared into my eyes for a moment, then opened his mouth to speak, shut it, opened it again, and then shut it once more.

"What?" I chuckled nervously.

Peter frowned. "When we had our fight? When you flipped the table? The night before you left the house?"

"Yes?"

I didn't want to ever again think of what Peter had said that had made me flip the table, but if we were going to work on our communication and inviting each other in, I couldn't ignore him. Hearing how he had fantasized about a coworker had drawn a rage from me I hadn't known was possible at the time. Now, in my living room in my apartment, the rage was manageable, but it was still there.

Peter was *my* husband. I didn't want to hear about anyone else making him feel the way that I was supposed to make him feel. Even if I hadn't been doing my job well for a while.

"You didn't let me finish my sentence before you flew off the handle."

"Oh?"

"What I was going to say that night was…"

"Just say it."

"When I saw my coworker looking at me, the thing I fantasized about was," he began, "the thing was that it made me fantasize that one day you would look at me like that again. I wasn't fantasizing about other men. Especially at work."

I managed to push down the unnecessary rage and smiled instead. "Okay."

"I needed you to know that."

"I'm glad you told me," I said.

"Really?"

"Yes," I said. "Now I don't have to find out who he is and kill him."

Peter laughed and pulled me in, wrapping me up tightly as his lips found mine.

The following morning, while Peter still slept on the left side of my bed, I knelt in the back of my closet, staring at the cardboard box. At first, I wasn't certain what had drawn me from bed before the sun was barely peeking over the horizon, and into the closet. So, I sat there and stared at the box, wondering what had come over me.

Peter was my future. For certain. I didn't know what that future fully looked like yet, but I knew he was the biggest and most important part of it.

I needed to accept my past trauma, come to peace with it, and move on. I needed to put it all to rest while still figuring out how to honor it.

I was exhausted and annoyed with myself. With my own bullshit. Finding a way to move on was the best thing for me. For Peter, our marriage...my future. *Our* future.

One cannot erase their history—their trauma. And they shouldn't. A person isn't who they are without those things, for better or worse. But finding a way to make sure they no longer have a hold over the future you is paramount. Finding a way to honor that they helped shape you into the person you are, while putting them to rest, is how one steps into their future with solid footing and hope.

One cannot chase after possibility if they are still stuck in the past.

Gingerly, I lifted the flaps of the cardboard box and looked down at its contents. And I made a decision that would help me step into my future with hope.

I quietly retrieved my phone from the bedside table, making sure not to wake Peter, and texted a friend.

A Sinful Christmas

"It's like we're living in sin," Peter said. "Which, I guess, makes it a little bit more exciting, right?"

My face broke out into a wicked grin as we stared out the window together. The living room had been decorated for Christmas again, prepared for the arrival of Peter's parents, who were parking in the driveway. However, we hadn't decorated the front room with the appropriate fake tree and matched ornaments and lights, only to decorate the den in a way that actually represented us. The fake tree never made its way down from the attic. The real tree we went and cut down at a tree farm was in the front window of the living room, decorated with the ornaments Peter's grandmother had left him, along with tinsel and lights.

The living room was festooned with the things that told a person, as soon as they entered our home, who we were as people. As a couple. It was warm and homey and inviting. It made me think of Christmases with my family. The laughter and warmth and joy of holidays with family. When Peter's parents walked into the house, they wouldn't be walking into a showroom. They would be walking into a home. One that represented both Peter and me and our marriage.

Of course, the den would always be our favorite room in the house, but we would no longer use it as a way of hiding the things we loved the most from people who visited.

"Makes me feel kind of feisty," Peter whispered in my ear, as though his parents might hear. He reached over to grab my butt. "Know what I mean?"

"You are a pervert," I said.

"So?"

"It wasn't an insult."

Peter laughed and wrapped an arm around my shoulders, pulling me into him as we stood there, waiting for his parents to park. The month that had passed since our talk before Thanksgiving had gone well. Perfect even. Not perfect in a way that meant every day was a breeze and never a single difficulty was encountered. It was perfect in that we were communicating, learning more skills to communicate, and we weren't shutting each other out. Peter had even gone with me to a few therapy sessions.

In that month, we'd begun to be playful with each other again. Our silliness and banter were returning. And when difficulties arose, we worked on them as a team. I was doing my best to show Peter that I wouldn't shut myself off when something was bothering me. I could speak up like an adult and tell him when I had an issue with something. Peter was proving to me that I was as important as him in our relationship—that we were equal.

But he was right. Knowing that I wasn't living at home and that we were going to pretend for his parents, made it thrilling somehow. It was still a lie. One I wasn't sure I was comfortable with, ultimately. However, if it was what Peter needed, I was going to go along with it.

"You okay?" Peter asked as the doors of his parents' car popped open.

"Yes," I said. "Why?"

He shrugged, still holding me against him.

"You're okay with all of this, I mean?" he asked. "It's four days."

"Yeah," I said. "It's fine."

"Sure?"

"Yes," I laughed and waved through the window at Peter's mother as she looked up from the walkway that led up to the house. She waved back excitedly. "I get it. Your parents…you want things to be perfect for them. And we're working towards fixing things anyway, right? It's okay."

Peter's arm slid from my shoulder and he gave me a small smile, though his eyes seemed sad as he made his way to the front door. Opening the door as his father raised his fist to knock—as though they hadn't seen us waiting on them—Peter's parents poured into the house with greetings and open arms, bags, frivolity, and crisp, icy winter air. Peter's mother swooped me into her arms before I had a chance to even respond to her greetings and "*Merry Christmas!*"

Of course, the front door wasn't even shut, and Peter was still hugging his father when the elephant in the room was addressed. Pulling back so that she could look at me, her hands clutching my upper arms, Peter's mother spoke up.

"I thought we wouldn't see you this year," she said. "After last year, I wasn't sure…"

Smiling, I gave myself a moment to collect my thoughts. Before I could respond, Peter spoke up.

"Enzo has an apartment downtown," he said evenly. "He's been staying there for a while. We're working through some things. But he's staying here with me over Christmas. So he could see you guys."

Peter's mother, to her credit, didn't gasp or resort to dramatics. Her hands tightened on my arms slightly, but after a slight pause, she gave me a smile.

"Well," she said, "I missed your cooking last year. My son is not the best chef."

The four of us laughed. It wasn't quite forced laughter, but it was a bit tense since Peter had dropped a bomb on his parents without warning. However, his parents handled it amazingly, taking the news in stride. Certainly, when they were ensconced in the privacy of the guest room upstairs later in the evening, they would whisper their thoughts to each other. But that was their marriage. We had ours. After a few moments, and more exchanged hugs and pleasantries, Peter ushered the two of them towards the den, telling them we'd bring in some snacks and drinks after we took their luggage upstairs. Then we could all catch up.

With his parents headed towards the back of the house, Peter stepped over to me and put his hands on my shoulders. Leveling me with his eyes, he stared at me for a moment. Then he leaned forward and kissed me.

"You didn't have to do that," I said.

"We're family. You, me, them. Family should be honest."

I gave him another kiss.

"They handled it well," I said.

"Well," Peter mumbled, "I'm sure I'll get some shit later for lying to them last year."

I laughed. "Maybe. But your honesty has earned you my admiration."

Peter grinned wickedly. "Does that get me something else once everyone is in bed tonight?"

"I can't believe you'd even talk to me like that with your parents in the other room," I turned my nose up haughtily and stepped around him to grab one of his parents' bags.

"And I won't tell you the answer even if you grab that other bag and follow me upstairs where no one is around to hear or see us."

Peter grabbed his parents' other bag and chased me, the two of us actually giggling as we raced up the stairs.

"*Real food,*" Peter's mother groaned. "Last year was a disaster, Enzo."

Standing at the kitchen island, Peter's mother seated on one of the stools on the other side, I was chopping vegetables. She was on her third glass of Chardonnay and her eyes were a bit glassy. I was no expert, but she seemed to be doing fairly well for an older woman with an empty stomach working on her third glass of wine.

Peter and his father were watching some American sports of some kind in the den, arguing loudly—but jovially—over one thing or another as they sipped bourbons. Since everyone was treating themselves, I had my favorite soda. Even after so long of not taking my medication, and having new rules I could follow, I found that I cared little for the idea of alcohol.

When I had been a teenager, and even in my early twenties, I had thought it would be nice to have drinks with friends. Alter my brain with a substance and see how I handled being altered. Dance wildly at parties and sing loudly to songs without inhibition because a chemical had changed my brain for a brief time. After my surgery, I found that I didn't want to change my brain any more than necessary. And I'd experienced enough life to know that if I wanted more experience, I didn't need to rely on chemicals.

Eventually, I knew I would drink. Why not try everything that life has to offer? Within reason. During Christmas with Peter's parents when I wasn't living at home was not the best time to take that step, however. So, soda was a perfectly acceptable treat instead. It had kept my head clear while catching up with Peter's parents in the den during the early afternoon.

When dinner time came, Peter had offered to help me cook. I knew Peter would have rather spent time with his father, watching sports, and the fact that he had even offered—something he hadn't done in the past—was good enough for me. Quite honestly, having him try to help in the kitchen had never been a good idea. So, I gave him a reprieve. His mother had insisted on helping, however, which basically meant she drank wine while watching me cook.

I was fine with the arrangement. Having Peter entertain his father while his mother simply sat back and watched me cook was best. Putting a drunk person in front of an open flame was a bad idea. Since Peter had been willing to help, that was all I needed to feel equal. Later, I would have to point out to Peter how easy it was to make me feel equal. Just to annoy him—but playfully. Not to instigate a fight.

"What do you mean?" I asked.

She rolled her eyes playfully. "My son—and I'm sorry to say so—cannot cook. God knows he tried last year, but we ended up ordering out every day we were here. Other than the meals I made."

"He has cooked for me before," I said, feeling as though I needed to defend my husband. "He's...well, he does okay."

She laughed. "That's very politic of you."

"He tries," I said, laughing with her. "Even when it's not great, having someone cook a meal for you is nice."

Peter's mother eyed me for a moment, long enough to make me nervous as I chopped vegetables. Finally, when she spoke, what she said was unexpected.

"Trying is what keeps a marriage together, isn't it?" she asked.

I glanced up, but didn't say anything; didn't stop chopping vegetables.

"Peter tries too hard for the wrong things," she said quietly, making it obvious these words were only for me. "He's in there with his father, carrying on like a loon about some game, drinking bourbon, acting a bit unlike himself. Don't you think?"

I shrugged.

"Politic again," she laughed, then lowered her voice again. "He thinks he has to behave a certain way or do certain things...*achieve certain things*...to make his father love him. I suppose it all has to do with the gay thing, but—"

"The...*gay thing*?" I asked, trying to control my voice.

"He's always thought we were disappointed in him," she said, waving the thought away. "And how stupid. I couldn't love him more if I tried."

I relaxed and continued chopping.

"I suspect he thinks that we wanted a *normal* son with a *normal* family."

"What's normal?" I asked.

"Hell if I know," Peter's mother responded with a laugh, which gave me a pleasant shock. "But I hope whatever he thinks it is, well, that's what he has."

I nodded along slowly.

"All we want is for him to be happy," she said with finality. "If he's happy, and he's a good person, nothing else matters."

Finally, I looked up at my mother-in-law and stopped chopping.

"All I want from life is to be happy," I said. "I don't know if it's a good enough purpose, but that's all I've ever wanted, too. And I am happy. Peter is happy. And your son is a good person."

"Then that's all that matters, right?" She tilted her glass at me in a salute as she winked.

"I suppose so," I said, smiling. "Do you like mushrooms? I wanted to add mushrooms, but Peter is picky about which kind."

She rolled her eyes. "His father is the same way."

I sighed as his mother leaned in conspiratorially.

"I love them," she said. "Put them in. Our husbands can pick around them."

Laughing at our evil, yet harmless plot, I retrieved the carton of mushrooms. As I continued to prepare dinner, Peter's mother drank, and we talked, I realized something about my husband. Almost always, when someone strives for perfection in one area of life, every other aspect of their life must suffer. Often, we focus our attention on being perfect to someone who already loves us, just as we are. If Peter and I could remember to remind each other that we loved each other, just as we were, and that we would love each other as we grew, that was all that we needed.

Christmas morning, though harried and eventful, was pleasant and joyous. Peter and I had breakfast with his parents in the kitchen, sitting around the small table, laughing, sharing stories, and drinking coffee as we ate. Afterward, we gathered in the living room and opened presents from each other. Peter's parents, as they had always been, were generous in their gift-giving to us, which always made me uncomfortable—yet grateful.

Peter and I had purchased gifts for them, too, of course, which they were delighted to receive, as always. I received a handful of wonderful gifts from Peter, and I had put a few token gifts under the tree for him. More coffee and conversation were had in the living room as the tree twinkled and the wrappings and trash laid in a heap in the corner. Peter and I made no effort to clean up when spending time with his parents was more important, especially since they had to leave before lunch.

When the time came, Peter's parents bagged their gifts, and Peter and I carried their luggage to their car. They had other family they wanted to stop by and visit before the holiday was over. Peter and I exchanged hugs and "goodbyes" with them, waving from the porch as they drove away. Once they were out of sight, snow began to fall once again, and Peter and I rushed inside, chilled to the bone, shivering and laughing.

Surveying the Christmas carnage in the living room, Peter and I heaved a sigh. Who wants to clean up a mess on such a festive holiday?

"Are you going to stay tonight, too?" Peter asked, his voice hopeful.

I shrugged. "I thought I would stay through New Year's Eve. If that's okay with you."

He simply grinned.

"Tell you what," Peter said. "If you will make coffee and something yummy, I'll build a fire in the den. This mess isn't going anywhere."

"Deal," I agreed enthusiastically.

Peter headed to the den, practically skipping with excitement as I made my way to the kitchen. I made a pot of coffee and arranged leftovers on a tray, gathered two coffee mugs, and the accoutrement needed for a Christmas lunchtime picnic in front of the fire. Before I carried the tray and coffee into the den, I dashed up the back stairs to our bedroom and retrieved two gifts I'd stowed in our closet.

Back downstairs, I carried the food and coffee into the den, asking Peter to drag the ottoman in front of the couch so we would have something to use as a table. Then I retrieved the packages from the kitchen and carried them into the den. When I entered the room, Peter was setting the tray of food and the coffee on the makeshift table in front of the sofa. He looked up with a smile, his eyes landing on the packages, and his eyes lit up.

"More gifts?" Peter asked like a child seeing that Santa had arrived.

"Well," I said, "they're for both of us. For our house."

"Does that mean—"

"We're working on it," I reminded him.

Peter nodded. "Well, are we going to eat first or open gifts first?"

I sat down on the sofa and handed the two packages to him.

"I'll let you open them," I said. "Or we can eat first if you want."

Giggling maniacally, Peter ignored the food on the ottoman and tore into the packages, practically unwrapping them simultaneously. When he was done shredding the wrapping paper, and the two gifts lay on his lap, I could tell Peter was trying to seem excited by what I'd given him. I wanted to laugh at his confusion, but I was equally interested to see what would happen when he realized what he'd been given. Of course, I was also nervous that what I thought was a good gift wouldn't be seen the same way by him.

Maybe I tried too hard? I thought to myself.

"Oh," Peter said, his forced happiness giving his voice a lilt, "pillows. For...for the sofa?"

"I thought they would look nice here in the den," I said. "Since it's our favorite room."

"That's very thoughtful, babe," he said, leaning over to give me a quick kiss. "Thank you."

"You're welcome," I said.

Peter gave me a quick second kiss, then turned his attention back to the pillows in his lap.

"It'll be nice to have a touch of you in here, too," he said, smiling down at the pillows. "It'll make the den feel more like—"

When he stopped, I knew he had finally realized what he was looking at in his lap. Peter paused; his mouth still formed to say the words he had been thinking. Then he blinked. Blinked again. His head turned slowly to look at me, an unreadable look on his face.

"What?" I asked innocently.

Peter looked back down at the pillows, stared at them for a few moments, then gently removed them from his lap and set them to the side on the sofa.

"*Jesus fucking Christ, Enzo,*" he said.

He stood from the sofa, his hand going to his face to shield his expression from my eyes. I didn't say anything as he walked out of the den. A bit nervous, but knowing he would eventually return, I poured coffee for the two of us and made little plates of food for both of us. When he came back, we would eat. I wouldn't say anything about what had happened unless he said something first.

When Peter finally did come back into the den—five or ten minutes later, I wasn't sure—he was sniffling and it was obvious he had been crying. He sat down next to me without a word and wrapped me in his arms, pulling me into him. Peter held me against him for what seemed like forever, then pulled back and gave me a lingering, soft kiss on the lips.

"*I love them,*" he whispered. "*Thank you.*"

"You're welcome. A friend made them for me."

Before we ate, Peter took the pillows and placed one at each end of the sofa. One made of black wool and the other made of puffy polyester that looked like a blue cloud that had once smelled of sugar.

We didn't clean up the destruction in the living room. Peter and I hid away in the den for the rest of the day, eating, drinking, feeding the fire, and enjoyed watching the snow fall outside as we stayed wrapped in each other's arms.

It was the perfect Christmas.

Something was wrong. It was the night after Christmas and Peter and I had crawled into bed at our typical bedtime and fallen asleep, snuggling, with his head on my chest. When my eyes popped open, I was uncertain what time it was, but Peter was no longer snuggled up next to me. His head wasn't on my chest. I reached over, searching for him in the dark, but my arm found nothing except empty space on the mattress. Fumbling in the dark, I grabbed my cellphone from the bedside table and checked the time.

Ten minutes after midnight.

As I lowered my cellphone, the human figure at the foot of the bed caught in the glow cast by my cellphone screen startled me. When I realized the shape was Peter, sitting on the bench, I chuckled and slowly sat up in bed. I set my phone on the bedside table and stared at Peter's back as he sat there.

"Couldn't sleep?" I asked softly.

"No," he said.

"Do you need some help getting sleepy?" I asked, suggestively.

I thought Peter would chuckle. Maybe even take me up on the offer. We'd had sex before bed, but I was not opposed to revisiting the activity if it would help him sleep. Even if it didn't help him sleep. Sex doesn't have to have any purpose other than to have sex.

I slid down the bed so that I was behind him and placed my hands on his shoulders, then leaned forward to kiss his neck. Peter chuckled, sounding hoarse, but gave no indication that he was interested in actual sex.

Something definitely had to be wrong.

"Are you upset about something?" I whispered.

"No," he said. "I just…I was having trouble sleeping."

I rubbed his shoulders gently in the dark.

"Do you need to talk about something?" I asked. "Did you have a bad dream?"

"No…no," he said. "I'm fine."

"Are you certain?"

When Peter tensed up, bending slightly at his waist, I froze. His arms went to his middle and he leaned forward, as though experiencing a cramp. A smile came to my face and I rubbed his back gently.

"Too much dinner?" I asked, chuckling.

Peter tried to laugh with me, but he cringed again. When I noticed how warm Peter's back felt, I scooted closer so that my legs were practically wrapped around him, and my hand went to the back of his neck. Then his forehead. He clenched up again.

"You're running a fever," I said. "Peter, what's wrong?"

"Nothing," Peter said, trying to sound fine, but not quite managing.

There was a twinge to his voice, the sound of someone not wanting to let on that they are in pain.

"Is it your stomach?" I asked as I pulled myself from around him and climbed off of the bed.

Coming around to stand in front of him, I knelt down in the dark, trying to catch his eye. Peter's arms were still laid over his stomach, his face was twisted up in pain, his teeth clenched together as his whole body stayed rigid.

"Maybe it's just gas pains?" Peter managed before his whole body jerked as another pain shot through him.

I felt his forehead again. Peter was beginning to sweat.

"Non," I said. "Needing to fart doesn't make you run a fever, babe. You need to go to the hospital."

Peter grumbled and tried to shove my hand away from his head before another pain ripped through his body, forcing him to clutch his stomach again. Before he could build a case and protest what I'd suggested, I rose and went over to flip the lights on. Peter shut his eyes at the sudden burst of light. No longer in the dark, I could see that Peter wasn't experiencing a typical stomach cramp. Pasty white, sweating through the t-shirt he'd put on before we went to sleep, his hair matted with damp, I knew he was not well.

"Don't call a fucking ambulance," he hissed.

"Do you prefer that we rely on my driving skills to get us to the hospital?" I asked, my hands on my hips. "Because you're going one way or the other."

I was not going to be nice to Peter when it came to the fact that he *was* going to the hospital. One way or another, he was going. I was no medical expert, but I knew danger when I saw it. Focusing on Peter and getting him to the hospital also helped keep the panic at bay that was rising in my gut.

"Enzo," he said.

Then another pain made him jerk once more. Nothing else came from Peter's lips as he looked up at me, his face painted with panic.

"Ambulance," I nodded.

Peter said nothing, but he nodded back. So, I hurried over to my bedside table and snatched up my cellphone once more.

Hospital waiting rooms are the worst. Over the years, I've grown to absolutely loathe them. They try to be cheerful, with muted primary colors, and beautiful landscape pictures on the walls. Or maybe they're ultra-modern so everything seems futuristic in an effort to remove visitors from the now. Televisions play the news to distract people. Magazines with covers displaying exciting headlines about celebrities with lifestyles everyone envies try to draw people from their thoughts. Vending machines with enticing, affordable, caloric-laden treats glow brightly from corners next to soda machines with more variety than anyone would need.

But the seat cushions are always a synthetic material that is easy to wipe free of germs and bacteria. The floors are scuffed and worn from the treads of wheelchairs, hospital beds, and other medical devices used to help people ambulate. Permeated with the combination of potent cleaning products and the smell of illness that can't quite be masked, the air is always stale.

Hospitals are cold. The blankets they provide are barely thick enough to deserve the name. I'd thrown on some jeans, a t-shirt, a sweater, and comfortable sneakers while Peter and I waited for the ambulance. I'd even helped Peter into some presentable clothes so he didn't have to be taken to the hospital in pajamas. When one can help another preserve a little bit of their dignity, one should always try. Then I helped Peter downstairs, his arms wrapped around me as he winced with each step.

Appendicitis.

That's what I told the 911 operator I thought was wrong. The EMTs, who I let in the front door so that they could attend to Peter in the living room, agreed with me. Peter and I were whisked away in the ambulance, me sitting opposite the EMT in the back of the ambulance with Peter lying on a stretcher between us. I did my best to comfort him as we raced to the hospital, but the EMT had work to do, so hand-holding wasn't possible.

Once at the hospital, everything became a blur. Peter was whisked into the Emergency Room, which was surprisingly not busy. Considering it was the night after Christmas, it was possible everyone was staving off addressing medical issues until the holiday was over. A doctor saw Peter within minutes, by which time, Peter could barely lay flat, such was his pain. Some tests and scans were done…and…I was in a surgical waiting room.

Peter had been whisked away from me, frightened and in pain, clutching at my hand as I followed his gurney as far down the hall as I could before he went into surgery. And then I was alone in an empty room designed to seat at least fifty visitors, waiting to hear anything about how he was doing. The hospital staff had been kind to Peter and me, treating us like a married couple instead of two gay men, but that did nothing to relieve my worry.

Should I call his parents?

A friend?

Alex?

It's not quite four o'clock in the morning. No one will be awake. Would they want to be woken up for something like this? Should I wait until someone tells me how Peter is doing?

How dangerous is an appendectomy?

Do I need to call his insurance or leave a message for his primary doctor?

Do I need to call his employer?

He doesn't go back to work until the new year, but surely, he will need recovery time?

Is...

Is my husband going to die?

The fear was mentally paralyzing, though I couldn't stop pacing from one end of the waiting room to the other. All of my thoughts slowly faded away and I could only focus on my feet moving beneath me, carrying me across the room, over and over. Finally, unsure of how much time had passed, I fell into one of the wooden chairs with a barely cushioned plastic seat and slumped.

Wait.

That was all I could do.

Outside, the lights of Minneapolis twinkled. The sun hadn't even considered rising for the day yet. I thought about buying a snack from the vending machine. And a soda. Something to give me energy and distract me from my thoughts when they started to return, but I had no money in my wallet. I didn't quite trust vending machines with my debit and credit cards because I suddenly remembered a news report I'd heard about stolen credit card information.

Then I thought of finding the cafeteria for a cup of coffee. And maybe they would be serving breakfast and I could get something to eat while I waited.

But then I would have to leave the waiting room and risk missing a nurse or doctor coming to tell me how Peter was doing.

You could order pizza.

Are there any pizza places open at four in the morning?

There's the all-night pizza place by your apartment, but do they deliver all night?

Their pizza isn't that good.

Am I even hungry?

Why do I always think of food during crises?

Food was always comforting. When nothing else seemed to help and the whole world was falling apart, food was there for me.

Why do I not have a weight problem?

Obviously, in the past, when I couldn't afford food, I would be skinny.

I eat all the time now.

I should really try to be healthier. Peter and I should always try to be healthier for each other. That's what good partners do—they make sure they stick around for as long as possible for the other.

Right?

What am I going to do if Peter...

"Are you Mr. Bradshaw?" I jerked at the sound of a man speaking.

Jerking my head up to attention, I found a man in scrubs, a surgical mask hanging around his neck, and a surgical hat still atop his head staring at me. He was looking down at me sternly, which made my gut wrench up in knots.

"Um," I said, "Mr. Barbier. Enzo. Enzo Barbier. Peter Bradshaw is my husband."

The man's stern expression brightened and he clapped his hands together.

"Wonderful," he said. "I hate having to look all over the hospital for family."

I didn't care about his professional problems. I wanted to know about Peter.

"I'm Dr. Sharif. Your husband did as wonderful as any patient I've ever had, Mr. Barbier," he said, smiling broadly. "Peter's in recovery right now. A little giddy from the anesthesia, but otherwise just fine."

A heavy breath I hadn't known I was holding escaped from me and I found I had to hold back the tears that had been lining up to escape my eyes.

"He's…he's okay?" I asked.

"He's great," the doctor assured me. "You did the right thing getting him here as quickly as you did. That appendix needed to come out now."

"It was so sudden," I whispered.

He nodded solemnly. "That's the thing with appendicitis. It can strike like that." He snapped his fingers. "You did the right thing getting him here. Sometimes patients just need some antibiotics and we can schedule a surgery for later if needed. Other times, it's a severe and acute case like Peter's and we have to act right away."

Nodding, I did my best to control my breathing.

"Can I…can I go see him?" I asked. "Now?"

"I don't see why not," the doctor said cheerfully, "just give us a few minutes to make sure he's cleaned up and settled in a recovery bed and a nurse will come get you."

All I could do was nod and say, "Thank you."

"He'll be a little," the doctor swirled his index finger next to his head with a laugh, "so don't expect him to be a great conversationalist. He might even be asleep when you get in there, but we'll make sure you get to see him in a few minutes."

I smiled awkwardly, suddenly feeling nauseated. "Okay. Thank you, Dr. Sharif."

"Of course," he said, walking away backwards. "A nurse will be out in a few minutes to fetch you, okay?"

"Okay."

Then he was gone again.

For some reason, the three minutes—I watched the clock—that passed between seeing the doctor and the nurse appearing to take me to the recovery room seemed longer than the wait for the surgery to be over. The nurse was as pleasant as the doctor, quick to let me know that Peter was fine, but my nerves were such that I could barely listen to her news of Peter as we made our way down hall after hall towards recovery. It wasn't until we were standing in a large, sterile room, one wall lined with hospital beds, and the other comprised of a nurses' station, and I was standing in front of a drawn curtain, that I actually began to listen to her.

"…he's being a little silly," she said, "but he'll be so happy to see you. He's been asking for you since he woke up. *Loudly.*"

"He's awake?" I asked softly as she reached for the curtain.

"Oh, God yes," she laughed. "Wide awake. For now, anyway."

I couldn't quite decipher what her laugh meant, so I waited. When she pulled back the blue curtain, and I found Peter laying in the bed inside the makeshift room, my nausea evaporated and my heart leapt in my chest. Peter, his color returned—though his hair was a mess—was looking around the room, his head lolling around on his neck like a balloon on a stick. He was smiling goofily and his eyes looked glassy. But he was awake. *Alive.*

At the sound of the curtain being pulled back, Peter's head swung on his neck to see who was coming to his bedside. His eyes landed on me and the biggest, dopiest grin overtook his face.

"*Enzooooooooooo,*" he crowed.

The nurse patted my back. "Good luck with this one."

She chuckled and walked away, leaving me with Peter. Padding over to the side of his bed, which Peter was patting heavily with his hand that had an IV sticking out of it, I lowered myself to the bed gently.

"Enzo," Peter repeated. "My sexy husband. Did you get handsomer?"

Peter's words were slurred and not quite pronounced correctly, but I didn't care. I wanted to laugh, but, instead, a tear slid down my cheek. I quickly wiped it away and slid my hand under Peter's, making sure not to disturb his IV.

"I'm still the same amount of handsome." I chuckled wetly. "Hey. Husband."

"*Heeeeeeeeeeey, husband,*" he repeated. "Did you miss me?"

I needed to sniffle, but I forced myself to ignore it while I was at Peter's bedside. Knowing he was fine had made me happy—and that's what I wanted him to see.

"Of course," I managed to chuckle. "I always miss you when you're not there."

When I had thought to say that sentence, it was simply to humor Peter's anesthesia drunkenness. However, as the words came from my mouth, it struck me how true they were. Like a punch to the gut, I suddenly wondered what the fuck had been wrong with me for years. My husband—the man I loved above all things, who meant more to me than even myself—was lying in a hospital bed after having avoided potential death.

How could I be so frivolous?

Why had I acted as though life wasn't so tenuous?

Did anyone understand that better than I?

"Aw," Peter said, "you're lying. You didn't miss meeeeee. You're just being nice. Don't be nice to me just because I got cut up."

I laughed and sniffled, not caring if Peter heard.

"I missed you very much, Peter," I said. "I promise. I love you."

Peter made a noise that was between a hoot and a bark.

"*I loooooooooove yoooooooooooou, toooooooooooo*!" he exclaimed. "I love you so much."

I could hear the nurses giggle at their station, which made me smile.

"Give me kisses," Peter followed up quickly. "I need Enzo kisses to feel better."

More giggles from the nurses.

"I won't recover if I don't have kisses, Enzooooooooo."

Instinctively, I wanted to tell Peter to lower his voice and not be so crass in public. Instead, I found myself leaning down, being careful of the tubes and wires, and not push against Peter, and kissed him softly on the lips. I didn't linger too long, afraid that I might cause harm, but I kissed him deeply enough that if he remembered the kiss later, he'd know I gave it my best, all things considered. When I pulled away, Peter was still making kissing motions with his lips.

Then, he fell asleep, his head rolling to the side, a smile on his face.

I'm uncertain how long I sat there on the side of Peter's bed, holding his hand, but eventually, I slid my hand from his. A sudden thought entered my brain and I did my best to comb my fingers through his hair and pat it down in an attempt to give him a little more dignity. I didn't want to leave him, but I had questions that he couldn't answer—even if he was awake. Making my way over to the nurses' station, the nurse who had brought me into recovery smiled up at me. The smile wasn't merely friendly, it was a conspiratorial smile, a shared joke between us about how Peter had been behaving under the lingering effects of anesthesia.

"Bless his heart," she said. "He's definitely the friendliest one we've had in a while."

I chuckled, wiping at my nose. The nurse smiled knowingly at me, then reached and pulled a tissue from the box behind her counter and held it out to me.

"Thanks," I said, wiping at my nose. "Um, he's okay?"

"Oh," she waved me off, "he's great. The best patient I've had in weeks. He did great."

"You're sure?"

She gave me an empathetic smile. "Absolutely. He'll be out of here late tonight or first thing tomorrow. Day after tomorrow at the latest. The way he seems, I'm betting tomorrow morning. We like to keep people for twenty-four hours to be sure, but if it wasn't for the anesthesia, I'd say he didn't even have surgery, he's doing so well. He might need your help a bit while he recovers, but he's going to be just fine. In a few weeks, this will all be an ugly memory."

Nodding, I exhaled heavily.

"Okay," I said. "Okay."

"He's lucky he had you."

"I'm lucky to have him," I mumbled.

She watched me for a moment before speaking again.

"Why don't you go get something to eat?" she asked. "Get some coffee? Catch a nap?"

"I don't—" I glanced over my shoulder.

"I'll make sure he's taken care of," she said. "We'll most likely move him to a private room in an hour or two, and then you can have him all to yourself when you get back. He'll be awake and lucid then, too. Go get a change of clothes for him to wear home. He'll appreciate that."

"The last time I left someone in the hospital to get a change of clothes for them to go home in, they died while I was gone," I said without thinking first.

When I looked back at the nurse, she was staring at me, blinking in disbelief.

"I'm sorry," I shook my head, a tear rolling down my cheek. "I'm…I'm sorry."

She rose from her chair and reached across the counter to grab my hands that were resting on the smooth surface.

"You listen to me. Your husband is going to be alive when you get back," she said firmly, staring into my eyes. "He might be sore and a little grumpy once the anesthesia wears off—most people are—but I won't let anything happen to him. I promise."

Nodding, I said, "Grumpy is okay. Alive is all that matters."

She squeezed my hands and smiled.

"I won't let you down," she said. "I promise."

"Okay," I chose to believe her.

I had to. The alternative was too much to consider.

She patted my hands and let go.

"Go get something to eat. Take a shower. Change. Get a nap. And grab him some clothes," she repeated. "If you give me your number, I'll let you know as soon as I know which room we'll be moving him to."

"Okay," I said, then gave her my number before asking another question. "Do you think I should call his parents? Anyone else?"

I had no one else to ask at the moment, and I figured a nurse would be familiar with what was most common in these specific situations.

"Well," she said, thoughtfully, "maybe wait until he's in his new room. He's going to be just fine. They might want to call and talk to him and that'll be easier in a room with a private phone. But, if you feel you need to let them know now, just tell them that you'll let them know later which room he's in so they can call."

"Okay."

She patted my hand once more. "Go. I'll take care of Peter until you get back. I promise."

Nodding, I said nothing else besides a "thank you," and I made my way out of the surgical recovery area. As I walked through the startlingly bright hallways of the cavernous hospital, my feet echoing off the walls due to their emptiness at such an hour, my mind raced. Equally excited that Peter was fine and traumatized by what had transpired in less time than it takes to braise a roast, I knew I was in a kind of shock.

My feet carried me on autopilot as I made my way to the hospital exit, my mind racing with what had just happened. Most prominently, I couldn't stop thinking about how Peter could have died. I could have lost him. Once again, Enzo Barbier could have watched someone who meant everything in the world to him disappear from that world.

I had no idea how I would have dealt with losing Peter.

Just as Peter would have felt if I had died having my surgery that I had been too selfish to even think to tell him about.

Like a punch to the gut, the last several years replayed in my head. My selfishness and foolishness washed over me. I had been so concerned with coming to terms with my past that I hadn't taken the time to embrace my future. I hadn't embraced my happiness. *I hadn't let the best thing that had ever happened to me become an important part of my existence.*

I had let my past rule my present.

Peter, our marriage, and our happiness were all that mattered. I still had to work on myself—and Peter still had to work on making sure I felt like an equal partner. But to think that working on those things separately was a solution was the dumbest idea I'd ever had.

Sometimes, in a person's life—though hopefully, it's rare—a person can fix a mistake. Correct a regret. That's exactly what I decided to do as I left the hospital.

By the time I reached the sidewalk outside of the hospital, I was running—running like I had done when I was in Montreal, trying to distract myself from my problems. Now, as a married man on the downward slope towards thirty in my new homeland, I was running towards my happiness. I couldn't wait to chase it down, wrap my arms around it, and refuse to let it go.

My feet didn't carry me to our house. Without being directed, they delivered me to my apartment. The sun was barely rising when I threw the first of my clothes into a suitcase that lay open on my bed. When I went to our house to grab some of Peter's things for his trip home from the hospital, I would drop off the suitcase. Peter's first day in the hospital would be the day that I started moving my things back home.

I would never spend another night in the apartment, away from my husband.

A half-hour later, I stood in the living room of my apartment, looking around at the unnecessary, empty life I had made for myself in an attempt to avoid pain.

When the sun rose from the horizon, filling the room with its golden light, I found I knew two things. Storms are unavoidable in life, so you may as well weather them with the people you love—the ones who want to help you adjust the sails. And since storms were unavoidable, it was fucking ridiculous to create more storms simply because you had become accustomed to them.

The Months the World Stood Still

"*Have you been watching the news?*"

Peter's voice was tinny, echoing through the cellphone as I sat in front of my computer in our shared office space in the house.

"Not really, no," I said back. "You know I've tried to avoid the news as much as possible ever since that asshole became president. I miss you."

"*I miss you, too,*" he said hurriedly, his voice cutting out a bit, "*go to the grocery store, babe.*"

"What?" I asked.

"*Sorry,*" Peter seemed to be moving around, shuffling noises echoing through the phone before his voice rang through clearly. "*I'm packing right now. It's a freaking ghost town here. Everyone's checking out and leaving. Go to the grocery store.*"

"Are you coming home sooner?" I asked, confused as I stood from my desk and headed down the hallway to the den. "Did you need me to pick up something specific?"

It had been almost three months since Peter's appendectomy. I had been living in our home since he returned from the hospital the day after his surgery, which was when they let him leave. In the past three months, I'd managed to move everything back to our house, sold the furniture I had acquired, and settled my lease with the building manager. She had been sorry to see me go, since, like most of her tenants, I had been quiet, paid on time, and rarely bothered her. However, she had let me break my lease without holding me to the fees I'd have to pay for doing so.

The Regal Building always had people on a waiting list, dying to move in, so it wasn't as if their bottom line would suffer from my leaving. Though I was excited to move home—excited to get my head out of my own ass and be with Peter all of the time—I knew I'd miss my apartment. Even though it hadn't really been my home as I'd said, I had enjoyed it for the time I'd lived there. I loved my living room and the view. My neighbors—some I'd made friends with—were wonderful. Even though it wasn't home, it held good memories. Saying "goodbye" had been difficult, but not nearly as difficult as thinking about not living with Peter any longer.

Within a month of having his surgery, Peter was completely back to normal and given a clean bill of health by his doctor. And he started traveling for his job again as needed. It was lonely, being at home alone during his trips to other cities, or even countries, for his work. However, like me, his work was important to him. He loved what he did and the trips were never longer than a week. So, as we'd been learning to do, we dealt with it.

His latest trip, to London, had been planned to last for two weeks. The longest trip yet. Neither of us looked forward to being separated for so long, but we decided that he would simply have to call me each night before bed. Staying up to date with each other that way was the compromise and the way we dealt with it. However, when he called me out of the blue in the morning—what would have been early afternoon for him in London—I was confused by his questions.

"That virus they first detected in Wuhan China?" Peter asked as I grabbed the remote for the television and began

searching for CNN. *"It's a bigger deal than we thought. It's everywhere now. It's serious."*

"You know I don't watch or read the news like I should," I mumbled into the phone as CNN appeared on the television.

I hit the mute button so that closed captions would pop up. I could talk to Peter and read the chyron and closed captions simultaneously.

Quarantine. Shutting down. Borders.

Words flashed out at me as Peter talked in my ear.

Chuckling nervously, he said, *"I know. Enzo...I'm heading home. It's...going to be a process. Getting back into the U.S. is going to be a process."*

"What?" I gasped.

"Don't worry," he said. *"My company is helping me get out of here. I'll get there. But I have to start that process now. Most likely, I'm going to have trouble at Heathrow. And then when I get to New York. A trip that would typically take a day is going to take two or three. It's going to be impossible to fly into or out of the U.S. within days, I'm sure."*

"That's insane, I—" I trailed off as I caught more words and images flashing on the screen. "What is going on, Peter?"

"People are dying. A lot," he said. *"It's a pandemic. And no one seems to know fuck all about any of it. It's a panic everywhere. Yesterday was...today everyone has lost their minds."*

I chuckled nervously. "Fuck all? The British are rubbing off on you, babe."

He laughed, and it was a genuine laugh.

"*Babe, don't panic. Be reasonable,*" he advised me. "*Get something to use like a surgical mask. Do the best you can. Some cloth or something, and go get enough groceries for a few weeks if you can. Take the car. Not the bus or something silly like that. Stay away from large crowds and be very careful.*"

"Peter, this sounds serious," I said. "Do I need to be scared?"

"*No. No. No,*" he said. "*Don't panic, babe. But I have no idea what's going to happen. I just know that pretty soon they're going to start mostly shutting down borders and entry points. I have no idea what each individual state is going to do. I don't know what's going to happen with food supplies or anything. Being prepared and not freaking out is the most important thing. I don't know how the general populace is going to act, so that's why I'm telling you to keep a level head.*"

"That sounds like I should be scared," I said.

"*Babe,*" he said, "*I would tell you if you needed to be scared. Right?*"

I took a steadying breath. "Yes."

"*I just want you to prepare in case things get prickly for a while. Okay?*"

"Okay," I said, nodding to myself as I stared in shock at the news. "You will come home. Right?"

Peter mumbled something that I didn't quite catch. "*Three days at most. I promise. They'll find a way to get me home.*"

"Okay," I said. "I have to work today, so—"

"*Use a PTO day,*" he said. "*Get to the grocery store. Trust me.*"

"Okay," I said, my concern growing.

"*I have to go. I need to get to the airport. A company representative that's over here is meeting me. I'll message or call you tonight. Okay?*"

"Okay. I love you."

"*I love you, too, husband,*" he said. "*I will see you soon. I promise.*"

The line went dead and it took me a moment to let my cellphone slide from my ear. Staring at the chyron on the television, I turned the volume back on. For what seemed like hours, I was glued to the screen, standing in the den, watching doom scroll across the screen. Finally, what was only minutes later, I turned the television off and sprang into action.

Peter had asked me to do something—and I trusted Peter. I knew that if he told me to do something, it was important. It took me a few minutes to find an old t-shirt I could fashion into what passed as a face mask. It looked ridiculous, and I knew I would be ridiculed when I got to the grocery store, but I did as Peter instructed.

It took me only a few minutes more to clear my work day with my boss. Within the first month of moving back home, I'd been made a manager, supervising a team of a few dozen interpreters. I knew it wouldn't be easy on my team to have me absent for a day without warning, but Peter had been clear. When I advised my boss that I could be reached via my cellphone, if necessary, he approved my day without further question.

Once that was done, I got dressed and hurried down to the car. A mild panic picked at my brain as I sat in the driver's seat, imagining what was going on in the world. The news can never be relied on for a clear and honest picture. The worst of the worst is what is always shown. Unless downplaying everything fits the narrative more. I've never been a conspiracy person or someone who loses their head thinking about how corrupt news organizations and politicians are, but I knew that there was only one way to find out how much I needed to panic.

So, I started the car and drove to the grocery store.

Peter stood in the pantry, looking around at everything I had purchased, chuckling to himself at the fully-stocked shelves. It was possible that I'd gone a little wild in the grocery store two days before. However, when I'd seen for myself how so many foods had been completely sold out, I couldn't control myself. I'd managed to stay calm for the most part, however. Peter had told me to get enough groceries for a few weeks. What I'd purchased for us would easily last a month or two. At least as far as non-perishable items went.

"We're going to be eating a lot of pasta and beans and rice," he said.

We hadn't even taken his suitcases down to the basement to start washing his clothes yet. The moment he had walked in the door, we had debated whether or not we should hug and kiss—concerned about whether or not we should stay apart for two weeks. In case he had somehow caught COVID-19 during his journey back home. It had proved impossible to stay separate. The two of us finally rushed into each other's arms, clutching at each other, kissing and holding each other, proclaiming how much we loved and missed each other.

After far too much holding each other in the foyer, I asked Peter to come to see if I'd gotten enough for us to get by. He immediately began laughing when he stepped into the pantry. I didn't really need an answer after that, but I waited for his verdict anyway.

"But we like those things, so…," Peter trailed off.

"I bought the pasta they had, so we have a variety," I said with a shrug. "People had bought most of the pasta. The ramen. Milk. Bread. If it was something you only have to add water to and heat to make a meal, it was gone. Ground beef and sandwich meat were gone."

Peter turned to listen to me.

"No one was buying fresh produce, so I bought a lot," I said. "I sliced and chopped and put a lot in bags in the freezers. The same with tomatoes so that we'd have the ingredients for easy pasta sauce. Whole chickens and pork butts were still available, so, I did the same with those."

Peter laughed.

"I heard toilet paper is—"

"Gone," I shook my head.

We both laughed.

"Of all things…"

"I know," I agreed. "It was stupid, but no one was behaving poorly. Not at the store I went to. They were all just concentrating on getting the items they needed. I talked to Alex. He said people are acting crazy in some places down there but he hasn't had any issues. Except with getting toilet paper."

Peter chuckled and glanced over his shoulder at the pantry once more.

"Well," he said with a sigh, "you took care of us. Like you always do."

"I did my best," I said. "I ordered some face masks, but I have no idea if we'll get them or when."

Staring at me for a few moments, Peter examined my face as though he had never seen it before.

"Are you okay, Enzo?" he asked softly.

"I'm scared," I said without thinking. "I'm really scared, Peter."

He moved over to me and took me in his arms.

"I am, too."

"We'll be okay together, right?" I asked, though I knew there was no way for us to see the future in such uncertain times.

"We'll be okay," he said, though I knew he was thinking the same thing. "Maybe it won't be as bad as the news and everyone is making it out to be, right?"

What Three Strikes Means if You're an American

Peter sat with me in front of my work computer, though we were turned to face each other instead of my computer monitors. Our knees were touching and we were staring into each other's eyes. I wasn't working even though it was a work day. I'd set everything aside, put my work phone on "do not disturb," and called Peter into the office for advice. He had been working in the dining room but took a break from his work to find out what I needed.

When I told him, he slumped, disappointed for me.

We'd been used to disappointments. Within our first year of living with the pandemic, hundreds of thousands of people were dead from COVID-19 in the U.S. alone. Protests against police brutality were ongoing across the country. The torture and murder of George Perry Floyd, Jr. by the police in our own city had brought the issue to the forefront of American minds a mere two months after the pandemic had been officially announced. We had watched in real-time with horror as insurrectionists attempted to storm the capitol and steal a legally won election.

The horrors in the U.S. were a mere percentage of the horrors we watched unfold on the news every day. We had been watching the world seemingly fall apart for a year. Though not ideal, we were becoming accustomed to bad news.

"That's a hard decision, babe," he said.

"I know," I said. "I'm...I know what the right answer is."

"Do you just want to hear it in my voice?" Peter asked.

I smiled, but I didn't respond. He knew the answer.

A year into the pandemic, and after months of Source Language, Inc. losing business, it became clear that business could not continue as usual. Mr. Barton had called me personally to let me know that restructuring would occur. A handful of employees at our company were going to lose their jobs. He hadn't indicated in any way that my neck was on the chopping block, he had simply been giving me a personal heads up.

The two of us had discussed the situation at length, and I could tell how much it pained him, knowing he would have to let any of our wonderful employees go. He had asked me if I was forced to choose if any of the interpreters on my team were underperforming in a way that would justify letting them go. Mr. Barton wanted to be certain he kept the very best employees if possible. Everybody on my team was wonderful—and I had enjoyed supervising them for over a year. Instead of giving him any of their names, I found myself asking:

If you got rid of me, how many would that save?

"Mr. Barton wasn't happy," I said. "About what I suggested. But he said if that's what I wanted to do, he would accept it—since I care so much about my team. He said if I did that, he would guarantee that none of my people would be let go."

"Do you want to do that?" Peter asked, rubbing my knees with his hands.

"A lot of my people are single mothers. Or the only income in their household. Or they really need the good insurance," I said. "I love my job. You know that."

"But?"

"Yes," I said. "That is what I want to do."

"Then that's what you should do," Peter squeezed my knees, smiling warmly at me.

"You'll be the only one with a job," I said, sighing and sitting back in my chair.

"So what?" Peter shrugged. "I make plenty."

"We won't be equal," I said. "Again. I'll feel like—"

Peter slapped my knee gently and drew my attention so that our eyes met.

"What's mine is yours and what's yours is mine," he said. "We're partners through the good and the bad. And how much you do or don't earn isn't what makes you an equal partner, Enzo."

"I just—"

"You do *so much* for us," he said. "You work full time. You cook for us every day. You keep this house sparkling clean and running. You're always there for neighbors. Family. Friends. We have a warm, inviting, happy home because of you. Even through all of the world's bullshit, you've made home feel safe. Like the one place in the world that doesn't seem messed up. If anything, I'm the one dropping the ball."

I chuckled. "No. But thank you for saying that."

Peter took my hands in his.

"I mean it, Enzo," he said. "This house is a home because of you. Everything works out because you work overtime on everything you do. If you want to quit to keep your people from losing their jobs, you have my full support. And we'll deal with it as a team."

Sighing, I nodded slowly. It was the right decision.

"But," I said, "what will I do? I guess I can find another—"

"Just live for a while, babe," Peter said. "Read. Watch T.V. Get a new hobby. Keep doing the other things you've been doing. Work on your writing some more. You haven't had a lot of time for that in months. It won't hurt for you to have one less thing to worry about. Selfishly, I'll be glad to have you free more often."

"I need a purpose, Peter," I said, though his last statement made me smile. "If I don't have a reason to get up each day…"

Peter shook his head lazily.

"I think you're confusing a job with a purpose, Enzo," he said. "A job is not a purpose. It's a means to make money. That's all."

"Your job is part of your identity," I said, nudging him playfully.

"I do love my job," he said. "It's boring as fuck, but I do love it."

We laughed.

"But it doesn't give me purpose, babe," he said. "That's you. Us. Our life. The dreams we have for the future. Not my job. My job helps us work towards that dream."

"The sweet things you say," I teased him.

Peter leaned forward and gave me a lingering kiss.

"You know what to do," he said, pulling back just far enough to speak. "But I won't tell you to do it. That's your decision. I'm behind you all the way no matter what you choose."

"Okay."

Peter stood, bent to kiss the top of my head, then looked down at me.

"I'm going to get back to work," he said. "Then you can sit here and think about what you want to do. Okay?"

I nodded and watched Peter leave, looking over his shoulder to wink at me. With the office at the back of the house to myself again, I stared out the window at nothing. Spring had arrived, and though still chilly outside, the sun shining down on the emerald green grass of the backyard made everything look summery. At least from the warmth and comfort of inside.

Since arriving in the U.S., becoming a naturalized citizen, running from my marriage, running back towards happiness, I'd had no purpose or meaning, found a job, nearly destroyed the most important thing in my life, nearly lost the most important person in my life, somehow fixed it…and now I was directionless again. In minutes, I would call the CEO of my company and offer myself up as sacrifice.

For a moment, I felt as though everything that I'd gone through since I'd left Montreal for the last time, had been pointless. Self-pity began trying to creep back into my brain, to convince me that I had failed yet again.

Yet, as I stared out at the backyard, my eyes unfocused and my vision glassy as I got lost in my thoughts, I pushed my doubts and pity away. I had Peter. He had me. We had our marriage. We had our home and our wonderful life. We had created that together.

The world was a messy place, but we were doing our best. Creating the future we wanted together.

Even without a job, I could continue to create. Peter and I could create together.

You Were Meant for Me

"Just one more time," Nancy said. "Please."

Rolling my eyes, I obliged.

"Deux croissants et deux lattés s'il te plaît," I repeated.

We were both wearing masks, but the bakery was empty of customers, so communicating was not as difficult as it sometimes could be.

Nancy squealed, her hands waving back and forth excitedly over the cash register. La Croûte had been mine and Peter's favorite coffee shop and bakery for years. We'd been patrons for years—the entire time I'd lived in the U.S. Nancy was not unfamiliar with me. She, along with the rest of the staff at the bakery, never got tired of asking me to speak French. Peter also was often amused, watching the women of the shop swoon over my native tongue.

Funniest to me was that I always had to order in English first since none of the staff actually understood French for the most part. However, they often also wanted to hear it in French. If the bakery wasn't too busy, so that I didn't seem like a sideshow, I would oblige. After a while, the staff began to realize that I was happy to do this simple thing for them, as long as they didn't put me on display for their other customers.

"Go sit with Peter," Nancy shooed me away happily. "I'll bring your coffees and croissants to you, hon."

Laughing, I pulled my card from the machine and slipped it into my wallet, which I then deposited in my pocket. Peter was waiting for me at our favorite booth by the front window, watching people on the sidewalk pass. It was a spectacularly windy, yet sunny day in Minneapolis. Everyone outside was struggling to keep their shirts or skirts from flying up with each gust of wind, which Peter found comical. It was funny to me, too, but I struggled with laughing at other people's misfortune. Especially since Peter and I had also fought against the wind on our walk into the bakery. Of course, the people who passed, holding down their clothing, were laughing about the wind, so I suppose it was funny.

"Nancy is going to bring our coffees," I said as I slid into the booth seat across from Peter and lowered my mask. "And croissants."

Peter smiled. "I was going to ask about the croissants."

"I would have been shocked if you hadn't." I kicked him softly in the shin under the table.

Peter feigned a shock of pain, before giving me a wink and pulling out his phone. I slid my jacket from my shoulders to lay in the seat behind me as Peter swiped through the news. Anytime we went to La Croûte together, we had a routine. I would order our drinks and snack. Peter would check the news for anything important. When Nancy brought our food and drinks to the table, we'd raise our masks before she was too close—to protect her and us. She never lingered for too long, so we would then lower our masks again and enjoy our coffees and snacks.

As we ate and sipped our coffees, Peter would occasionally mention something newsworthy he saw as he scrolled through his phone. I would stare out the window and watch people pass. On gloomy days, I'd watch the rain trace rivulets down the window. On sunny days, I watched the sun glint off of the windows of the surrounding buildings. I'd simply spend time disconnected from everything the world could throw at a person in a day.

Once done with our coffees and snacks, we might linger for a few minutes, but we'd eventually leave La Croûte for a hand-in-hand walk around our favorite downtown neighborhood. The pandemic had changed our routine in that we didn't pop into as many shops to browse anymore—especially if they were busy—but being outdoors and keeping a reasonable distance from others finally felt safer. Even if every shop was too busy to feel safe to venture into, at least Peter and I could have our walk, our hands never separating.

When the world is constantly threatening to fall apart, at least you can hold on to someone who matters to you.

"Thank you," Peter said for us when Nancy delivered our order.

She told us we were welcome through her mask, and her eyes were such that I could tell she was smiling underneath it. Nancy was a smiler. It was one of the things I loved about her. I never felt unwelcome in La Croûte.

Aside from our home, La Croûte was one of the few places in the city where I felt comfortable and safe. I tried not to spend too much time at the bakery, but when you find a welcoming place with genuinely friendly people, and it also serves coffee and wonderful baked goods—it's hard to stay away for long.

"You know," Peter said, "no one ever needs to go to France. The croissants here are the best in the world."

I laughed loudly. "I wouldn't go that far."

Peter frowned playfully.

"They are delicious, though," I relented.

Eyeing me for a moment first, Peter said: "Do you think you ever want to go back to France?"

"To live?" I asked.

He shrugged.

"No," I said. "Never."

"What about to visit?" he asked. "You could show me where you were born. Teach me more about the culture. Those kinds of things?"

"I suppose," I said. "If it was important for you to take a vacation to France one day, I would go with you."

"But it's not important to you?"

"No."

"So...you don't miss your home?"

"This is my home," I said. "*You* are my home."

He grinned widely. "I feel the same. But you know what I mean. America is...well, *America*. Our marriage aside, don't you think that—"

"I think that I'm where I'm meant to be," I said, cutting him off as I kicked him gently under the table again.

Peter simply smiled.

"However," I said, knowing what he was getting at, "no, America is definitely imperfect. It can be awful, yes."

"But?"

I shrugged. "It's my home. I don't want to run from it, either. What kind of person would that make me if I didn't hold onto hope that it will be better one day?"

"I suppose," he said, lifting his coffee to his lips. "It's just frustrating. Ten steps forward, nine steps back, you know?"

Sighing, I said: "I guess we'll just have to keep making steps together. Because this is where we're meant to be."

Peter grumbled playfully, pretending to be upset.

"It's just the worst," he said, "knowing exactly where you belong. Being with the person you're meant to be with. I don't know how we'll manage."

Laughing, I tore at the top of my croissant.

"You think you'll be okay?" Peter asked. "Knowing you were meant for me?"

"I was meant *just* for *you*?" I asked playfully. "No one else ever would have done? We're soulmates?"

Peter stared at me.

I let him stew for a moment, then smiled.

"Yeah," I said. "I can't imagine anything else. I wouldn't want to."

Sighing happily, Peter mimicked me, tearing at his croissant.

"I suppose there's only one thing left," he said.

"What's that?"

"What's the next step?" he asked. "Since I guess we're stuck with each other…what do we want to do with that? Things are kind of getting back to normal. As normal as they'll probably ever be again. What do we do now?"

"There are so many possibilities," I said. "Which one to choose?"

Peter shrugged. I shrugged. We took bites of our croissants. He went back to scrolling through his phone as I stared out the window, listening each time he mentioned something interesting he ran across.

What was next?

I think I knew what was next for me.

And I was certain Peter would be happy to go along with my idea.

You Can't Dream the Same Dream Forever

The blistering sun had turned our car into a sauna on an exceptionally warm and muggy summer day. Our activities in the backseat hadn't helped cool it down. We'd left the car on with the air conditioner running, but it could only do so much to keep us cool. Peter was still astride me, his bare chest slick with sweat against my bare chest. Naked and unashamed, and kissing in the backseat of our car that we'd parked down a rarely traveled country road, we were coming down from our orgasms. In the mid-afternoon hour, we knew we couldn't spend as much time as we'd like, doing the thing we were doing, but we didn't rush, either.

I took my time, kissing Peter, nibbling at his neck, running my hands up and down his back, feeling every inch of his body that I could. Peter had his arms around my neck, sighing happily as I explored his body. Our lovemaking was over, but we were still connected, refusing to separate so quickly after such a high. We were both still trying to catch our breath.

Finally, I pulled my mouth away from Peter's flesh so I could look up at him. He bent his head to give me a soft, lingering kiss on the lips, then shifted enough to elicit a moan from me. We both laughed as I reached up and ran my fingers through his damp hair. As I looked up at him, all I could think was how much I wished that certain moments with Peter would never end. If we could be frozen in time for…well, forever…at certain points in our history, I would never feel sadness for the rest of my life.

Then again, what are the happy times without the sad times?

When it became obvious that we needed to separate and slide back into our clothes, we both did so begrudgingly. Laughing, we both slid into our pants and shirts, doing our best to not elbow each other as we redressed in the backseat. Finally, fully clothed again, we sat at opposite sides of the bench seat, smiling at each other wickedly, proud of the fornication we'd just committed in broad daylight.

"I think I've found a new favorite way we do that," Peter spoke first.

"I'm definitely not mad at it, either," I said.

The first "tip-taps" of rain sounded on the roof of the car and splattered on the windows. The warmth and thick mugginess that had hung like a wet blanket over our city all day had culminated in the only logical result. Peter and I grinned at the sound of the rain. Not because we had been particularly excited for another rainy day, but because the heat had been unbearable. In Minnesota, you only get so many hot days in summer, but when they arrive, they are relentless. Especially after all of the temperate days of early and mid-summer.

"Should we sit here and just enjoy the rain for a while?" Peter asked.

"I don't have anywhere to be," I teased.

Our Sundays, as we'd planned since our first meeting in Montreal, were always dedicated to each other, as long as we were together. Leisurely breakfasts in our bedroom in the tiny sitting area. Not showering until the morning was nearly gone. Sex. Lots of sex. We'd recently taken up driving out to the country for fun outdoorsy intimacy. It hurt no one as long as we weren't caught—and we never were. We didn't necessarily need more spice in our marriage, but extra excitement in any marriage never hurt.

I leaned back against the door and kicked my feet out, trying to lay them in Peter's lap. He laughed and pretended he would push them away before, ultimately, pulling them into his lap. Moaning with satisfaction, I laid back and enjoyed having Peter massage my feet as we listened to the rain begin to fall harder and faster, until a symphony was playing above our heads on the windows around us. Even though it was mid-afternoon, the storm clouds had blotted out the sun, casting the interior of the car in dark shadows.

So, relaxed and satisfied, I felt as though I could fall asleep with the doorhandle digging into my back and the hard glass of the window against the back of my head. The sound of the rain and Peter's expert hands working on my feet chased away thoughts of anything important. It struck me at that moment how perfect our life together had become. We were happily married, financially secure, loved our home, loved each other, we had plenty of food—the world was a crazy place, but we had carved out a little piece of sanity and security for ourselves.

Privileged for sure, but we weren't going to disrespect that by pretending we were sorry for it.

"I never knew life could be this good," Peter said, clearly reading my thoughts.

I responded with a chuckle.

"Are you happy, Enzo?" he asked.

"I am," I said as my eyes lazily shut. "I'm very happy."

"Can I tell you something?"

"Of course."

"I never wanted a family of my own," he said quietly, "because I never thought I'd meet someone I'd want a family with."

I laughed.

"I never thought I'd meet a guy I'd actually want to marry," he continued. "But then here you come and just shit all over my assumptions."

"I do what I can," I said. "I live to serve."

Peter tickled my feet, and I kicked softly, actually giggling. When we settled down, he went back to rubbing my feet, but not as attentively as before.

"What do you say?" he asked.

"About what?"

My eyes were closed again and I was enjoying the sound of the rain as it assaulted the car.

"Starting a family finally," he said. "You always wanted a family of your own. I...I think I'm ready, babe."

Peter's sudden decision to bring up starting a family— seemingly out of the blue—had me sitting up, my eyes opening as I slid my feet out of his lap. Picking up on the sudden change in my mood, for how could he not, Peter winced. We'd just had sex in the back of our car down a country road and were relaxing and enjoying the rain. The last thing I'd thought would happen was that we'd bring up one of the last bones of contention in our relationship.

For years, I'd repressed the life goal of having my own family. A husband, kids, a boisterous, happy home with homework and family meals at the table and big holidays and fights and making up and warmth and love and...everything.

I had pushed that desire down for so long that I'd forgotten it had once been my greatest desire.

Now, sitting across from Peter in the backseat of our car, I didn't know what I wanted.

"Well?" Peter asked nervously.

"Well...what?" I asked.

He frowned at me.

"Why now, Peter?" I asked with a sigh.

"What do you mean, *'why now*?'" he grumbled. "Is there a better time? I'm going to turn fifty before too long. Do you want to wait until I'm sixty? And you're forty?"

I rolled my eyes. "Are we going to fight now?"

"I'm not trying to fight," he said, though his tone didn't match his words. "But why are you upset that I brought it up?"

"I'm not upset."

"You look upset."

"Well, I'm not."

"Well, you sound upset."

"Good Lord, Peter," I grumbled, turning to sit with my feet on the floorboard. "I'm not upset. It's just that...why bring it up? Now?"

"Isn't that what you've always wanted?" he asked, sliding across the seat to be closer to me. "I thought you'd be happy. What's going on here?"

"Nothing's going on," I said, and even I knew I sounded grumpy. "I just don't know why you brought that up randomly today. That's all."

"Babe," Peter slid closer and put his arm around me, "what's going on?"

Sighing, I did my best to deflect Peter's question. I knew that I was falling back on bad habits of pushing things away when I didn't have the words to explain how I felt. Or, maybe, even I didn't know how I felt. But I couldn't force myself to address Peter's question in a way that expressed what I was thinking and feeling.

"Nothing," I said, lifting myself and, preparing to climb into the front seat. "Let's go home."

"How did you suddenly go from *'yay, we just had great sex'* to grumpy Enzo?" Peter grumbled. "We were having a good day."

Annoyed, I grabbed the door handle and popped the backdoor open. A sheet of rain slapped against me and assaulted the interior of the car as I jumped out, slamming the door behind me. I had barely made it to the front of the car, marching angrily away, before Peter caught up to me. Dashing through the rain from the other side of the car, he met me at the hood. Peter grabbed me by my upper arms, stopping me.

"What are you doing?" he shouted over the rain.

I refused to look at him.

"Look at me, Enzo!" he shouted desperately. *"Don't ignore me!"*

Forcing myself to comply, I turned my head into the rain and look into his eyes, the rain droplets stinging my face as we stared at each other.

"What's going on?" he asked again.

"I don't know!" I shouted back.

Not angrily—just loudly so that I could be heard over the pounding rain.

"Do you not want a family with me anymore?" he asked. *"Is that it?"*

"It's not you! I want you in my life forever, Peter!"

"Then...what?"

Staring off over Peter's shoulder for a moment, I found myself wondering if there was any way I could simply explain how I felt. How could I explain why his question had bothered me?

"I'm happy, Peter!" I shouted over the rain. *"Does it make me a bad person to not want to do anything that might fuck that up?"*

Peter's expression softened and he gripped my arms tightly in his hands, a gesture of reassurance.

"Even if it's something I've always wanted?" I asked loudly as the rain drenched us. *"Maybe dreams aren't worthwhile if they might interfere with another dream. You know?"*

"That doesn't make you a bad person, Enzo."

"Why? Now it's something you want and...maybe I've changed my mind. Maybe I...I'm scared to do anything that will change what we have, Peter."

Peter stared at me.

"And how could we bring a child into this world, you know?" I shook my head. *"Just because you want something doesn't mean it's the best thing. Everything is so messed up and scary and...do we want to bring a life into it?"*

"I don't know."

"I love you so much, Peter." He smiled and squeezed me tighter as I spoke. *"That will never change. I don't want* this *to ever change. This—us—is the most important thing to me."*

"You're the most important thing to me, too, Enzo."

"Maybe I wanted to have kids and all of that because I didn't understand what all a family can look like. We have a family. You and me. And...maybe my dream is different now? Maybe somewhere along the way, without even knowing it, I decided that I can't dream the same dream forever. You know?"

Peter nodded slowly. And I'd run out of words. Maybe I still wanted to be a father. But was it the best dream for me? Was it the best next step for Peter and me?

"Then what's your dream, Enzo?" Peter asked over the rain. *"What do you want? You've got me. I'm along for the ride, babe."*

I stared at him.

"Do you want to expand our family? Or not?" he asked. *"Is it something else? You know I'm here for you until the end, and I know you're here for me until the end. So, all we have to do is decide what the end is going to be, right?"*

"I suppose. Yes."

"What do you want, Enzo?" he asked again. *"Just tell me what you want."*

A Home
Present Day

Grief, by definition, is "*deep sorrow, especially that caused by someone's death*." That's the dictionary definition. In psychology, grief is defined as "*a powerful emotional and physical reaction to the loss of someone or something*." Psychology further goes on to explain grief as "*characterized by deep feelings of sadness and sorrow, and often by a powerful yearning or longing to be with that person again*." Grief, therefore, is a logical response to trauma one experiences via loss. It's a method to process those feelings associated with said trauma.

Almost everyone agrees that there are five basic stages of grief, as first described by Elizabeth Kübler-Ross. Denial, anger, bargaining, depression, and acceptance. When a person has their life—their whole world view—turned upside down by loss, the process to work through it is layered and, often, life-long. A person doesn't want to believe what is happening in an effort to parcel out the grief so it is not overwhelming. Then they're angry. Next, they try to barter with anyone—but most commonly God—to fix the loss. To reverse the irreversible. When that proves impossible, depression follows. Finally, and hopefully, they settle into acceptance and moving on with their life, leaving their grief behind, or at least, shoving it to the back of their mind.

I've found the definitions of grief to be adequate. The stages, and their definitions, however, do not resonate with me.

For me, grief has never been regimented, even if there are distinct ways to categorize the period of grief I have been going through at any given time. However, they are not linear; they are cyclic. Passing the anger stage doesn't mean it won't return. And anger doesn't have to be the second stage, either. Grief is not structured; it cannot be confined to a definition or outline.

Because grief has triggers.

Birthdays. Christmas. Family occasions. Holiday times. Those are when people, supposedly, have their grief triggered in the strongest ways. Those are the times when grief—even if someone feels they have moved past it—returns. Because it's cyclic.

However, this theory of grief triggers is predicated on a Western and Christian cultural ideal.

Grief is universal, but how it is felt, triggered, and dealt with, is not.

Ultimately, psychology and the dictionary cannot define grief for me. Because nothing that big can be explained simply with words. The theorized triggers are inadequate as well. Because there is really only one trigger for grief; for loss.

Life.

One doesn't need to have a special occasion to grieve someone they've lost. They merely need to be alive...and remember that a person they love is not.

So, definitions are inadequate, but they are also unnecessarily complicated.

The side effect of living is, often, grief.

To grieve is to be human. To grieve is to be alive.

There is only one cure for grief. It's not working one's way through the posited five stages and coming out the other side with a fresh perspective. The cure is to live and to be grateful one is alive. However one can manage to do that. A person may spend their life dealing with grief because all of life is a trigger, and grief is cyclic. Each person figures that out in their own way because grief is not universally felt, triggered, or dealt with the same way.

Does grief ever go away? In my experience…no.

When does it get better? I'll let you know.

When does it get easier? Every day.

That's the thing about grief. It never gets better because better would be to have the person or thing back that you no longer have in your life. However, the skills one learns to deal with grief get honed when it returns on a random Tuesday while one is making a spreadsheet for work and they are eating a snack their deceased loved one enjoyed. Dealing with it gets easier each day. Each time grief is felt, each time a dark cloud of sadness forms above a person and rains down on their unsuspecting head, their umbrella gets bigger. Stronger.

Grief is a crack. A cavity. A place for the niggling, intrusive thoughts to invade and wiggle around. All anyone can do is evict the pest and temporarily patch the hole. But like any pest, grief will return, finding a flaw in the new construction.

I suppose, if grief is a side effect of life, then life is a side effect of grief, too. Because does one ever feel more alive than when they are grieving? What reminds one more that they are alive than when someone they love is not? And what better way to honor that loss than to make the most out of one's life—to be grateful for it?

Gratefulness doesn't make it better; it simply makes it easier.

So, I choose gratefulness. I'll deal with grief as it comes. Its less frequent visits have become less severe each time. Maybe one day it will decide to no longer stop at my door. Only time will tell. Only more living will tell. The trick is to want that life; to live.

Life is easier with purpose, meaning, and possibility.

When I'd walked into the house, going around to the backdoor, up the back steps, and into the kitchen, I found I could go no further. I sat down at the kitchen table, holding the bundle I'd carried all morning against my chest. I laid my plastic bag of cherries on the table.

The kitchen was warm and yellow from the sunbeams shining through the windows, bright enough that turning the lights on in the room was unnecessary. Our gloomy day in Minneapolis was burning away and the early spring sun was making itself known. As grief is to life, so is winter to spring, existing to give each other meaning.

Grief for my family was mostly a distant memory, since thinking of them as the days since my thirtieth birthday had passed by made me smile instead of sad. In the kitchen of my home—*our home*—I no longer felt like I was living with ghosts. I felt the ghosts were living with me. Hopefully, honored by the life I'd built from the rubble created by their loss. My home was their home, because, while moving on is the most important stage of grief that no one talks about, those ghosts would always be a part of my life.

I hope that, in some way, that had given their lives some meaning.

You can't really give dead people much, but you can always offer your gratitude. And a little space in your memory and your home for them to occupy from time to time.

So that they never truly died.

Holding the bundle against my chest, thinking about my life in its entirety, those I'd lost, I knew for certain that I knew nothing. I was no closer to understanding life. I was uncertain if I'd decided on a perfect purpose, or if anything I'd done or would do had any meaning. But I knew that my life had held possibility, and possibilities laid out before me.

I'd learned to create something out of my life. Peter and I had created something together.

We'd keep creating together. And separately. Because even if you have someone to create with, it's still rewarding to also have a little something of your own.

So, I pulled the bundle away from my chest gently and stared down at it, a broad smile stretching my face as the sun seemed to glow in the kitchen windows, chasing away the cold.

If you're fortunate enough to live, maybe the most important thing you can do is to give life to something else.

I guess that's the purest definition of "creation."

Bundle of Joy

"When did you get home?" Peter's voice woke me from my daydream.

Unknowingly, I'd closed my eyes and smiled as the sun from the window shone on my face, warming my skin as I sat at the table and held my little bundle. When Peter spoke, I slowly opened my eyes, my smile widening as our eyes met. He stared at me with a goofy, confused grin for a moment—the smile I could never get enough of—then looked at the bundle in my arms. Grinning, he made his way from the kitchen door to the table and sat down in the chair across from me.

Holding his arms out excitedly, he said: "Give it here. Let me have it. I've been waiting all day!"

Laughing, I felt frozen for a minute, but then managed to let go of the box I'd picked up at FedEx and slid it across the table to Peter. Having missed the delivery the day before, I'd been deflated. However, having a morning alone with the box, contemplating its contents had been good for my nerves. For the longest of seconds, Peter stared down at the plain, cardboard box with a single shipping label affixed to the top. Then he looked up at me, concern etched across his face.

"You haven't opened it," he said. "I don't—"

"Open it," I said.

"You really should," he said, shaking his head.

"I've been too scared to," I said.

"Scared?" He laughed. "Why would you be scared?"

I shrugged. "Do the honors?"

Sighing, Peter nodded and smiled.

"Only if you want me to?"

"Yes," I said. "Please."

He didn't need any further prodding. Peter stared into my eyes as his fingers worked expertly to strip the tape from the box and pry back the top flaps. When the box was open, we took a collective deep breath, and he plunged his hands inside. Suddenly, Peter was smiling at me. His hands had found the object held within.

"Babe," he sighed, "I see what you mean. This is a huge moment."

"Don't prolong it. I'm dying."

Peter chuckled and lifted the book from the box. His eyes went wide with wonder and a small gasp escaped his lips. I was dying to see it for myself, but I tried to be patient as Peter held the book in front of himself, staring down at it as though he'd never seen a book before.

"*Repainting the Universe*," he whispered with awe. "*A novel. By Enzo Barbier.*"

"It's just the proof," I said, shrugging as a way to convince myself to not lose my mind. "It's…it's not finished, I suppose? Not final."

Peter looked up at me and shook his head.

"Don't do that," he said. "This is *amazing*, babe."

He turned the book proof in his hands so that I could see the cover. At first sight, the book, with my name on the cover, made my eyes go wide and my breath to catch in my throat. Nothing makes creation more amazing than when you can hold the product in your hands for the first time. It makes what seemed so impossible for so many years a possibility.

"Do you mind, if…" Peter trailed off.

"No," I said, gesturing emphatically, "please."

Giddily, Peter began flipping through the book, examining the wrap-around cover, reading select passages, possibly as excited as I was—if not more so. Like me, he was elated to see the product of all of my work in a physical, tangible form. He held my years of work in his hands—it was real. *And it was beautiful.* Even if it was likely imperfect.

"I am so incredibly proud of you, Enzo," he said, though he couldn't pry his eyes from the book as he slowly skimmed through the pages.

Peter had read the book at least twice, kindly offering himself up as an advanced reader as I made my way through the arduous, heartbreaking, and exhilarating journey of writing my first novel. To see that he was still as enamored with it as he was during his first reading made my heart fill for him even more.

I had a book that would be published. But most importantly, I had someone who had always believed that I one day would have a book published. A dream I'd barely had the courage to dream was a reality, and I had my family. What more could I ask for?

"Thank you," I said.

"You are so fucking impressive," Peter said. "I'm not kidding."

"Oh, shut up," I said, kicking his shin gently under the table.

"I just had to say it," he chuckled. "I won't keep making you uncomfortable."

The minutes ticked by as Peter examined the book, the joy on his face only growing with each page he turned or each sentence he read over carefully. When he finally closed the book and held it out to me over the table, I couldn't take it. I needed more time to let the moment sink in before I could hold it in my hands. So, Peter laid it on the table between us, turned so that the writing was where I could read it, and we simply stared at each other.

"How do you feel?" he asked.

"I don't know, you know?" We both laughed. "I feel as if I should feel certain things but I'm...scattered. It's a lot. You know?"

Peter reached over and took my hand, giving it a squeeze as we both simply sat with the moment, letting it be what it was. Finally, I remembered the bag of cherries on the table next to the book, amused at how easily they'd been forgotten by a box being opened. I cocked my head at the bag and squeezed Peter's hand to make sure I had his attention.

"I got cherries at the store," I said. "I think I'll make a clafoutis for dessert tonight."

"*Yum!*" Peter exclaimed comically. "You treat me so fiiiiiiine, babe."

I laughed at his nonsense and let my hand slip from his. When I rose from the table, Peter frowned up at me. He knew the look on my face. Peter had become familiar with that look over the last six months.

"Where do you think you're going?" he asked.

"To check on—"

Peter cut me off with a shake of his head.

"Noe fell asleep ten minutes before I found you in here." Peter gestured for me to sit, so, smiling happily, I did. "If you wake him up, we're going to have words."

I laughed. "But I missed him all morning."

"You can snuggle him after he wakes up," Peter warned me. "Not before."

"Fine, fine," I said, waving him off. "I'll get Noe snuggles in later."

"Good," Peter said, taking his turn to kick my shin playfully under the table.

"Even with all the fussiness," Peter said, "I think these are going to be my favorite years as a father."

"Oh?"

"Cherry clafoutis for dessert?" He shrugged. "He's too young to eat it. When he gets older, I'll have to share all of your wonderful cooking with him. I'm not *quite* ready for that yet. I already have to share your snuggles, and I'm not *entirely* happy about that."

"I'll give you extra snuggles later," I said.

Peter bent and pulled my foot into his lap, sliding my shoe off and setting it gently on the floor. Then the other foot followed. I sat back in my chair as he massaged my feet—one of the ways Peter showed his love—making me as comfortable as possible. With a content sigh, I turned my head to look out the kitchen window at the new buds barely sprouting on the trees. Soon, the black, skeletal arms that had been clawing at the sky for months would be clothed in lush emerald leaves once more. The cold would be gone, for the most part, and we'd have the warm days of summer once more. The sun would shine and life would return; it would go on.

Except on the days Minnesota decided we simply had to have gloominess.

We could endure gloom, the three of us. Peter and I had picked up enough experience over the years that our umbrella was now big enough for three.

"Hey," Peter squeezed my calf, "that's a big smile you got there."

Chuckling, I continued to look out at the day that had decided it preferred warmth.

"What do you have to be so happy about, mister?" he asked.

Turning my head to smile at him, I said: "Everything."

The End.

About the Author

Chase Connor spends his days writing about the people who live (loudly and rent-free) in his head when he's not busy being enthusiastic about naps and Pad Thai. Chase started his writing career as a confused gay teen looking for an escape from reality. Ten years later, one of the books he wrote during those years, *Just A Dumb Surfer Dude: A Gay Coming-of-Age Tale*, was published independently. Now with The Lion Fish Press (and 20 books later), Chase has numerous projects in various stages of completion lined up for publishing. Chase is a multi-genre author, but always with a healthy dollop of gay.

Chase can be reached at chaseconnor@chaseconnor.com
Or on Twitter @ChaseConnor7
He can also be found on www.chaseconnor.com
Or on Goodreads

SIGN UP FOR THE CHASE CONNOR BOOKS NEWSLETTER AT CHASECONNOR.COM

He does his very best to respond to all DMs, emails, and Twitter comments from his reader friends and loves the interaction with them. Chase has several novellas/novels for sale in e-book, paperback, hardback, and audiobook formats wherever books are sold.